# The Changelings

# The Changelings

## Jo Sinclair

Afterwords by Nellie McKay and by
Johnnetta B. Cole and Elizabeth H. Oakes

Biographical Note by Elisabeth Sandberg

The Feminist Press
New York

For Helen Ban, Grace Meyette, and Pearl Moody

Library of Congress Cataloging in Publication Data

Sinclair, Jo, 1913–
    The changelings.

    Reprint. Originally published: New York: McGraw-Hill, 1955.
    I. Title.
PS3537.E3514C46  1985        813'.54        85-6875
ISBN 0-935312-40-4 (pbk.)


Cover design: Gilda Hannah
Cover art: L.A. West


This publication is made possible, in part, by public funds from the New
York State Council on the Arts.

The Feminist Press at The City University of New York gratefully
acknowledges Barbara Smith for recommending the republication of this
book.


Distributed by The Talman Company, Inc., 150 Fifth Avenue, New York, NY
10011.

# Contents

# Chapter one

All that summer, as no white people came to rent the empty, upstairs suites of the Valenti house or the Golden house, tension had mounted in the street. Only Negroes came.

It had been an exceptionally hot summer, with not much relief at night. The street watched, from behind windows, from swings or chairs on front porches, from the walks where garden hoses threw meager streams toward the dry lawns. These black people, who came so eagerly and stubbornly to ask for rooms, seemed part of the heavy fantasy the heat had made of their lives.

All that summer the street had watched the Valentis and the Goldens shake their heads, and the black people leave, and new ones walk down from the corner to take their place. The word, rustling and shrilling from house to house, was that many of these people had even offered to buy.

It was July, it was August, it was almost September; still the heat would not budge out of the street, nor lift much after the sun went down. And still the black people walked up and down, from Woodlawn to the edge of the Gully and from the dead end back to the corner, until the entire fantasy of heat and alien color and unuttered threat seemed to have been there forever.

Then suddenly, on the third of September, the Rosens moved out of Zigman's upstairs suite. A third house was open to the enemy.

## 2

The name of the street was East 120th. It was short, rather narrow, with just a few single-family homes in a predominantly two-family neighborhood.

The three empty suites were in houses rather close to each other, and near the Gully. A horizon—like Woodlawn Avenue at the opposite end of life—the Gully had been partially filled in for years, but

1

the street still called it by the old name. The two adjoining streets emptied into it, too, but not as dead center, not with as straight and wide a mouth, or as direct a jumping-off point. In feeling, the Gully was East 120th's back door.

Long ago, it had been a dump. A mile or so across the enormous, always-smoking crater in those days, other streets had backed into the Gully; and a factory had stood at that far edge, with its own railroad siding, its hills of slag and sand and stone. Gradually, the dump had been filled in, until now it was almost level in some spots. Sudden rises remained, shallow but rough hills of packed dirt faced a walker who stepped down from the curve of sidewalk onto the first gravelly slope. Abrupt turnings materialized, led into level areas large enough for baseball games. There was complete privacy as soon as one of these turnings was reached. At night it was possible to disappear from view of the street at once, as soon as a person moved away from the lamppost and stepped down from the sidewalk onto the slope leading down.

Where the factory had stood, there were only rusty chunks of rail now. During the war, the government had filled the faraway streets at that far edge with low houses like barracks. Negroes lived there, but the vastness of the Gully was like an ocean between them and East 120th. At the farthest lip of that ocean, people small as toys walked sometimes, but they never came close enough to be eyes or voices.

Year after year, mild election promises had been made. The Gully was to be a park, a housing project, a school and playground. That was still good for an occasional laugh around Election Day. There was another stale joke in the street's clipped vocabulary: the city was saving the Gully for the best offer from big business, and when the great day came all the houses would sell for a million dollars apiece.

The Gully could have been created for children. No matter how many adults walked there occasionally, it was a children's place, honeycombed with their ways of living. In winter, they slid down the shallow hills on sleds or sitting in discarded wash buckets. In spring, they searched as if for buried treasure for the partially burnt objects which came to the surface in certain muddy spots, through layers of old ashes. In summer—when the evenings were as open as the days—the gang unlocked its clubhouse, nailed tight the boards loosened by winter, and took over ownership.

2

For in the summer the Gully really belonged to Vincent and her gang.

## 3

Outwardly, the summer's tension had not touched the gang. There was no change of pace in the snitching, in the clubhouse meetings to plot the next raid on a store or the next training period of climbing and running. The roasting of hot dogs and potatoes at the club fireplace went on, planned by Vincent and directed by her or by Dave.

The regular Friday-night meetings went on, with their careful plans for Saturday's job. Meetings on other days or evenings had always been haphazard, called on whim, but the Friday meetings remained iron ritual because Saturday was the best day for snitching in stores.

The gang had built the clubhouse in a small, level area at the end of a turning that was perfect: not too far from the mouth of their own street and yet hidden enough by the turn to seem like a private corner.

The back wall of the little house was one of the packed-dirt slopes. There was a flat roof, a square hole in each side wall for a window, and the door was on real hinges, with a spike for a knob. The clubhouse was big enough to hold ten people, sitting close together on the floor. Vincent and Dave always sat on up-ended orange crates, on either side of the larger crate used as a table. Angelo had come up with two wine bottles, to hold candles.

They had snitched all the materials for the house the summer Vincent had started the gang. The large outside fireplace nearby had been her idea, too, and they had snitched the bricks and smooth rocks from lawn edgings in other streets. In their vocabulary, the word was "snitch," never "steal." Stealing meant money or jewelry. Snitching meant high adventure, challenge, an excitingly dangerous nose-thumbing at the world. In the four summers they had been together as a gang, not one member had ever been caught in a snitch.

The vocabulary of the entire street was sparse, yet in this children's place of Gully, dream and emotion flowed like a rich language. Without the words for it, Vincent's heart could have described the fireplace, the careful placing of potatoes, the leader's privilege of striking the first match, the waiting for the moment when potatoes were done: hot and mealy inside the blackened skin, the grains of salt standing out like shining sand on the streamy white.

Only her heart could have explained the secret music floating from fire into person, from fire up into sky, as she stood poking at a potato with her special firestick, in which she had cut a V. In the darkness, fire music could be like an arch of tenderness over the Gully. Or it could be a long story chanted with the stars, with the slowly moving clouds and the reddish moon. Or it could be the gathering together in her of a thousand questions into one flame-colored core of feeling.

Her heart could have described how, even now, the clubhouse seemed enclosed in a magic ring, as if her fire burned high as a wall all about it; how even now, when they left the houses where adults cursed and shouted about the empty rooms-for-rent, the gang could still disappear over the edge of the Gully and enter a hidden world.

And yet, before half that summer was over, Vincent had felt the queer, intangibly frightening touch on all of them of the feeling in the street. She could not understand what was happening. She could not name a single concrete difference in the gang. They still raided stores and yards, swooped down the slopes in yelling, laughing races to train for a big snitch.

It was Dave, she finally decided. All the difference she sensed in the gang seemed to center in him. For example, Wednesday afternoon, the day after Phil Rosen had moved. Walking to the corner, Angelo had just happened to mention Ziggy, the way the whole gang did once in a while, with honest admiration. Like a sudden eruption, Dave had shouted, "Shut up! My brother's none of your business. I'm the only one who's going to talk about him. You, too, Vincent—hear me? Better tip off the gang, I'm warning you!"

For example, Wednesday night. Dave had come out on his front porch, was standing so close to Vincent's porch, where she was sitting on the swing, that she could hear a quick breathing from him. Instead of jumping the rail and climbing up on her porch, the way he did so often, he just stood there in the shadows made bunchy and uneven by the lamppost nearby.

"What're you doing, spying?" he said. "In case we let some *Schwartze* in to see the joint?"

"Hell, no," Vincent said, turning to stare at him. "I'm just sitting here. It's too hot in the house."

4

This was Dave, her friend? The guy she had made second in command of the gang? she thought indignantly.

"That bastard, Phil," Dave said, his voice needled through with hatred. "What'd he do this to me for? He shouldn't have let them move, the punky sissy. Acting like a friend of mine—then putting me in a spot. Making an empty right upstairs of me!"

"What the hell'd you expect him to do?" Vincent said in a low voice. "Since when can a guy tell his old man what to do?"

"Since now! You just watch me—if my old man tries to get funny with our empty! Tell that to your mother. Or Mrs. Levine. Go on, tell the whole street! If he gets funny and makes my mother rent to. . . . Crap!" he finished, his voice cracking.

After a while, she said, "Hey, what the hell got into you?"

"All right," he cried, "you got to sit there and spy on me and my mother? In case of a double cross, huh? Bet your whole house ain't sleeping nights since the Rosens moved. Well, don't get funny with me—I'm warning you!"

"Hey, listen," Vincent tried to say, but Dave had rushed into his house, the screen door slamming like a gun shot into her mind. A few minutes later a colored man had come up on Dave's porch and was ringing the bell.

God damn it, Vincent had thought, is it my fault he's got an empty upstairs? What's he warning me for?

# Chapter two

The regular Friday meeting of the gang came up three days after the Rosens moved. Vincent was late. It was six-thirty when she suddenly became aware of the time at her sister's apartment. A man's voice on the kitchen radio blared it. Quickly, she put Manny back into his crib and said, "Hey, Shirl, I got to go. See you Monday."

Shirley lived on East 110th, north of Woodlawn. As Vincent ran the ten blocks with an easy, loping stride, she thought about Phil Rosen. He was the first to disappear from the gang. Only girls, and boys too small for the gang, had lived in the two suites which had been empty all summer. Phil had been good, fast and daring, always ready for dangerous work. She hated to think of him lost to the Heights.

It was still burning hot out. At her street, she turned south and stepped up her speed until the Gully came into view. Then she slowed down and disciplined her breathing, wiped her perspired face, so that the gang would not know she had been running. By the time she stepped off the sidewalk at the dead end onto the slope where the Gully branched downward, she was breathing easily. With her usual leader's poise, hands in her pants pockets, she strolled toward the clubhouse, her face lifted to the slightly cooler air of the big open area.

The entire gang was at the fireplace, and the usual group of outsiders were hanging around. Vincent gulped as she saw that the fire was going full blast, that potatoes already were being poked and turned. Who had signaled the start of the fire? Yeah, who in hell but Dave would have had the nerve!

The street ate supper early. On most Fridays, Vincent had Shirley's stuff delivered before supper but today her mother had got a late start in the kitchen because the stores had been so crowded. Vincent had not been able to take Shirley the extra fish and chicken soup, prepared secretly by her mother every Friday, until after her father had eaten and settled down on the front porch with his paper. Then she had grabbed the basket and climbed over the back fence, run up East 121st. She had several secret ways of getting to Shirley's, and no questions asked; her father had never yet caught her.

Today, somehow, Vincent had lost track of time because her nephew was even sweeter than he had been on the Monday visit home. Playing with Manny, she had forgotten the meeting and her uneasiness about Dave. He did such magic tricks with his chubby feet. He was such a laughing baby. Even now, his round merry face hovered in her, a memory of love, as she stood guardedly at the entrance to the world she had made and owned.

In the moment before she could be seen, she spotted everybody very carefully. The outsiders consisted of Santina, Becky, Anna and Louis Levine. Most of the gang, firesticks in their hands, were tending strictly to the business of potatoes, but Dave was stretched out on the ground, leaning on one elbow as he smoked and frowned at

6

the fire. And Alex was monkeying with Santina in the new, sexy way he had learned all of a sudden this past summer. It was another threatening difference in the gang, like Dave's change.

Vincent hated these inexplicable changes; they loomed over her tight little, safe world like the black people standing in front of the empties. Who had permitted them in her Gully, her gang!

"Hi," she said in her arrogant, leader's voice, and stepped around the bend into the level, big space of gang headquarters.

"Hi," everybody but Dave called back.

After a second, he said tonelessly, "Kind of late, huh?"

"Yeah," she said, and swaggered to the head of the fire—her place. The first time; nobody had ever done anything without her before—not fire, or meeting, or most casual plan.

"We started," Dave said. Without moving, he flipped the tiny remainder of his cigarette into the fire.

"Yeah, I see you did," she said carelessly. "Anybody put in a potato for me?"

"I did," Leo Levine said eagerly. "It's right in front of your place, Vincent. I got your stick out of the club, too."

She nodded, and Leo brought her firestick, held it out with his usual air of worship. "Okay," she told him graciously, getting the first whiff of the stale urine odor as he moved.

He smelled of his brother Louis, with whom he slept, and of Anna, whose cot stood in the same room. They still wet their beds at night, though Anna was almost twelve and Louis ten. "Especially that Lou," Leo had confided once. "He's got to sleep with me so's Moe and Chip can have beds to themselves, the lucky bastards. Honest to God, Vincent, there's a regular puddle in the bed in the morning. It dries out by night, though."

Vincent poked at her potato, and Leo wandered off to his own place at the fire. The clubhouse smelled like the three kids sometimes. So did the back hall at home; the Levines lived upstairs.

Alex Golden smacked Santina on the bottom. Her giggle and Dave's growl hit the air at once: "Come on, cut the funny stuff! What do you think this is?"

Santina gave him the eye. "Want me to tell you?" she said in her ripe voice.

"Aw, cop a sneak," Dave said, and sat up jerkily.

Vincent watched his every movement from the corners of her eyes, but she said in her crisp, business voice, "Hey, Joey, the club all ready for the meeting?"

"Yeah," he said; and Angelo added, "We got about half the candles left for tonight. Plenty of matches and butts."

She nodded. The meeting itself was never held until dark. This month, Joey Simon and Angelo Rinaldi were the appointed sergeants-at-arms. It was their job to sweep the clubhouse and ready it for business, and get rid of all outsiders before the meeting began.

"Hey, Vincent, where's those new candles?" Dave suddenly flung at her. "That whole box we snitched in the dime store?"

She gave him a cold look. "I got them hid. For after we use up these. You the sergeant-at-arms this month or something?"

"I'm sick of those garbagey pieces of candles we use," he said with a cocky grin.

"Tough luck! We're still following rules around here—use up old stuff first." Then she said with rough irony, "Who's turning your potato? Got yourself a nigger servant all of a sudden?"

One hand fisted in her pocket, she stared at him until he jumped up and grabbed his firestick, lunged over to his place. He poked so violently that sparks erupted under his stick.

Nigger servant, nigger servant! The words repeated themselves like a feeling of danger in Vincent's head as she poked her potato with pretended casualness and listened to the hoarse, contented sounds Becky Golden made as she stood rocking, smiling at the fire.

Vincent had seen Dave several times in the three days since his upstairs had turned into an empty. They had spoken, they had walked from the corner together and turned into their yards. He was the same Dave, and yet he was entirely different. The change she had sensed in him, inch by inch all that summer, seemed to have gone like an arrow into a fierce, glowing space directly behind his eyes. She heard it, constant jerk and vibration, in his voice.

From a good tough guy, best in the gang next to her, he had changed into. . . . She could barely put it into words for herself. It was as if he had become ready, with frightening suddenness, to turn into his brother Ziggy, who was in the state penitentiary. Or into his brother Al, who was a gambler, one of the best card dealers in town. She could not understand that confusing picture, so she tried to paint herself another one: from

8

a kid who had run and laughed and snitched with her, Dave had turned into somebody sour and nervous as a man. Mr. Levine, or her father, or Mr. Miller; he acted like one of the men of the street, who were always looking over their shoulders for colored people or something.

"Hey, Alex," Dave said with a hard snicker, "who in hell's doing your potato? Your sister Becky? Or you got a nigger servant, too?"

A laugh came from Alex. "Sure, I got one—Santina!"

Angelo guffawed, slapped his thigh. "Hot enough to turn black, Santina? You tell 'em!"

Even laughter was different this summer, Vincent thought coldly. A fresh, free exuberance was gone—out of laughter, out of adventure.

"Want to feel how hot, Dave?" Santina said, her giggle crawling up and down Vincent's back.

He did not even glance at her as he said, "I'm busy. The boss says I got to tend to business."

Vincent looked at him. There was a strange cruelty in his voice and eyes, so new that again the confusing picture leaped at her: Dave teetering at the edge of the split second of turning into Ziggy.

He wants my gang, she thought with a feeling of shock, putting it into words for the first time that summer. He wants to steal it, grab it for his.

The baking potatoes had begun to scent the hot, still air. As the delicious odor reached into Becky Golden, her familiar bellow burst out: "Ma, Ma, gimme eat!"

"Shut up," Alex told her casually. "They ain't done yet. You got to wait a while."

"Hey, what you do," Dave said in a hard voice, "put one in for your sister?"

"She's eating mine when it's done," Alex said, scowling. "She's got to eat all the time or she cries—everybody knows that. My mother made me take her along, so she smells the stuff and she hollers for eat. What the hell! I was in on the snitching, wasn't I? So I can give her my potato fair and square."

"Since when do we snitch for anybody else but the gang?" Dave demanded.

"Yeah?" Vincent said curtly. "Since when you giving orders around here? If Alex wants to give his potato to Becky, it's his potato."

9

"Well, how come Leo can't give me his?" Anna Levine shrilled.

"Me, too!" Louis said. "Leo's my brother, too!"

Vincent turned, with anger. "Are you a dummy, like Becky? Now shut up or you'll get kicked right out of here." She glared at Angelo, said in her leader's voice of harsh arrogance, "All right, sergeant-at-arms, bring another potato for Alex. He snitched that whole bag yesterday—I'm reminding everybody! So if he gives his away because he can't help it, he gets another one. What the hell!"

As Angelo ran toward the clubhouse, she thought ragingly that Dave had better just guard his empty and lay off her gang. She resented his sudden attack on Becky Golden, who played with kids as if she were one herself, instead of a grownup who was simple in the head. He was acting like he owned her private world.

"Who's getting more wood?" she said; another order.

"Come on, Alex," Dan Buckholz said. "That's fair—you're going to have two potatoes in there now, huh?"

"Yeah," Alex said hesitantly. "Want to come, Santina?"

"Wait for you," she said. "Right here, okay?"

The minute Alex and Dan disappeared into the reaches of the Gully, Santina came over to Dave. "Got a cig?" she said softly.

"No," he said, without looking at her.

Vincent watched Santina's eyes examine Dave's body, the way they studied Alex's so often. The hungry stare made her a little sick at her stomach. If Jules could only explain what had crept into her orderly world this summer, while her back was turned!

If he could write a poem about what happened to a gang, to a Dave, one empty after another to be guarded and the bell ringing, the strange black faces bobbing in and out the street, up and down the front steps; but it was the gang that was changing all the time! To hell with the empties, with Santina trying to touch a guy's leg all the time and Alex's hand creeping over the high-pointed breasts or grabbing the pinched-in waist while Santina flung back her long hair and smiled, smiled all over her dark, smooth, wise face. Yeah, to hell with Dave jumping off that porch he was guarding and trying to grab her gang, her club! Could Jules write a poem about that?

Dan and Alex were back, throwing fresh wood on the fire. Santina stood with Alex again. The heat, the light of day, were permanently

10

fixed in the sky; Vincent longed for darkness, for the night, for the striking clock of a business meeting.

"Hey, it sure is funny without Phil, huh?" Joey said.

"That punk?" Dave said nonchalantly. "He belongs on the Heights, where sissies live. Who needs him?"

That's a lie, Vincent thought as no one answered him. Phil was a good guy and Dave knows it.

At that moment Dave took some loose cigarettes out of his pocket. They were whole, never even lit, and he had a lot of them. She groped in her pocket for the folder of matches she always carried. New cigarettes tasted wonderful, not like the butts the gang picked up on Woodlawn. No matter how long the salvaged butts were, they always tasted of other people to Vincent. She hated to put them in her mouth but knew she had to because the rest of the gang did.

"Snitched them," Dave said airily. "From the guy who kills chickens in our store. The sap left his jacket around—open pack in it."

He handed the cigarettes around to the gang, but walked past Vincent as if she were one of the outsiders who never expected anything or got it. She pretended to poke at her potato, keeping her face expressionless, but the shock of Dave's action stunned her for a second.

Like a blurred image of the companion he had been so long, he grinned. That familiar, Polack-blond head might have been a stranger's. The blue glint of eyes, the dimples catching light in their holes, the grace and prowl of the hard body—all were the same; but where was the Dave who had run with her, craftily worked the stores with her, and then shared the laugh as they had run to the club with the snitch? They had had complete fearlessness between them, like a rope tying them together on the highest roof or most rickety fence. She remembered a kind of wonderful brotherhood.

Once, on a summer Sunday, after they had sneaked into the show by one of the fire doors and seen the movie twice, then strolled out like paying customers, Dave had stopped her in the lobby and pointed to their reflections in the big mirror. "Black-and-White, huh?" he had said, grinning. In the remembered mirror, next to his yellow hair hers was black, curly and tousled all the way down to its tip-of-the-ear

11

length, as if the Gully wind were still in it. Her dark skin, tanned as his was gold, had light freckles sprayed over nose and cheeks. She was almost as tall as he in the mirror, and as slim in her navy-blue pants and short-sleeved middy blouse.

What had happened to that tough, good brotherhood? Vincent heard Angelo say, "Boy, this sure tastes swell, Dave." The first satisfied puffs were being released from pursed lips all about her.

Vincent dropped her stick, pretended to stretch, then swaggered over to the clubhouse to get herself a butt from the cigarette box kept on the table. It was a rectangular candy box made of thin brown wood, which she had begged from her sister. Shirley had kept needles and pins in it, but she had emptied it with a smile when Vincent had explained that it was perfect for the clubhouse. That was Shirl, sweet as sugar.

As Vincent selected the longest butt in this box, she thought absently: How in the hell can Pa stand it, not even seeing Shirl all this time?

She closed the box. Hell! she thought, how can Pa stand it—never even seeing Manny once? That fat little laughing face, the way his hands and his pink little feet jump up in the crib?

For a long time Vincent had lived in three separate worlds: one was the gang-Gully, one was the street, one was Manny–Shirley. There were three levels of thinking and feeling in her, to match these separate worlds in which she moved so methodically. Rather suddenly, lately, her worlds had begun jumping out of their boundaries, fragments from one mixing confusingly with bits from the other two. Sometimes all these fragments merged abruptly, making a peculiar composite of emotions she did not know how to handle.

Now she stood very still in the shadowy clubhouse. This was the first time Shirley-Pa-Manny had made actual words in her. All questioning had been nebulous before, the feeling of her stomach sinking or her heart banging too hard when the phone rang sometimes on Sunday while the Grandmother was visiting—and what if it was Shirley (never mentioned by those stern lips), or what if it was about Manny being sick, and Vincent would have to yell his name and Shirl's even though the Grandmother and Pa were in the house and would hear those forbidden names?

Somehow the questioning was all mixed up with Dave's first

12

concrete steps of revolt in the gang today, with the way an empty in the street—Dave's—had hit her personally out of all the summer's complaining, bitter talk. Her other two worlds had jumped out of focus and grabbed on to Manny–Shirley.

As she stood there, scared, voices drifted into the clubhouse; Santina's, saying, "Gimme a puff, Blacky, huh?"

And Anna's shrill, curious voice: "Hey, Santina, how come you call Alex 'Blacky' sometimes?"

Santina's laugh, her slow, meaningful tones, came crawling into the open doorway: "You're too little to know. You just wait."

"Wait for what?"

"See how black his hair is? On his arms, too, huh? Well, it's blacker somewhere else! Huh, Blacky?"

A high whistle came from Angelo, and Alex said jubilantly, "Black as hers, huh, Ang'?"

Then Dave's voice came, that jerky and meaningless anger: "Shut up! This Gully's got so much hot-pants in it today, I'm going to throw up my guts."

Silence, then Louis begged, "Hey, Leo, gimme a puff."

"Scram," Leo said. "You're not big enough."

"I'm going to be in the gang next year," Louis cried eagerly. "Vincent said!"

"Since when," Dave said with a contempt that shoved Vincent out of her numbness, "is she telling pisher kids they can be in the gang?"

"I ain't!" Louis said, and Leo added quickly, "He don't—not every night any more."

"Yeah?" Dave said. "Just smell him."

Trying carefully to figure out the best moves to make as the leader—untouchable, inviolate—Vincent got the big box of salt snitched at the beginning of the summer. Then she went to the open door and stood there to light the butt, so that they could all see how she was thumbing her nose at Dave's new cigarettes.

The butt between her lips, she strolled back to the fireplace. "How's your potato?" she said to Leo. "I brought the salt."

"Not even done," he said, and dragged on his new cigarette with such a look of smug triumph that she flushed.

Glancing about her quickly, she saw how they all looked at her

13

as they held their cigarettes jauntily, as if taunting her. That was different, too! Her hands were sweating on the box of salt as she silently cursed the daylight for not moving an inch toward dusk. The whole world seemed fixed and immovable, even as it slid slowly toward a feeling of disaster. She yearned for night, for the order and ritual of a meeting.

"Hey, Dave," Dan said eagerly, "the Rosens leave anything around when they moved?"

Vincent saw a lump pop into Dave's jaw, then he drawled, "Yeah, a lot of crap."

"Going to let us look around?" Joey said. "Finders keepers?"

Dave was still drawling: "Too late—the Zigmans don't sit on their cans. Me and my mother cleaned it up next day—their basement lockers, too. We got people coming in to look it over."

Nobody believed him, and a second later Alex laughed in proof. "How does it feel to have an empty upstairs?" he said slyly.

"You ought to know," Dave shot back. "What do you and Santina do—play around in yours after dark?"

An appreciative snicker came from Angelo. "Good idea, huh, Alex?"

Vincent had to notice Dave's eyes. They seemed to be looking two ways quickly, first to the left and then to the right, but too fast, as if he were trying to watch a lot of people all at the same time. And there was such a peculiar expression in them—so ashamed, or something—that she tossed her cigarette end into the fire and said roughly, "Hey, come on, you guys, cut out the crap. Who wants salt?"

She put the box of salt down and leaned over to poke her softening potato. "About time to eat," she said.

"Yeah?" Alex said sullenly. "How do *you* feel, living right next door to an empty?"

"What the hell's it to me?" she said, faking a frown.

"Boy," Anna Levine cried with the ridiculous air of importance she had copied from her mother, "you ought to hear my brother Moe."

"Yeah? What's Moe have to say?" Dave said instantly.

"Well, we're the ones, ain't we?" Anna said. "Vincent's downstairs, but our kitchen looks right in your upstairs. We used to see the Rosens eating and everything."

14

In Vincent, the waiting for disaster focused into a sharp fear as she saw Dave's face twitching. She did not know why, but his empty was tied to her, to her private world. She did not know why, but suddenly her prayer started saying itself in her head, slow, hard as fists.

Then, after all the fencing, the hidden explosive came bursting out as Alex said, with a dirty grin: "Going to rent to *Schwartze*, Dave?"

Even Dan and Angelo, even Santina—none of them Jewish—knew that word. The whole street knew it, and Dave said murderously, "How come you think we'd do that?"

When Alex laughed meaningfully, half-muffled echoes of his laugh came from the others. Dave wheeled and glared around. "How come?" he shouted.

Anna said, with her perky importance, "My father says maybe your father and mother don't care who lives upstairs of you."

And Louis added, "Sure, your family ain't afraid of *Schwartze*, because when Ziggy gets out of—"

"Shut up!" Dave interrupted, his voice thick. "You two pishers get the hell out of here before I kick your teeth in!"

"Make me," Anna said, and ran to the opposite side of the fire.

"Don't pay no attention to her," Leo started to say nervously, and Dave threw his firestick at him.

As Leo dodged, Dave said, "One more crack, and I'll show you what Ziggy does to this whole stinking street when he gets out. Me and Al standing right next to him. I'll show you—right now!"

He strode toward the clubhouse, disappeared inside.

"God damn it," Vincent forced herself to say in level tones, "I'm going to bust up this gang or something. Screaming around like a bunch of regular girls. Cut it out."

"Boy, ever see him that tough?" Angelo muttered with respect.

"Know what?" Santina said in a low voice. "He's going to be twice as tough as Ziggy one of these days."

"You ain't kidding," Leo said, picking up Dave's stick.

The tense, admiring voices rose and fell about Vincent as she listened to the way Dave was banging stuff in the clubhouse. She knew she should stop him. She should throw out the outsiders, somehow pull the gang back into the old orbit of work and adventure. But something had paralyzed her mind and she could not think out her next step.

One of Becky's howls came: "Ma, Ma, gimme eat!"

"Hey, Alex," Anna said impatiently, "give her that potato. She don't know the difference if it ain't done."

"The hell she don't," Alex said. "What do you think she is, a dog? Becky, shut up—it ain't done yet. You ain't eating raw potatoes! You don't pee in bed, either!"

"We ain't got no empty upstairs of us, either!" Anna flung back.

"So you got one next door. You'll have *Schwartze* near you before we do—want to bet?"

"Well, it won't be our fault! If Mrs. Zigman don't care, on account of Ziggy and Al being gangsters and—"

"I told you to shut up!" Dave shouted, appearing in the doorway of the clubhouse. "Don't talk about my mother. You talk about my mother and I'll kill you."

He lunged out toward the fire, and Anna ran to Vincent and hid behind her. "Vincent's mother said it, too," she wailed. "She said she bets your mother'll leave in *Schwartze*—"

Dave leaped, thrust Vincent aside, and slapped Anna's face so hard that she lost her breath.

Vincent's arm throbbed from his push, and she said harshly, "What's the big idea of hitting a girl? We got rules in this gang."

"Crap on your rules," Dave said. "We got another rule, too. How come you don't mention that?"

"Yeah?"

"Yeah! No girls in this gang!"

Vincent blinked, felt the complete silence of the gang around her like an enormous, sucking hole. "Who the hell do you think you are, all of a sudden?" she said.

"Ziggy's brother. Al's brother. Ask any stinking cop who we are!"

"Your brothers hit girls, too?" she said caustically.

Red soared into Dave's face, but he laughed. "Hey, girlie," he said, "what about that rule? No girls in the gang, huh?"

Not one of the gang said a word for Vincent. Their silence made her scalp feel prickly with apprehension.

"Hey, who the hell do you think you are?" Dave went on scornfully. "A guy?"

16

It was an accusation. She had never actually called herself a boy, but neither had she ever thought of herself as one of the girls she despised for their soft, plaintive weakness. She was simply Vincent, with the proud right to walk with the strong. She had proved it—in a thousand ways. As she turned away, with her old disdain, she was stunned to see that the other faces reflected Dave's ugly laughter.

"Who's eating potatoes with me?" she said gruffly, but the apprehension was choking and dry in her throat by now.

"Hey, girlie," Dave called, his tone like an insult. "Who's eating potatoes with this girlie, huh?"

Suddenly a wild shout pushed out of her. "Shut up, you dirty liar!"

"Ha ha," Dave said insolently. "Hey, gang, did you hear girlie?"

"Know what?" Santina said. "Bet she thinks she's a guy!"

Angelo rocked with laughter. "Vincent thinks she's a guy!"

Even Becky was staring at her, the dull eyes as unbearable as all the bright, excited ones. With difficulty, one of the old, working statements came from Vincent: "What's the matter, Dave, looking for trouble?"

"Trouble from a girl?" Dave's arms were crossed over his chest. "Because you wear pants when you don't go to school? That make you a guy?"

"You brother Nate's old pants," Leo said, like a dirty betraying enemy. "You copped 'em when he went to New York."

"What do you have to wear in school?" Dave went on inexorably. "Dresses—ha ha. Middy blouse, skirt. What do you get called in school, huh?"

"Judith," Alex said derisively. "Judith Vincent."

"What does your mother call you?" Dave said.

"Judy, Judy!" Dan's taunting voice answered.

But the gang had always called her Vincent, she thought numbly. Her friends, Jules—it was her name! With a carelessness she had to fight for, she began walking toward the clubhouse. "Who wants a butt?" she said.

"Where you going?" Dave said. "No girls in this gang—get it?"

She turned, shouted, "Lay off! Get home to your empty, you rat. This is my gang."

"The hell it is," he said. "No girl's going to be my boss."

"Me, either," Angelo said.

"Hey," Alex said suddenly, "what you got under Nate's pants, girlie?"

An excited laugh burst from Santina. "Go on, Dave," she cried, "show her what guys got under their pants, huh?"

A wave of snickers and howls came from the gang, but Dave said airily, "You cop a sneak, will you?"

"Aw, come on, Dave," Santina said. "Show her what you got and she ain't. Come on."

"Save it," he said. "Save it for that guy they got all lined up to marry you, hot pants."

"Hey, lemme show her!" Alex said, and unzipped his pants, began to grope inside.

"That a boy, Blacky!" Santina cried.

Dave pushed Alex, so hard that he fell. "Show hot pants," he said. "If she wants to see so bad."

"What the hell?" Alex shouted, getting up.

"Button up or I'll bust you one," Dave said coldly, moving away. "Come on, gang."

They all assembled in a tight group, leaving the outsiders at the other side of the fire. After a second, Alex came, too, smoothing his pants shut.

"All right," Dave said with assurance. "So we prove it she's a girl. Nothing dirty. All we do is pull off her clothes and prove it, see?"

There was an outburst of admiring whistles and catcalls. Across the three or four yards separating her from the gang, Vincent said unbelievingly, "You dirty bastards. You touch me and I'll kill you."

Another wave of whistling and taunting laughter came floating across, and Vincent's hands began to sweat in her pockets. It was as if they smelled her hidden fear, as if the whole summer of waiting had ripped her open suddenly and they knew—before she did—that she was no longer the fastest, the smartest.

Her three worlds tipped dizzily, smeared together: Who had described Manny's sin to the gang? Who had told it in the clubhouse, once while she was gone, that Jules might die, might disappear as abruptly as Nate out of her life?

"Let's go," Dave said, his voice clipped, and the gang moved behind him. Vincent saw a wedge of sullen faces and big, hunched

18

bodies. Suddenly they all looked towering as men, lumpy with muscle.

Her hands came out of her pockets in fists. For the first time, she felt like the youngest. There had always been an agelessness about the gang before, a magic stretching to fit the particular adventure. When they had leaped from garage roof to tree, run the slopes and hills, they were kids. When they had entered a store, cool and full of distracting talk to make the snitch easier, they were adults. When they had sat in the candlelit clubhouse, watching their cigarette smoke in the air and the shadows thrown by the flickering candles, they were dreamers —young or old enough to match any wish.

But now, as she watched the slow, deadly advance, she knew she was only twelve: to Dave's almost and Alex's full fifteen, to Angelo's and Leo's fourteen, to Dan's and Joey's over-thirteen.

"Surround her," Dave ordered, and the gang fanned out, and inside of her Vincent was saying her prayer with every ounce of her faith: Dear Lord, kind Lord, gracious Lord, I pray Thou wilt look on all I love tenderly tonight. . . .

"Grab her arms first," Dave said.

"How about if I dive for her legs?" Leo said.

Weed their hearts of weariness, Vincent prayed. Scatter every care, down a wake of angel wings winnowing the air.

"Show her what she ain't got!" Santina screamed joyously. She, too, pressed Vincent's sudden youth back on her. She was Dave's age, Alex's; her outcry was full of mysterious knowledge, like their expressions.

And with all the needy, Vincent prayed, oh, divide, I pray, this vast treasure of content that was mine today. Amen.

The wedge came closer. Her prayer began again, faster, more dogged in its reaching for a miracle; but the slitted eyes and the taunting men's grins came closer.

Amen, amen! she called in her head, and Dave jumped into her flailing fists. Then the other bodies hit, on all sides of her, so that she could not see single members of the gang but felt all their knobby hardness at once. She was punching one gigantic face, one chest, one belly taut and solid.

"You got her!" Santina cried, a wild exultant voice.

Then every precious memory she had been hugging turned anonymous for Vincent, as if she had never had a Manny or Shirley, a

19

Jules, a Nate, a prayer. One pair of hands with the strength of a hundred had her pinned to the ground. Gigantic hands—strangely powerful but still smelling of the Levine kids—were tearing off her blouse, peeling Nate's pants off her, down her thighs, down her legs and past her socks and shoes.

She went on fighting, with the automatic fury and skill of the old Vincent. Lying on the jagged stones of the ground, she kicked and buckled against the grabbing weight, cursed like the old Vincent, until they had her underwear pants off. The sensation of unshielded softness was so new and terrifying that she could not move suddenly. A weeping, so shrill with weakness that it sickened her, dinned through her head.

Then she felt that gigantic pair of hands seize her undershirt and tear it off, over her head. The weight lifted, the smell went away. She felt the hot Gully wind on her closed eyes as she lay twisted into herself, her thighs pressed together convulsively. The wailing inside her head made her think of Manny, that time he had been sick.

She recognized Dave's voice, breathless and gulping, above her: "All right! Still think you're a guy?"

It thrashed her to her feet. She leaped for her clothes, fumbled on her underpants. When she straightened, holding the other pieces against her, she was unable to think what to do with them.

Everybody stared at the whiteness of her skin next to the tanned arms and neck and the triangle of brown pointing into the small, beginning breasts. Her hair looked curly and soft; her naked back and the long legs, the slim waist, the rounded thighs, all were of a strange and pretty girl they had just been fighting.

Suddenly blood started like pinpricks near one corner of Vincent's mouth. Leo mumbled frantically, "Hey, I got to go!"

He ran to the fire, seemed to tap Anna and Louis, and the three disappeared as if wind had carried them out of the Gully. Dan backed off. Then Joey and Angelo moved, as if at a signal, slouched out of sight. Alex went to the fireplace and took Becky's hand.

"Come on home," he said shakily. "Ma'll give you eat."

"Alex!" Santina whispered. "Wait for me, Alex."

They were gone. Vincent and Dave stared blindly at each other. "Hey, Vincent," he said painfully, "you got blood on your mouth. Wipe it off, for Christ sake."

20

"Go to hell," she said dully.

He winced. "Does your face hurt?"

Her eyes looked wide and empty. There was such a ghastly loneliness about her that he felt scared. He turned away, almost falling as he ran.

Slowly, Vincent began to feel the quiet, the heat of the air on her bare skin. The first of the dusk was creeping into the Gully, the misty blue color she loved. It'll be dark soon, she thought, time to light the candles, start the meeting, plan tomorrow's snitch, and. . . .

Suddenly, as if she had just walked into a room, she smelled the burnt potatoes in the fireplace. Her face was wet, forehead and upper lip, and she felt the heaviness in her arms, aching bruises all over her body. Quickly, she dressed herself, wiped the blood from her face, smoothed back her hair. She brushed leaves and dirt from her pants. Then she did not know what to do, so she stumbled back to the fire. Bits of wood were still smoldering, and she leaned numbly and tucked in some paper, made a latticework of thin wood to catch the first flame. The reek of burnt potatoes was smothering.

Little flames jumped up. Across the area, the clubhouse was just a blotch of shadow and she wished the candles were lit, but she was too tired to walk over and do it. She sat down in front of the fire, hugging her knees. The blue color was all different today; it made a lost place of the Gully, and she could not bear it. She hid her face against her knees.

And then, as she fought to keep herself from sobbing, a girl's voice behind her said scornfully, angrily, "Hey, if you're crying, you're a jackass."

Vincent jumped up, shouting, "Who's crying?"

Turning quickly, she saw the girl, standing with her hands in the pockets of her slacks. She was colored.

There was a mechanical tensing for action in Vincent, weight on her toes, arms ready to fly up at the first move from the enemy. In one flashing instant, her heart thudding heavily at the abrupt danger, she took in everything about the girl: brown pants, white blouse, tennis shoes, a chain or cord of some kind around her neck and the ends disappearing inside the front of her blouse. They were as tall as each other, and the girl's straight, black, shining hair was ear length too, parted on the side.

For a fantastic second, it was like staring into a mirror—except for the brown color of the face. Then Vincent became aware of the girl's direct, angry eyes, and she said, "Who the hell do you think you are?"

"I don't think—I know," the girl retorted. "Clara Jackson, that's who. If you don't like it, lump it."

All the words she had heard at home, and up and down the street, tangled in Vincent's mind. The suspicion and hatred, the fear, which had made strident echoes all the past summer, clanged through her like a warning. Should she run, fight? Should she walk away airily, holding her nose?

"What do you think you're doing in this Gully?" she said roughly.

"You own it? Is it private property or something?"

"It's my gang headquarters. That private enough?"

"No," the girl said. Then, with that intense anger, she said, "What do you mean, your gang? That blond guy just took it away from you, I'll bet. I saw the whole thing. I wanted to kill him! Why'd you let them do it?"

Vincent flushed. "Six to one?" she said bitterly.

The girl stamped her foot, making a savage, insulted gesture of it. "Why didn't you use your knife? Cut the bastards to pieces? I hate guys like that. They think a girl is a punk! I've been watching you for a long time—the whole bunch of you. Ever since I moved around here. Why'd you let them get you that way?"

"I don't know," Vincent said with desperate anger. "I was dumb —I should've been ready for it. Boy, dumb!"

In the blue light, they stared at each other, sharing fury and bitterness, a mutual intense pride. Vincent forgot this was her first close encounter with the enemy. "Where'd you move?" she asked.

"Over on East 112th," Clara said, then she came a few steps closer and said with a new surge of anger, "Why didn't you take your knife and cut off that damn thing they're always talking so big about?"

"I haven't got a knife!" Vincent shouted, overwhelmed by frustration.

"Stripping you! Next time they'll do it all—the works. That's all they ever want. You got to show them who's boss."

Clara was shaking a fist, as if it had been she thrust to the ground, undressed, humiliated. Her outrage encompassed both of them. Abruptly, she pulled something out of her pocket and thrust it at Vincent.

"Here," she said, "I'll lend you mine. Cut that blond guy to pieces. Cut it right off of him."

It was a small but thick knife. Vincent did not take it, and Clara said, "It's got two blades. Good and sharp. Go on—give it back in a couple of days. I'll meet you here."

"I'm not coming here any more," Vincent said. "The hell with it."

"Scared?" Clara cried, scorn lacing through her anger. "If you let that bastard get away with—" Again she stamped her foot in that proud, outraged way. "Show him you're better. I can't stand it if you don't! You hear me? See if you can get up enough nerve to show him."

"What do you mean, nerve?" Vincent demanded.

Clara looked her up and down. "No guy'd undress me," she said, her voice smoldering. "No twenty guys."

She threw the knife at Vincent's feet. "I'm lending it to you," she said contemptuously. "If that guy grabs you again you'll need it, hear? Bring it back. Monday night—that gives you three days. Meet me here, in your fancy, private place—*I'm* not scared."

As she turned, began to walk away in a leisurely way, Vincent said, "Hey, wait a minute."

Clara looked back at her. "Make it Tuesday," Vincent said, flushing. "My sister and her baby come every Monday night."

"Tuesday, sure," Clara said, "I don't care. Same time as now, huh? Cut him good—where he'll know it, you. You, Vincent," she added, giving the name a powerful, fisted sound.

Vincent watched her long, casual stride until she disappeared into the turning. Then she picked up the knife and put it in her pocket. In a daze, she went to the clubhouse to shut the door before she realized that it was no longer hers.

The knife lay in her pocket like a present, and she thought with amazement: But why did she lend it to me?

It was almost dark when she started out of the Gully. As she walked toward the slope leading up to the dead end of her street, she remembered the brown skin, the way the nostrils had flared, a sharply etched line of upper lip.

She remembered the shared bitterness and fury. This was the

23

enemy, described from house to house all summer with fear? She had never stood as close to a Negro, or talked to one. On lower Woodlawn they were black faces to walk past. In school she had passed them in corridors without looking for the color of eyes or the shape of a face. One or two of them sat in some of her classes, but they had never focused for her outside of vague names. What color were Clara's eyes? She remembered only the blazing shade of anger.

As she approached the beginning of the slope, she groped to touch back to the way things had been before today. It was not the abrupt savagery of the act of violence that came with her out of the Gully but the protecting fierceness of the girl she had met there. And again the realization came of how alike they were—not only the pants, the way of standing on guard with their bodies, but the whole inner reflection of pride and arrogance. Had she dreamed Clara Jackson? No: her hand felt the knife in her pocket.

Vincent climbed the shallow slope, stepped onto the curving sidewalk of the dead end. It was always a little like stepping over a boundary line, one country into another, but tonight both countries were unreal.

She stood under the lamppost, trying to get her bearings. Kids were playing near the next lamppost, and a dog barked somewhere. The street smelled hot and used, and she was so lonely suddenly that she began to run toward the Golden house. Jules would help her. He always did.

## Chapter three

Early that evening, Sophie Golden was sitting at one of her living-room windows, near the foot of Jules' big bed, peering out and making her usual comments on what was going on in the street.

She spent a lot of time at this window in hot weather so that she could amuse her son with gossip and with the nicknames she delighted in pinning on people, fight his boredom with clever remarks about life. And she came to the window, too, because she keenly enjoyed seeing her world go by.

The living room had three large front windows, and the screened door opened onto a good-sized porch. Because it was the largest and airiest room in the house, it was turned into a bedroom for Jules in the summer. He could see a slice of the street; it was his mother who looked up and down several times a day to tell him in exact detail about the parts of the street he could not see when he was ordered by the doctor to stay in bed.

Sophie Golden was a tall, big-boned woman in her fifties. An intense vitality shone through her tiredness. Her black, curly hair had gray in it but her grainy skin with its scarlet patches, her loud voice, her large firm body, made a youthful exuberance anywhere she went. Her children resembled her—even Jules, the sick one.

"Ah hah," she said now, her face near the screened window, "there's another one going up Zigman's steps. That makes six *Schwartze* today. Already, and look how early it is."

She groaned. "Like they heard on the radio the Rosens moved! The sign isn't even up yet. How do they find out the magic news?"

"From God," Jules said, looking up from his book. He prided himself on the cynical way in which he could speak to fit an occasion.

"Sure, now you're studying religion," his mother muttered.

"Yep. Oh, God, soften this woman's heart to the needs of her fellow man," he intoned sardonically.

Jules Golden was seventeen, tall, extremely thin. His face was marked by the years of heart disease he had battled as if the sickness were a person. Propped against three large pillows, half sitting, he looked too long for his bed.

His neck stretched skinny and gaunt out of his immaculate, white pajama jacket, the swell of his Adam's apple almost grotesque in that fragile length. He had a large, bony nose, a bit beaked below the shell-rimmed, thick glasses he had to wear, and he had a habit of tilting his head and peering at people. His skin was rough and reddish, like his mother's, and his soft dark hair was as wavy as hers. One long lock fell often over his eyes, and he kept brushing at it restlessly.

"God," Mrs. Golden said with distaste, "if I ever meet Anna Rosen in the street somewhere. What I'll tell her!"

"Those rats," Heidi called in corroboration from the kitchen, where she was drying the supper dishes.

"Jealous the Rosens got to the Heights?" Jules said, grinning.

His mother glared at him. "They moved out like a secret. Did they say one word, before, to the street? All of a sudden a mover comes and they're gone. Not one word to a neighbor. She was afraid to tell us!"

Jules' grin deepened. "Ma, you know what? You're finally going crazy. Why does a family have to check with you before they move?"

"With me? With everybody! The street is so mad it feels like steam heat when you walk past people. What are we, dogs, that she couldn't at least tell us she's going? She lived here fifteen years and she goes without one word. God! You get a little money, so you stick a knife in your own kind? If this is what money does, I don't want it!"

As she took a breath, Jules said with a snicker, "Not much."

Mrs. Golden looked out the window again. "Hah," she said with calm enjoyment, "you should see the *spunyitze* watching the Zigman porch. Like she'll go over and choke the man with her own hands."

It was the name she had bestowed long ago on Mrs. Valenti, Santina's grandmother, who had mourned her dead husband for more than twenty years by wearing only black, long, full dresses which swirled about her ankles as she walked in her garden and yard. As Mrs. Golden had explained it, *spunyitze* in Yiddish meant a big, long skirt.

"Who answered the bell by Zigman?" Heidi called.

"Dave. He slammed it right in the *Schwartze's* face. Ah hah! The Rich Woman is watching, too. From her porch. A hundred-dollar accident wouldn't make her feel good now, I'll bet. With empty rooms right next door."

Both Jules and Heidi knew she was speaking of Mrs. Levine, whose dream had always been to somehow get involved in a streetcar accident or to fall in a large department store, and in this way collect money without even having to sue.

Mrs. Golden's nicknames for certain people in the street—called out so long and so often that the street itself used some of them—rose out of a crude, salty sense of humor that was half sorrow. She jeered at Mrs. Levine but in a kindly way, for she understood every facet of the need for money. She knew exactly why the woman pushed each of her boys into the trade known as "hustling papers" as soon as he was big enough to carry the newspaper bag; but it was still another means of entertaining Jules, and she used it to the hilt.

26

"We'll have another Rockefeller family in our street, hah?" she would say. "A big family business—hustling papers. A million-dollar business for my son's son."

"A dynasty—the du Ponts of the hustlers," Jules would answer, sometimes playing her game. She loved it when he thrust back, salt for salt.

"While the mother of the dynasty schemes to collect from the streetcar company. What's a broken leg? Money heals everything."

Now Heidi called with irritation from the kitchen, "Ma, should I or shouldn't I give Becky some more chicken? She ate three pieces of bread but she's still sitting and looking."

"No, wait till she starts hollering," Mrs. Golden said. "She smells Papa's supper warming, that's all."

Her loud voice always sounded hoarse, and the voices of her children had this quality, too, as if they were mimicking her. "Light the boiler for Papa's bath," she said.

As Heidi clattered down the basement steps, Mrs. Golden shouted, "Make a big fire, Ida. I'll give Becky a bath after Papa's."

Jules looked up from his book again. "So do you have to yell all the time?" he said. "Where's Alex?"

"In the Gully—where else?"

"Stupid half-wit," he muttered of his brother, but he meant it as little as he meant most of the derisive words he flung at his family. His mother, who knew him well, shrugged off the cursing tones.

They were very alike, these two. They soared easily into brief but furious arguments, in which they seemed to despise each other. They were both lonely, frightened, deeply loving, but hid their emotions in different ways. Mrs. Golden trusted her family as she trusted herself, and clutched at each one. Jules, distrusting them and pretending to push them away, needed them near him all the time.

"Where's Papa?" he said. "His supper's stinking up the whole house."

"He went to the Heights right after work," Mrs. Golden said. "To Uncle Nathan—for advice."

"Advice, huh? What to do about the *Schwartze?*"

"So?" she said. "Is it your business?"

Jules sneered. "Uncle Nathan, the oracle. Please, please, Uncle

Nathan, tell us! You live on the Heights—tell us what to do—there are three houses with empty suites now!"

"We need advice, he likes to give advice," Mrs. Golden said coolly. "Why shouldn't I keep on the good side of a rich brother?"

"Crap," Jules said. "Heidi, turn on the radio."

"In a minute."

"Now!"

Heidi came to snap on the radio. She was a stocky, muscular woman of twenty-two, with restlessly sullen eyes. The radio, a big floor model purchased the last time Jules had been ordered to bed, stood in the dining room in the summer.

"Why don't we move it near you?" she grumbled, a question she had asked hundreds of times. "Then you can do anything you want to it."

"Because it would be too loud," Jules said, one finger on the line of print he had read last in his book. "Try another station. No, no—another one. That's it. Now make it softer."

"Who was your nigger servant last year?" she said, but she was beginning to feel more cheerful as she sensed his good humor. Jules' moods affected his family powerfully.

Heidi went to the buffet, leafed through a pile of pamphlets covering more than half the top of it. "The mailman didn't bring anything today," she said with a sigh.

A taunting smile appeared on the gaunt face. "Too bad! No pamphlets on how to fly? No brochures in color from a Florida chamber of commerce?"

"Shut up," she said jauntily as she came into the living room. "There's always a lot on Saturday. Tomorrow you'll be begging me to show you the pictures."

"Yep," he said, still smiling. "I'm going to write you a poem about Florida some day that'll fly you right down there. I'll get rid of you."

He took half of the cut orange lying in a saucer on his bedside table, and sucked on it. Scattered over this large table were library books and a box of paper tissues, medicine bottles and spoons, a glass of water, a big red loose-leaf notebook, and a number of pencils, which he kept sharpened with the razor blade lying near them. Curled pencil shavings were in a neat pile at the edge of the table.

28

At intervals, Mrs. Golden swept them into the large paper bag pinned to the side of his mattress; it was swelled with soiled tissues.

Heidi was at the screen door, staring dreamily into the darkening street, and Jules said slyly, "Who's out there? Chip Levine? Prince Charming, ready to grab you?"

She flushed but she liked the words. Turning and examining the dark, soft fuzz on her brother's face, she said affectionately, "You need a shave, bum."

"Juley, now?" Mrs. Golden said immediately. "I could cut your hair, too. It's three weeks already."

"Tomorrow," he said, and began reading again.

For an instant his mother was unable to glance away from the fast pulse at the base of his throat. In the lamplight, the beat was too sharp, too quick, a dreadful rhythm in the jump and retreat of the skin. She forced her face back to the window. She talked; words had always been an antidote for fear of any kind.

"Al Zigman used to come every Friday to eat with his mother," she mused aloud. "Why doesn't he come any more? I'll bet he doesn't even know yet the upstairs is empty. Maybe a gambler doesn't care who lives upstairs of his own mother? But he's a Jew—gangster or not. He's got to care."

"You think Mrs. Zigman would let them in?" Heidi said.

"No. Just like I wouldn't. She's a good woman. Stubborn—how else would she still be alive with such sons? And the *spunyitze*? No! Everybody knows how Italians hate *Schwartze*. Thank God, the landlords of the empty suites are iron people."

"Are you starting that crap again?" Jules said, continuing to read.

In the kitchen, Becky's bellow turned on. "Ma, Ma, gimme eat!"

"Ida," Mrs. Golden said, "give her paper to cut. Maybe it'll keep her quiet till Papa comes and eats. He likes to give her from his plate."

As Heidi settled Becky on the kitchen floor with a stack of newspapers and the blunt toy scissors, Mrs. Golden perked up at her window and said, "Ah hah, the Reb is taking a little Friday-night walk. Look how he puts down his feet—slow; every step golden: here comes the prophet, look me over!"

Jules' head jerked up as his mother began ridiculing Ruth's father.

"Look at the holy man. One son is holier than him but not so good with the ladies, hah? One son divorced. A wife who gets crazier every day—and still he walks like he's a rabbi. Where is his daughter, the Queen? Who walks in a street like she won't spit on any man? She doesn't know she's an old maid?"

"Enough is enough!" Jules spluttered. "Don't you get tired of cutting people up and down?"

"Who's cutting?" Mrs. Golden bit her lip. She could not bear to think of Jules' secret love for Ruth Miller, and never failed to disparage her.

"What about your beautiful daughter?" he cried. "Turn it around—men won't spit on her."

Mrs. Golden shouted back at him, instead of weeping. "And I—I spit on you. Heartless brother. Genius. Insulter of sisters and mothers."

"Cheer up," he said in the cruel, sniping way of which he was a master. "Florida's full of millionaires, doctors, and rabbis. They'll all fight to marry your gorgeous daughter."

She glared at him. "And you? I suppose you'll be a famous writer?"

"I will be dead," he said, in the ominous voice with which he punished them so often. "Becky in an institution. Alex in a school for delinquents. In Florida, the Goldens can start over again—minus their cripples—far from the *Schwartze!*"

Mrs. Golden shuddered as she turned back to the window. "Juley," she said, "I'm not listening to you, that's all. I'm watching the street, so you can just shut up. Stone is softer than you—I'll watch the stone street."

"Go on, watch," he said. "Watch my funeral out there."

His mother suddenly laughed, with relief. "Here comes your little pet—the *schwartze kuter*. Out of the Gully, running like a real *kuter.*"

"And I want to warn you," Jules said in his dramatic way. "If you ever insult Vincent to her face you'll lose your son."

"Me?" she said with hurt surprise. "Would I insult your best friend? I'm proud I made up such a good name for her. She likes it. She told me herself once how even her own brother called her *schwartze kuter*. Sh! She's here."

30

Vincent was on the porch. At the screen door, she said, "Hi. How do you feel, Jules?"

"Hot. Full of poison," he said. "Come on in. We'll have poetry and tea, huh? Like on the Heights."

As Vincent opened the door, Mrs. Golden said, "Judy, maybe you saw Alex in the Gully?"

"No," she said shortly.

"He came, he ate, he went away again." Mrs. Golden went off to the kitchen, now that Jules had someone else to entertain him.

"Come on, sit on my bed," Jules said gently. He had seen Vincent's pale, scratched face at once, her dirty blouse.

"What's the matter?" he said in a low voice when she was sitting near him.

"Nothing," she said.

"Come on, what happened?"

She shook her head as she felt him prying. "I told you, nothing," she said, staring at his red notebook.

After a minute or two, he said softly, "Want to hear a poem?"

She nodded.

"How about 'The Changelings'?" He took his notebook from the table, opened it.

"No," she said quickly. She did not want the strength and drive of that one, not after what had happened to her in the Gully.

As Jules looked at her with surprise, Vincent said awkwardly, "Got a new one? Maybe about—colored people?"

It was the only way in which she could ask for help; the red notebook was Jules to her, its contents a kind of oracle advice. It was inconceivable to her that she could tell Jules the sudden mystery of having Dave turn enemy, and the enemy turn into a girl named Clara, who had thrown a present of protection at her feet.

"My favorite subject," Jules said grandly. He drew his bony knees up under the blanket and made a table for the notebook.

"Hey, Ma," he called. "Heidi. I'm going to read a new poem."

They came out of the kitchen at once, their eyes shining at the prospect. Heidi snapped off the radio as she passed it.

" 'Die Schwartze,' " Jules read. He prided himself on his Yiddish, and rolled the title out as he tasted the words. "Translation: 'The Black Ones.' "

Mrs. Golden frowned. "Since when is a poem about such things?"

"Since yesterday," he said gloatingly. "I thought you two like my poetry."

"Wise guy," Heidi said, trying to sneer.

"Here goes," Jules said to Vincent, and began to read with sly enjoyment from his open notebook:

"The immigrants come to America.
Freedom, freedom!
But the years go by—they get fancy ideas.
Look at them!
They can't even talk good English,
They're still greenhorns in their shivering hearts,
But overnight they're demanding ownership of a street.
Overnight they dreamed America melted them into a new
    shape:
Landlords of a city."

Mrs. Golden's frown deepened. "This is a poem? Go to Public Square for your lectures!"

Jules went on reading calmly:

"Oh, fable of democracy!
Having come, a pilgrim,
You can now deny a new kind of pilgrim:
*Die Schwartze!*
Having stepped foot upon a new shore, like a forefather,
You can now order off the newest invader,
The enemy which once you were:
*Die Schwartze!*
Oh, democratic vistas!
My son's son will have no need to remember
When his immigrant blood was enemy,
When his own difference was the flaw
In the fragrant American night!"

Vincent had not understood all the words, but she sat quietly waiting for more, or for the explanation he sometimes gave her, like a teacher interpreting a page of Shakespeare or history. She loved to hear Jules read his poems. There was a wonderful gleam in his eyes, even now, when he was so obviously taunting his mother.

"Shame on you," Mrs. Golden said angrily. "Why do you have to learn such things to children? Judy, don't listen to him. He is against decency, against Jewishness."

Jules looked at her, suddenly swept by excitement. "My God, you just put your finger on it! Maybe that's why these so-called poems have been leaking out of me all this time. For Vincent. For children. Because—sure!—who ever really talks to himself when he's got something to say? Yes, for children—to learn how to be braver than their parents. Better!"

"My genius!" Mrs. Golden cried. "He knows everything. Even about mothers and fathers. Sure, he knows how to pay them back for their suffering, their sweating. Sure, give them the *Schwartze* for a present—they'll sweat for good then, hah?"

"You think you're afraid of them?" Jules said, blinking with excitement. "Oh, no. They're simply what's in your heart—black, terrible. You're simply afraid of what's in your own heart, Mrs. Golden."

"Boy, I could kill you sometimes," Heidi said helplessly.

Vincent fingered the knife in her pocket and waited for Jules and his mother to stop spitting at each other. She wished the women would leave, and then she would get Jules' real explanation of the poem.

"I know all about your heart," Jules accused his mother. "Now you listen to this. Stanza Two, '*Die Schwartze*.' Vincent, you listen, too!

"Now comes The Black
From out the secret dark cell of my heart.
Now comes The Black Enemy, unnamed, unseen,
For I fear his name, his face,
For I will not admit his name is mine,
His face is mine!
Now comes The Black to overwhelm me,
From out the sky, from out the street,
From out the heart of me!"

Vincent touched the knife, the secret, the memory of the brown girl who had been watching her and the gang for a long time, unobserved. Would that Clara ever have showed herself if Dave and the gang had not attacked? From out the heart of me, from out the heart of me!

By now, Mrs. Golden stood trembling near the foot of Jules' bed. "Crazy philosopher," she cried, "you don't know that our street—with three empty suites—is the responsible one? Everybody else knows it, white and black! You say let them in. Crazy! You know that 117th, 118th, 119th are still white streets. And not one empty in any of them. You know that from our street up is still white. If 120th falls—if one *Schwartze* is permitted to move in and we fall—the other streets go, too. Then the whole neighborhood goes. It is a war. And we, we on 120th are the ones who will win it or lose it for a whole neighborhood!"

"Crap," Jules said, his face splotched with anger.

"Dirty mouth," his mother said. "This is still a good street, remember that, Mister. This is not a slums yet—we should give it to them."

"No," he shouted. "Make it a slums before you let them have one stinking empty."

"Stinking?"

"Ma," Heidi said in alarm, "come on the porch. He's nuts."

"Shut up," her mother said, not looking away from Jules. "This street stinks? Look at the pretty lawns. Look how people keep up the paint, the roof, on their little bit in the world."

She made a spitting sound of disgust. "On you! That's the way I spit on all children who can't realize a mother's worries. I remember suffering. In Russia, in America! I remember the depression. My house went to the bank. Other houses on this street went. We know how to squeeze a penny on this street, Mister! Tears ran in this street. Sweat —till we were able to buy back our houses. So now we'll throw them away to *Schwartze*?"

"Crap on the depression. How long can you go on using that excuse? And let me tell you, lady, this isn't Russia—it's Ohio. Even *Schwartze* have jobs today. The—the right to spend their money on rent. Stop acting like a White Russian landowner."

"Don't shine your genius on me! I'm a dumb woman in history but I know what a bread costs. I don't need books for that!"

"I cry for you! You and every money-hungry pig in this street."

"Don't talk to me about money," she flung back at him. "Every

34

scream in the depression came from me. Me, me! Who'll help me scream the next time the bank grabs? You, maybe? Or the *Schwartze?*"

"Ma!" Heidi begged.

Jules slammed the red notebook down on his table. "Vincent, get out of here," he said in a choked voice. "I don't want you in this ugly, dirty house. Go home."

As Vincent jumped up and sidled past Mrs. Golden's big, taut body, she heard Heidi's low cry of warning: "Ma, he's getting out of bed."

"Juley, you stay right there!" Mrs. Golden cried, and Vincent was out the door, off the porch.

Calmly, she ran across the street toward her house. In ten or fifteen minutes the Golden shouts would be over, Jules would be reading his book, and his mother would be bringing him grape juice. Then, later, in the middle of the night, he would write another poem. It happened all the time.

Now comes The Black, she thought as she ran. From out the sky, from out the heart of me.

In the Golden house, Jules was in the throes of a coughing and retching spell. His mother stood near him, holding his heaving body and pleading, "Juley, darling, be quiet. See what happens when you holler?"

Heidi came running with the basin, and Jules spat out the bloody phlegm which gathered in his mouth. Tenderly, Mrs. Golden wiped his perspired forehead, his lips, with the tissues she seized skillfully from his table.

Finally he waved away the basin. His mother helped him back on the pillows, straightened his legs, and smoothed the blanket over him. She went to the kitchen, where Heidi was drying the basin she had scrubbed, and whispered, "He's still mad, but he feels better. Go look."

Then she leaned toward Becky, who sat in deep drifts of the pieces she had cut out of sheets of newspaper. She took the scissors away, said softly, "Go to Juley. Go, darling. Juley wants you."

Becky jumped up and ran into the living room, and with a sigh Mrs. Golden took a coin from her purse and opened the broom closet. On its back wall was nailed a blue-and-white tin box with a

Star of David on it. This charity box was known as the *pushke*, and into it went small sums of money for Palestine.

Mrs. Golden threw her coin into the box. At the sound, Jules called cynically in a tired voice, "Well, how much did you throw in this time because I didn't die?"

"A quarter."

"Cheapskate! How much will you offer God to save me from a real attack? Huh?"

His mother smiled patiently as she closed the closet door. "Don't worry—He won't let you suffer," she said softly.

When she came in with a glass of grape juice, Jules was gravely handing Becky one pencil after another in a kind of game they played sometimes. Heidi stood nearby, watching them with an anxious grin.

"That's a good girl," Jules said absently. Only Becky, of all the family, was untouched by his disease. She accepted him as he was, a playmate, a gentle or comical voice; he loved her for it.

The lamp lit up the coarse, bristling, black hair, which her mother kept cut short for cleanliness. Becky looked much older than her twenty-four. She was a short, squat woman with a puffy body. Her features seemed blurred, her mouth loose and shapeless with an almost constant bland smile.

"Juley, a little grape juice?" Mrs. Golden said. "It's cold."

"Thanks," he said. They smiled at each other as he sipped.

"Want to hear the other poem I wrote last night?" he said.

She nodded, recognizing one of his ways of apologizing to her. "I know, it was a long night," she said gently.

He opened the red notebook again, began reading:

"The lampposts are like yellowed stars
Strung on a long piece of night, over our heads.
Cannot love float with these lights into our street?
Cannot the heat make love blossom in our flowerless street?
As the lampposts pretend they are stars
Strung on a long dreamy string of night?"

"Beautiful, beautiful," his mother murmured.

"Gee, Juley," Heidi said breathlessly, "that's wonderful."

Mrs. Golden pressed one of her hands to his face, and Jules kissed it with a darting, shy movement. Then he took his glass of juice and held it to his sister's mouth.

"Come on, Becky," he said, "let's have a party."

## 2

Sitting on her porch swing that Friday evening, Vincent touched the bruised places on her arms. Her legs ached when she moved them. But it was the brown-skinned girl who lingered in her mind, along with Jules' new poem, not the knowledge that she had lost her position in the gang.

She took the knife from her pocket, opened it and tested the sharpness of the blades. She thought of Dave's face, beginning to gush blood, and she shivered as she quickly put the knife away.

The upstairs screen door banged, and she heard Mr. Levine's heavy tread on the porch. He shouted a favorite cry: "Get to the hell out of my house. That's all!"

This was usually addressed to his oldest son, Moe, who now came noisily down the front-hall stairs. Moe was dark and lean, and he always walked as if he owned the whole street.

"Anybody using your phone?" he said in his insolent way.

"No," Vincent mumbled, and he went inside. He was one of the men on the fringe of her life that she hated for scaring her.

In a moment, Anna Levine came running out of the yard, a pitcher swinging from one hand, and went off toward the corner. On the upstairs porch, the man groaned softly. He had stomach trouble and drank a lot of Seltzer water, which Anna brought him from Newman's grocery. It was cheapest by the pitcher, and Mr. Levine claimed that it had more bubbles than bottled soda.

Through the window, Vincent saw Moe turn on her dining-room light and sit down at the phone. The screen door upstairs banged again, and she heard her father: "Well, Hersch? Your wife told me you have some business. She is on our back porch, with my wife. It's a little cooler there."

"Sit down, Abe," Mr. Levine said in his gloomy way.

They were speaking Yiddish, as usual, and Vincent listened absently. She understood the language well, though her own Yiddish was a stumbling mixture, half English.

37

"I hope you have been thinking," Mr. Levine said, "of what I mentioned the night Rosen moved his family to the Heights."

"I have been thinking."

Vincent heard the hesitancy in her father's voice, and sneered. He always sounded so wishy-washy with Mr. Levine, as if the big, loud man was his landlord instead of his partner.

"The third empty suite, Abe. And right next door to us. One black face in the windows and our house is worth half."

Anna came walking carefully with the brimming pitcher, disappeared into the yard. Mr. Levine's laugh sounded peculiar. "Do you realize that on the Heights they have gas furnaces, mostly? Not coal? Who could call it an accidental fire there?"

"Here comes your Seltzer—sh!"

Soon Mr. Levine's loud, rumbling belches started. "Ah, that's better," he said with relief. "Thank God for Seltzer. All right, Abe, a coal furnace. It becomes overheated sometimes. People put in too much coal, then they go away. To a party, for a visit—the whole family. Near the furnace is paper, rags, the things kept in a basement. Fortunately, houses are insured."

"Well, it is only September. God knows how long this heat will continue!"

Vincent heard the badly concealed fear in her father's voice, and began listening with interest.

"Winter always comes," Mr. Levine said firmly.

There was a pause, then she heard her father mumble, "My wife says the Black Ones came to Zigman's all day."

"Well, what do you expect? What stupid white man would rent in this street? On the edge of quicksand? Better a fire—let others stay and be sucked in."

Moe Levine turned off the light in her house, came out the back way and sauntered off toward the corner. For a second, as she watched his prowling walk, Vincent remembered Mrs. Levine crying to her mother in the downstairs kitchen: "Why does Moe have to go only with gentile girls? He's not a boy, to try out forbidden tastes. A man, twenty-seven years old! He works, he even took in his brothers and gave them paper routes. Like a responsible man. Why can't he find a good Jewish girl?"

For another second, quietly and with love, Vincent touched

38

Shirley and Manny in her mind: "forbidden tastes," or else mothers and fathers called it "sin" in the sibilant Yiddish that could give words such stern and accusing import.

Then she tried to visualize her house burning, saw herself running in to rescue her treasure box and the school supplies left over from last semester. It might be fun, she thought with a faint stirring of excitement.

"Who do you think will be the first to sell to a Black One?" Mr. Levine asked.

"It won't happen. They won't even rent to one."

"Abe, stop dreaming! You know what I thought today? Maybe Simon'll sell first. He's already got a butcher shop on the Heights. So why not live there, too, eh?"

"He can't afford it. Anyway, Simon wouldn't do it."

"It'll be a Jew who'll do it first. Not an Italian, not a gentile. Mark my word, Abe—a Jew will take the first dirty step!"

Mr. Levine belched, poured himself more Seltzer. "Who else would have the courage?" he said. "Buckholz, Mrs. Anderson? Connors doesn't even own a house—he rents. Rinaldi, Rini, Valenti? Oh, no. Italians won't do it, that I know. The gentiles? Oh, no! They're the kind of people you forget are even living in your street—they never open their mouths."

Her father did not answer, and Vincent thought absently of how they all had this habit of grouping the street: there were the Jews, the Italians, and then all the others were called the gentiles—*die goyim*. She smiled as she wondered if Jules would write a poem about them some day, too.

Mr. Levine cursed. "If only the first house had been sold already. When I think of what the Italians might do to us if we were the first! You know how they hate the Black Ones. Think of Ross Valenti—one look at his face and I get cold."

"And what if somebody did it to us?"

"Ah, but if one could only sell a house without these hundred worries," Mr. Levine said wistfully. "They pay double, you know."

"Do banks lend them money? I heard of a man on 105th who sold his house three different times—to three different Black Ones. He is still living there—no bank would give them the loan."

39

"Do you believe everything you hear? I tell you, Abe, fire burns out the biggest worry!"

Vincent shrugged as she stretched her aching body. It was none of her business. Grownups took care of things like that. Yeah, but maybe Dave could get in on this fire deal. If his house burned, he would not have to worry about all those *Schwartze* either—like Pa and Mr. Levine. Then maybe he could be the old Dave again, the brother and pal, if he did not have to worry about the terrible enemy grabbing his empty.

Only the enemy was no longer terrible, she thought abruptly. The enemy had a face, was named Clara. The enemy had loaned her a knife, had been as furious and bitter over her lost kingdom as if it had been her own ripped away.

Hey, how come? Vincent asked herself.

She heard her father's voice, plaintive, meek: "Why does it happen so often? That is what I can't understand. Since I came to this city I have seen it twice, and now it's the third time. It happened to me on Cedar—what a beautiful Jewish neighborhood that was in the old days! Then, all of a sudden, the Jews started to run."

"We ran, too! Others ran to 105th. And what happened there, not five years ago? Like a flood! Finally the Black Ones even bought the synagogue for their church. That beautiful temple. God, it was the talk of the city when they built it. Do you remember?"

"Yes, yes, of course. What happens, for God's sake?"

"It is an American habit," Mr. Levine said. "It has to happen. For years a neighborhood is peaceful, pretty, well kept. Then, overnight, the Black Ones start hammering to get in. They want it! No matter where you move: in ten years, in fifteen years, they're here again! They're hollering, 'Let me in, give me your house!' "

"They say the same thing happens in other cities, too."

"Certainly," Mr. Levine said. "It is one of the American habits. And it always goes the same way. First a few Jews with money move. Then some of the Italians start getting nervous, so they move, too—they always follow the Jews, you know. Then the gentiles start running. And the Jews without money? If they're frightened enough, they go, too. They mortgage their old age to the eightieth year, but they go! And all the while, more and more of the Black Ones sneak in. Soon a whole neighborhood is rotting."

40

Vincent had never heard him so eloquent. There was a bitterness in his voice, a sound of hurt she could not associate with this coarse man.

"And by then," he said, "the rabbis have gone, too. All the leaders of a Jewish community have run, too. They have forsaken us who are left, who cannot run. The organizations have abandoned us—welfare, religion, the groups which give a Jew safety in his thoughts. All right, we can take a bus and go to them—on the Heights. But is it the same? No! In our hearts we know they have left us."

"Yes, when the Jewish community abandons you—"

Vincent, listening intently, heard the same tone of hurt in her father's voice.

"It is an American habit, I tell you. And when your leaders run, can you fight? Should you? If they run from the Black Ones, like sheep?"

There was the gurgling sound of Seltzer pouring into an empty glass. To Vincent, the shouts and laughing cries of the children at their lamppost games sounded very far away as she waited for her father to make some kind of bold, unfrightened answer.

A scornful laugh came from Mr. Levine. "Without money you are dead. What else is there to say? This is the American habit, Abe. You think we can break such habits? Me, a poor carpenter, and you, a painter, just as poor?"

Vincent frowned as she heard the shakiness of her father's voice: "I'll tell you the truth, I never got used to this country. With its habits! For me, America was always hard, a strange place."

There was a silence, then Mr. Levine said gruffly, "Well, did I ever get used to this country? Am I a millionaire—or even a building contractor? I am still going to work on the streetcar, on the bus. Like you."

The two men were *lantzman*. They had come from the same village in Russia and belonged to the same benevolent society, which was made up of men and women from that village, and their families. Doggedly, they paid sickness and death dues, attended meetings. Each Monday evening they went to talk and to play cards with fellow members at brotherhood headquarters, which recently had moved to the Heights. Their wives attended sisterhood meetings on Thursday evenings; they, too, played cards after the meeting, which was devoted

41

to plans for parties, cake sales, and raffles for the benefit of Palestine. Neither of the partners had ever wanted the responsibility of being a boss, of estimating the cost of jobs or directing other men's work. Both were uneasy in any language but Yiddish. They were transplanted men who had never become accustomed to a new soil.

All of these things Vincent knew, without the words to describe them. And she knew that the partners were weak and ineffectual, her father in a soft, silent manner and Mr. Levine with the shouts and curses which often made her father wince as he sat downstairs with his Yiddish newspaper or library book. They were two more of the men on the fringe of her life who frightened her.

The girl without the words to go with her feelings and instincts listened to the partners and wondered why there was so much talk about only the *Schwartze*. What about love (Shirley and Manny)? What about friendship (Jules, once upon a time Dave)?

"I remember," her father said, "that people had fires during the depression. Before the bank could take away your house. There is no depression today."

"What is the difference between a depression and the coming of the Black Ones?" Mr. Levine said bitingly. "Both roll like a flood over you until you are naked and penniless as the day you came to America. A nothing again. With one difference! Then you were young, with a tomorrow. Now? Old, old! No longer the dream of love to help you. The dream of sons." He made a loud, spitting noise. "Sons? I laugh!"

Vincent's eyes smarted at the queer sadness in his voice. She had to think of her brother Nate, of tiny laughing Manny.

"Believe me, Abe, there is always a new name for suffering. Each year—when a man must fight the flood or be destroyed. Hitler is gone, eh? There is no depression? So this year it is the Black Ones. The same flood, to wash away tomorrow. Only the name is different. Who will take care of us when the flood comes? Our sons?"

Across the street, the *spunyitze* had come out on her porch and had begun her nightly cries. For as long as Santina stayed out each evening, her grandmother called her; the imploring, stern cadences were part of the night music of the street.

"Sahn-tina! Sahn-tina!" she cried, her foreign pronunciation of the name giving it a strange, singing quality.

42

Tonight it was like a mourning in the street, as if the old lady keened a powerful sadness up at the moon: "Sahn-tina! Sahn-tina!"

Vincent took the knife out of her pocket; a gift—what a puzzle. And what a puzzle that the men had blamed all their losses on the mysterious, terrible *Schwartze:* rabbis and money and love and sons. For her, tonight, their enemy had a name, a face.

"Sahn-tina! Sahn-tina!"

"Listen to her," Mr. Levine said. "A voice like iron. That one will never rent or sell to them. They are more her enemy than ours, even. Remember, Abe, even an Italian has his Hitler."

But Vincent stared at the knife, remembering how the enemy had thrown it to her like a gift of protection.

## Chapter four

On Saturday mornings Ruth Miller went alone to open her father's pawnshop. He came after sundown, when the Sabbath was over.

At eight-thirty on these mornings, Jules began to watch through his window for Ruth to leave her house, on the opposite side of the street. She left at any time between then and nine—Shylock's daughter, his beloved princess, in her arms the perpetual book, the package of lunch, and the big purse in which he visualized all the sweet-smelling, secret possessions of a beautiful woman.

She never wore a hat in warm weather, and Jules was grateful. He loved to see her hair, long and black, worn straight back and tight above the ears, then coiled in a loose, soft knob at the nape of her neck. She was quite thin, so that her face often seemed stark, the bones pushing hard in her cheeks and at her chin and temples, and yet her lips were very full under the carefully applied lipstick. With her dark, smooth skin, her graceful hands ungloved on a book, she seemed like one of the beautiful, fiery women whose pictures he stared at in books about long-ago Italy and Spain.

Sometimes, when he was well enough to be on the porch and she came over to ask him how he felt, she looked quiet and deep as an ocean; but sometimes her eyes seemed burning dark, feverish, poems in her face. And sometimes she waved to him as she walked in the street. And sometimes his mother called her "The Reb's Daughter" or "The Queen," and deep inside his head he told his mother how he worshiped Ruth, how he wrote love poems to her which no one but God could read, for he did not write them in his notebook.

At a quarter of nine, Ruth came out of her house and began to walk toward the corner. From his bed, Jules watched her raptly, guarding his face so that his mother or sister would not take him by surprise if they came suddenly from the noisy kitchen.

He had an idealized picture of Ruth Miller, to fit his dream. She was strong, very quiet and wise, invulnerable to fear, ugliness, lust, any weakness. She was a boy's beautiful dream of love.

Watching her, he could taste a kind of peace, and almost touch the day when he would feel rest inside of him. Watching her, he could feel that some day his constant turmoil would stop and he would no longer have to struggle not to be afraid. His heart always followed Ruth to the corner, all the way to her father's pawnshop.

## 2

When Ruth got to within a block of the store she saw her brother's shabby little car at the curb in front of the store. She smiled, walked faster. She was never sure Herb would be there Saturdays until she saw him.

She came up to the car and Herb lowered the newspaper he had been reading. "Hi, honey, how are you?" he said in his slow voice, and got out to help her open up.

"Been here long?" Ruth asked as she took the huge bunch of store keys from her purse and began working on the locks.

"Maybe fifteen minutes," Herb said. "You missed two customers. Frankie, and Jack Vanta. They'll be back later." He grinned. "In time to get some dough for their bookies."

He knew many of the customers from the years he had worked in the store, and most of them had come to his store occasionally, or to Ben's, when his father had irritated them.

Ruth had opened the locks on the master gate, which protected the door, and Herb lifted the section off, leaned it so that he could

44

remove the sections of gate which barred the double windows. Ruth selected the other keys for the door.

Sometimes she felt like a jailer, opening her own cell. Her father believed in a variety of locks, for protection. It took three different keys to open the gates, and two before the door could be swung; then there was a key for the inner door of the safe, after the combination had been twirled, one for the strongbox, and two for the back door to the store.

She pushed the door open, then propped the screen door so that Herb could carry in the gates. As she entered the store and pulled the light cords, the dank, dusty smell hit her like a presence; but at least it was cooler inside.

Dropping her book on the counter, she carried her purse and the package of lunch back to the office, with its grilled open window and high stools, the cot where her father napped. She removed her dress and put on one of the cotton smocks, pinned another smock around her dress before hanging it up. Then she opened the safe, unlocked the strongbox, and removed the cash and the expensive jewelry which would go back into the window for the day.

The gun she put on the shelf just below the cash register, close to the grilled window. The money she put into the register. The large, heavy books, with their thousands of careful entries, she placed on the counter, and then readied the many forms for customers and for police records, made sure the ink and pen were in place. She locked the little plump sacks of diamonds back into the strongbox and then closed the safe, hid the keys in a dark corner under the counter.

Years of opening the store had made her movements mechanical, very fast. As she carried the rings and bracelets and several flashy necklaces to one of the front windows, Herb bumped the heavy steamer trunk over the floor and outside. Mr. Miller always kept a trunk outside the store to show the world that second-hand luggage could be bought, along with tools, shoes, clothes, musical instruments.

Ruth placed the jewelry on a piece of black velvet, then leaned farther into the window to rearrange a trumpet and violin, a microscope, the cheaper gaudy jewelry which drew Negro customers. She could see Herb at his car. He was taking out the pieces of his latest invention; he would spend most of the day in the store working on it,

45

using one after another of the pawned tools in the big section back of the luggage.

She saw how carefully he handled the pieces of wood and metal as he piled them in his arms to carry them in. His tired, battered-looking face was perspiring in the hot sunlight, and as he turned, the glare picked up his scar for a second. It ran the length of his cheek on the left side of his face, almost a half inch wide, puckered, a dull red, giving him a quizzical, rather endearing look.

Herb was a big man with sandy, cropped hair. He was only ten years older than Ruth but looked more like fifty than his thirty-five, with those carelessly hunched shoulders. She thought his eyes wonderful, moist, soft brown, almost too gentle for a man. She loved him with an intensity that was half hurt. Sometimes she could not bear even to think of his fumbling, shabby life in the three years since he had left his wife and child and walked out of the pawnshop their father had opened for him.

When he came back into the store she was at the second window, replacing micrometers and the other expensive items moved each night into a section of the glassed showcase which ran the length of one side of the store. Mr. Miller did not believe in tempting potential thieves, left only cheap things in the windows overnight.

Herb began to set up his invention, called from behind the wall of trunks, "How's Mom, Ruthie?"

She sucked at her full lower lip, then said, "The same."

"Still think the neighbors are stealing from her?"

"Still."

"Even with the hall door locked? I brought her a lot of extra keys last week. Didn't do any good?"

"Herb, she forgets what she's put out in the hall closet! Uses up the potatoes and onions, and—she forgets, that's all!"

"Yeah," he muttered tenderly. "I'll try and get over tomorrow. Bring Alice—she'll pep Mom up."

"I wish you would," Ruth said, turning from the window. Then she added carelessly, "Want to phone before you come?"

"Why?" Herb said, startled. "Dad's always out of the house by ten on Sundays. At the store, no?"

"He's going to another board meeting. There's some kind of fuss at *shul*. He—well, he's so nervous and angry. The board's being odd."

46

Herb's laugh was hard. "Well, well! You mean he can't crack the whip at the board meetings any more? They used to kiss his feet."

"Herb, please don't talk that way," Ruth said quickly. "Dad's got so many troubles. The board is talking about moving the *shul*, selling this building and buying one on the Heights. Or even building there."

"Don't make me laugh! He'll remind them whose money started that *shul*. He'll make them sweat out that five thousand bucks before he lets them move. Don't they know the *shul's* in hock to him?"

"Herb, that's rotten!" she cried hotly.

"All right! So what's needling the board, all of a sudden?"

"I suppose it's the *Schwartze*. The neighborhood's changing." Ruth was dusting the wall shelves, their packed contents of cameras, binoculars, fishing supplies, rifles and cartridges. "That's another thing that's bothering Mom, too. She's frightened. Doesn't want to go out alone after dark."

A heavy flush of anger swept into his face. "Poor little peasant," he said gratingly. "He locked her up in a city. He put high-heeled shoes on her, and—"

The screen door slammed. A man had come in with a suit to pawn. "I'll take him," Herb said, his voice slow again. "Hello there, Bert."

Bert was an old customer. There would be a long, quiet argument about how much he could get on the worn suit. Ruth wiped the glass top of the long showcase, which was used as a counter. Her heart was still beating too fast at the way Herb's voice had turned murderous for a minute.

She could hear his ordinary voice now, patient with a customer, hearty, crafty. Yes, the right answer would always be at the tips of their tongues, no matter what secrets hid in their hearts; and the quick knowledge of an article's value, the instinctive slashing glance to see if a thief hid in a customer, the guarded step back toward the gun in the office.

The pawnshop was in their blood, she thought dismally. None of them would ever escape it. Even Herb had not escaped, though he was a salesman now. He sold storm sash and screens, or something of the sort; he had never gone into detail about his job.

He never went into detail about anything. That reticence hurt her as much as the tiredness written all over the man. He had never

**47**

talked about why he had walked away from his wife after eleven years of marriage, or from his business, from his father. Herb came to the store only on Saturdays because he knew Dad would not be there until dark. They had seen each other rarely during the three years and then only by accident; Herb brought his daughter to the house often on Sundays, and occasionally Dad happened to get home earlier than usual from the store.

Ruth could still wince, remembering her father's rage, the horrible things he had said after the divorce. He had even brought up the inventions, accusing Herb, to his face, of wasting hours every day with his puttering: "In my store—before you were married! In your own store, instead of earning bread for your wife and child! And why? What crazy idea—inventions? What ever came of them, these—these toys!"

Why hadn't Herb answered their father that day? Ruth asked herself for the hundredth time as she went back to the office. There was a tiny, closetlike room at one end, with a toilet and a stained sink, a mirror, the towels which she brought from home. She washed her hands and rubbed in a skin lotion, combed her hair, freshened her lipstick.

"Ruthie," Herb called, "get five bucks for Bert. Two-week loan. And he wants his suit cleaned."

"Coming up," she called back through the grilled window. Yes, it was in the blood. Trust Herb to sell the old man a dry-cleaning job, too!

And Alice? she thought bleakly, as the cash register clanged open and she began filling out the receipt for the suit. She's crazy about him now, but she's only ten. How will she like the gentle failure when she grows up? Will she want to see him even that one day in the week that the court gave her father?

She carried the receipt and the money down front. "How are you, Bert?" she said mechanically.

"Fair, fair," the old man said as he wrote his name, and went on telling Herb about the roaches in his room.

Ruth pulled a stool out of the office and sat down to read the book she had brought along with her. Wonder if Herb has roaches, too? she thought. Since the divorce, he had been living in furnished rooms here and there. He had never asked her to see any of them. When

48

she phoned him once in a while, a woman's coarse voice answered, then shouted: "Hey, Miller—phone."

The screen door slammed, and Herb said with a chuckle, "Bert's going to sue his landlady—roaches. The suit's okay. Not even a bedbug."

He put it in the box for the cleaner and came to her, on the other side of the counter, flipped her book around to see what it was. A quietly sardonic smile came to his face. "Well, well, Dostoevsky this week, huh? Keats last week; Proust next? Looks like Flo's written you out a list of her good old favorites."

"It's a good book," Ruth said, tapping her cigarette jerkily.

"Classics, culture—Flo's recipes for anybody's troubles."

"How's Alice?" Ruth said brightly.

His smile changed. "Sweet as sugar. You know, we've got a new game. Take turns phoning each other. I call her in the morning; she calls me at night, just before she goes up to bed. My landlady's fallen in love with her, right over the phone."

He pushed the book back. "Seeing Flo tonight?" he said.

"Concert," she said, flushing at his amused tone. "I'm meeting her at the Museum. It's one of those summer, outdoor affairs."

"Chopin, I'll bet," he said cheerfully, and went off to his bench. Soon a light, irregular hammering came from there.

Ruth pretended to read. Flo was Herb's former wife, and the concert tonight was Chopin. She hated the contemptuous way in which he spoke of things like literature and music. That was a failure, too, the forgetting how hungry his little sister had always been for the new language, for the cultural richness of the country—even before Flo had come into their lives and offered so generously to share her friends and intellectual activities.

It was not that she loved Flo, or felt close to her. Herb and Alice were in her heart, but Flo was the figure before whom her mind bowed. She had always been dazzled and rather awed by Herb's wife, her knowledge of conductors and composers and authors, her poise at a piano as she played to a crowded room, the way she surrounded herself with brilliant, successful people.

After the divorce, she had gone right on seeing Flo and her crowd. It had taken her months to get over her fear that Flo might ask her to stay away because of Herb. The blond, energetic woman was her only contact with a life she wanted ravenously, even though it continued to make her feel so small. It was like books, when she thought of the richness of Flo's evenings and weekends; she was starved for them, and she would never get enough of them, or be completely at ease with the language in them.

The screen door slammed, and then, almost immediately, slammed again. Saturday began in earnest, still the best day in the week for pawnshops. Part of the morning was taken up by old customers on their way to bet on the races. White and Negro, they were in a hurry, and they brought in luxury items like radios, traveling clocks, suitcases.

Ruth filled in all the receipts, as well as the careful records for the police. Between customers, she kept up with most of the bookkeeping. Herb sold a suit and a pair of shoes to a strange Negro. Ruth sold a cheap violin to a strange, white woman who told her that her son was going to be a famous musician.

She threw in an old music stand for free, and when the woman left she called softly, "Herb, how's Alice making out with her piano lessons?"

"She hates 'em," he said, snickering. "Bet she cheats like crazy on practicing when her old lady's not around."

Ruth went back to her book. She was never able to tell Herb how she loved his daughter, just as she was never able to face herself, in actual words, with her deepest hunger. She had constant, nebulous pictures of herself bending over her own child, opening books for him, and singing lovely old songs, while in the background hovered a man who was always gentle, loving, sensitive, and a complete success in all the ways a man could be.

The vise squeaked as Herb tightened it on one of his pieces. "I hear the drugstore was held up Wednesday," he said.

"Two *Schwartze*."

"Yeah," he said hesitantly. "Is it such a good idea for Dad to be here alone Saturday nights?"

"Mom's coming, too, these days."

"Good, good." Herb's head came up, and he frowned at her above a trunk. "Say, honey, I don't get this *shul* argument. Any *Schwartze* move into your street yet?"

50

"No, but another Jewish family moved last week."

"But there are plenty left for a congregation. What's up?"

"Don't ask me," she said impatiently. "I don't pay any attention to the street. I hate to see Dad so disturbed about the *Schwartze*, though."

He stared at her. "Why in hell is he so disturbed? He's been selling them junk for years, making money. All of a sudden they're poison?"

"Oh, Herb!" she cried, irritated.

"The fools," he said. "Dad and the whole board. In the first place, why should the *shul* move?"

"I told you—Dad doesn't want that!"

Herb snorted. "Sure, because he can't go with them. Isn't that the only reason? Now take Ben—he's a real member of that congregation. Is he—"

"How can you compare Dad and Ben?" she broke in.

"Hey," he demanded softly after a second, "what's so terrific about Dad?"

Ruth's heart slammed. She could not bear the dreadful potential of emotion trembling so often these days in Herb's voice when he mentioned their father. Carefully, she said, "All I mean is, Dad would be heartbroken if the *shul* moved to a new neighborhood. He's not a young man, to flit around."

"No, he's getting old, thank God," Herb muttered, his jaw tight.

"Listen, I'm starving," Ruth said with a smile. "Going to run out for some coffee? I brought chicken sandwiches, on the chance you'd be here. And Mom sent one of chopped liver."

He smiled, too. "She figured I'd be here, huh? Split it with you."

"No onions! Not to a concert."

Herb came around the wall of trunks, rolling down his shirt sleeves. "The Chopin lady come up with any professional men for you yet?" he said.

Ruth flushed, but she said lightly, "Oh, everybody knows I'm an old maid by now. Even Mom doesn't nag much any more."

"And Dad?" he asked quietly. "Has he started to nag yet? Who would open the store on Saturdays if you got married? Who would look at him with girlish, worshiping eyes?"

51

She jumped down from the stool and went to the cash register, brought him a dollar bill. "Coffee's on the house. Want to pick up some pie?"

Herb took the bill, suddenly leaned and gave her an affectionate kiss on the cheek. The endearing smile was back as he said, "Chip always brings dessert. Why waste good Miller money on pie?"

Her eyes stayed expressionless, and he said quizzically, "Chip doesn't read Proust, huh? He doesn't go to *shul*. Ruthie, Ruthie, where are you?"

But he sauntered out without another word. She felt, a little breathlessly, that she had escaped a moment of horror when she had gotten him to stop that hammering about their father. Why had Herb started to talk, all of a sudden? After all her longing for an end to reticence, she discovered that she was frightened at what Herb might say to her.

### 3

They had finished their lunch, were drinking their second containers of coffee—Herb back on the workbench and Ruth at the counter, reading—when Chip Levine came in with the big paper bag of fruit he always brought on Saturdays.

"Hey, wake up," he said, letting the door slam. "We just rented a house to *Schwartze*."

"Who did?" Ruth cried. "You're lying, aren't you?"

He slid the bag over the glass toward her. "Have some fruit," he said, grinning. "Boy, I really scared her, Herb, didn't I?"

"Hi, Chip," Herb said, and came out for an apple.

"You're disgusting," Ruth said. "I can think of better things to joke about."

"Me, too," he said, staring at her with enjoyment. "Bed—me, you. Want to laugh?"

"Oh, please!" She lit a cigarette with a gesture of scorn.

Chip Levine had been named Sigmund at birth, but only his parents remembered that. He had been called Chip since the days, at eight or nine, when he had gone about the streets earnestly begging all sizes of kids to knock the chip off his shoulder and get their blocks knocked off. In later years he had become quite well known as a Golden Gloves fighter, and he still did a lot of amateur boxing.

Dark, with a rather square, guarded face, Chip flaunted his muscular, graceful body. He had been in love with Ruth Miller for years, with a hopelessness which he had converted into bold, crude words with which to kid himself. They were a lot alike; he felt as inferior to her as she to Flo. Both were tense and emotional, deeply sensual, but they covered in different ways. The pattern was an old one by now: Ruth was cool and supercilious, overly careful of diction, and  Chip was deliberately coarse, quick to jeer at every stilted thought she held up like a wall between them.

Herb was smiling as he ate his apple. "When's your next fight?" he said to Chip.

"Tuesday night. Want me to leave a couple of tickets at the door?"

"That would be swell," Herb said, and took a bunch of grapes from the bag before he headed back to the bench.

Chip began to peel a banana. "Eat some fruit, skinny," he said to Ruth. "Instead of smoking like a furnace. I rode all the way downtown to the market for it—you're so God damn particular."

She pushed the bag toward him, said petulantly, "Why do you bring me bananas? I hate them—you know that."

"They cost like diamonds," he said calmly, and took a big bite, went on talking with his mouth full. "I like to see you eat—the best. Bananas'll fatten you up. How in hell do you expect to warm a guy's bed, that skinny?"

"Oh, Chip, stop it," she said in a low voice.

It was like a game they had to play. The more she winced, the harder he drove at her. The more priggish her voice became and the more she cringed inside at the idea of lying down with a man, the more she thought of his body and of his warmth, his strength.

She had never gone anywhere with him. They saw each other as they passed in the street, sometimes talked briefly. He came to the pawnshop for an hour or two every Saturday on his way to the gym, where he boxed. They both knew, without ever having discussed it, that he never came any other day because of her father.

A buying customer came in. He asked to see some fishing tackle and a rod, and Ruth led him back, stood talking to him as he fingered items. Chip twisted to see the name of the book she was reading, then turned again to watch the Ruth-of-the-pawnshop: shrewd, sly, a business woman. He was dryly amused at the way she still mystified him. What a hell of a combination in one woman! Passion and snobbery, Jew smartness and—Jesus, the sweet, dreaming mouth!

Saturdays were painful for him, though he looked forward to their exquisite sharpness all week. When he had come back from the army after three years in Europe of being a big-shot boxer between battles, he had planned to get the hell out of town—away from Ruth, away from the family.

One look at that icy, beloved face and he had gone right back to hustling papers under Moe. His brother had put in his own time in Burma and India by then, and the *Beacon-News* had held out a better job like a medal, had made Moe a supervisor in Eastside distribution. The job was the same, his family, Ruth, and the sunken hopeless feeling in his stomach was the same every Saturday when he left this place and got to the gym, began punching out his loneliness.

Every other day he worked until four-thirty, but Saturday was free because of early shift on Sunday. Yeah, good old Saturday! That night he would have to get himself a good lay somewhere, then home for a few hours of sleep before his mother woke him and the others at four in the morning for the Sunday work. It was the same every Saturday after he stumbled out of this rotten, wonderful time near Ruth.

As he watched her, he made a little talk over the trunk. "Ever know it so hot, Herb? They finally had to air-condition the gym."

"It's not too bad in the store," Herb said. "Throw me a banana, Chip." Peeling the banana, he said in a low voice, "What's all this stuff cooking in the street about *Schwartze?* Or is Ruthie being dramatic?"

"It's the same old crap," Chip said, with no interest, "only the Rosens moved. So it's number three on the empties and all the folks are crying harder, that's all. They got to cry about something, don't they?"

"Yeah," Herb said with a frown.

The customer left without buying anything. Chip watched Ruth walk to the back room, to wash her hands. Then she stopped at the small, electric phonograph on a table just outside the grilled window, selected a record, pushed the lever. Music began softly, a piano, and a thin sourness trickled into Chip's mouth as he watched her standing there in the clutter of a thousand unredeemed articles, listening.

Dreaming of some college guy, he thought. Professional man, doctor, rabbi. Or a guy like her old man—without the beard—forty years younger.

"Hey, skinny," he called, "come here and eat some fruit. Before you turn around I'm scramming over to the gym."

And he thought again: Why does a guy have to find a star, way up somewhere, and keep looking? You can go blind! In the guts!

Ruth came, reluctantly ate a few grapes. "Chopin," she said, nodding toward the phonograph. "Isn't it lovely?"

Anger, the need to grab her up close to him, turned his voice taunting. "How would I know? The Levines are strictly from *Eli Eli* and *borscht*. Me, I don't know Chopin from my bunghole."

"I'm going to ask you to leave," she said, at her coldest. "Unless you stop talking that way."

"Why don't you stop making me talk that way?" he said pleasantly. "Be yourself for a second, will you? I know I'm low. I know I'm nothing but Levine trash, but stop rubbing it in for a second, will you?"

She ran to lift the needle, which was scratching in the last groove, and so he did not see her flushed face. Be yourself, he had said, as if he knew that she acted most of the time—with everyone, even her father and Herb, even with the kids of the street. Sometimes she could not remember the Ruth hidden in the woman who dressed so carefully each day and fussed with hair and shoes, who spoke slowly with painstaking diction and carried books as part of her princess costume.

But here stood the only man who had ever loved the princess, like a caricature of the lover-husband for whom she had perfected herself. Herb's hammer made a light, delicate sound, and for an instant she saw his intent eyes—a million miles away. When she turned, Chip was leaning on the counter, eating an apple. She slipped behind the showcase and sat on the stool.

"Don't you get tired of all those fat books?" he said in his mocking way. "What good'll they do you in bed?"

Somewhere inside of her, Ruth felt this inarticulate way Chip had of making love to her; no language at his fingertips, no music in his mind to soften and color a phrase, only the stubborn, crude words with which their whole street identified love. This was the only man who had ever loved her.

She thought of her father, visualized him in the big mohair chair at home, right now. Temple services over, the big Saturday dinner over, he sat with head sunk, eyes shut, as he began to sing. Other men had music in their minds! Her father's deep, powerful voice—steeped in memories of his father's prayers, his grandfather's—could make a concert hall of a house.

As she lit a cigarette, absently pushing the ashtray back and forth on the counter, Chip tossed his apple core into the bag. He saw her a million miles away from him, reached for her anxiously.

"Hey, remember me?" he said. "Before you turn around I'm going to get tired of trying to make you. Then watch me go out and lay some broad just as low-class as a Levine."

She looked at him scornfully, playing their game, but inside she shivered. A lover-husband could be like her father, too, and gentle as Herb. But who else, what else! A hundred-headed man with her father's mind, Ben's devout eyes, Herb's secret Godless heart?

"Remember me?" Chip said again. "Waiting to drag you to bed, is all."

"Go home," she cried in a low voice, under the hammer sound.

"I am home," he said in the taunting voice. "You're it."

It was the first time she had heard music in him, an inside language. As she stared unbelievingly, the screen door crashed, and a customer stood peering in the dusty, cool gloom of the store.

Chip's longing eyes followed the Ruth-of-the-pawnshop as she stepped briskly toward the customer.

### 4

Shortly after three o'clock that afternoon, Ben's wife came into the pawnshop. Chip had been gone almost a half hour, and Ruth had turned on the phonograph again.

It was grinding out an aria from *La Traviata*. Herb was whistling along with the recorded voice as he puttered at the workbench, and Ruth was making entries in one of the books, when the screen door opened. She looked through the grilled window and saw Ilona's shy, plump face, her smile as she caught Herb's eye.

"Honey," Ruth called in surprise, and came out of the office to greet her sister-in-law.

"Well, well," Herb said, pleased. "Look who's here."

"So nice," Ilona murmured happily. "The phonograph, and Herbie—I was hoping you'd be here, Herbie. I haven't seen you for so long."

His arm was around her in a hearty squeeze. "How are you, Ilona? Look how pretty this lady stays! A mother of two big boys—impossible."

She laughed, delighted. "You should care! Why don't you come and see us sometimes, Herbie? Little Alice should see more of my boys. She'll forget her own family."

Herb winced, but he said smoothly, "Now, now, Ilona. We'll make up for everything some day. How are the boys?"

"Fine. They're taking a nap downstairs, on Ruth's bed—your mother is watching them. Your father is sleeping, too. I—all of a sudden, I had to go for a walk! It was so hot in the house. I—I had to— Oh, I knew you would be here, Herbie! What are you doing, inventing?"

"What else am I good for?" he said, pretending to chuckle.

As Ilona took off her hat, Herb's eyes questioned Ruth. There was a strange unrest in Ilona today; ordinarily her quiet, lovely nature made a shine wherever she went. He brought one of the high stools, set it behind the counter for her as she stood listening to the last of the aria. When she sighed, Ruth felt a flutter of warning in her chest. She reached up to pull the cord of another light bulb.

"You'd think it was evening in here," she mumbled.

In the sudden push downward of light, Herb's face looked too craggy under the quizzical smile. They both studied Ilona in the new brightness.

"It's like a furnace outside," she said absently, still listening to the music. "Even in the Gully, when I went in there for a minute."

The record came to an end, and Ruth ran to lift the needle. What had brought Ilona to the store today? she wondered. Some evenings she kept Ben company in his store, but she never came here.

"So beautiful," Ilona murmured.

"Caruso," Ruth said. "I got this whole lot for a dollar."

Herb laughed. "Your father will give you hell, young woman. What good is music in a pawnshop?"

"I wish they weren't so worn," Ruth said, and put on another record. As the voice began again, pulsing under the cracked surface, a customer came in and she said, "My turn, Herb."

When she had led the Negro toward the counter in the rear, begun to examine the small radio he had brought in, Ilona said anxiously, "Herbie, were there a lot of customers today?"

He leaned on the counter, trying to figure out her nervousness. "For a Saturday, not a crowd. A pawnshop sure isn't what it used to be. Well, Ben can tell you that."

Shaking his head, he said, "Every time I remember how much money Dad used to take in on a Saturday—at that first store. Customers enough to keep us all happy—Ben, Ruth, me. Even Mom came evenings to help out. Yep, that's where we learned our first English. Boy, what a gold mine it was."

"Once Ben showed me where it was," she said.

"Pretty close to downtown," Herb reminisced. "We lived two streets over. It was still a Jewish neighborhood then, if you can imagine that. The only reason Dad moved here was he needed a bigger store. Yeah, then came the house, the *shul*."

"Then stores for Ben and you."

"Sure! A chain—a Miller store wherever a man needs money! One for each son. Later, a store for each grandson, huh? Dad had big dreams there for a while. Too bad one of the Miller boys took a flop, huh?"

She looked at him in such a pained way that he chucked her under the chin. "*Nu*, Ilona, is it so bad that I finally knew I should've been a farmer, instead? A carpenter, a man who likes to use his hands?"

Her eyes blinked as she said slowly, "A farmer. Sometimes I think: Ben—out in the sun. The children with him."

"Even a salesman gets out in the sun," he said, shrugging.

The customer was on his way out, and Ruth got to the phonograph in time to raise the arm for the end of record. She caught the look of their strained faces, heard Herb say with an effort at heartiness, "Well, going to visit with Ben a little bit on your way home? Give him my best."

"Oh, Herbie!" Ilona's voice was so frantic that Ruth rushed toward her.

"What's the matter?" Herb asked, amazed.

"Ilona, what is it?" Ruth touched her cheek.

"Ben didn't go to the store today," Ilona cried. "He's not going to open Saturdays any more. Until sundown."

"My God," Ruth said, "Saturday is the best day in the week. He can't afford to close."

"Don't I know that?" Ilona said tearfully.

Herb's jaw looked lumpy as he stared at her. Half frightened, Ruth muttered, "All right, Dad doesn't open on Saturdays. But he sends me. Ben hasn't got anyone to open for him."

"Right!" Herb said. "Dad can keep the Sabbath and the best day in the week, too. It's easy to be religious."

"Herbie, what should I do?" Ilona begged.

"What did Dad say?" Herb lashed out.

"He doesn't know yet! He went to *shul* early, for only a little while. I heard him come home. He was hollering at your mother. I—I heard all the way upstairs. I think he had a fight with the rabbi. And Ben— He's going to stay in *shul* all day, he told me."

"Not to open the store on a Saturday," Ruth said, a little dazed.

"The store, the store!" Herb suddenly shouted. "That's all we ever heard. From the day we got to this country."

Ilona touched his arm timidly. "Sh, Herbie. It's a living, if a man does it the right way. Like your father—"

"That pig?" he said in a strangled voice. "He's ruined us all. With his right ways."

Ruth felt sick at the look in her brother's eyes. "Ilona," she said quickly, "you've talked to Ben?"

The patient, wet eyes were lovely. "My poor Ben," Ilona said. "We talked so much. For almost a year already he's been looking in his heart. *Davening*, till I thought I would go crazy—a young man should *daven* away his years. I even tried to fight with him, but how can you fight with a man who's so good? Well, I lost—today he's in *shul* all day."

"Dad fights with the rabbi and Ben *davens*." Herb's laugh was ugly.

"He *davens!*" Ilona cried. "Every night, before he lets himself eat. In the morning, before he puts one bite in his mouth. For a whole hour."

A shudder thrust through Ruth. That was the word, all right:

59

*daven.* The Yiddish word made a righter sound than "pray." It made a stern, chanting sound of doom. *Daven,* Ben, poor little Ben.

In her head, she could hear the chanting sound Ben made as he prayed. She had a picture of his slight body leaning, his head bent over the prayer book which he had opened and placed on the flat-topped refrigerator. Before he was married, he had stood in exactly the same spot in her mother's kitchen. His voice was as deep as his father's but with no ardor, no swelling joy of song. Its insistence, its mourning, came down through the entire house sometimes like a raw, warning wind.

Herb walked away abruptly, muttering with a kind of astonished grief: "What the hell? Only thirty years old—what did Dad do to him?"

Ilona looked after him, said entreatingly, "Ben is so good. He never spends one penny on himself. He's like an angel."

Herb was at the door, his stooped back to them. He slammed it, then locked it, stood staring out. Ruth lit a cigarette, her hands shaking. It was Herb she was frightened for, his complicated, tired heart in mysterious battle with their father.

"I tried," Ilona's wailing love plaint went on. "Think of the children, I told him. Have we got so much money that you have to throw it away? Forget about me! We don't have a good stove, a car. We don't go away to vacations. All right, I don't care—I love him. But your own boys, I told him. Ben, Ben, your own flesh and blood!"

Ruth felt as if she were under a double, simultaneous barrage; from Ilona came that terrible patience and love, and from deep in her head Ben's stern *davening.*

"I talk to him and he just looks at me out of those eyes—till I only want to hold him and rock him, that's all. He's so good."

"Jesus Christ," Herb said, only half aloud.

"But should he be like that? Was it the war, maybe? The Jews in Europe? I don't know! He's not an old man who's got nothing to think about but *davening.* He's got the children, me. He's young. I'm young yet!"

Herb motioned savagely at somebody outside the door. "We're closed," he shouted. "Come back later."

"This whole year," Ilona said. "Honest to God, sometimes I had to cry. I woke up—in the middle of the night sometimes—and Ben
60

wasn't in bed. Then I heard him, in the front room, in the boys' room. *Davening*."

Mom always said Ben was a plain boy, Ruth thought numbly. Be kind to him, don't hurt him, he's only a plain good boy, Mom said. But Dad would beat him because he acted so dumb. On the head, across the face. That was after we came to America, Ilona. Long before you met Ben. Mom crying in the kitchen, Herb standing with fists in his pockets. Don't, Mom would scream; leave him alone, he can't help it if he makes mistakes in the store!

"Can I fight God?" Ilona said helplessly. "He's not going to open on Saturdays. I know Ben—he made up his mind."

Suddenly Herb spun around, came quickly to her. Ruth was stunned to see his gentle smile as he leaned across the counter.

"Hey, honey," he said cheerfully, "we've all gone a little nuts. This isn't so terrible—take it from an experienced man! Do you know what'll happen on Saturdays? Ben's customers will come at night. Or Sunday morning."

"You think so?" Ilona asked breathlessly.

"Sure! They're his customers, they like the guy. After they get the idea, they'll keep his hours. After all, honey, they need him. When you need somebody you go when he's around. Don't you?"

"I guess so." Ilona smiled. "Oh, Herbie, I feel better!"

Ruth stared at her with envy. Already, Ilona's face was calm. A strong man had told her not to worry. It was as simple as that! she thought, thinking of Chip.

Ilona kissed Herb. "I knew I should come today," she said happily. "Honest to God, I feel like a different person, Herbie. I'll go home—the boys will be up. My little devils."

She put on her hat, came out from behind the counter—miraculously the old Ilona again, a matronly young woman with a quiet face. "Come soon, Herbie," she said. "Bring Alice upstairs on Sundays. There's time for us, too, no?"

"Sure, sure," Herb said, walking ahead and unlocking the door.

"Good-by," she called. "I feel fine, don't worry!"

When Herb turned to walk back, his face looked ghastly, the scar like a heavy bruise across the pallor. His voice shaken, he said incredulously, "How is it possible? One man can do such things to a whole family?"

61

"Is it Dad's fault," Ruth said very quickly, "that Ben—"

"Ruthie!" His voice made her cringe. "Look at me. Why does that man make me feel like—like a punk? Soft, weak—a nothing!"

His fist came down on the counter. "Ask him what he did to all of us. To Ben, to you. Yes, you too! And my poor little mother— alone, alone in the city! Scared, wondering every night where he was —so I taught her to play solitaire. I was a good son. I showed her how to be alone in the city!"

Ruth was filled with panic suddenly, that he would say too much about her father.

"What the hell did he do to me?" Herb demanded. "Ask him. No, better ask that ex-wife of mine, instead. Get her on the subject of Herb Miller. What a brilliant man she married. A money-maker! How sorry she is that she ever had a child by him. Oh, yes, the unfortunate comparison between the sterling Sam Miller and his oldest son—"

To Ruth's enormous relief, the screen door slammed. The customer, a Negro woman, was a little drunk. She came to the counter and threw a coat on it, said sullenly, "Who's the boss?"

Herb stumbled toward the tool section. Her voice shrill with her panic, Ruth said, "Can I help you?"

"I want five," the woman said. "That's my winter coat."

"Pawn or sell?" Mechanically, Ruth examined the coat.

"Pawn, pawn! I'm getting it out next week. Think I'd leave my good coat here for five bucks?"

From the corners of her eyes, Ruth saw Herb leave the store, the pieces of his invention bundled in his arms. The woman's truculent voice went on and on; then the sound of Herb's car starting cut across the blur of words.


# Chapter five


Saturday at Zigman's poultry store was the best day in the week for gentile customers. For the Jewish trade, all day Thursday, and Friday mornings were best.

Dave Zigman, early that Saturday afternoon, swept the concrete floor for the third time. The store was a former double garage, about fifty feet back from Woodlawn Avenue, behind several stores. As Dave swept up the litter of droppings and feathers, he was still thinking of Vincent and what he had done to her the day before in the Gully.

It was so hot that his dog, Nicky, lay panting under the truck, which was right outside the doors, waiting for Dave to load it with the crates of chickens and ducks for his father's Polacks. Nicky was the combination rat catcher and watchdog for the store, and Mr. Zigman insisted that he stay there day and night, instead of coming home sometimes with Dave.

In hot weather the stench was intolerable, but Dave had become a master at breathing through his mouth. He had found the way, too, of not listening to the incessant racket of the live poultry, packed into crates in the storage half of the store, or to the abruptly strangled shrillness of a chicken getting its throat cut behind the partition by Mr. Silver, the kosher slaughterer.

There were only three customers. Dave's father and the two helpers were waiting on them, and his mother and Mrs. Newmark were plucking chickens. There were still six or seven birds draped limply over the table, each labeled with a customer's name, waiting for the women to strip them of feathers. In hot weather, his mother moved this table, the hooks, the tubs of water, over near the doors for air.

Dave tossed the litter into the rubbish can and began loading the truck with crates of live poultry. He made sure the scale was on the truck, and a big stack of the surplus newspapers Mrs. Levine sold them, then he began yanking the crates, grunting as he lifted them.

The hard work, all that day, had not eased him. He was still sick at heart about Vincent; he could not understand why he had led the attack. He kept visualizing Vincent on the ground, motionless and unable to move any part of that suddenly soft, white body. For some horrible reason, when he had looked down at her yesterday he had thought of the word "rape." The violence of the word had seemed to permeate the entire Gully. Ever since, the word had hung in his mind. And the picture of Vincent had hung there, a naked, suddenly ravished body—of a pal.

Christ, why didn't people leave him alone! he thought desperately. Why didn't they stop knifing him with Ziggy and Al?

Sometimes it seemed to Dave that the world had created a certain way for him to be. He had to act like their conception of Dave Zigman, the big-shot brother of a big-shot crook and a gambler. He was heir to plunder; even if he did not want it he had to steal it—potatoes, a pack of cigarettes. Sure, even the gang—he'd finally stolen that, too!

He took a quick, glaring look into the store. His father had passed a weighed chicken to Mr. Silver, who was already holding it head down, his stubby fingers stroking the feathers at the stretched neck, as he sauntered toward the slaughtering tub.

Cop a sneak, you bastard, Dave said to his father in his head.

Morris Zigman was a big man with white hair. He limped. His left leg was swollen, all the way up, and every once in a while he went to Mt. Sinai Hospital for a few days of treatments. When Dave had to look at his father, he tried not to see his leg. For close to a year now he had kept himself from glancing at any part of his father below the waist. He would look at his hair, which had been blond at one time, or at his handsome, weatherbeaten face, hating it.

He hopped up into the truck, began to push the crates back into stacks and tie them to the little, dirty truck against the trip ahead. On most Saturdays and on the days before big gentile holidays, his father drove to outlying neighborhoods to sell live poultry and eggs to the Polacks. It was a joke around the store that he spoke better Polish than his customers. For some reason these people liked his father; sometimes he spent Saturday night at one of the faraway houses, and when he came back in the empty truck he told his wife about the meals and the homemade wine the customers had pressed on him.

He liked these trips much more than selling in the store. It was Fanny Zigman who really ran the business anyway. Morris had never had her smooth way with customers. His voice was gruff, and any joke he attempted turned out flat. He had a stubborn way—the direct opposite of his wife's—of arguing about the price and weight of a fat chicken. Often, at the end of one of these loud sessions between her husband and a customer, Fanny would say with a quiet smile, "Go to your Polacks, Morris. Who else can understand you?"

Dave piled the crates of ducks closest to the scale; they were a popular item on the trips. There was a sudden cackle from the chicken Mr. Silver had carried behind his partition, then the scream, the strangled gurgle. Bastards! Dave thought.

As he tied the ducks, he heard his mother say, "Mrs. Newmark, singe these chickens, please. Joe is already late with the first delivery."

Mr. Silver, who always wore his hat and a long, bloody butcher's apron, strolled over to her with the chicken he had just killed, draped it across the pile waiting to be plucked. He, too, spoke in Yiddish: "Did you notice how many Black Ones were in today, Fanny?"

"Am I blind?" she retorted calmly, her hands not stopping for a second. "I noticed. So?"

Dave spoke a lame Yiddish, but did not understand the language half as well as Vincent did. Sometimes, when they snitched in Jewish stores, she translated a complicated sentence in a low voice as they waited for exactly the right second for the snitch, the right tempo in customer conversation. He winced, remembering the perfect snitching technique they had perfected.

Mr. Silver shrugged. "So money is money, eh?" he said. "As long as we don't have to live with them."

"Is somebody forcing you to live with them?" Fanny Zigman said.

Dave tensed over the crates. Was that bastard making cracks about their empty? he thought, and watched until Mr. Silver walked away.

Mrs. Newmark had gathered up an armful of drooping, naked birds, carried them to the gas burner and turned the flame high. The smell of singed pin feathers came wafting into Dave's nostrils. His mother stood alone now near the doors, her hands moving like machines as she deftly turned the chicken hanging from the big hook, began stripping feathers from its breast and legs. The familiar, hurting impulse was in Dave immediately: pick her up, run, run with her until she turned soft and laughing and scented, as beautiful as her eyes.

Under the dirty, bloodied apron, his mother wore a long-sleeved, cotton sweat shirt which had once belonged to Ziggy, and which came down almost to her hips over her dress. On her head, covering her gray hair completely, she wore a dark shawl known as a *babushka*. This was made of a knubbly material which seemed to pick up feathers and the chicken fuzz drifting about her as magnetically as the sweat shirt did. Fanny's theory was to protect her hair and body by catching as many of the feathers as possible on outer clothing.

Sometimes Dave told himself that he hated her, the dirt and smell and blood surrounding her at the store, the tired face which she kept smiling for customers, the way her mouth looked slack with exhaustion so often when nobody was around, and yet her hands kept moving all the time as she picked a chicken clean. *Flick*, it was called in Yiddish. "Mrs. Zigman, you'll *flick* my chicken right away, please? I'm in a hurry."

*Flick*, or pick, they were too fast for hands. He wanted to hate those reddish, lumpy, machine-fast hands, but he wanted to kiss them, too. He wanted to clasp a bracelet around one of her wrists—twinkling and glimmering with diamonds—and make his father look at it, laugh like crazy as he forced his father to look at that shine coming from his mother's hand.

He wanted a fragrant, young mother with long beautiful hair and white hands, in a cool green dress; somebody like Ruth Miller as she passed in the street, only older, a mother. He wanted someone lovely and happy and full of love, a mother, to hold and worship and kiss right out loud in the house, instead of only in his heart.

In his heart, he loved her as if there were a hole there, burning, filling and emptying all the time. They were very close, he and his mother, but without words. It was a feeling, so choked and packed that they seemed always on the verge of some tremulous, wonderful outburst that never happened. He helped her in the house, scrubbing the bathroom and kitchen floors, the back-hall steps all the way down to the basement, the way she liked it. He would take the bucket and brush and rags out of her hands and do it, on a Friday afternoon when she rushed home to cook and clean, or some evening after she had been in the store all day.

In their house, his mother was always clean, and the rooms and floors were clean, the tub shining after her bath every night. It was just that his senses carried her the way she was at the store: a pinched, grayish face under the feather-clotted *babushka*, the way her little button nose got redder and redder as she moved so fast, as she smiled and gabbed at customers, the way her apron got bloodier hour by hour, and the whole world stank more around her.

She had dimples, even deeper than his, but they did not show often; the smiles to customers were only acting, not dimple-real. Her eyes had been beautiful for as long as he could remember. Even today, even with the sadness way down in them, his mother's eyes were liquid and deep, brimming with a brown, rich color under the thick lashes.

Every Thursday night, because she had no time to do it on Friday

66

itself, she insisted on baking the braided Friday loaves of bread. She would take the last Sabbath loaf out about midnight. He was still awake, at the radio or reading, and she called to him quietly, "Dave? Maybe you'd like a piece of hot *challeh* with butter?" They would eat a steamy slice, yellow with melted butter, sitting silently at the kitchen table. Every Thursday night, like a wonderful ritual, and then he would help her clean up the kitchen.

His mother never talked about Ziggy to him, or about Al or that bleached blonde, Elaine, Al had married. She talked about the street, the store, neighbors, aunts and uncles. The silence between them was of heart things, and neither seemed able to touch one word of that close, beautiful language trembling around them like delicate waves of feeling.

Fanny Zigman had finished the chicken. She had taken off the *babushka*, the apron and sweat shirt, and was hanging them on the wall spikes. She was smoothing her hair and brushing off feathers, and Dave knew she would leave the rest of the *flicking* for Mrs. Newmark and go home soon, walking fast, start cooking supper the minute she hit the house. When he got there, after helping his father load the eggs at the market for his trip, the house would be full of good smells and she would be dusting or mopping, or sweeping the front porch. Maybe sprinkling the lawn; she liked to sprinkle. The table would be set for him. Even if he went to the Gully first, or hung around the gym for hours, watching Chip and the other guys box, the table would be set.

No, he could not show her the boy inside his world's conception of Dave Zigman. There was a gentle dreamer of book life he could not describe. There was a boy scared he would be like his father, his brothers—wounders and hurters of women. Inside the snarling, punching tough guy who was learning how to box, how to slam out the indescribable shame and anger and pity against the sandbag or punching bag, was the Dave who feared the sucking pull toward the dark corner where his brothers waited for him.

As he was finishing the last crates, his father called from the doorway, "Hey, hurry up already."

Cop a sneak, punk! Dave sneered, inside his head. As he worked faster, he watched his father limp toward the tub of water where his mother stood. She was dipping the whisk broom and then brushing fluff from the bottom of her dress.

Don't touch her, you hear! Dave warned the man, in his head.

He heard his father say in his accented English, "Fanny, you finished *flicking* the Valenti turkey? The girl just called up again."

"I'll take it myself," his mother said. "I'm going home now, so I'll give it right into the *spunyitze's* hands. You're ready for the Polacks?"

"I have to get the eggs yet. I'm late already." For some reason, he lingered, and Dave heard his mother say crisply, "Well, why don't you go help Dave finish up?"

"So it'll take another ten minutes," his father said. Then, his voice lower and suddenly speaking Yiddish, he said, "When is the last time you spoke to Al?"

Dave made the knot tight, thinking idly of Al's big, light-blue Cadillac. Sometimes Al came on Friday night, to eat. Sometimes with Elaine; but it was better when she wasn't there. Sitting like a bleached, rouged broad in his mother's kitchen. Yeah, and outside the Caddy drew people like flies for an hour or two. Kids came to touch the big white-wall tires, a piece of chrome, or they peered in at the luxury as they talked excitedly.

"The last time?" his mother said. "Three weeks, isn't it? He came for supper, a Friday. You were by the Polacks. Why?"

"Elaine telephoned. I thought it was a customer first—I never heard her on the telephone before. Like a gentile. I didn't know who she was."

"What happened! Did they arrest him?"

Dave jerked, stiffening at the sound of his mother's voice. He strained to see her face. Al had managed to stay out of real trouble. He had been in county jail two or three times, but that was peanuts compared to Ziggy, who had got himself buried in the state pen.

"They didn't arrest him," his father said. "They just closed down his place. Almost three weeks ago. He went out of town, that's all. Elaine said he told her to phone you if he wasn't back in a few weeks. Not to worry."

Suddenly Dave was watching his mother stagger, tip grotesquely, fall to the floor. For a second he was rooted to the truck, staring at the limp, stretched-out body. She looked so small.

"Fanny! What's the matter?" His father sounded astounded.

Dave leaped from the truck, the scream in his head coming out in a bubbling moan that made Nicky bark and race him to his mother. "Silver!" his father shouted, running wildly toward people. "Mrs. Newmark, quick! My wife, my wife!"

Dave stood over his mother, but he was unable to move for a horrible moment because it was suddenly like having Vincent there at his feet, that second when she was finally undressed, stretched out like a soft, ravished girl—so small, so still.

His mother's face was very white but almost smiling. He saw some fuzz in the thick eyelashes, and he kneeled, started brushing with tenderness at the stuff. At the first touch of her face against his fingers, he cried, "Ma. Ma, get up now. Please, Ma."

Nicky was whining, trying to lick her face, and people came running from the other part of the store, calling alarmed questions. Dave pushed Nicky away, doggedly went back to smoothing the fuzz from her eyelashes.

Fanny Zigman came back to consciousness, listening to a voice inside her exhaustion crying: God, help, help! She felt how easy and sweet it would be to slip into death, to rest finally, to forget Ziggy, Al, Morris. God, help!

A gentle, shivering hand was on her face. No, she was too tired! But her eyes opened. There was Nicky, trying to lick her ear. There was Morris, Mr. Silver, all the assistants, leaning over her like a dropped ceiling of scared faces. But it was only Dave she really saw.

His hand had brought her back, and it was only his frozen face she saw. Lost, her lost little boy: she made herself laugh. She made herself sit up, then scramble like a girl to her feet.

"Well, how do you like that?" she said, still laughing, her hands on her hips. "She faints from the heat. Like a regular movie star!"

"You're all right?" her husband asked.

Her dimples flashed, and the scared faces began to smile as she winked. But Dave was watching like a frozen, lost boy.

"Sure I'm all right!" Coolly, she picked up the newspaper-wrapped turkey. "What is today, *Yom Kippur?* Nobody's got work to finish up?"

Everybody snickered, wandered back to work. To her husband, she said, "I thought you were late for your Polacks."

"Ma," Dave said harshly, "we'll drive you home."

She smiled at him, her heart twisting at the look in his eyes. "Oh, no," she said carelessly. "The walk home is my biggest pleasure. Fresh air, sunshine. I should sit in a noisy truck?"

"Wait," her husband said, his voice relieved. "We'll get the eggs, then I'll drive you. Why are you rushing home?"

She did not know how she would get home, heart and body were so tired, and she giggled into Dave's frantic eyes, cried gaily, "A movie star should ride with ducks? What a joke!"

When she walked out, and started down the driveway with the Valenti turkey under her arm, Dave thought: I'll tell Vincent to take back the gang! She'll have to!

## 2

Early that evening, Alex Golden rushed into the house. "Hey, Ma," he bellowed in the kitchen, "gimme eat, huh? I got to go."

Mrs. Golden came out of the bathroom, leading Becky, who was already echoing Alex's cry: "Ma, Ma, gimme eat!"

"I told you a million times," Mrs. Golden said, "don't holler 'eat' in front of her."

"Well, how about it, huh?" he said.

"Where's the fire?"

"He's going to a concert," Jules called balefully from his bed. "To the Art Museum. To college."

"Aw, I got to be back in the Gully," Alex said to his mother.

"I'll make you salami-and-eggs. Go wash. Ida, cut bread. We'll all have delicatessen—it's Saturday night."

Alex stood in the doorway, looked across the dining room at Jules. How pale his brother looked, the red notebook so close to his face. "You go to college?" he said with a sneer.

"Beat it," Jules said, and turned on his lamp.

As Alex washed his hands, Heidi said, "Should I cut for Papa, too?"

"No," her mother said. "Papa's late—he must have gone to Uncle Nathan's. Put back Juley's bread."

The Goldens ate day-old rye bread, which was cheaper. Jules was given white bread. Heidi voiced an old plaint: "Ma, it's Saturday night. Can't we have fresh tonight?"

"No. You know yesterday's is healthier. The doctor told Papa—

70

even for his nervous stomach. Are you a baby that I have to tell you every day?"

Sullenly, Heidi cut thick slices from the big round loaf, and Mrs. Golden called, "Alex?"

"Yeah?" he said, staring at his face in the bathroom mirror.

"You saw a lot of *Schwartze* in the street?"

"Yeah, by Zigman. There's a sign on the house."

"So, she put out a for-rent already," Mrs. Golden said, breaking eggs into the skillet.

"You've got a sign out, haven't you?" Jules said. "So've the Valentis. What do you want the Zigmans to do—live upstairs and down?"

In the bathroom, Alex stared into the mirror, poked at a new eruption on his chin. He wondered if Santina would meet him in the Gully, if she had finished all the Saturday cleaning the old lady made her do.

He thought of the way she called him Blacky. Boy, what a sexy babe. Her whispers ran through his mind: "Hey Blacky, come on, show me. Come on, how black are you all over, Blacky baby?" He liked it that she talked so much and so hot all through a loving, in breathy whispers that way. Last night, coming back after Vincent had been stripped, they had decided to go into the clubhouse. She was as hot as he felt, kissing and biting as if they were undressing Vincent all over again. They left the door open, in case anybody came, and the danger made it twice as exciting. Lying on the floor, in the thick black heat, sometimes they thought they heard footsteps, the slither of watchers all around the little house, and then Santina and he would stiffen all over, their hearts banging against each other. Boy, exciting!

Would she be there tonight? Last night had been the other end of the world from where Jules was when he started to cough and spit up that bloody stuff. Santina was the other end, a million miles away from dying. He knew now that he wanted to be with Santina as soon as Jules' eyes closed, as soon as his mother started to cry soundlessly at the kitchen table and Heidi came to stand near her and pat her head, while Jules lay white as a ghost and Becky ate her bread as if nothing had happened.

Jesus! he thought, his scalp prickling at the picture he had drawn for himself. To Alex, as to all the family, Jules was the soul and spirit of their life. He loved Jules inarticulately, painfully, with awe. And he felt death in him all the time.

The doorbell rang, and he heard his mother say, "Sure! As soon as a light goes on in the front room they're here."

When he came out of the bathroom, his plate was waiting on the table and Becky was sitting and staring at the hot food. He began gulping his supper, half listening as his mother spoke curtly through the screen door.

Heidi was measuring out Jules' drops. "Here's your orange," she said. "What do you want Ma to do with them, make a party?"

"Shut up," Jules said with his usual disdain. "If you didn't pay so much attention to *Schwartze* at the door, you wouldn't spill my drops."

Alex ate faster, his eyes narrowed, and passed Becky a chunk of salami. He felt surrounded by danger. The ring of a doorbell and the black face waiting there to grab a house, Jules gaunt and pale in the bed, Becky. She, too, was a kind of death in the house. He loved her and could not bear to look at her. Pushing his plate, with the remnants of his meal, in front of her, he fled toward life.

"So long," he shouted, and slammed out the back way.

Mrs. Golden came back to the kitchen, her face splotched with annoyance, and stirred the rice-and-milk she was cooking for her husband. The radio blasted on, and Jules said, "Softer, softer! Will you open this other window? I'm burning up. Is Vincent on her porch?"

"I can't see," Heidi said. "It's almost dark."

She came into the kitchen. "Ma," she said, "can I go to the show tonight? They got that picture about fliers I told you about."

"Ask Papa. Take Becky, if you go. The show quiets her."

"Okay," Heidi said, her eyes bright. "I'll get dressed up—it's Saturday night."

The back door opened. "Here's Papa," she cried.

Herman Golden was carrying a fur coat over his arm. He was a slight, gray-haired man who dressed very neatly and was as precise in speaking and gesturing as an old-fashioned schoolteacher.

"Hello, Sophie," he said. "Hello, Ida. How's Jules?"

"The same," his wife said. "What's the coat?"

"Nathan called me in the shop. He found another customer in his street. A Mrs. Gold—you should see her house. Like a palace. Her husband is in real estate."

"So?"

He sighed. "So it's a collar job, rush. I have to deliver it tomorrow, before one."

Giving the coat and his hat to Heidi, he sat down at the table and took Becky on his lap. "Hello, darling," he said, and patted her cheek.

"Mink," Heidi said, smoothing the fur.

Mrs. Golden leaned to examine the coat. "Mink-dyed muskrat. Don't get so excited."

"Hello, Juley," Mr. Golden called, above the music, and Jules called back an absent greeting.

"Where's Alex?" Mr. Golden asked his wife.

"In the Gully. You're hungry?"

"No, but I better eat. I had nausea on the bus."

Herman Golden worked in an exclusive downtown fur shop. He was extremely proud of his place of employment, but his earnings were so low that his brother-in-law had taken it upon himself to find after-hours jobs for him.

"You saw Nathan?" his wife asked.

"For a minute. I wanted to tell him the Rosens moved, and—"

"Not now," she interrupted in a whisper, and gestured toward Jules. He nodded, went to wash, and Heidi ran to change her clothes.

When Mr. Golden sat down to his meal, he said, "And you?"

"I'm not hungry," his wife said shortly, from across the table. Alone, they had fallen naturally into Yiddish.

He had a mouthful of his rice soup, then he said hesitantly, "What is it? Many of the Black Ones rang our bell today?"

She shrugged. "It's too hot to eat."

He buttered a piece of bread for Becky, sitting next to him.

"The sign is out at Zigman's," his wife said, talking lower than the radio bumble.

"Well? Did you think they had a Jewish tenant in their pocket?" he said impatiently, and gave Becky a spoonful of his soup.

"Herman, don't give her too much. She'll get cramps."

"What other pleasures does she have?" He fed Becky another spoonful.

"I said, don't! She'll get sick one of these days, and—what do you want? That we will be forced to send her to the institution?"

He looked at her reproachfully. "Over my dead body you'll send her."

"I want to send her?" she said harshly. "I?"

As they stared at each other, their faces slowly reddened. Mr. Golden ducked his head, took a quick bite of bread. Then, not looking at his wife, he said, "If we send her—would you sell, go to Florida?"

She felt breathless. This was the first time he had put into words an old question each had argued alone. "And Juley?" she said.

"They say we could get a second-hand car and trailer. You put a mattress in the trailer, drive slowly. They say it's like being in your own bed. No matter how sick you are. And in Florida—you get well."

He looked at her, saw a softness in her eyes, a wistfulness. "Sophie," he said hoarsely, "is it true, what Heidi says? That she would have boys here—many boys—but she's ashamed of Becky?"

His wife came out of her little dream. Her face hardened, and she said grimly, "No."

"No?" he said, his voice helpless.

"If there were boys who wanted to be with her, they would come! Florida— Why should we blame life's disappointments on Becky? What did she ever do that I should blame her for my heartaches?"

"Sophie," he said brokenly, "what kind of talk is this?"

"That's enough! No institution. I am not ashamed." She got up from the table and walked around, her hands twisting together.

"Am I?" he said, his voice muffled.

She faced him, hands on her hips. "What is happening here?" she said, her eyes glittering. "Shame or pity are not for me! No tears. No falling to my knees. I refuse!"

Silently, Mr. Golden ate his soup and listened to the music flooding in from Jules' radio. Heidi came out of her room, humming to that music. She wore one of her good dresses, high heels, and her face was made up.

"Papa," she said eagerly, "can I go to the show?"

Mr. Golden stared up at her rouged lips. "You went twice this week already," he said.

As her face turned sullen, he said with a kind of tenderness, "Ida, darling, you have nowhere else to go, just to the show?"

"I like the show!"

"A dance, a wedding, a nice little walk with friends?"

"Herman," Mrs. Golden said sharply, "I had enough today!"

"A dance, a wedding," Heidi cried. "Who'll I go with—Ross Valenti? Or maybe a *Schwartze*?"

"All of a sudden," her father said angrily, "there's no place a girl can go to meet boys? Why don't you go to the Council, at least? There are clubs there, parties. It's a Jewish settlement house—for girls and boys, no?"

"The Council," Heidi said bitterly. "What happened to it since *Schwartze* began to move in the neighborhood? It stinks, that's what! They opened that branch on the Heights—and that's where they've got the swimming pool and the big gym. That's where they got the live orchestra for dances. Hell, they don't even have dances here any more. *Schwartze* guys might come!"

He glared at her. "You're talking to your father, Ida!"

"Is she so wrong?" Mrs. Golden said. "Haven't they begun to abandon us?"

"They? Who is they?"

"The Jewish community," she said very quietly. "A community follows the thousands—it does not stay with the few. The dances and clubs, the Jewish stores, the halls for weddings and parties. Where are they?"

"On the Heights!" Heidi screamed. "They left us garbage. The fancy things are for the fancy Jews!"

"For God's sake," Jules said nervously, "why do we have to holler every second? Ma, I've got to have some peace."

"All right," Mrs. Golden called back instantly. "This minute."

Heidi ran to her room, banged the door. Mr. Golden, his face gray, drew Becky back on his lap and said, "Sophie, since when does a girl talk like that?"

His wife took a comb from her apron pocket, began to part and comb Becky's hair. "She is not a girl. She is a grown woman, looking for life."

"That is my fault?"

She stared him down with a weary look. "You didn't want her to work. You said she should be a home girl—get ready for marriage, cook, clean. Meet nice boys. Are you looking for a miracle? So she wants to be a flier. Go to Florida. Be in love. With a Chip Levine!"

"Phah!"

"Certainly! But a woman sees only what is in front of her eyes."

She went into the bathroom, brought back a wet washcloth, and wiped Becky's face and hands. "Florida," she said softly. "You pick oranges in your backyard, the sick are well again. People dream."

"Somebody will buy the house," he said. "Then we'll go. Is it a crime to dream?"

"A crime? For me, it is bread." She smiled. "Go take a little rest on the swing, then you'll fix the rich woman's coat."

She kissed his cheek, took Becky's hand and pulled her gently from the little man's lap. He sighed, went off toward the front porch. As he passed the bed, Jules said, "There's a little breeze out there, Papa."

Mrs. Golden went to Heidi's room, opened the door. "Come," she said, "you'll go to the show. Take Becky—she's clean, all ready."

She counted money out on the table. "Here's for candy—don't give Becky too much. And here, you'll bring back ice cream for Juley. Have a good time."

On her way to the porch, Mrs. Golden stopped at the bed. "Juley, maybe you feel like eating now?" she said.

Jules shook his head. She watched him, the pencil in his hand, the notebook open against his raised knees, his head tilted to the music.

"I'm saving up for a radio-phonograph," she said. "Like Uncle Nathan's. And I'll buy you any records you want."

"In Florida," he said, not looking up.

"You think it can't be?" she asked, but he did not answer.

After a second, she went out to the porch. People were walking in the street. She heard voices, laughter. Mrs. Zigman was sprinkling her lawn. Mrs. Golden watched Santina run past her house, toward the Gully.

"I'll bet the *spunyitze* will be the first to sell," she said.

"It should only be," her husband said, from the swing.

"They'll marry off the girl and sell. Italians! By sixteen they've got a baby already!"

She came to sit next to him. The music, from the open windows, put walls around them. She could see Jules pushing his hair back, one hand tapping now and then to the tune.

"Talk softly," she said warningly. "I don't want Juley to be upset —he seems weak tonight. Oh God, why should I have to fight him every minute? Why did he take the Black Ones into his heart that way?"

"Those books," her husband said. "People who read that much—"

"Like a sick child takes a doll into his arms for comfort. He won't put the Black Ones down for a second. I can't understand my own son!"

"When is the doctor coming?"

"Wednesday. Well, what did Nathan say about the Rosens moving?"

"He said three empty suites in one street is not good," Mr. Golden said. "His advice is to sell. Before somebody rents and property goes down."

"I can't be the first," she burst out. "Sell or rent—not the first."

He hesitated. "Nathan says if you're afraid, let an agent do it. It's worth the commission, and the agent takes the blame. If a bomb goes off we're not here by then."

"Nathan gives advice," she said bitterly. "Sometimes I could hate my own brother. With his brick single on the Heights. A rich man gives advice! When I speak to him of ethics, he laughs. 'Let the rabbis be ethical,' he tells me—they can afford it, you can't.'"

"You're afraid to sell to them?" her husband asked in a very low voice. "We could go at once to Florida. Be out of reach of—of threats."

"Afraid! Nobody understands," she said, her voice very tired. "I am alone—one finger on a hand. Herman, can't you possibly understand me? I can't do such a thing to my neighbors. To my fellow Jews. In my heart I can't do it!"

After a long silence, Mr. Golden said helplessly, "Maybe somebody else will sell soon."

## 3

All that afternoon Santina had cleaned the house under her grandmother's probing eyes. It happened every Saturday. Then, when Dave's mother had delivered the turkey, she had taken time off from the cleaning to have a lesson in the basement on how to prepare poultry the way an Italian man liked it.

They ate all their meals, prepared and cooked them, in the basement room. Sink and stove, the old icebox, the old kitchen table and chairs—all were in this room. Upstairs, they used the bedrooms and bathroom, but rarely the spotless kitchen with the new breakfast-room set. The living and dining rooms were never used except for holidays or when the priest came once in a while.

Even when relatives came to visit, they used the basement room. They never had other visitors, except Sam. When Sam and his mother came, they all sat in the living room, and her grandmother showed the other old lady the tablecloth Santina had crocheted, and the new towels and sheets in her dowry.

She was engaged to Sam, she guessed. He was a thickset, spectacled man in his middle thirties, and he had a very successful meat stall in the market, near the fruit-and-vegetable stall that her brother ran with two of their uncles. Their father and mother had been there first, before Ross, but after they had been killed in that automobile accident Ross had taken over their share of the business.

When she was sixteen she would quit school and marry Sam. That's what her grandmother said. And Ross said it—her stern-faced, balding brother who would not get married until she was married and in her own home. He said that all the time.

Santina rarely thought of Sam and marriage. She learned about cooking, sewing, cleaning. She went to church with Ross and her grandmother and learned further nuances of the word "sin." She visited the many cousins and aunts with her family, and smiled in silence as she served her grandmother's wine and pastries to their own visitors. In the house, she rarely spoke unless she was asked questions by her brother or the old woman.

They were strangers to her, just as the upstairs rooms seemed the house of strangers when she cleaned there. Sometimes she stood in front of the picture of her mother and father, so grave and stiff in their wedding clothes, and watched their strange faces for a while; but she could never remember them too well, voices or smiles, so she wandered back to her cleaning.

The two rooms smelled of furniture polish and mothballs. She dusted all the wood, the two Madonnas, brushed the mohair pieces,

78

then ran the sweeper. It was like working in two precise, cold places belonging to other people. She had no desire to touch the ornate scarves her grandmother and her mother-in-the-picture had crocheted long, long ago, or the dark wood crucifix carved by her grandfather, who had died many years ago but for whom her grandmother still wore black.

Late that afternoon, the old woman brought down into the basement room a peck of tomatoes and a chunky, huge broccoli like a deep-green flower from her backyard garden. "For supper," she said with satisfaction. "Prepare them. Remember, Ross is late on Saturdays so do not start cooking too soon. I am going to weed the flowers now."

Mrs. Valenti spoke very little English and had no use for even the few sentences she had to speak on occasion. She was a strong, healthy woman despite her seventy-three years, and prided herself on her house, her garden, and her appetite and digestion. She spent as much time in her flower garden, at the front, as in her big vegetable garden, in the back. In the summer, her skin seemed to turn dark as the earth. She looked happy as her peppers swelled on the bushes and her flowers grew tall and red near the porch.

Early that evening, as Santina sat in the basement room crocheting lace for a table scarf, her grandmother gave the tomatoes one last stir and said, "I am going to see Anna Rini. She is sick. I will be back before Ross comes from the market. I will prepare the cheese sauce myself."

She left. Santina, alone in the house, with not even the thought of the old woman near, permitted her heart to take over the entire place where she existed.

Her heart was a secret room in which lived a dream of delicate, exquisite love. The rough words which she spoke to the street, the excited ones to Alex, were not the language she spoke in her heart; nor were the stilted, sparse words she exchanged with Sam and his mother, her own family. The language in her heart, like the dream of love there, was musical, beautifully pure. When she was alone, the room in her heart opened. She stared into it with bewitched eyes until she could no longer sit still.

Today, it happened again. The beauty, the music and the delicacy, drove her into restlessness. She wanted to dance. Her body wanted to run and leap like the wildest wind of grace. There was always a kind of translation of her secret language into familiar excitement, an interpretation she could understand in her body, so tightly leashed most of the time.

And so today, she thought of Vincent undressed, lying at the feet of Alex and Dave, the other boys. She thought of Negro men walking in the street and coming up to ring the bell and her grandmother running from the backyard to scare them away. She thought of Alex, the smooth heat within the clubhouse, the smells in there of baked Gully earth, of bodies perspiring and Leo's pee smell, of old candles and old cigarettes burning, of the summer-hot wood of ceiling and walls. And Alex, and Alex! His hands were as frantic as his body, and he never talked but kind of grunted. Yes, and Alex! Frantic and groping and black—funny how a body could seem lustrous and hot and black as the night seeping into the clubhouse.

Santina sat in the basement room a little while longer, pressed into her chair by the remote weight of the word "sin." She thought of Sam and of getting married, of her grandmother's angry descriptions to Ross of the men who rang their doorbell, of the expression in her brother's eyes sometimes when he asked her if any of these men had ever tried to talk to her. She thought of Alex, of Vincent standing naked in the first dusky light of the Gully; of Alex; of Ross saying to their grandmother: "It is a responsibility—an unmarried sister." And Alex, and Alex!

The music of the secret heart language beat higher and higher, then rushed completely through her, swept her out of the basement room. She locked the back door, put the key under the mat. Night time was beginning all about her in the street. It would be dark as she ran past the Rini house, where her grandmother sat visiting the sick. It would be dark in the Gully. Would Blacky be there?

As she ran, the restless wild-wind music sang in her of love, and she thought, giggling: I'll tell Grandma I went to church, to pray for my husband-to-be, my wedding-to-be.

### 4

Saturday merged, in the street, with Sunday morning. At four o'clock that morning, Lizzie Levine woke her sons, one after another. This Sunday was different; it was Louis's first time. She went to him first, touched the bed. It was dry, and she chuckled tenderly, said to him in softest Yiddish, "Wake up, little wage earner. Hurry, run to the bathroom before the others. Hurry, you are a big boy today."

The house was still hot from the blazing sun of Saturday. God, she thought, the heat stays like the threat of the Black Ones, to wear us out. Yet this morning she felt hopeful. Louis's entrance into the working world was like another weapon against life.

Anna slept on, heavily. So did her husband, as the little woman hurried on bare feet from one bed to the next, shaking each of her sons until he sat up and yawned. Sometimes she wished Anna were a boy, so that she, too, could go into a hustling job.

Already the kitchen was full of good, brisk odors: coffee for Moe and Chip, cocoa for Leo and Louis, the big frying pan full of slowly sizzling eggs-and-lox. On the table were rolls and bagels, hot from the oven. This Sunday-morning meal was an important one, and she did not begrudge the money spent on extras. The meal was a bribe for her wage earners on the most difficult morning of their week.

She had been up since three. Humming, she stirred the eggs, poured the coffee and cocoa. She was as excited about Louis's debut as she had been about Leo's. She remembered what fat tips little boys were often given as they sold the huge Sunday paper, especially in the downtown district—hotels, bars, restaurants, the places where men grew sentimental about boys who had to earn their bread.

Chip was the first into the kitchen. He sat down, blinking in the bright light as his mother brought him a plate. The salty, hot fish smelled good to him after the close bedroom.

"Take a biscuit and a bagel," she said gaily. "I got plenty for everybody. This is a big holiday for me."

"Did you wake the kid?" he said, and sipped his coffee.

"He jumped from bed like a bridegroom on his wedding day," she said, laughing. "Today I don't have to dress him—he's all grown up."

Over the years, she had fashioned a language predominantly Yiddish, from which the important English words shone out like diamonds. "Excited! He feels like a regular man. Sig, let him hustle his papers downtown. You know how they tip little boys. And he looks like a regular baby, not even his ten years old. They'll give him plenty."

"Okay," he said. "I'll keep an eye on him from the truck."

81

She scurried from stove to table, and he watched her as he ate. His mother was a little, twisted-looking woman but hard as a rock. When she laughed, six or seven teeth were disclosed; the others had been pulled one by one as they crumbled. She was "waiting" for new teeth, as she waited for everything that cost money.

Now she peered through a window. "Plenty dark yet. Will the little wage earner be afraid of boogiemen?"

A sigh came from her. "I never enjoyed an empty house next door to me," she said. "No faces in the windows, no curtains."

"Oh, somebody'll move in," Chip said, yawning.

His mother turned from the window. He noticed how sunken her cheeks looked because of the missing teeth, and flushed in round patches like rouge.

"Have you a lot of Black Ones for customers these days?" she said.

"Well, they read the funnies, too," he said, smiling.

"Be careful with Louis when they are around! He's only a baby. He never went out of the house before in the middle of the night."

"Don't worry, Ma," he said, watching her go to the hall door.

"Moe, Leo, a black year on you!" she called cheerfully. "You'll miss the streetcar."

Chip blinked, suddenly. It was a little like seeing his mother for the first time. He was not watching the whining, driving Lizzie, whose curses could be as rich and elaborate as her life was skimpy, but a woman of fear, a woman who had been made by fear, whose every step was drawn by it as automatically as a boxer leaped away from his opponent at the right second.

And his sudden picture of her contained fresh details: the tenderness for her baby boy, a kind of joyous participation in Louis's excitement at growing up, the vigor with which she greeted and forced, and yet still tried to prevent, another man in the family. Her bare feet looked frail to him—the big reddish bunions and contorted toes—slithering across the newspapers she spread each Friday after washing the kitchen and bathroom floors.

Jesus, her feet hurt! Chip said to himself, thinking of how she rarely wore shoes in the house, winter or summer. And he remembered—for the first time making it more than a hazy fact that had

82

been kicking around for years—that she had lost four babies in her lifetime, born too soon or dying within a week after birth.

Now what the hell? he asked himself, amazed at his peculiar feeling of hurt. She made him think of Ruth, not with the old familiar distaste at the comparison but with a fierceness that encompassed both women.

Leo stumbled into the kitchen, sat down sleepily, and began stuffing food into his mouth. Then Louis came, his round face glowing with elation.

"Sit, little man," his mother said. "Moe!"

"All right, all right." Moe came in, his eyes looking even smaller as the glare hit them. Slouching into his chair, he said, "Now listen, Ma, I'm warning you. I haven't got time to find him toilets all over downtown."

"It's hot," Mrs. Levine said placatingly. "Wet pants don't hurt in the summer. Take a hot biscuit, Moe. Here's your lox."

"I won't wet," Louis cried. "Honest, Moe."

"You won't," his mother promised him eagerly. "You're a big boy, with a brand-new *torba* Sig brought home just for you."

On the floor near the door lay the old, stained canvas bags they wore slung across one shoulder to hold the newspapers they sold. Even Moe and Chip, supervising the distribution from trucks and street corners, wore them. The clean one for Louis, to which she had referred, lay on top of the pile. The entire family used her Yiddish term for the bags.

"Eat, eat," she said to them. "The car doesn't wait for anybody. Louis, drink the cocoa and run to the toilet, so nobody'll have to worry."

"Hey, take it easy," Chip said with a laugh. "We're not going to a wedding. We're just going to work."

"I'll go to your weddings yet, too!" she cried happily. "Get up, Leo. Louis, they're going."

At the door, she draped the bags over the younger boys' shoulders. "Be careful with your *torba*," she warned Louis. "There's a deposit. If you lose it like a baby you'll have to pay like a man. You hear me?"

"I won't!" Louis cried.

Her sons clattered down the back stairs, and Mrs. Levine went to

83

her front porch to watch them out of the street. She stayed there until she heard the clang of the streetcar on Woodlawn. This was the signal to her each Sunday morning that her sons were on their way downtown, and she could go in.

She lingered for a few minutes. It was almost cool on the porch, and she remembered with a lump in her throat the look of Louis in the lamppost light, the big *torba* almost down to his ankles, how he had half run to keep up with Moe, the boss.

How beautiful a street could be! she thought as she stared down. Quiet, no enemies walking and ringing bells and smiling at every "no" and coming back the next day with a new smile. Oh God, would someone sell, give them the first "yes"—and destroy her children?

There was a light in the Golden house, across the street. She shivered as she thought of Jules, and went quickly in to clean up her kitchen.

# Chapter six

On Sundays Mrs. Golden was at her window early. There was the going to church and the coming back to report on, fresh activities for the amusement of Jules. There was the parade of Negroes, much thicker on this day, when so many men and women came together to ring the bells.

It was almost noon when Alex came running from the corner with the thick Sunday edition of the *Forward*, a Yiddish daily newspaper. Both Mr. and Mrs. Golden read only this Sunday edition, which had a rotogravure section and was filled with special stories about Jewish activities all over the world.

"It just came," Alex said, dumping the paper in his mother's lap. "Lucky I was there, waiting. Mr. Newman was squawking to the driver. They only sent half as much as he ordered."

"Sure," she said, opening the paper and scanning the headlines eagerly. "First they send to the Heights—the leftovers are for us. Did you see Papa?"

"He took the streetcar. Nobody was driving to the Heights."

"Well, what's new in the jolly old *Forward?*" Jules said.

"Plenty," his mother said. "The world moves!"

She read bits aloud on Sundays, sometimes entertaining him, often infuriating him. The news stories were stale, translated from the English dailies, but he liked to hear the features and the human-interest stories.

"The voice of the ghetto," Jules said, stretching and getting into a more comfortable position. "Mrs. Golden will now read the most slanted writing in the world. By Jews, for Jews, about Jews."

"Shut up," she said absently as she turned pages.

Heidi came from the kitchen, stood at the screen door, and looked out with complete boredom. "Did the Italians come from church yet?" she said.

"No, only the *goyim,*" Mrs. Golden said. "Where's Becky?"

"Cutting paper." As a car pulled up across the street, Heidi said, "Ma, Herb Miller just came."

"His little girl is with him?" Mrs. Golden turned to her window. "Look how pretty her mother dresses her. She *looks* like she lives on the Heights. Juley, can you see? Look how big Alice is getting."

"Herb's starting to look like an old man," Heidi said.

Mrs. Golden's voice was gloomy. "That's what sorrow does."

"Crap," Jules said.

"When children have to wait till their fathers are out of the house before they can bring grandchildren to a mother. Herb, Shirley Vincent. God, people wait for grandchildren and then look what—"

"Come on, cut it out," Jules interrupted with annoyance. "Where are your grandchildren? Gossip about them, why don't you?"

"When it's time," she said calmly, "I'll have grandchildren. Ida, if any more *Schwartze* come up on the porch, I'll go."

"They're concentrating on Zigman's house," Heidi said.

"I wish they would leave her alone. Mrs. Vincent told me today in the grocery that Fanny Zigman fainted in her store yesterday. It's enough to make anybody sick, an empty upstairs."

"So how come you aren't sick?" Jules said. "Ladies and gents, a woman of steel—Mrs. Herman Golden."

"Steel and iron," she said. "Now shut up and I'll read you."

Mrs. Golden began reading aloud, in her excellent Yiddish, short

85

articles about a famous author at home, a great British diplomat and his most recent stroke of brilliance, a youthful banker who had made a million.

"Is he married?" Heidi asked about this last man.

"It doesn't say," her mother answered. "Ah, here is a story about a doctor who is working to cure cancer. His picture is here. A young Jewish boy, like a doll."

"Hurrah for the Jews," Jules said, bored. "Rich, famous— geniuses."

"So?" his mother said. "It's bad when a Jew is a big man?"

"Does that make you and me big, too?"

"To me," she said with satisfaction, "it always feels good to know that a Jew did it."

"Ma," Heidi said in a low voice, "here comes one."

She moved away. The bell rang, and Mrs. Golden sprang to her feet and went quickly to the door, stepped out on the porch.

"Want the radio?" Heidi said.

"No," Jules said with irritation as he stared out the window at the scene on the porch. "Did anybody bring the Sunday paper?"

"I'll ask Chip for one," she said. "He's always got extras."

He gave her such a scornful look that she reddened. "All right, save your cracks," she said, and went to the kitchen.

Mrs. Golden came in, slamming the screen door hard. "You know what he had the nerve to tell me?" she said indignantly. "That he works in the main post office—inside job!"

"And he doesn't?" Jules asked, his annoyance turning to anger. "What then, he does? A *Schwartze?*"

"My God," he said, "why should my mother be so dumb?"

"Dumb? I'll show you how dumb I am. I made up my mind—I'm going to advertise in the Jewish paper for a tenant. That's all!"

Jules laughed derisively. "Better put the money in the *pushke.*"

"I'll take Italians if I have to. Look at the Simons—they never had trouble when they rented to the Rinaldis."

"How about Chinese, Mrs. Golden?"

"He asked me if the house is for sale. Imagine." She sat heavily, turned pages and muttered, "Who will sell to him? You'll see, some-body'll do it. It'll be a Jew. Who else would have the nerve?"

Jules heard a kind of black, bitter pride in her voice, and he said furiously, "Then do it, coward. Get it over with!"

She glared at him. "And get bombed? Stoned?"

Her fist came down on the newspaper, and she cried, "There are stories here I never read you. I don't want to start up your sewer mouth. In Chicago, in Washington—it's happening all over America."

"Read me," he said tauntingly. "I dare you."

"All right! Look, right here. In Chicago thousands of people went to burn down a big apartment house. Why? They heard *Schwartze* were moving in. In Washington a family moves in and all the white neighbors throw stones. Windows break. A fire starts. Who would carry you out in a fire, wise man?"

"God!" he said.

Heidi and Alex had come into the living room, lured by the crackling voices.

"Listen to him," Mrs. Golden said. "He doesn't know that soon they'll move God out of here, too. They'll buy our *shul*, and then? The end."

"Aw, Ma," Heidi said.

"I'll kill 'em first," Alex said, his voice furry.

"Sure, go kill," Mrs. Golden said. "It's right here, in this paper. It happened right in this city—they bought a *shul* and made it a church."

Jules had begun to sweat, the pulse lunging in his throat. "That scandal sheet!"

"All right, it happened in a neighborhood almost all black. But don't think it won't happen to us, too."

"Crap," Jules said, his hands trembling as he wiped his face. Alex stared at his face, then abruptly ran out of the house, his feet pounding down the porch steps.

"Boy, do I love this," Jules said. "When do you go to *shul*? Or your husband? On the Day of Atonement—period. How come *shul* is so holy to you, all of a sudden?"

He grabbed one of his books from the bedside table, opened it, and pretended to read.

His mother tapped the newspaper. "It's right here. It happened on Berkeley Avenue. They bought the *shul* and the property next door,

87

where the rabbi used to live. For fifty thousand dollars—that big, beautiful stone place. Where do they get such money?"

"From God," he muttered.

"The Greater Abyssinia Baptist Church," she read with bitter relish from the paper. "Such a name will be on a *shul*."

Jules felt like crying, for some reason. "I'm trying to read," he said. "Kindly scram out of my bedroom, both of you."

## 2

By two-thirty that day the Levine boys had stumbled out of bed, appeared in the kitchen. Lizzie was frying potato pancakes; a large platter held a towering heap of those ready to eat.

Chip and Leo were the first ones at the table. "Hot dog," Leo said, "*lotkes!* I want a hundred, Ma."

She filled two plates. "I found the money," she said to Chip. "Where's Louis's?"

"Ask Moe," he said. "He took charge of the kid."

"Look in his *torba*," Leo whispered, grinning.

"For his gentile girls he'll take my bread?" she muttered.

Mr. Levine came into the kitchen. "Where is Anna?" he said. "I need Seltzer."

"Maybe in the Gully," his wife said. "Moe! Louis! Come eat."

"How much did Louis make?" Mr. Levine said, patting his stomach.

"I'll tell you later," she said shortly. "Call Anna from the porch."

Suddenly suspicious, his mustache quivering, he did not move. When Moe came into the kitchen, his eyes fastened on the face of his oldest son.

"Boy, I'm starving," Moe said.

"And money?" Lizzie said coldly.

"I left my dough on the table," Moe said with an insolent glance at his father. "Is there a crook in the house?"

His mother studied him. As Louis sidled into the kitchen, his eyes blinking sleepily, she said, "Your new employee earned nothing?"

"That punk?" Moe said, picking up two pancakes from the platter. "All he did was pee all over Chester Avenue."

When he bit through both pancakes, she stepped up to him and

88

snatched the remainder from his hand. "You want to eat?" she said. "Pay what you owe me."

As she tossed the fragments back to the platter, Mr. Levine said angrily, "Crook. Get to the hell out of here."

"Yeah?" Moe said. "Then my dough goes with me."

"Did Louis make, or didn't he?" his mother said ominously.

Chip grinned as he finished his coffee. He especially liked her at times like this. She was like a dirty, hard little rooster, planted solid on those bare feet.

"How can a pisher make money?" Moe said, and Louis finally burst out: "He took it, Ma!"

"Aha," Mrs. Levine muttered, and suddenly ran to the bedroom, returned in an instant with Moe's canvas bag.

"Hey!" Moe shouted, but his mother turned it upside down and shook.

Several copies of the Sunday paper, rotogravure sections sliding separately, fell to the floor. Then came the rain of coins, rolling over all the papers she had spread on Friday, already dirty and jagged.

"So there!" Louis said, and ran to pick up his earnings.

"Thief," Mrs. Levine said triumphantly. "You're stealing from your own mother? For your *shikse* girls? Your dates you find in the street?"

"Phah!" Mr. Levine said in disgust, and went to the porch.

"Call yourself a mother?" Moe said, shrugging, and sat down.

"You don't call me?" she said with a smile, and brought him a plate heaped with pancakes.

At the table, Chip had another of those new, startling sensations about his mother. Why should Ruth feel superior to her? he thought. Here's a strong woman. Here's a funny kind of love that people have to see!

He went to his bedroom closet and took his boxing gloves from the hook, thinking quietly of Ruth's fragrant, beautiful body as he smelled the sizzling chicken fat which had permeated all the rooms by now. He left by the front door, jumped lightly over the canvas bags with the unsold papers that he and the kids had left in the hall, coming home that morning. Louis's bag was filthy, after the one night, and he smiled as he remembered the little, dumpy boy hustling his papers so earnestly that he had forgotten to look for a toilet.

Dave was waiting on the porch next door. "Hi, champ," Chip called. "Ready for your workout?"

"Yeah," Dave called back and got up from the swing, his own gloves dangling from one hand. He had bought them with the money his mother paid him on the sly for working in the store. "Don't say anything to Pa," she had told him very unconcernedly, and he had gone out and bought the gloves as carefully as if they were a gun.

Vincent was on her swing. Dave had sat watching the back of her head, her stillness, until Chip had come and he could jump up out of the thick, explosive stuff in him.

"What's new?" Chip said, putting his gloves on. They practiced boxing on the small Zigman lawn every Sunday, in good weather.

"Nothing," Dave said, starting to tie on Chip's gloves.

"Coming up to the gym Tuesday? I told Max to let you in for nothing."

"You fighting?" Dave asked.

"Yeah."

"I'll be there." Dave jammed on his own gloves, and Chip turned to look at Vincent.

"Hey, *kuter*," he called with surprise, "you asleep or something? Aren't you going to tie on Dave's gloves?"

Dave's jaw clenched as he pulled the gloves on tighter. Would she come? Vincent had always been around on Sunday to tie his gloves, ever since he had bought them.

His face turned hot and his teeth ached a little as he saw, from the corners of his eyes, that she was coming. Silently, she pulled the strings tight, tied them. She did not look at him once as Chip began to dance around the lawn, loosening up.

"Thanks," he said, his voice barely audible.

She went back to her porch, sat on the top step and hugged her drawn-up knees. As Chip and Dave began to box, slowly the usual audience assembled on the sidewalk in front of the Zigman house. Vincent saw members of the gang show up, but made no sign of recognition. Santina ran across the street, and in a minute Alex was at her side. Then Heidi, leading Becky by the hand, came across the street.

Good-natured advice and laughter began to dart from the audience, but neither Chip nor Dave paid any attention. Vincent saw Angelo peering at her, and pretended to dust off one pants leg. A gay, rather breathless remark came from Heidi, and Chip answered her with a chuckle.

Vincent thought of Jules, who always jeered at the way his sister ran after Chip. She had not seen him since Friday night. She missed him bitingly, but she could not run across the street in the old, eager way and plunk down on his bed, watch him open the notebook, listen to the teacher-brother-friend words. Just as she could not go to the Gully any more; the clubhouse had a banged, locked door in her heart.

Then, abruptly, she thought that she would have to go to the Gully Tuesday, to meet Clara, return the loan. Her hand slipped into her pocket and she fingered the knife. Clara: she looked out into the street and peered hard at the faces of the Negro couple leaving the Golden porch. Was he Clara's father? Was she Clara's mother, aunt, cousin?

She had been watching the Negroes in this new way for the last two days. It was the first time she had ever looked for anything beyond the dark color—eyes, shape of a face, an expression of yearning or of laughter. Funny!—to be looking for such things. She wished she could tell Jules about it.

The two boxers were motionless for a moment on the little lawn, burned brownish by the sun. Both wore tennis shoes; the boy was as graceful as the man as they both rose on their toes a few times, their gloved hands in front of their chests.

"Careful how you stand," Chip said. "Most guys don't know about standing right."

"Yeah," Dave said.

Chip's glove reached in suddenly to stagger him. "See? You shouldn't of even rocked on that one."

They started again, gloves tapping face and chest, steps cunning in a thrust forward or a sidestep, a pulling back.

"Dance it out," Chip said, phrases bouncing out between bits of action. "Stand right—dance it out—the guy gets careless. Then smack on the kisser. But you got to dance."

"I'm dancing," Dave said, breathing hard.

"Hey, Chip," Heidi cried, "want a good dancing partner?"

"Come on, cop a sneak," Dave shouted at her.

91

Today, the terrible sensation of inner violence had mounted as the boxing lesson went on. Usually, if he punched hard enough and long enough, it abated somewhat. Not today! The exploding inside of him felt like fire as it waited to go off, and the boxing was making it burn hotter. Today, the whole street felt like an explosion all around him. Just waiting to go off, just burning underneath; all of them, every person he had seen today, starting at the first ring of the doorbell that morning and the look on his mother's face as she had gone slowly to answer.

He punched with all his strength. Why wasn't his old man home, instead of out drinking wine with the Polacks? Why was Vincent sitting there like a—a slap? He punched, dodged, punched at Chip's bobbing head. And the stinking gang, all lined up and waiting for him to take over—waiting since Friday night!

Everybody in this street—he punched and punched—today they all looked like they were going to explode. You could smell their insides burning in the sun. Even Herb Golden—the way he had slammed the car door, led his little girl by the hand into the yard. Bang! Then the *Schwartze* could step over the pieces of everybody and walk right into the empties, take over.

"Good," Chip said. "That's real slugging, champ."

Vincent watched, her eyes expressionless, how the new leader of the gang was showing her that he was stronger than she, that he had the right to dispossess her. Her hand was tight on the knife in her pocket.

"Keep nursing your left," Chip said. "Come on—dance."

Then, suddenly, the boxing lesson was over. Ruth Miller came walking from the corner and Chip said to Dave, "Okay, that's it for today."

He walked quickly to meet Ruth, untying his gloves with his teeth. Dave saw Heidi's face flush very red as she stared at them. He smiled back uncertainly at Ruth as she walked past with Chip, and he remembered that violin his mother had bought from her so long ago, the few lessons he had taken.

His mother had put the violin away somewhere after he had stopped playing it. A fluttering wildness, half fear, lay in Dave's chest as he remembered the bracelets he had seen from time to time in the pawnshop windows. They looked beautiful behind the glass, the sun

making them shine so that he had to think, with anguish and loath-
ing, of what such a shine would mean to a young woman in love,
her arm held up gracefully as she looked at her slim wrist and smiled.
Oh, those dimples, little holes, deep holes of gaiety!

Santina had turned to continue her admiring study of Ruth, who
was wearing a white linen dress and shoes to match on this steaming-
hot day.

"Hey, Blacky," she said, her voice so low that no one else could
hear, "think she's hot stuff? Look at Chip sweating."

As Alex and she went into a shrill giggling, Dave stared coolly at
the gang, lined up on the sidewalk. Joey Simon said eagerly, "Hey,
Dave, how about going to the Gully?"

Vincent went into her house, and grief gnawed like a sudden,
secret animal in Dave's chest.

"Let's have a meeting or something, huh?" Angelo said.

"Or figure out a snitch for tomorrow, huh?" Alex said.

Dave gestured at the Negro couple walking slowly toward them.
"Look who's coming," he said carelessly. "I'm going in and tip my
mother."

He swaggered into the house. Chip was on his way back from the
Miller house, his gloves swinging, and Heidi took Becky's hand and
went toward him.

"Want a paper?" Chip said. "I got some extras in my *torba*."

"Swell," she said, blushing, and followed him up on the porch.

Across the street, Jules and his mother still watched from the
window. For the past fifteen minutes or so, Jules had permitted himself to swim in jealousy. He had studied Chip Levine's strength as
he boxed, had watched his rush toward Ruth the moment she appeared in the street, and the way they had walked together toward
her house. He felt like a sick punk, gawking near-sightedly on the
boundary of other people's love.

Mrs. Golden, feeling the familiar lunge of heartbreak for him,
said tauntingly, "A reb's daughter lets a hustler of papers walk on the
same street with her? A new world!"

He did not answer, nor look in her direction. She tried harder:
"That whole Levine family is right out of the funny papers. When I
met Lizzie in the bakery today she was like a new woman. Why? She
has another breadwinner in the family—Lou went out hustling Sun-

93

day papers today. She's so happy that she's got a new scheme. Better than falling in a streetcar! You hear, Juley? You'll die laughing."

"I'll die, period," he said spitefully.

Like a cunning clown, she salted her voice with irony to lure his interest. "Now listen, Juley, to her new scheme. After all, they know her on every streetcar in the city, every bus, so now she's got something new. She told me on the way home. 'I heard about a woman who fell in a big department store downtown,' she says to me. 'She was pregnant, so they handed her a thousand dollars. You know how they are in America about motherhood. You don't even have to go to court. If you're in your fourth or fifth month, they push a fortune at you.' Juley!"

There was a glimmer of a smile on his wan face, and his mother said, "So I told her, without even a laugh, 'Lizzie, don't tell me you're pregnant!' She laughed, fresh like a girl, and said, 'So you fall, not pregnant. They won't give you so much, but do I need a fortune?' You hear, Juley?"

She watched gratefully as his amused smile took some of the gauntness from his perspired face. Then Heidi came in, said triumphantly, "Free paper!"

"Free hug and kiss, too?" Jules said sourly.

Heidi looked pleased. "Look up the travel section," she said. "See if there's any new Florida addresses for pamphlets."

"Taking Chip with you?"

"Shut up," Heidi said with a grin. "Gee, wouldn't that Florida ocean breeze feel good right now?"

"When we sell the house we'll go," Mrs. Golden said, looking dreamily out the window, and Heidi sighed as she led Becky to the kitchen.

Florida, Jules thought bitterly. The big pipe dream. Like Jerusalem must sound to some people when they say it out loud. That's how it looks in Ma's eyes, in Heidi's. Next year in Jerusalem!

"Come on, sell me one of those breezes?" he said. "I'll give you a second-hand heart for it. Sell me a pailful of ocean? Half a rotten heart!"

"Don't get excited," his mother said.

"Why not? That sappy daughter of yours talks about Florida breezes and here it's weather for rape."

94

"I'll bring you grape juice, with ice."

"Bring Heidi a lover, better. A husband."

Mrs. Golden looked at him shrewdly. "Want your bottle?" she said.

Jules tried to go on glaring, but a giggle came through, then a grin. "Okay," he said. "That'll take care of my sex urge, huh? Smartie!"

Smiling, she went for the shining, scrubbed milk bottle he used when he was confined to bed. She had refused to buy a urinal. To the entire family, including Jules, she had explained this by saying with a careless laugh: "I should spend good money on such a thing? When the boy will hop out of bed soon and run to the toilet like anybody? Hah!"

In her heart, she always said: If I won't buy one, he'll get better —he won't need one.

She brought him the bottle, wrapped in a white towel, and went out on the porch. As she stared toward the corner, she saw a familiar figure approaching on the other side of the street and she smiled with pleasure.

"Ah, thank God it's three o'clock," she announced to Jules through the open window. "Here comes the old Mrs. Vincent to bring me peace. Fresh air in a dirty room."

She had a habit of slipping into Yiddish when she was strongly moved and making overly dramatic but honest speeches. "A picture of home in an alien, unholy land. It's a joy when three o'clock Sunday comes—rain or shine, she is here. She will blow away the Black Ones with one of her strong breaths."

"Listen to the great actress," Jules said sardonically. "Too bad the play stinks. Come on, Juliet, take this damn bottle out of my bed."

Mrs. Golden came in, took the wrapped bottle to the bathroom. "Ida," she said, "go wake up Papa. Tell him the old Mrs. Vincent is in the street. He likes to know when she's on their porch. The minute she comes."

She rushed back to her window. "Look. Look how everybody is smiling, saying hello. Like she is a queen—and she knows it. How she walks, so straight, not afraid of God or the devil. Would anyone know she is almost eighty?"

Jules opened a book as his mother went on admiringly: "They say she is a very rich woman—in money and in down pillows and feather beds. Bolts of silk left over from her business. They say her sons' basements and attics are overflowing with her possessions, stored for the day when she will give them to her children. After all, until five years ago she still had that big store. She must have made a fortune, selling remnants to the gentiles. Smart! I should have half her mind."

Jules groaned. "Do I have to hear the same story every Sunday, as soon as she hits the street?"

"It strengthens me to talk about her, to look at her. Religious— she prays like a man in temple. She doesn't even have to look in the book, she knows it so well. She lives alone in a room, goes to her daughters and sons when she wants—leaves when she wants. Money she has, strength inside and out, independence. Is this an extraordinary woman?"

"And a Jew on top of everything else!" Jules said. "Hurrah."

"I should be so learned in Hebrew."

"She's here?" Mr. Golden called from the kitchen.

"Almost by Zigman's," his wife called back.

"Too bad Shirley isn't here, with the baby," Jules said, frowning at their ridiculous excitement. "That would give the old gal something to be a queen about."

Mrs. Golden made a scornful sound. "She would turn around without one word and leave—that's all. She wouldn't be on the same porch with them."

"Boy, what crap," Jules muttered, hunching down behind his book.

"Shut up! There is real religion—a person has to respect such things. Did it matter to her that the baby was given a Jewish name? Mendel—named after her own dead husband? No! Shirley could have named him Tony, for all the difference it made to that woman. She is Jewish to the heart. Like—like a Moses! Wrong is wrong, and what is more wrong than a Jew married to a gentile?"

Heidi laughed as she washed dishes. "Emmanuel O'Brien. Boy, what a name," she called.

"Manny," her mother protested. "They call him Manny. It's not so bad when you don't say the last name."

Her husband came to the window to take a look at the slow walker

96

in her long dress made of a heavy, shining, brown material that looked rich and very hot in the sunlight.

"You know what I have to remember all the time?" he said admiringly. "How smart she is—a man's brain. A widow thirty years, with a business of her own, then she wants to be a citizen—for business purposes. So she marries an old fool, becomes a citizen by marrying a citizen. Then, when she doesn't need him any more, she divorces him. I tell you, a brain like a man's."

"True, true," his wife agreed.

On the porch across the street, Vincent and her parents sat and waited for the Grandmother to complete her slow, dignified walk.

"The water is on for tea?" her father said nervously.

"It's boiling," her mother said, as nervously. "The sponge cake is cut and on the plate. The lump sugar is ready, the jelly. In one minute, Judy and I can have everything out on the porch."

Next door, Mrs. Zigman sat on her swing and Dave on a chair nearby. They did not speak to each other, but Dave had pulled his chair very close. Vincent could see Mrs. Zigman's face, tired and pale, and she remembered how jolly that face could be. In the back yard, hanging out her clothes, and when Vincent took the garbage out she could see the dimples, just like Dave's, going in and out when she smiled and talked about Dave to his best friend.

She watched the Grandmother walk past Dave's house. Mrs. Zigman, her voice a little breathless with respect, called out in Yiddish: "A good day to you, Mrs. Vincent."

The Grandmother nodded, called back in her vigorous, lordly voice: "A good day," and continued walking. Then she had turned in, was climbing the porch steps, and her son and daughter-in-law waited, fiddling with a chair for her, and Vincent waited stiffly to kiss her cheek after she had seated herself and put on her glasses, placed her enormous leather pocketbook on the floor next to the chair. It was all ritual, each step done the way the Grandmother wanted it.

Sitting as erectly as she had walked, in the chair placed so that she could observe the street and be seen by the street, she did not seem tired or out of breath in the least bit.

"A good day, Mother," her son said, and his wife echoed him, and Vincent stepped up to kiss the harsh cheek, scored by hundreds of lines.

Then she followed her mother in to help bring out the glasses of strong tea, the sweet jelly and sugar, the cake. Summer or winter, on the porch or in the living room, her father and the Grandmother drank many glasses of burning-hot tea in the few hours of the Sunday visits. They sweetened the tea by holding part of a lump of sugar in their mouths as they sipped, or they spooned in the jelly her mother had made.

Ordinarily, Vincent sat around for a while until her father and the Grandmother became engrossed in talk, then she quietly disappeared toward the Gully or went to Jules. Both destinations seemed so impossible today that she sat on the top step and carefully did not look at Dave, next door.

Sonia Vincent sat uneasily on the swing. The Grandmother never paid much attention to her. She never pretended with people; the rather disdainful superiority she felt for her son's wife crept into her voice when she occasionally addressed her. As far as she was concerned, her son had been unfortunate enough to fall in love with a girl who was not only as illiterate as Abe was scholarly, but three years older. Sonia had always been afraid of her mother-in-law, and in awe of her. It would be a great relief to her when the weekly visit was over and the big, erect woman was on her way again.

"Today," the Grandmother said with distaste, "it looks like a street for the Black Ones. From week to week, there are more walking past your home."

Vincent watched her surreptitiously, the way her big, brown-splotched hands shook slightly with the glass and saucer, the thick neat brown wig so youthful-looking above the crisscrossed skin, the gold watch pinned to the bosom of her shiny dress.

Her father's voice was gloomy. "Since you were here last Sunday, the house next door is half empty."

"Another dish of honey—more flies," the Grandmother said.

"And your street?" her daughter-in-law asked hesitantly.

"All white, of course. Would I continue living there, otherwise?"

"Of course not," her son said eagerly.

"Moving has never been difficult for me. A clean, kosher house. Within walking distance of the temple. Quiet, privacy—otherwise, one house is like another. Nevertheless—"

"Yes, Mother?" The nervousness tiptoed through his voice, and Vincent thought how strange it was that her father seemed to act like a kid with the Grandmother, a boy who was almost afraid to answer her.

"Nevertheless," the Grandmother continued, "the longer I live in this country the less I feel trust. Jews are surrounded by disasters here, too. I, for one, will not sit and wait too long for the American disasters to bury me like an avalanche."

"Of course not, Mother."

"Morris writes me that in New York the problem of the Black Ones is the same," she said. Morris was her oldest son, the only child who was not within walking distance. She quoted him often, as if the miles between them somehow invested him with authority.

"In New York, too. Imagine!"

Vincent suddenly disliked her father's manner with the Grandmother. He was a mediocre-looking man with graying hair; not tall, not short. She was used to him in his daily garb of paint-splashed overalls, the white painter's cap ridiculously out of place with his long, scholarly face. The only time he seemed truly happy was when he was reading one of the thick library books at the kitchen table. Often she had seen him smile over a page of print, the look of dreamy pleasure on his face seeming to put him, all alone, in a locked room.

The street passed languorously back and forth. Constantly, men and women nodded at the Grandmother as she sat in full view, and she nodded back majestically, her eyes probing every movement on the sidewalks.

"And how is Nate?" she asked, one of the implacable questions of a visit.

"Fine, fine," her son said hurriedly.

"He writes regularly," his wife added. "He sends money."

The old woman frowned. "Morris writes me that Nate never comes to his house. Like a stranger."

"He works too hard!" her son said. "He is determined to be a success. You are the first to know how much time that takes, in this country."

As the Grandmother nodded, and as her mother chimed in with another lying, glowing remark, Vincent hated all three of them for a second. Their talk made her brother a king, a prince, but Shirley's name

99

was never said by the old woman, or by anyone in her presence. All the screaming denunciations were over. Judgment had been passed, and a silence was there instead of a name.

She is as if dead, as if dead; the familiar words went through Vincent's head. Shirley married a *goy*, she is as if dead to us. Stubbornly, she said Manny's name to herself. It was a little like stepping up to the Grandmother and pushing a fist into her old, cold face of authority.

Next door, Dave was pulling the hose toward the sidewalk. "You got to take it easy," he said to his mother. "Don't worry, I'll get everything wet, Ma."

"Judy," her father said, "go bring the Grandmother another glass of tea. Mother, you are ready for cake?"

"Sponge," her mother said. "I baked it fresh, this morning."

"No cake," the Grandmother said.

When Vincent came out of the house with the steaming tea, her father looked flushed and unhappy, and she knew one of the other implacable questions had been asked: "When are you going to stop working for other men, like a nothing?"

She thought jeeringly: Don't make me laugh! That was in the past, too, like the way Shirley had run away and married Johnnie, and the way Nate had refused to learn the painting trade, the way the Grandmother had finally talked Pa into trying to be a painting contractor.

She carried the glass of tea to the old woman and went back to sit on the top step, listening with that jeer to her father's flurried questions about his brothers as he tried to change the subject.

The few months in which Abe Vincent had been a contractor were a painful memory to him. He had lost the money his mother had insisted he take as a loan with which to pay his workers. He had gone through a nightmare of anxiety in his attempt to be a boss. Not only had he found it impossible to direct other men and give them orders but he had not been able to discover the magic formula of figuring a job. He was always afraid his price would seem too high, and the figure with which he came up after hours of pencil work invariably was absurdly low. Even now, he could remember the smiles on men's faces as they heard his estimates. His own workers had laughed.

So he had been a miserable failure. He had gone back with relief to the safe and simple life of working for other men. Why did his mother continue, Sunday after Sunday, to punish him with the memory of how he had disappointed her? Her scorn, her insistent question each week, simply highlighted the way she had been able to walk through America and take from it the success all men sought when they emigrated to a new country.

"Have you heard any of the rumors about the temple?" she asked now.

"People talk, Mother," he said. "Surely it is impossible that our temple can be driven away?"

"There have always been disasters for the temple," she said. "From the earliest years. If a man's own family can open itself to the enemy, shall we be surprised at the enemy outside the wall?"

Vincent saw her father wince, her mother's spasmodic clutch on the arm of the swing, and she felt their strange guilt as keenly as if she understood it. Somehow, the Grandmother was blaming them for Shirley and Manny, and at the same time blaming Shirley and Manny for everything bad—the *Schwartze*, the *shul* maybe moving to the Heights, and—yes!—even her father having to work for other men and being a nothing.

An anger that was mostly grief came into her as she sat motionless, so near the three. So a beautiful Manny could be an enemy of a *shul?* If the Grandmother said it—sure, she was a big shot in the *shul!* Even Mr. Miller stopped to greet her when he passed the house on a Sunday. The voice of authority: Manny was an enemy, like a *Schwartze.*

Like that girl, Clara? her mind went on. She's an enemy, too. But she loaned me the knife. Manny, Shirley, Clara: name your enemy!

Dear Lord, kind Lord, gracious Lord, she said fiercely to herself. It was a weapon against the three on the porch, her God against theirs, her prayer against the memory of theirs as it made a sibilant or chanting sound in the *shul.*

She had never asked any of these three for answers. And they had never heard her urgent silences; not one of these three elders had explained the stern, threatening wrath of their God against Shirley—and then against Manny.

Nobody in her world had ever known about her need for God, nor about the ways in which she had looked for Him. Sometimes she had followed Dan Buckholz and his family, and the Connors; stood outside their white frame church and waited for some kind of explanation to come out for her.

Sometimes she had followed Santina's family, Angelo's, to stand outside their church, named St. Joseph's. It was stone, with smaller buildings clustering like a tiny village within the stone wall stretching almost a block along lower Woodlawn. No meaning came soaring out of St. Joseph's with the organ, the singing voices. And then, suddenly, strangely, it was Manny's church—a completely distorted meaning.

What was God to people? she had asked herself again and again. If she knew that, would she have God, too? How many times she had longed for her father to order her to *shul*—the way he did her brother. But it was only Nate he had hollered at, for years: "I want you in temple! Like a decent Jew, like a man!"

In her father's temple, the men sat downstairs and the women upstairs. In her father's temple, sometimes—wandering, as all the children did—she had found him in his row downstairs and sat next to him and listened, secretly touching the tasseled fringe of his prayer shawl. Or she had gone upstairs and sat next to her mother, to the Grandmother or her aunts, once next to Dave's mother. The sound of men and women praying half aloud had come into her—a strange language of sternness, of sorrow, of awe—and she had yearned to understand and to possess her father's God.

It had troubled her more and more to know that she did not belong to any God she saw. The tougher she had acted, the higher she had jumped and the faster she had run, the emptier she had felt inside—with God untouchable, unseeable.

And then, one day, as she had sat in the library and looked through books, the entire search had ended. When she remembered back, it did not matter when she had opened that book but only what she had found in it. She had found a God she could understand.

There had been a prayer in that book. When she had read it, at once it was hers. In the simple words, in the gentle, compassionate words of that prayer, was all she had ever wanted of God. Love, pity, strength; these she could understand. And the calling out to a God to help her beloveds in the world—this was the kind of praying she had looked for so hard in her father's temple and on the sidewalks in front of the other churches where her street went.

To be able to talk to God as if He were kind and strong and used to giving—this was the beautiful meaning of the prayer Vincent had found. She said it to herself every night, as she lay in bed. And then, after a while, it had taken to saying itself inside her head whenever she was in danger, or when Jules was particularly sick, or when Shirley had run away and her mother had cried and her father had hit himself on the head with his fists—over and over, his face writhing, until Vincent had run out of the house to the Gully, the prayer rushing all through her like sudden courage enough to bear even this: ". . . and with all the needy, oh, divide I pray! . . ."

That night, when she had come home from the Gully, her mother had whispered, "Never say Shirley's name to Pa or to the Grandmother. Never—she is as if dead to them." But in bed, saying her prayer, Vincent had given life back to her sister in her heart.

Then the next despairing whisper, after the baby had been born: "Never say 'Manny' to Pa or to the Grandmother. Oh God, they took him to that church—St. Joseph's! They made him a Catholic! Never, never say his name to Pa." But that night, in bed, Vincent had shouted the new baby's name in her heart with each word of her prayer.

Now, as she sat on the porch, the prayer said itself. But there was a bared rawness in her today which could not be soothed. That forced stripping in the Gully on Friday somehow had left her mind naked, ready for a different kind of awareness.

Always before, she had been sensitive only to her own fears, attuned to a secret song of power and tough philosophy. But all kinds of walls had toppled in her private world on Friday. There was an enormous silence in her now, instead of the singing, and she could hear a new, painful kind of questioning—about other people. In this silence, she seemed to hear the Grandmother and her father and mother in a completely different way.

So if Shirley is "as if dead" to Pa and the Grandmother, she thought carefully, what does that make Manny? Never even born—that's what it makes him! Can they do that to a baby? Can even the Grandmother do that? Act as if a baby wasn't even born in the world? And Pa! God damn it, Pa, who said you could do that?

The idea was so horrible that she jumped up and ran. It was too new, too confusing, like looking into the faces of *Schwartzes* for laughter or sadness, instead of for just the color of fear.

## 3

At three o'clock that afternoon, Ben Miller was still in his pawnshop. He had caught up with the bookkeeping and police reports he had not been able to finish the night before, but there was still one watch to repair.

He went outside for some air before tackling the watch. The heat was stifling, but he lingered for a minute to lean against the wardrobe trunk, which—like his father, at the home store—he pushed outside each morning to advertise the pawned leather goods on sale.

So hot, he thought as he watched the Sunday-quiet action of the street. Harvest time, and the heat continues.

But then he smiled, pushed his hat back to cool his forehead. In the city, harvest time? He was still thinking like a Hungarian peasant of sun and crops, remembering the cool, scrubbed days of autumn in the village, and how the New Year approached with them, and the Day of Atonement. Here, in the city, seasons never seemed so excitingly and beautifully separated; a time for planting, for work, for harvest, for holy days.

He went back into the gloom. His father, in opening a new store for him, had patterned it after the home store: the tools in one corner, the suits hanging in another, the showcase cutting a similar line across the floor under the hanging violins and guitars. The office was in exactly the same spot, so that going back for pen and receipt card sometimes was like going back to the years he had spent in his father's store; and often, stepping into the office, Ben looked mechanically for the bearded man—napping on the cot, or reading his newspaper—having forgotten for that second that his father was in his own store, almost fifteen blocks northwest, on Central Avenue.

In the office, Ben sat on a high stool and screwed the jeweler's glass to his right eye. He had learned from his father how to do minor repair work; it was a way of making extra money on pawned watches or clocks which needed only cleaning or slight adjustment.

As he probed in the works of the watch, the screen door banged.

104

It was Herb, carrying his invention. Ben smiled with pleasure as he called out a greeting and came out of the office.

"On a Sunday?" he said. "What a nice surprise."

Herb grinned. "I took a chance you'd still be here. I need about fifteen minutes with one of the Miller tools. How are you, Ben?"

"Fine. How's Alice?"

"Wonderful! I saw her this morning, and I'm going to pick her up later. Take her out to dinner, maybe a movie."

Herb went to the tool section and began to fiddle with a vise. "How come you're still here?" he said carelessly. "Don't tell me customers have started coming Sunday afternoon."

"I had to catch up with a few things. I'm going soon."

"Anything doing this morning?" Herb asked.

"Two customers," Ben said. "Business could be better, huh? Dad's going to be worried."

"What the hell's Dad got to do with your store?" Herb said, smiling. "Maybe you'd better start worrying, yourself."

Ben's rather mournful smile came in answer. "Maybe," he agreed.

"A living you got to make, huh?" Herb said immediately. "Which reminds me. I hear the holdups have started on Central. They'll be working up here soon. Is your gun in good condition?"

Ben grimaced. "Would I shoot a man?" he said.

"Is there a gun in back?" Herb said, his voice suddenly harsh.

Ben looked at him. "Dad put one there when he first opened the store for me. You, too, Herbie?"

"Me, too, what?"

"You're afraid colored people will come? To hold us up, to murder?"

Herb flushed at Ben's quiet, wondering tone. "Why kid ourselves?" he said. "Facts are facts when you're in business. There are more holdups. And more *Schwartze*. Two and two are how much?"

"I will not use the gun."

Herb sighed to himself. There was a dignity about Ben, as honest as their father's was pompous. His brother's gentleness, his absent look, brought a dryness to Herb's throat.

"Listen, Ben," he said abruptly, "what would happen if you walked out of here? Took a nice, simple job somewhere—nine to five

—no headaches, no guns. Just a living, see? You come home for supper every day on time, the kids are there, Ilona."

"Herbie, don't make jokes," Ben said, smiling. "Dad is already a disappointed man. If I left the store—"

"Palestine would fall!" Herb finished the sentence vehemently. "Did it fall when I walked out?"

"Herbie, please," Ben said in his slow way. "Dad has enough troubles these days. Even in *shul* he is not happy—you can see it on his face. He says the old respect for him is not there any more. They don't ask his advice, the way they used to about everything."

"You're breaking my heart," Herb said, and began to hammer violently.

Ben went back to the office, put the watch and tools away. The familiar sadness came into him as he looked at his brother from behind the grilled window. Herb had turned his back on many things, arrogantly, and yet he was not happy. And Ben wondered, as he had so often, if Herb was afraid of their father, too. Dad had always loved Herb. A person could see it in his eyes, the way his hand had gone out to touch Herb's arm or shoulder when they stood talking. The old days, when they talked; but even then Herb had not looked happy.

As Ben walked back toward his brother, he remembered how Herbie had seemed just like a father in Europe—strong, and always laughing, even when they had to beg in the street. He had known how to divide food, how to cover a mother with a blanket at night, how to make Ruthie stop crying, how to smile at Ben and say: "To-day, little brother, we play a game. We pretend it is the Day of Atonement and we men are fasting. You and I, we pretend we are in the temple and food is not even permitted in the thoughts of devout men."

These years, he always missed Herb more keenly at the High Holy Days. As he stood in the temple, wrapped in his prayer shawl, it was Herbie he looked for at his side, hungry for the expression in his eyes, the sense of his companionship.

Fiddling with the hammer, Herb looked at him so somberly that Ben said, very softly, "Come home with me. We'll eat together. You'll play with the children for a while."

"God damn it," Herb said tremulously, "you're going to lose your
106

shirt if you close on Saturdays. Either keep open or get the hell out of here and find a job where you don't have to work that day."

For a moment, Ben felt a sapping helplessness. He had expected anger and accusations from his father, not from Herb. In a low voice, he said, "What would I do if I left the store? What other trade did I ever know in America?"

"In Hungary you'd have been a farmer! Wheat, potatoes. In the evening, you'd walk with your boys and wife under the acacia trees—"

Herb slammed the hammer down. "All right," he said in a moment, very quietly, "why now? Why are you closing on Saturday, all of a sudden?"

"I don't know," Ben said hesitantly. "For almost a year—the whole street, Dad—so worried and scared about the colored people— Herbie, people are ugly! About other men, their families. I—I don't recognize people any more. My own father. I—I have to have help!"

Herb swallowed. "Help? You mean from God? On Saturdays?"

"The Sabbath," Ben said, with his queer, boyish dignity. "I have not kept the Sabbath. The store, my children's future— All right, I opened on the Sabbath all these years; but Herbie, it was a mistake. I feel this."

"The colored people," Herb said carefully. "I don't get that."

Ben shook his head. "Do I? I just feel something. And—well, that Dad should be so disturbed— Herbie, they are people! Like me, like my boys. And in our street, in our *shul* even, the men talk of these people like—like—I don't know! Is it good?"

The screen door slammed. Ben saw their father standing there, as if he had leaped out of the sudden passion of their talk, and he started nervously.

"Good afternoon," Mr. Miller said in his heavy way. He was trying to smile, but Ben saw that he was flustered, his eyes eager in Herb's direction. "I stopped in for a minute. Is it possible that business is any better here than in my store?"

"Hello, Dad," Herb said, fumbling with a cigarette, trying to turn away from the familiar neat beard, the big fleshy look of the man, the sensual mouth which the reddish beard had never hidden. At once, the eyes behind those glasses had fastened on him, asking, begging.

"Things are as slow as usual," Ben said.

Herb lit the cigarette, his stomach turning with the old mélange of emotions. His father was as carefully dressed as always, in a summer suit, a rich-looking tie, white shoes. The assured dignity seemed more unreal than ever as he pushed his hat back and disclosed his hair, still youthful and thick, as virile-looking as the powerful neck and flushed face. When he thought sometimes of still loving this man, unable to stop loving him, he cried; sitting in the darkened, lonely room, his stomach hurting with the convulsive heave.

Mr. Miller cleared his throat. "I was going over my books all morning. Very slow by me, too. The store is not what it used to be, that's all. We just can't get used to it, eh, Ben?"

Herb began to put the pieces of his invention together. His head was pounding, and he thought: Oh, I know, that crack was for me! You stopped making big dough because I flopped on my face.

"How is business with you, Herb?" his father asked.

"Not bad." He went on moving his hands, not looking at the man.

"And how is Alice?"

"She's fine," Herb said, wincing from the heavily accented, careful words. His father prided himself on his English; but Herb, waiting with dread, knew it would be Yiddish as soon as the moment of stress or fury grabbed.

"You're not seeing her today? It's Sunday."

"Oh, sure," Herb said quickly. "I'm late now. I was just leaving."

His father's words came rushing now. "Why don't you bring her, you'll both eat by us? She likes that. Ruth will be there—Alice is crazy about her."

"No, no, I—well, I promised her a movie, you see. A kid—promises."

Mr. Miller looked around; Ben had begun to close up. He was carrying out the gates for window and door, would soon push in the trunk.

"Listen, later I'm going to *shul*," he said, his voice so low and hesitant that an ache pinched along Herb's chest. "You we.en't there so long and— You know, some of the men still ask for you! I—it's a kind of a meeting tonight, business. The future of the whole congregation. I'll tell Ben to come, too. I would like it if both my sons—"

"Thanks, Dad," Herb said miserably. "But I really can't, honest."

As his eyes met his father's and he saw the open pleading, he

108

turned very pale. The scar on his face seemed to bulge with color and movement, and Mr. Miller's eyes swung away.

Herb grabbed up his invention. "I have to go. Good-by, Dad."

When Ben came back into the store his father was in the office. He had begun looking over the books. Like a child anticipating punishment, Ben had to force himself toward the frowning face behind the grilled window.

Mr. Miller looked up as he walked into the office. "Yesterday," he said, "the best day of the week—you did almost nothing."

"I did not open until after sundown," Ben said.

"A Saturday!" Mr. Miller was honestly shocked. "Even Herb knew better than that."

Then, a moment later, he said in a strained, kind voice, "Ben, I am the first to appreciate a man's feelings about the Sabbath. Do I have to tell you? But I have Ruth. When one of your sons is big enough to open for you—all right. The store is your bread, especially Saturdays."

"I can't open on the Sabbath any more." Ben's voice was very low.

His father burst into Yiddish: "Every Saturday? Crazy boy! Look at these books."

"Don't look at my books if they make you worry," Ben said, automatically speaking the same language.

"Your books? I gave you this store! Do I sit by while you lose it? The way Herb lost the store I gave him?"

Ben saw the scorn and anger in the man's eyes. His father still considered him a stupid boy, the son who had never been able to compare with the older son, physically or intellectually. Quietly, with respect, he said, "I will keep my store closed on the Sabbath. I see no other way for me."

Mr. Miller got down from the stool, closed the book. Ben saw his sudden uneasiness. He felt, with a kind of wonder, how unafraid he was and almost at the same time he realized that the ugliness he had sensed in his father all this past year was fear. His father, afraid!

"Ben," Mr. Miller said, "the Black Ones are at our heels. We need all the money we can earn. All the business success. Power, strength. Don't you understand? We have to keep them back, push them away from what is ours. We must put up that kind of a wall, for protection."

A wall? Ben thought. Remember the village we came from, Father? How the Jews lived in one part, the gentiles in another? A wall, in our heads. And in our blood we saw a wall.

As he remained silent, his father said in a stifled voice, "Ben, can't you realize that they are forcing the temple itself out of our community? Why must you close on the best day? Now—when they are almost upon us?"

"Perhaps because of them." Ben was almost stammering with earnestness. "Is it possible that a temple can be forced by people? Mere people—like we are people?"

"What? Think like a man, Ben! A man with children, responsibilities—not like a young student, arguing philosophy and—and the soul!"

"The soul," Ben said, and his father stared at him. "The Black Ones, Father—how is it possible that they can change the soul of an entire street, a temple, a neighborhood? Is this good? I was in temple all day yesterday. I—I needed help. I prayed to know why it should be that men can be changed so by other men. I, who have God to ask. I asked for help."

His father turned from the glowing look in Ben's eyes. "I must go home," he said. "We will talk some other time."

At the door, he said, "You will come with me to the meeting this evening?"

"If you want me, Father."

Mr. Miller nodded, left abruptly, but Ben could not move for a while. When at last he went to put the last gate up over the door and to snap shut the locks, a confusion of walls and gates and locks swirled through his head.

Don't make a wall in my head, he thought tremblingly. That's all I ask. Please!

# Chapter seven

It was Monday, after supper, and Mrs. Golden came to sit at her window to the world while Heidi did the dishes and Becky entertained herself on the kitchen floor with the blunt shears and the Sunday paper.

"I think she likes colors," Mrs. Golden said to Jules. "I gave her the funnies to cut."

"Where's Papa?" he said impatiently, closing his book.

"He went on the Heights straight from work, to fit a coat. God, will it ever get cool?"

"Snow," he said dreamily, his head back on the pillows. "Ice, kids coasting down the Gully on sleds."

"You want ice cream?" she said. "I'll call Alex and send him."

"Later. What's happening out there? I'm dying of boredom."

"It's too early," she said, peering toward the corner. "Even the *Schwartze* haven't started their parade yet for the night."

Suddenly she spotted someone. "What, already? It's the *pushke* collector—I didn't know it was time. I'll go meet him. He always comes the back way."

Jules groaned mockingly as she went off to the kitchen. "Sure, it's nearer the *gelt*," he said. He disliked the arrogant, bearded man who came twice a year to collect the contents of the charity boxes.

"Ida, the table is clean?" Mrs. Golden said. "He uses it to count."

"Hurry up," Jules called. "He's coming, with his neat little belly, strutting like a pigeon. Gimme your *gelt*, O Jews!"

"Sh, he's in the yard," his mother said, then snickered. "Look, he's still got the little belly."

At the screen door, she said in Yiddish, "Good evening, good evening. The time goes fast."

"Good evening," the collector said; he spoke what Mrs. Golden called a high-class Yiddish. "I hope all are well in this house?"

"With God's help," she said, and went to open the door of the broom closet while he placed his kit on the table.

Becky came to watch him open it, take out a lightweight claw hammer, a box of nails, a new collection box, a pad of receipts. His soft, white hands moved with meticulous speed. As he went to the

111

closet with the hammer, he said portentously, "Yes, the time goes fast, but the need is greater each day, believe me. There is now a whole world of Jewish suffering."

Jules snickered loudly at the professional tone of mourning, and his mother answered quickly, "Terrible. The heart bleeds at each newspaper story."

The collector had clawed the box from the back wall of the closet. At the table, he emptied it and made little piles of dimes, quarters, fifty-cent pieces, counted each pile into his hand so swiftly that Becky gaped with joy at such a fast game. He put all the coins into a leather pouch, which sagged back into his kit when he drew the strings.

Mrs. Golden pretended to busy herself at the sink, and Heidi made a clatter with pots, but they both saw the frown on his face. As he took up the new box, with its fresh blue-and-white colors and Star of David, he said sternly, "It is not so much this time, Mrs. Golden."

"Oh, I'm sorry," she cried, with real feeling. "I just wish the times were getting better, believe me."

"What my mother means," Jules called out in loud, insistent English, "is that there hasn't been enough sickness in this house lately. Not enough disaster. Too bad! Palestine suffers, huh?"

"What?" the collector said, and Heidi leaner closer to her dishrag and tried to keep from giggling.

"Disregard him," Mrs. Golden said softly. "It is the bitterness of a person too long sick."

"Do you understand English?" Jules said sweetly. "This is America, isn't it?"

The man went to the closet, quickly nailed up the new box. Mrs. Golden hid a smile as she saw his pursed mouth.

"See what I mean?" Jules said when the brief hammering had stopped. "The *pushke* is like a book of disasters. Scare people enough, fatten the book, and there is a fortune in dimes, huh? Each piece of money is another paragraph of trouble in the book, in the house. Little coin, little trouble. Fifty cents—oh, that's a big trouble! My son had a bad attack, but he got better, thank you, God! My husband lost a customer, but he didn't break a leg walking home—so here's a quarter, O Palestine!"

"I'll write out a receipt," the man said curtly as he came back to the table. Becky was playing with the box of nails, and he took it from her with a sigh before he leaned over his pad and wrote. He tore off the receipt and handed it to Mrs. Golden. "Perhaps next time you can do better," he said.

"Oh, I'm sure!"

"Blame this poor showing on me," Jules said, his eyes glittering with malicious pleasure. "It's not her fault I wasn't sick enough for plenty of *pushke* money. I'll try and do better, honest!"

The man shrugged, hurriedly packed his equipment and snapped shut the valise. As he walked toward the door, he said, "Are any of the Black Ones living in the street yet?"

"Not yet," Mrs. Golden said grimly, "though there is one Jewish family less. You knew that the Rosens moved?"

"Yes, we have the record. Well, God will take care of you, Mrs. Golden. A good year to all in this house."

"Thank you. A good year to you and yours."

The screen door slammed, and Heidi said with relief, "Boy, I was getting nervous. He was really going to bawl you out, Ma."

"I'll have to be more regular. It's a shame to have such a little bit in the *pushke*."

"Why don't you put in a penny every time you say no to a *Schwartze* at the door?" Jules said slyly.

"Give Becky a piece of bread," Mrs. Golden said to Heidi, and walked back to her window, watched with interest. "From the Millers he'll get. From Lizzie? Not as much as from us."

Jules snorted, and his mother frowned at him. "You have to insult him every time he comes? A holy man like that?"

He pushed himself up straighter against the pillows, damp with his perspiration. His feeling of elation, at having made everybody in the house uneasy for a few minutes, turned into anger.

"Listen, Mrs. Golden," he said, "I, too, am representing God on earth. I don't have to prove it by going from house to house, threatening people whose *pushkes* aren't full enough."

"He threatened?" she demanded.

"With his eyes—his voice. Woman, collect more money for Palestine or God will smite you and yours!"

"Shut up," she said quickly, her voice worried.

"Listen, I'll ask you a favor! Next time I'm real sick, don't buy my life with a dime in the *pushke*—please! Go buy me a red, red

113

rose. I'll bet God'll like that better than threats in His name."

"Boy, listen to him," Heidi said admiringly from the kitchen.

"Yeah," he said. "Rent your upstairs to the first family who rings the bell tonight. I dare you. That'll fill your *pushke* for God."

"Look who's a specialist in God," she said.

As they glowered at each other, Jules said, "I just don't get it! This street's like a—a European village or something. Who's doing it? The whole damn street—every Jewish house—like there's a sign on it, inside and out. Not only for that man to come and bleed us. No, that's the least! It's a sign for—for rotten things. Lock up empty rooms—kick people off the porch. Say no, no, no to people begging for—for room to live!"

"So—only the Jews are rotten? The *spunyitze* turned into a Jew overnight, with her empty? That she, too, doesn't want to rent to them?"

"Is this an American street?" he demanded. "My God, sometimes I wonder where this street really lives. In what crazy dark age?"

The little pulse in his throat was banging so hard that his mother winced and turned back to the window. "Stop beating me," she said. "I'm a tired woman. They should put money in the *pushke* for me today."

She made a half-hearted attempt at her usual game of entertaining him: "Well, the Zigman truck just drove in. Maybe they'll give the collector a fat chicken, with the money? Lizzie is on her porch next door, watching. Tomorrow she'll tell me about the fortune he got out of her *pushke*."

"Ma," Heidi called, "after I finish I'm going for a walk in the Gully. I'm so hot I'm melting."

"Take Becky. If you see Alex, tell him I want him home."

Mrs. Golden's voice brightened as she looked out. "Ah hah! Mr. Vincent and Mr. Levine are leaving for the lodge. So who'll drive into our street soon with her little *goy*?"

"Hey, listen," Jules said with irritation, "what do you mean, 'our street'? Why do you act as if you own the street? You and the other Jews? There are plenty of others here."

She thought about that for a moment or two, her eyes becoming very interested in the essence of his question. She loved a good discussion, leaped into one as avidly as Jules did.

114

"I'll tell you," she said, thinking it out slowly. "We feel how we are the owners here. We built up a whole neighborhood. With our sweat, raising our families, worrying. We were the first in the neighborhood with our bakeries and butchers, our *shul*. No? After us came the Italians, the gentiles. All right, maybe a couple of gentiles were here before us, but we came by the hundreds, no?"

"So?" he said.

"Well, what more do you need to own a street? That you came first, that you opened up business places. Worked to raise children from babies, to keep your house in good condition. Brought in movie shows and doctors, schools, the Council—all the things people bring into a neighborhood."

By now, Jules was engrossed in the discussion. "And the gentiles? They own houses, too. They keep up the lawns, the roofs. Their kids grew up in this street, too—but *you* own it?"

She nodded, her eyes glistening with the enjoyment of participating with him in serious talk. "In a street, always only certain people are close. They are the strong ones. The talkers, the leaders. Others sit on their porches and listen. When it comes time, they follow the leader—like a game by a lamppost for children. So here, the Jewish families are the leaders. Strong, loud mouths, hollering do this, do that. The others don't even want to be leaders. You know why?"

"No," he said, looking at her intently.

"I'll tell you why! They are safe. They can sit and be quiet inside. Can we? When is a Jew safe? Only when he is a landlord who watches every second—day and night. Only when he owns the street. When he can holler out like a bell if anything comes to remind him he's only a Jew. If anybody tries to slap him in the face with the fact, like —like it is garbage!"

She paused to take a deep breath of satisfaction. Heidi and Becky passed through the living room, went out to the porch. Jules studied his mother.

"See, that's what I don't get," he said. "Here is a good woman. Passionate, strong. She respects houses and people. She works like a horse and she admires others who work. Proud. You're proud to be a Jew, a mother, a landlord."

She was looking at him with happy eyes. Praise from him was a rare gift.

"And this woman," he continued with scathing quiet, "is afraid of colored people."

"Ma," Heidi called from the porch, "here she comes."

Mrs. Golden turned from Jules with relief. When he spoke in this way, hurt in his eyes, she felt a confusion about all the things in life which seemed so brutally clear-cut at other times. He no longer seemed a sick, embittered boy but a wise man questioning the core of her being.

A little dark car had pulled up at the curb across the street. Dusk hung over the street, and Mrs. Golden could barely see Shirley's face as she walked toward her family's porch.

"Still alone, with her baby," Mrs. Golden said. "Never with her husband by her side. I never saw that man once, and she's married more than three years already. No, she has to wait for her father to leave the house before she can sneak home with her baby for a visit. Look what happens when a Jew marries a *goy*."

"What happens?" Jules' voice was no longer the one she dreaded hearing. It held the familiar sneer, the quality she could fight.

"Better never to marry," she said with calm distaste.

"So why don't you and Papa quit hounding Heidi to get married?"

"What's the matter, you want your own sister to be an old maid?"

"But what if a nice Irishman came along and proposed to her? Miracles happen!"

"A Catholic baby she'll never bring me," Mrs. Golden said, still peering across the street. "How Mrs. Vincent can walk in the street, look anybody in the face, poor woman."

## 2

After her mother had kissed Manny and held him for a while, Vincent was given the little boy and she carried him to the swing and sat down. She held him carefully, pushing the swing slowly as she looked at him in the faint light thrown by the nearest lamppost. She was sure he liked being swung on Monday evenings. He seemed to laugh and gurgle more, and make wider gestures with his strong arms.

"Well, as soon as Moe is through on the phone we'll go in," her mother said nervously.

"Let's stay on the porch, huh?" Shirley said. "It's so hot in our apartment. It's kind of cool out here."

116

"It's hot inside by us, too," her mother admitted.

"And it's dark already," Shirley said quietly. "They can't see us on the porch."

"All right. Sit in the iron chair—it's cooler. Don't let me forget later, I've got chicken and soup left over from Friday. You'll take it home with the cake."

"Okay, Ma." Shirley looked through the window, following her mother's fixed stare. Moe Levine was at the telephone in the dining room, had switched on the lights and was watching the porch as he talked.

"Don't look in the house," Shirley said. "He won't come out here."

In an indignant whisper, her mother said, "Every Monday, like a clock! As soon as Pa leaves for the lodge and Moe smells you're coming, he's down at my phone. I wish she would get her own telephone."

"What's the difference?" Shirley said soothingly.

"It's none of his business when you come! Such a family! She still won't let them buy a car. All right, when Nate was here he felt sorry for Moe so he used to drive him. But now? A grown man, and she makes him take the bus or the car. But a phone she ought to put in!"

Vincent moved her lips gently over Manny's soft cheek, and he laughed. Her mother was always very nervous throughout the Monday-night visits. She was uneasy about any of the neighbors seeing Shirley and Manny at the house. She was ashamed of them, and yet she could not bear passing up the opportunity of lodge night; as soon as her husband was out of sight, she ran to the telephone: "Shirley? Pa went already." By the time Shirley had driven from East 110th, her father was on the bus, well on his way to the Heights.

By the time Manny was in her mother's arms, being kissed over and over—her mother whispering in that happy yet half-crying way: "My little sweet, beautiful boy! My sweet love!"—her father was halfway to the other end of the world, and Shirley was smiling at Vincent, saying, "Hi, honey."

The lights in the dining room snapped off. "Moe is through with my phone? Good!" The woman relaxed a bit in her chair.

Shirley had taught her how to use her telephone by dialing the figures corresponding to the alphabetical letters of the numbers she wanted to call, and had prepared a list of these numbers, headed by her own. Her mother could not read English, but she spoke it passably and understood it well. Shirley and she listened to three of the same radio serials each day, and then talked to each other on the telephone, discussing the newest bit of tragic action. She had never been to Shirley's apartment, but they spoke to each other four or five times every day before her husband came home from work. Saturdays, she waited until he went to temple before she ran to the telephone and dialed, said eagerly: "Shirley? How's the baby?" Sundays, there were no calls unless he went to the corner for a paper.

"What's new, Ma?" Shirley asked.

"The *pushke* collector was here," her mother said with satisfaction. "He found four dollars and ten cents. The most I ever had. He gave me a compliment and a blessing for the whole family."

"That's swell," Shirley said. "That buck I put in helped, huh?"

Vincent remembered that dollar. Manny had not come that Monday night; he had stayed home with Johnnie because of a bad cold, and Shirley had gone to the broom closet and thrown four quarters into the *pushke*. Vincent remembered, too, how often her mother threw in a coin directly after a telephone conversation with Shirley, or on Mondays after the little car had moved out of the street. A sigh, then the clink of the coin, and sometimes there were tears in Ma's eyes as she turned back from the box.

It was still another facet of religion Vincent could not understand. By throwing a dime or a quarter into a holy box, did you placate God for Manny having been baptized a Catholic, for Shirley having married a *goy*? Would even the sternest God frown on sweet Manny?

She touched the baby's cheek, unearthly soft, and heard her mother giggle, say in a lower voice, "He bawled out Lizzie. I heard every word down the back hall. She puts in only pennies—she told me herself."

Shirley laughed. "How's the latest flop on the streetcar?"

"She's trying the Heights cars now. But she complains that they're so smooth that it's going to be hard to fall."

"How's Pa feeling?" Shirley asked.

"Tired out from the heat. But there are plenty of jobs for painters."

"That's good. How's the Grandmother?"

"The same. An iron woman. Yesterday, in that hot weather, she came walking like a young girl. Nothing bothers her. She's never sick."

"That's wonderful."

Vincent became aware of the wistfulness in her sister's voice, a tone like loneliness. Suddenly she thought: Ma never asks her how Johnnie is. Not even on the phone. Is that what makes Shirl lonesome?

The street seethed with the noise of kids playing, people trying to cool off by walking or by sprinkling their lawns. Manny jumped in Vincent's arms, his sturdy legs kicking at her stomach. She smelled his fragrant, silky hair as she ducked her head and nuzzled him to make him laugh out loud in that wonderful, wholehearted way he had of responding.

In describing her sister to herself—not with words but in feelings colored by her love—Vincent always had a picture of Shirley's warmth and her gaiety of smile and words, the way she hummed in the small apartment as she cleaned or gave Manny a bath or started supper for Johnnie the nights he could come home from the station. Her brown, curly hair, the way she was not really pretty, but clean and plump and smiley; and she and Johnnie always looked so happy together! Then, after Manny was born, it seemed to Vincent that her sister was overflowing with laughter and kisses for her family, with little pieces of joy that came out in open, breathless love words.

But the picture of Shirley also contained her manner when she came to visit on Monday nights. Even before Manny, who was eight months old; it must have started when she married Johnnie, Vincent finally figured out in her secret thoughts. There was a frightened, guilty side to Shirley on Mondays, as if she agreed that she had done something bad, and would be punished for it.

And tonight, Vincent thought with a troubled frown, Shirley sounds real lonesome. Like she's homesick—for Pa. For the Grandmother, for crying out loud!

She thought of the old woman sitting on this same porch yesterday, pretending Manny had never been born. Quickly, she bounced the little boy up and down, leaned over him to feather-kiss his chin and ear. It's a damn lie! she said to herself. He *was* born. He's right here. I don't give a damn what the *shul* says—or the Grandmother and Pa, either!

119

A man climbed the steps of the porch next door, rang the bell, and her mother said, "All day long, every night, since the Rosens moved! How is it in your neighborhood?"

"They never bother anybody," Shirley said, answering in Yiddish mechanically.

"Just wait! They say on Central there's a holdup every week. Always by the Black Ones."

On the porch next door, the Negro pushed the bell again. Vincent heard the long peal at the back of the house. Then Dave's voice came leaping: "No rooms, Mister!"

Vincent's arms tightened around Manny as she heard that tense, strained voice behind the screen door. The man went away, and Shirley stretched, said, "It's so much cooler here. Maybe some day we'll have a house with a porch."

"And a back yard for Manny," her mother said. "A little grass. It's good for a baby to play in a yard."

Was she afraid God would strike her dead if she even said Johnnie's name? Vincent asked herself with a sudden resentment. That big, blond guy who could hold Manny as gently as if a baby were a cream puff?

"Look at my six-foot-two," Shirley would say about her husband, right in front of him, the two grinning at each other so wonderfully that Vincent could taste a kind of joy in her throat. "Ever see such a bull? Hey, six-foot-two, I love you!"

Johnnie looked terrific in his fireman's uniform. Shirley loved to see him all dressed up in that uniform. She had made him go and have his picture taken in it. It stood on a table in their living room, the biggest, sweetest grin Vincent had ever seen in her life. But every time she looked at the picture she had to remember the night Nate had told Ma and Pa that Shirley had gone out of the state with Johnnie.

"John O'Brien?" Pa had said in a terrible, stunned way. "She married a man with that name?"

And Ma, crying bitterly, had said, "A fireman? Even his job— God! Did you ever hear of a Jew being a fireman?"

"Who is he? What is he?" Pa had shouted.

Nate had shrugged as he had begun to undress on his way to the living room, where his rollaway bed stood. His cynical, after-the-war voice; Vincent, sitting up in her bed and shivering, had heard her brother say: "The guy's about five years older than Shirl. He's Irish. He's a fireman—with a damn good civil-service job. This is not a bum. He's a good scout, and Shirl's no baby, and she said to tell you she'd be back after they're married. Now leave me alone. Don't cry on my shoulder until I go out and marry a *shiksel*"

But on the porch tonight, as on each Monday night, the feel of a little body, the sound of a baby's hearty chuckle, could erase any memory of that night of shouting and weeping. Vincent said, "Hey, Shirl, does Manny have to eat or anything? Could I do it?"

Shirley laughed. "He ate like a pig before we came. If he cries later, you'll give him a cracker."

"When are you training him to a bottle?" her mother said.

"Oh, I love to feed him," Shirley said. "I'm in no hurry. My milk's good for him and he likes it."

"How about changing diapers?" Vincent asked.

"Is he wet?"

Vincent smoothed the round bottom. "No, I don't think so."

Shirley laughed again. "Just wait! You'll have plenty of chances to change him before we go."

"Sweet little pisher," her mother said, so affectionately that Vincent's throat felt scratchy with the always-recurring fierceness of *why*. Why can't Pa love him? The Grandmother? Why can't he come here every day, all of us together, and Pa could bounce him, too?

"How's Nate, Ma?" Shirley said.

Her mother brightened, her voice, her whole manner. "I haven't heard from him since the letter Judy read you over the telephone. It's time for another one soon. She answered right away."

Manny was falling asleep in Vincent's arms. As she watched the little jerks of the body as it fought sleep, she listened to the talk about her brother Nate.

He was a wound in her, which she nursed in complete secrecy. She did not touch this wound often, or press it to see if it hurt. When she remembered Nate, she tried to think of the way he had been before the war, permitting herself to remember him until the week he got back.

In his uniform, dazzling all eyes; he was even slimmer and taller than when he had gone away, and so dark and polished, his laugh so fresh, that her chest ached at the feel of him back in the house. She had worshiped him more than ever, had run like an excited little wildcat to fetch cake and tea, to shine his shoes. She had stared and stared at how beautiful a brother she had as he talked to neighbors on the porch, near the lamppost on his way out of the street.

Nate was always opening what Ma called "little stores" and Pa called "bookie joints." In these places, where he sold out-of-town newspapers, cigarettes, candy and hot dogs, there was a curtain or a door at the back; Pa's scornful descriptions always included that item. Nate would open a place, and a month or two later he would close it and open one in a different neighborhood. She had been to only one of his stores—the last one, next to Johnnie's fire station. That was after the war. That was the Nate she hated to even remember.

She preferred to remember the Nate who had stayed out late every night, and then in the morning had strolled in pajamas and bathrobe to the kitchen from his rollaway. "Hey, Ma," he would say, "brought you a souvenir from my date." And he would toss a spoon on the table, a fork, or a knife, which he had put in his pocket the night before. Each was stamped with the name of a hotel, or a dine-and-dance place, or a restaurant. The table drawer was full of silverware marked: "Chinese Gardens," "The Statler," "Little Italy. . . ."

After Nate had gone to New York, Vincent began to hate eating with those forks and spoons. She began picking the unmarked kitchen silver out of the drawer for herself, though it was still fun to remember Nate's lazy laugh on the mornings when he presented Ma with new souvenirs, and Ma's eager questions about the dancing, the fancy food, the clothes his date had worn.

It was more fun to remember, long ago, when he had brought home the puppy and named it Prince. Ma had hollered because of the dirt it would make and because she was afraid of dogs, but Nate had built a box and lined it with clean rags, and the little fat puppy had lived under the stove. For three whole days, she and her brother had loved Prince. Nate had brought home cans of dog food and a collar too big to fit yet, and a dog comb. He had just started hustling papers with Moe Levine, and he had spent his first money to buy Prince. Three wonderful whole days; she and Nate had taken Prince for walks, and fed him and cleaned up the kitchen floor the minute he had an accident. But Ma had moaned and hollered until Nate had suddenly picked up Prince and run out of the house, given him away to somebody—comb and collar and box and all. That was the only dog they had ever had.

Or, when she wanted to think of Nate, Vincent could remember the twenty-two sandwiches the night before he hitchhiked to New York. Ma and Pa were at the big lodge party. Shirley was in bed with the measles, and she and Nate had been all alone in the kitchen, making sandwiches for his secret trip. Ten sandwiches of peanut butter, twelve of salami; she had counted out loud as he put them into the knapsack he had bought a week before and hidden in the basement. After he had put the packed knapsack behind the couch, where nobody could see it, they sat on his rollaway and he told her about the fancy job he would get in New York, how he would make a million dollars, and maybe she would come and visit him all the time. In the morning, he was gone when she woke up, and Ma was crying, Pa hollering: "Let him go, it'll be a good lesson for him to be hungry, he'll know how to be a man with a job!" Nate was back in two days, all the sandwiches gone. Dirty, tired, but still the big-shot brother she adored, he had said to her: "I walked my head off—nobody picked me up. Next time I go to New York I'll be driving my own Caddy."

But he had gone by bus. And Vincent, rocking Manny slowly, heard her mother say to Shirley, "He doesn't go to Uncle Morris' house. The Grandmother is very angry."

Shirley giggled. "Nate never did like his relatives."

"Shirl," Vincent whispered, "I think Manny fell asleep."

"He'll sleep right on your lap, honey, don't worry. He'd sleep on a big, pointy rock—my little fatty."

Her mother came to the swing and leaned over the sleeping baby. "My sweet child," she whispered in Yiddish, and kissed one of the curled hands.

With her lovely warmth, Shirley said, "Ma, look how cute they are together—the *schwartze kuter* and little Mendy."

A chuckle came from her mother as she went back to her chair. "A *kuter* holds a kitty. Soon he'll be climbing fences after her."

Vincent nodded grimly to herself. Yes, she would teach the kitten how to take care of himself! Some day she would show him all the tricks a big alley cat knew of running fastest, of fighting best. Let the Grandmother put that in her pipe and smoke it!

123

Across the street, Heidi and Becky came walking from the Gully, turned into the Golden yard, and Shirley said, "How's your friend Jules?"

"Pretty good," Vincent said, "but he's still in bed. I sure hope the doctor lets him get up soon. On the porch, maybe."

"All summer," her mother said darkly. "Why she doesn't send a sick boy like that to the hospital. All she talks about is the empty suite over her head, the Black Ones."

"Nobody likes hospitals," Shirley said, with pity.

"Why doesn't she at least send that poor Becky to the institution? That woman has two heartbreaks in her house."

Yeah? Vincent thought, her resentment deeper. But she *wants* her heartbreaks. Not like Pa. She loves them, she wants them right in her house. Why doesn't Pa want Manny? He's not sick, or like Becky. He's perfect.

Again the Zigman bell rang as a stranger stood on the porch next door. And, across the street, the light streaming from Jules' windows fell upon a Negro couple standing on his porch. From the Gully lamppost came a fast, high chorus of children's voices: "Red rover, red rover, let Anna come over!"

"Oh, Shirley," the low Yiddish burst out, "if a person could only run to the ends of the earth from these Black Ones! I am afraid to look into their eyes."

Yeah? Vincent thought bleakly. Is Pa afraid to look into Manny's eyes?

Suddenly she thought of that girl, Clara. She remembered the girl's eyes, proud, fierce with anger at Dave. Why in hell would Ma be afraid to look into her eyes? Was it fair and square for Ma to say that?

The new thinking clicked on and on, in confusing spurts: Well, hell, what's so fair and square about Pa or the Grandmother? To say Shirley is "as if dead." To pretend Manny was never born.

She rocked the baby in her arms. Clara—a name with eyes, fists, a voice. Where does she live? Why did she lend me her knife? Maybe she won't be there tomorrow night? Oh yes, she will! Just like I will. We meant it—fair and square.

Her resentment was clotted with anger as she thought: Is it fair and square for Ma never to mention Johnnie? She acts as if there isn't any Johnnie. Like Pa and the Grandmother acting like there isn't any Manny!

"Shirl," she said harshly.

"What?" her sister asked.

"How's Johnnie?"

There was a pause, then Shirley said in a startled voice, "He's fine, honey."

Her mother was silent, and Vincent thought: See? There *is* a Johnnie!

Shirley began to talk, very fast, about a pattern she had bought for a housecoat. Next door, Dave suddenly rushed out and was down the porch steps before the screen door could slam. Vincent heard his muffled curse as he ran off toward the corner. She turned, watched him sprint past the lamppost, and wished they were running together, laughing, like all the times they had raced the moon.

Then she became aware of a woman crossing the street. She stopped on the sidewalk in front of their house, her face turned toward the sound of Shirley's voice.

"Hey, Ma," Vincent said in a low voice, "the *spunyitze* is out there. I think she's coming up on our porch."

Her mother stiffened. "Shirley, take Manny inside!" she cried.

"Now, Ma," Shirley said uneasily, "don't be silly."

Mrs. Valenti started slowly up the little walk leading to the porch, and Vincent's heart began to beat hard as her mother jumped up in a panic. She hoisted Manny up to her shoulder, got ready to run.

"What can she want?" The whispering Yiddish sounded breathless. "She never comes here. Why on a Monday, suddenly? Judy, give me the baby! Go stop her. Find out what she wants!"

"Ma, you cut that out," Shirley said in a low voice.

Manny yawned against Vincent's cheek. She felt his warm breath, that little soft opening mouth plastered against her skin, as he began to dig his head into her. She took a deep breath as Shirley got up.

Mrs. Valenti said hesitantly from the walk at the foot of the steps, "Hey, Missus."

"Hello, Mrs. Valenti," Shirley said, and walked toward the steps. "Come on up."

"Shirley, not on the porch!" her mother whispered frantically.

"Come on up, Mrs. Valenti," Shirley said again.

As the woman climbed up, Vincent made out the somber face and had to remember Santina's jubilant outcries Friday when the gang was stripping her. Sitting far back in the shadows with Manny half hidden in her arms, she noticed the water glass. The *spunyitze* was holding it out to Shirley, gesturing with her other hand.

"You got milk? Extra?" she said eagerly.

"What?" Shirley asked.

"My Ross sick! You want give me little bit milk, Missus?"

"God, what can she want?" The Yiddish was like a moan.

"Sick? What's the matter?" Shirley said. "Did you call the doctor?"

"No doctor! He take knife! My Ross got in ear—big, swoll'. Hurt bad. Swoll' in ear. You know?"

"A boil?" Shirley said. "Has he got a boil in his ear?"

"Yes, yes! Boil—you call that!" Mrs. Valenti took a step forward, touched Shirley's breast with delicacy. "Is baby milk in ear. Wash out, huh? No hurt no more."

Shirley laughed. "Oh!" she said with delight. "Sure! I'd love to."

She turned to her mother. "Ma, you know what she wants? Some of my milk. Ross has a boil in his ear. She thinks some of my milk'll cure it, I guess. Isn't that cute?"

Mrs. Valenti nodded excitedly. As Manny squirmed and kicked in her arms, Vincent watched her sister begin to unbutton the top of her dress. There was something so comfortable and pleased about Shirley's laughter that Vincent had to smile. Her sister acted as if the *spunyitze's* request for milk was a compliment or something.

She noticed that her mother had sort of sidled up to the two women. As Shirley took the glass, her mother said with a reluctant chuckle, "Shirley, tell her it's a small world. Tell her in Europe my own mother used to doctor ear trouble with breast milk. Abscesses and such things."

"I'm tickled to death to give you some, Mrs. Valenti," Shirley said, talking slowly so that the woman would understand. "You know what my mother just told me? In Europe, her people used milk for ear trouble, too. Just like you."

She uncovered her breast. Vincent saw the faint gleam of white in the shadows, heard the stream of milk hit the glass. Mrs. Valenti made a cooing sound of joy.

"God bless you," she said. "God bless baby."

"Oh, I'm tickled to death to do it," Shirley said, laughing.

Her mother chuckled again. "How small a world!"

Then Mrs. Valenti laughed, too. "Thanks, thanks," she said. "God bless baby, Missus."

Vincent put her face next to Manny's, suddenly feeling so good that she could hardly stand it. The three laughing women, the glass filling with milk, the little boy making his own laughing noises as he jumped in her arms; it was, in a queer and wonderful way, as if Manny had become part of this street.

# Chapter eight

The next day Vincent stayed on her porch until the first weight of dusk began to color the air, then she went to the Gully. The girl had said to meet her the same time of day. It would be dark soon, and nobody would see them.

She whistled as she sauntered down the slope and toward the clubhouse turning, in case anybody was around, but when she walked into the little level area the place was deserted and safe. She stopped whistling, walked the rest of the way to the fireplace and stared down at old charred paper and wood.

For a second of intense hurt, she remembered all the fires, all the joy of those yesterdays which had merged so quickly. There had never been a calendar to life; excitement and fun had been timeless. Every day had been the present, fast and dangerous, the never-ending moment of leadership.

Vincent glanced about her. The place looked strange. When she thought of Friday and the gang moving toward her, the memory seemed blurred, the tragic poignancy of the entire incident already stale. She had a past, suddenly, and she felt queerly older.

Something moved at the side of the clubhouse, came toward her, turned into a striding figure. Pants, white blouse, tennis shoes; an excitement came back into Vincent as she saw the girl. Clara was exactly as she had remembered her.

"Hi," she said.

Clara's answering nod was just as wary as her greeting, and after a second Vincent said, "What you doing up there?"

"Playing safe. I got a hiding place right behind your club. I always get there before it's dark. I can see but nobody sees me." After a little pause, Clara said carelessly, "You never came back after Friday."

"No," Vincent said.

The scornful smile she remembered so clearly was back on the brown face. "A couple of others come. Every night. Phooey!"

She spat straight down, then wiped her shoe over the spot. "Not that blond guy, though. He ain't been back, either."

Then she said coolly, "Well, did you cut his tail off?"

"No!" Vincent flushed, dug the knife out of her pocket and held it out.

"Afraid, huh?" Clara said, and snatched the knife, slipped it into her pocket.

"I don't want to use a knife," Vincent said, glaring at her.

Clara sucked at her lower lip. Then she said, "Hell, I never used it, either! But you got it in your pocket, you know you can always pull it out, see? If white people get funny. Hell, they're always looking to hit us, rob us. My mother and father told me all about that."

Vincent stared at her. But they had always told her exactly that about *Schwartze*. Who was lying?

"You never cut anybody?" she muttered.

"Not me. All that blood? I'd just throw up or something. But you got to carry a knife. All the guys in my gang did. You got to show guys you're just as good as them, don't you?"

Vincent nodded. "You got a gang, huh?"

"Fifteen guys and me. I wasn't leader, but I sure was first lieutenant." Bitterness suddenly ravaged Clara's voice. "Yeah, but my gang's down there on 55th Street and I'm up here on 112th. And what in hell for? We ain't even in our own house. Had to move in with my auntie, like a bunch of sardines. My father's so mad he won't talk to us sometimes."

"How long you been here?"

"About a month. I hate it!"

Vincent took a cigarette out of her pocket. Leo had given it to her that morning, trying to get on her good side because of Friday. It was new and quite straight, and she had taken it for one reason only.

"Want a cig?" she said, and broke it in half, fair and square.

128

"Sure do," Clara said, as Vincent took out the packet of matches she always carried.

They sat on the ground near the fireplace, and Vincent held a match for the girl.

"Tastes good," Clara said. "We used to smoke all the time. There was an alley behind the barbershop—that's where we held our meetings. When it rained we could crawl under the back porch there."

"Well, how come you moved, huh?" Vincent said earnestly. "I mean, in with your aunt that way? Like sardines? No money?"

"You crazy? We got plenty of money! My father works in the post office. My mother's got a swell job in the beauty shop. Hell, even Frankie and Bill, they work. They're my brothers—they hustle papers. We always paid our rent in that old joint we lived in. That's why my father's so mad. He paid on time every month—not like plenty of people. But we had to get the hell out anyway. Boy, he's twice as mad at white people."

"Why? What'd they do?" Vincent was fascinated. Like Clara, she paid no attention to that "white people." By now, the phrase meant simply "they," the enemy.

"Plenty!" Clara said. "Down on 55th there's lots of houses that just plain stink. You ever see them? They're so lousy and broken down, my father says they ought to be bombed. Those white people never fix them or paint them or anything. Well, ours got so bad the city hall condemned it. The whole damn street. See, they're going to tear down all the houses and build some kind of a project. Yeah! My father says that'll take forever and a day, even if it ain't a lot of big talk from the city hall."

She looked at Vincent, said in a flat voice, "So we moved. My father kept cursing them out, said he was going to shoot them all—but we just moved anyway. Like sardines. My mother cries every night, and he keeps saying he'll shoot them. Big old talker!"

"Why's he want to shoot them?"

"We didn't have anywhere to move, did we? We still ain't got anywhere, that's why. He looked all over town for a place. So'd my mother—kept asking all her customers. There's just no houses around."

Vincent thought of the empties in her street, and she suddenly remembered Jules' poems. They had always seemed like mystic, ex-

129

citing songs, charged with the wonderful fireworks of Jules but to her merely a singing about unreal things.

This girl had just made the poems real. She had put people's faces in them, and crying and cursing. She herself seemed to have jumped out of one of those poems.

"My father's always talking," Clara said scornfully, but a bleakness stuck through like bones. "All this money we got saved in the bank. What a big shot he is in the post office. But we had to move in with all our relatives anyway. Hell, I even have to go to a new school this fall. Lincoln Junior High—nuts!"

"Hey, that's where I go," Vincent said.

"Yeah?"

Suddenly they were both wary again, as if trying to visualize meeting in a corridor at that school, stopping to talk.

"Wish we had another cig," Vincent muttered.

"Me, too." Clara threw the tiny remnant of her cigarette butt into the fireplace, near Vincent's.

The dreamy, blue dusk gathered slowly, taking its time. After a while, Clara said, "I sure hate to go home from here. Boy—quiet! You can hardly hear those kids up there, huh?"

"Hey, listen," Vincent blurted, "would you move in a place where there was a fire?"

Clara studied her. "I don't know," she said cautiously. "Would it be fixed up or anything—after?"

"I guess so," Vincent said, suddenly shocked at what she had said.

"Sure I'd move! How would you like to live in somebody else's place? Nervous about sitting somewhere, or—or taking too long in the bathroom! Sleeping with your cousin, and two more in the other bed? Hell!" But then her voice softened: "There's a little baby there."

"Yeah? How old?"

"Almost a year. She's the cutest, prettiest baby. Fat!"

In the brown face, the eyes dreamed a little, and Vincent marveled about the mounting list of things she and Clara had in common. Would she tell her about Manny some day?

"Hey," Clara said, "what did you mean about that fire?"

"Nothing! I mean—I got to thinking—you know, if I saw a house like that?" Vincent's heart slammed. No, her father would never do it! Why had she even mentioned it?

130

"You going to—well, kind of keep your eye peeled for a place?"

"Maybe I could, huh?"

As Clara looked at her, in a wondering way, Vincent tried to think of something else to talk about, said: "That's tough about you had to move. This guy, Phil Rosen, next door to me—he had to move. Boy, he sure hated to leave the gang. He told me. You—do you miss your gang bad?"

"Hell, no!" Clara's voice was gruff with bravado. "I like to be by myself. Those guys were always talking so big. Like they were the only ones who could do things. Just because they were boys. Zipping their pants open, like—like that's all there is!"

"Yeah," Vincent muttered.

After a minute, Clara said, "But you could have fun once in a while. I even had a couple of nicknames the guys called me. Well, it got so even a lot of grownups called me that, too. 'Jack' was one. You know, for Jackson—my name. Then they'd call me 'Hi-Jack,' too. I'm a pretty high jumper, is why."

Vincent was grinning. "Hey, I got one, too! I mean, that's got to do with jumping and running fast. Lots of people in my street call me the *schwartze kuter*. That's Jewish, see? It means the black alley cat. You know, one of those tough cats in the street? It's a compliment."

"Black cat, huh?" Clara said.

"Yeah, but not just any cat. One of those tough-guy cats who's the best fighter, the best climber."

Clara chuckled, and Vincent added eagerly, "This friend of mine, Jules. He lives across the street—his mother made up the name. Lots of people call me that. Even my sister sometimes."

"Say it again?" Clara asked.

"*Schwartze kuter.*"

"*Schwartze,*" Clara said, stumbling over the pronunciation. She chuckled again. "That's me, huh?"

Vincent's face felt hot, but she said, "It means black."

"Well, I'm going to call you Vincent," Clara said.

"Okay! And I'll call you Hi-Jack."

"Uh-uh," Clara said. "I'm not in the gang now. You call me Clara."

Anger spurted in Vincent. Her gang, like Clara's, was gone, too. "Well, God damn it," she cried, "don't be calling me Judy!"

"I said I'd call you Vincent, didn't I?" Clara shouted back. "What're you getting so tough about?"

"Okay!"

They both frowned, stared into the fireplace. Finally Clara said with a sneer, "Every time I think of guys—acting like kings or something. That blond guy who did it to you. Boy, you looked so little and—and like a kid when they got you on the ground!" Her disdain had turned into anger again. "See, that's why I loaned you my knife. I been around—I know what those bastards can do!"

"Don't worry, I'll get even," Vincent said.

"Yeah. But what if he tries it again? Or one of those other guys? Or if they try the real works on you?"

Vincent looked at her. "I'll fight," she said.

"If I'm around, I'll help you. I'm bigger than you—we'll both kill them."

"Okay," Vincent said gratefully.

But Clara frowned. "Yeah, and what if five or ten guys jump you? And you're by yourself?"

Vincent was silent, and Clara said, "I used to pull out my knife. Just hold it."

"Aw, the hell with them," Vincent said, trying to sound careless.

"Used to scare me," Clara muttered. "I used to go home, after, and throw up." Then she said thoughtfully, "If you don't want a knife, would you wear a medal?"

"A what?"

"A medal." She fumbled at her neck with both hands and drew the cord up, over her head: "See, I'm Catholic and we wear medals. I've got some more at home so you don't have to worry about giving this back. You wear it, and no guy'll ever be able to even touch you. See, it's as good a protection as a knife."

Amazement tingled in Vincent like a sudden shock as she stared at the medal Clara was holding out. Here was one of the secret, different things out of Manny's life, out of a Catholic's God-ways. But how could a *Schwartze* be a Catholic? Like Santina, Angelo—Johnnie? Yeah, but look at Manny!

"Want to look at it?" Clara said.

Vincent took the medal, the long cord crumpling in her palm under it, and studied it intently. Once there had been straight lines

132

like boundaries around each religion touching her life; separate boxes into which people fit. Manny, who belonged in one box, had been pulled somehow into a different one. How confusing to see the box for Catholics open again—and there was a brown face, alongside the other mistake of Manny's face being there.

"It's a St. Anthony medal," Clara said.

An exciting mixture of feelings rushed through Vincent, and at the core was Manny's name, like a shout. The queer closeness between Clara and her seemed to pivot on him, and she tried to figure things out as she stared at the medal—a man's face, next to it a baby's head. In her mind, suddenly, Manny and Clara stood close as a brother and sister.

"Want it?" Clara said.

"Gee, I—it sure is swell of you," Vincent said awkwardly. Her face very hot, she added, "But I can't. See, I can't wear it. I'm Jewish."

"Oh," Clara said, her voice troubled. "Jewish people can't, huh?"

"No."

They both stared down at the medal, frowning. Suddenly Vincent had an idea. "Hey, look," she said, "I've got a treasure box. You know —where I keep special stuff? Secrets and everything. Could I keep the medal in my box?"

"Sure you could," Clara said excitedly. "It's your own treasure box. Nobody'd know it was in there. And it would be protecting you just like you're wearing it. Only you ain't wearing it, so that part's okay, see?"

"Okay!" Vincent said.

They grinned at each other.

"I got one, too," Clara said. "Used to be a cigar box. It's still my secret, but boy, it sure is tough to find a good hiding place when you haven't got much room. People peeping at you all the time. Except real late at night."

Vincent nodded. As she put the medal in her pocket, she tried to visualize how it would feel not to be able to look in your treasure box when you wanted to because of a lot of people there always. She could not quite imagine it.

The medal was the biggest gift she had ever had in her life. Nobody had ever taken a piece of God—right off herself!—and offered it for protection. "Hey, thanks," she said. "Thanks for the protection."

"Yeah. You'll see—it's going to be better than a knife, even."
Clara gave her a darting, sidewise look, then she mumbled, "You know
what? I sure feel like I know you for a long time. Like—well, look
how we do lots of the same things, huh?"

"Boy! Isn't it funny?" Vincent said.

"Yeah." Then Clara said, "See, I never knew no white kid before."

"Me, too! I never even talked to a colored kid."

"Funny, huh?" Clara mused.

A desire to give Clara something made a yearning all through Vincent. Something precious, like that medal; and she said, as the wish
burned deeper in her: "You go to that St. Joseph's Church? Down on
Woodlawn?"

"Yeah, since we moved up here. It sure is pretty."

Wonder if she ever saw Manny in there, Vincent thought. So it's
pretty? Manny has a pretty church.

The first real darkness of night was drifting about them. They
could see each other, but not expressions or color of eyes. The Gully
looked like it sounded in one of Jules' poems: cool and peaceful, with
dreams floating down from the sky and up from the ground like dark-
blue smoke.

Thinking of his poems, Vincent suddenly knew what she could
give Clara. It was her most precious possession, and she said eagerly,
"Hey, I want to tell you something! You ever read any poems?"

"Poems? You mean like in school—Longfellow or something?"

"Yeah, but different! I mean—well, this friend of mine across the
street. Jules—I told you about him. He's sick all the time, has to be
in bed, or on the porch swing. He's got a leak in his heart, see? Well,
he writes poems. He's got this big red notebook and—well, nights a
lot, you know, when he can't sleep? It hurts him, his heart, so he has
to kind of sit up. So he writes these poems. They're wonderful!"

"He a kid?" Clara asked.

"Hell, no! He's seventeen, going on eighteen. He's going to be a
famous writer some day—everybody knows that."

"Yeah?"

Her voice rough with feeling, Vincent said, "He wrote me this one
poem. Just for me, he said. It's—well, it always makes me feel terrific
when I even think about it. It's got a name, too. 'The Changelings.'
Know what that means?"

"Uh-uh."

Vincent laughed. "I didn't, either. Jules had to tell me. It means somebody who's left in a place secretly, instead of the person who's supposed to be there. And especially kids. Say there's a little kid in a house. You know, a baby. Well, all of a sudden it disappears and some other kid's there—and its parents don't know. They think it's the same kid, see?"

"But it ain't?"

"No." Vincent added thoughtfully: "But you got to remember something. It sounds crazy, but Jules wrote this poem about the *insides* of a kid. The kid's heart—you know, the way he thinks inside of him. There's this new kid—this changeling—in a house, and his parents think he's theirs. But he isn't—not in his heart. They think one way and talk one way, and the kid who's a changeling thinks entirely different. What Jules meant in that poem is that the kid just feels like a changeling. Inside of him, see? He says lots of kids are like that. They don't really belong with their parents, or their grandmother either, because they want different things out of life. They don't talk—well, the same language. I mean, in their hearts! You know what I mean?"

"Not for sure," Clara said doubtfully.

"Well, take me. My mother and father are always crying the blues about things. How they're scared of—of people coming and taking what's theirs. They're always crying about no money and—and hating people. You know, people who're different and don't go to the same church and don't look like them? I mean, they're just plain scared of a lot of stuff."

"Yeah, that's right! Mine, too."

"So take me," Vincent said, words pouring out excitedly. "I'm the changeling in my house—the way Jules has it in my poem. I'm not scared. I'm not going to run around crying and hating people. Spying to see who's going to do me dirt. See? I'm not going to talk their language. I'm going to be free, so I can go out in the world. And—and beautiful. That's in the poem. You can't be free if you're scared of everybody, can you?"

"I guess not."

"Listen to this," Vincent cried. " 'All doors are open, for we are young and strong and full of hope. Come, Changeling, be a son of World, a daughter of Life.' That's a piece of the poem. Like it?"

"Boy!"

"Jules says he's a changeling in his house, sometimes," Vincent

135

said. "He says you can be a sometimes-changeling, too—depending on how lousy your mother or father acts sometimes, see? Or how they holler and cry—scared."

"How about the other kids in your family?" Clara asked.

"Jules says that it's usually only one kid, when it happens. In lots of families there aren't any, but when it happens it's one kid. Like somebody sneaked it in at night and sneaked out the one whose place you take—only it's you inside that they change. And nobody knows. Not even the kid."

"What! Not even the kid himself?"

"Well—after a while. I mean, he starts to know that he and his parents are different. And his brother and sister, and—and even a grandmother. They talk different, they feel different. So that's where you're a changeling—way inside your heart. Sound crazy to you?"

"No," Clara muttered.

"If you'd hear my poem," Vincent said glowingly. "See, I can't say it the way Jules does. He makes it—well, I mean when you're a changeling you believe in loving a lot of people. Not hate them. You're real strong. You're real free. And—and the whole world is waiting for you to come in. You belong to the whole world, see? Not just in a house where there's all this crying and squawking. They're so God damn scared of everybody!"

"They sure are!" Then Clara said, "Hey, I like that idea. That's neat."

"I knew you'd like it. But you know what? That poem is hard to explain. You've got to sort of know what he means. Inside, huh?"

Clara nodded slowly. "Yeah. Like that stuff about mothers and fathers being different than you. They are, and they aren't. You love them and you want to punch their faces in sometimes."

Vincent looked at her, the darkness cupping them in a more wonderful closeness but not obscuring their vehemence, their fierce agreement.

"They are, and they aren't," she echoed. "Hey, that's it, all right! They're really our mothers and fathers, but sometimes it's just like they aren't. We're different. We—we want different things. And the way they talk. Well, who in hell cares about some of that stuff they're so scared of? Or so damn private about. Take religion! I mean, you got to be a Jew if you're a Jew, or—well, they treat you like you died. They don't call your name. They—they pretend you're not there."

"Like you can't wear my medal, huh?" Clara said. "Sure, I know! They get you all mixed up. Like that 'sin' stuff they're always hollering. And how you'd better stay with your own kind or you get slapped around. If I told my mother about you—"

Vincent snorted. "You think I'd tell my mother about you?"

They both snickered.

"Yeah," Clara said thoughtfully after a while, "but how're you supposed to know what the hell to do? You take my parents. Even my auntie and my cousins. All of them! 'Girl, you stay away from them white folks,' they keep saying. 'You colored, you stay with colored. Those white folks're waiting to get you. Take anything you got. Hurt you, kill you. Girl, you watch out!' So what do you do? Wherever you go, you got your fists all ready to let go."

Vincent's head buzzed with the echoes of all the voices in her street shouting the same things—only the colors were reversed.

"And then what?" Clara said, her voice suddenly spurting grief. "You go to church. You kneel down—everybody's kneeling together, praying. And it's so pretty in there. You open your eyes, you look right at Him, our Lord. His eyes are so— You—you want to cry! You don't know what to do. So—so where are you?"

So where are you, Manny? Vincent thought with her own grief, visualizing the *shul*, Pa and the Grandmother in there, keeping him out.

"So maybe you're a changeling, too," she said tremulously.

A deep breath puffed out of Clara. "Yeah," she said, "could be." But suddenly she giggled. "You know what I just thought?" she said. "What if some white lady was to find me in her kid's bed? Some morning? Walk in to wake up her kid—and there's me! My little old black face peeping up at her. 'Mama, Mama!' I'd holler. And she'd fall flat on her own face in that room, screaming for the police."

Vincent guffawed. "Oh, boy! Mrs. Levine. Or Jules' mother."

They giggled luxuriously for a while as the darkness settled into every inch of the Gully, bringing a slightly cooler air to their cheeks.

Then Clara said, "That poem is yours, huh? He wrote it just for you?"

"For my birthday last year," Vincent said. "Nobody even knows about it. Just Jules and me."

"And now I know, too. Hey, when's your birthday?"

"November twenty-third. When's yours?"

Clara laughed. "Saturday. This coming Saturday, I'm thirteen. I'm going down and see my gang. Celebrate. How old are you?"

"I'm going to be thirteen, too."

Another of those rather shy laughs came from Clara. "I knew I was older than you. You looked so—little, that time on the ground here. But we sure got a lot of stuff together. Gangs and—and changelings, huh?"

"Yeah!" And Manny, Vincent thought eagerly. "My sister lives near you. On East 110th, the other side of Woodlawn."

"I live this side of Woodlawn," Clara said. "You go to your sister's a lot? To visit?"

"Sure, almost every day sometimes. I'll look for you."

"I'll look for you, too. And here. See you here, too, huh?"

"Sure, see you here, too," Vincent said.

Then a sudden little panic shattered her feeling of closeness as she thought: If we stopped and talked, near Shirley's! Who'd see us? What would they say? What if she came to my house? Yeah, and—and her house?

She shivered as she pictured herself walking into an all-black street, past a thousand houses with black faces peering from porches, from behind windows.

"Sure is cooler," Clara said, and stretched. Then she got to her feet, said reluctantly, "I better go. My father squawks if I'm not home after it's good and dark. Well, so long."

Vincent got up, too. "So long," she said, still fighting that abrupt fear.

The girl wandered off. At the turning, her dark bulk paused for an instant. "I'm sure going to remember that changeling stuff," she called back, and the shadow disappeared.

Vincent's hand groped in her pocket, touched actual shape and coolness, a tangled cord. Yes, Clara had given her the medal. It was real, all right. And again she tried to imagine not having room enough in your own house to take out your treasure box without a lot of people spying on you.

She strolled toward the clubhouse, touched a wall, the door, trying to feel the old excitement. But the only real feeling in her was the confused puzzle of Manny and Clara, together in one God-place. A *Schwartze*, and a baby who was half Jewish.

138

Vincent opened the door and walked into the clubhouse. There was a candle stump in one of the bottles, and she lit it, sat down on the leader's crate from which she had directed a thousand meetings. Looking around, she saw the familiar shadows cast on the walls by the candlelight. She could remember every detail of her life here, the power, the excited joy of certainty, but the memories were oddly blurred.

Which was real in life, which had she dreamed? She pulled out the medal and examined it. Yes, it was real! Then so was Clara, and so was the way she and Manny stood, hand-in-hand, in their church.

For an instant, Vincent wanted intensely to put the cord over her head, see how it would feel to wear such a gift of protection. The idea frightened her, as if the Grandmother could see into her wish, and she shoved the medal back into her pocket.

As she sat staring at the candle, Dave Zigman suddenly appeared in the doorway. Real, blurred memory, dream?—no, he was as real as the medal she had just studied! Her stomach lurched and seemed to sink as she thought: Hey, did he see me talking to a *Schwartze!*

Dave just stood there for an endless moment. Then he said hesitantly, "I was taking a walk. Saw the light in here, and—well, I figured I'd better see who was in the club."

"Sure!" she said. "You got to investigate for the gang, huh?"

"I didn't know it was you."

She could see him clearly in the candlelight, his face taut. His eyes looked so queerly pleading that for a moment she thought: He's changed, too! Like me. He looks different.

"I'm scramming." She jumped up.

"Wait a minute!" he cried.

He had stepped closer. His eyes looked so lost, so changed, that she was frightened. "What the hell do you want?" she muttered.

"Hey, Vincent," he said, "how about taking back the gang?"

"You go to hell," she said.

"I don't want your gang," he said, like he was begging.

"Take the lousy gang and shove it," she shouted, wild with confusion.

She stumbled past him, leaving him in possession of the kingdom, and ran as fast as she could toward the turning.

Dave stood where she had left him. I've got to get that bracelet for Ma, he thought numbly. Right away. Before it's too late.

He could not move, as if Vincent's proud, disdainful shout had taken away his strength. Right now! he thought frantically. Go to the pawnshop, spot one. Later I could bust in the window.

Then he, too, began to run.

## 2

That evening, as Vincent put the medal in her treasure box, a quarrel began upstairs. She could hear the shouts clearly in her bedroom as she hid the box in her bottom dresser drawer.

"Get to the hell out of here!" Mr. Levine screamed.

"God damn you, lay off," Moe shouted. "I broke Chip in and I broke Leo in, but I ain't taking Lou until he's big enough. I'm not going to change a kid's pants all over downtown. One Saturday was enough."

I'll look at the medal once in a while, Vincent thought. Some day, show it to Manny? He'll know. Right off her neck—he'll know.

The familiar, anger-choked cry came again: "Get to the hell out of my house! That's all!"

When Vincent came out of her bedroom the quarrel was over. Her parents were upstairs, the house dark as she sauntered out to the porch and sat on the swing.

At the Gully lamppost, a game of kick-the-stick was being organized. Across the street, a Negro couple stood on the Golden porch. Next door, the Zigman doorbell rang under the eager hand of a Negro woman. The traditional evening was in full swing, but to Vincent each familiar voice and step seemed unreal as her old life.

Mr. Levine and her father came out on the upstairs porch, settled themselves in creaking chairs. Mr. Levine groaned.

"God," he said, "when your oldest son spits in your face it is time to do some serious thinking."

Next door, Mr. Zigman said, "No rooms, no rooms! Go to some other street!" His door slammed, and Vincent heard the woman swear very softly as she left. From the swing, she watched the tall, slow figure with new curiosity.

She was crossing the street, heading toward Jules' lighted windows, when Mr. Levine said angrily over Vincent's head, "Did you

140

hear that woman? When they have the gall to curse us on our own porches!"

"You—talked to Moe about the furnace?" Vincent heard the scared tone in her father's low voice at once, and began listening closely.

"I talked. Don't worry—he likes to holler, to act like he's the landlord here with his paper jobs, but I know my son!"

Seltzer poured into a glass. The belching came, then the comfortable "Ah!" Vincent watched the Negro woman go up on the Golden porch and ring the bell. Was the woman related to Clara?

"What happens with the bank?" her father said. "It's their house."

"What does the bank care where money comes from? Has the bank a heart? This is still another American habit, Abe. If money is there, no questions are asked."

Crap, Vincent thought. Clara's father has money but he can't get her a house.

"One thing must be clear," Mr. Levine added, his voice crisp. "The women should not be told. This is men's business."

"I don't talk of such things to my wife."

"Or your mother! I don't care how smart she is. A woman is a woman."

"You're right, you're right."

"All right, I have been thinking—of afterward. The insurance is paid to us, we fix up the house. But not too good, Abe. You understand? We don't spend much money. We fix up the house so that it *looks* fine, and then we sell it at a fine price."

"And the unspent insurance money?"

"It fattens the down payment on the next house we buy. On the Heights! The larger the down payment, the lower the monthly payments on the mortgage. Right?"

"Right, right."

As Vincent heard her father's tremulous voice, she felt an intense uneasiness. Would he ever do it? Such a rotten, cheap trick? If she told him about Clara, how she and Manny went to the same. . . .

She huddled in a corner of the swing, listening to the joyous, carefree game at the Gully lamppost. For a second, she wished she were there, just kicking and running and shouting, not having to think of anything else.

141

"I have to think!" her father said abruptly. "In all my years in this country— Well, I have always worked for any money I received."

"That is obvious," Mr. Levine said dryly. "A poor man you have been since first I knew you."

"And you are rich?"

"Not yet. It has taken me all this time to learn the American habits." Mr. Levine's voice turned hard. "Now I will tell you another thing. I have to—because you cannot make up your mind. If nothing happens, I will rent my half of the house to Black Ones."

"What!" her father said, with a despair that made Vincent wince. "You would put them into the same house with my family?"

"If I have to. Abe, I will not stand by and see my children destroyed."

The dirty sonofabitch, Vincent thought with fierce resentment. Why didn't Pa tell him he didn't want to, instead of just acting scared that way? Scared! Scared of doing something wrong. A fire *was* wrong, wasn't it?

Her father's voice was so tight that it seemed to shake: "This must not happen, Herschel."

"It is up to you, Abe."

In the silence, Vincent heard the gurgle of Seltzer poured into a glass. Did Clara's father have enough money to buy this house? she wondered. If there was a fire? Yeah, but what happened if a *Schwartze* was your landlord? All right, say there wasn't a fire—come on, Pa! Say the Levines moved—could she get anybody to rent the upstairs to Clara?

Her head ached. For a minute she wondered what a burning house —your own house!—looked like. Would she be able to rescue her treasure box, her school stuff?

Nothing she touched in her head made sense. Why would a burning house keep the Levine kids from being destroyed? Why was Manny an outcast? Why was Clara an enemy, and Johnnie the reason for Shirley to be as if dead?

A big ball of confusion rolled idiotically in her head: Manny . . . *Schwartze* . . . make a fire and collect insurance . . . Clara gave it to me from around her neck . . . a brother changing and disappearing . . . guys grabbing at you but Dave's all different now, all changed, too—like me. . . .

Across the street, on the Valenti porch, the *spunyitze* began to call, "Sahn-tina! Sahn-tina!"

The ball whirled more aimlessly in Vincent's head. She could scarcely remember last night's laughter, when Shirley had given her milk to this woman and Manny had been a part of the street, as if he had been born here and lived in one of the houses.

"Sahn-tina! Sahn-tina!" The cry was a threatening shiver in the street, to match the one in Vincent's heart.

# Chapter nine

There was a letter from Nate the next day. Vincent heard her mother running in from the front porch. She could always recognize her son's handwriting, whether it was in pencil or in the green ink he used sometimes.

"Judy," she called excitedly. "A letter from—guess who!"

When Vincent came out of her room her mother was sitting at the kitchen table. The envelope had been carefully opened and she was holding a five-dollar bill.

"I knew I would get a letter this week," she said jubilantly. "You'll read it to Shirley later, when I phone her."

"Okay," Vincent said. Nate's scrawl made her bite her lip as she unfolded the sheet of paper.

"Well?" her mother said, and chuckled. "It starts: 'Hello, Ma.'"

Vincent began to read her the letter: "'Hello, Ma. I have been too busy to write but I know you will excuse me. Before I forget, here is five bucks. Buy yourself some perfume.'"

A soft, girlish laugh came. "Last time, he said I should buy pretty underwear."

"'Haven't seen Uncle Morris yet. But honest, Ma, that trip to Brooklyn is a killer. And then, after I get there, he'll cry the blues about business and serve me tea until I work up a real sweat. Tell the Grandmother I went to Cuba. Or tell her Uncle Morris is gone—bored himself to death.'"

Her mother giggled, but Vincent went right on: "'Guess what,

Ma? I started to collect souvenirs for you again. Guess I'm homesick. I already have one knife from the Paramount Hotel and two spoons (one for tea and one for soup) from the Red Barn. I figured I'd get a dozen or so and then send them home. Remember all the laughs we had when I brought home the other souvenirs?' "

"I have every piece! God, the places he took girls in those days! The meals, the orchestras he talked about the next morning—and out of one pocket a fork, out of another a knife. Every time I eat with one I see him standing in the kitchen, laughing."

Me, too, Vincent thought. He can go to hell.

"Well?" her mother said.

" 'I hope Pa is still working. Let me know when things get slow and I will try and send some dough for the house. Maybe I will have a winning streak, you can't tell. Is the old witch still walking over every Sunday and making you and Pa sweat? What a dame!' "

Her mother laughed until there were tears in her eyes. "God, she should hear him! Oh, if only he could come for a week or two. He would make me young again."

"Here's the rest of it," Vincent said sullenly. " 'How's Shirley and the kid? How's Judy? Well, Ma, take care of yourself. Don't go on any streetcars with Mrs. Levine without taking your lawyer along! Buy that perfume and think of me when you put it on every day, honey. Best regards, from your son Nate.' "

Her mother wiped the tears of laughter from her eyes. "Get the paper and the pen," she said. "I'll be right back."

She opened the back door, called up the stairs, "Lizzie! Lizzie, I just had a letter from Nate, from New York. You know what? He sent me twenty-five dollars—I should buy perfume!"

Vincent sneered to herself as she brought writing materials to the table. As her mother began happily to dictate, she wrote the answer to Nate. It was simply a matter of translating her mother's Yiddish. She hated it when Nate's letters arrived. Reading them—first to her mother and then to Shirley over the telephone—answering them, made the bad memories come. She could not stop them, as if Nate's amused, cynical voice had crept into the kitchen.

She had to think of his last store, the one he had opened after he had come back from the war, so changed, so terribly and mysteriously changed that he was not Nate at all.

First, he had moved out of the house (no longer the companionable rollaway in the living room). Ma had cried, Pa had hollered: "Fine! Now the neighbors can really talk—an unmarried son moves away from home!"

He had opened the store. Shirley had told them about it, where it was, how she was helping him at the cigar-and-candy counter every evening and taking in plenty of money. She had raved so, and it had sounded so successful, that Pa had not even questioned her going every night and some Saturdays and Sundays to help out. (And all along it had been Johnnie, but nobody but Nate knew that.)

Every time Nate phoned, or some Fridays when he came to eat, Ma asked when she could see the new store. Nate said, "Oh, as soon as it's all set." And Shirley said, "Not yet. When it's really rolling, then you and Pa and Judy'll come." So one Sunday afternoon Ma had said, "Well, I waited long enough. It's a nice day, Abe—we'll go and surprise Nate and Shirley in the new store."

All the way there, on the long streetcar ride, Vincent's heart had raced ahead, anticipating Nate's grin and the way he would let her take any of the candy, any flavor ice cream. Maybe Shirley would let her sell something? Or Nate would let her help cook the hot dogs, split the buns and spread mustard? When they got off the streetcar and walked toward the store, she noticed the fire station next door, and that added to her excitement.

Then her father had found the right address and was opening the door, her mother and she had stepped in, her mother crying gaily in Yiddish: "Nate? We decided to surprise you! Shirley? Come, show us your place!"

But Shirley was not there. And Nate's face had turned red, his eyes so furious that Vincent had stopped just inside the door. She had become aware of all the men and women standing around and smoking. All the blond women and the men with their hats on had turned to stare at her, at Ma and Pa.

Nate had come very fast, had taken his mother's arm. Vincent heard his low, enraged voice: "Jesus, Ma, why did you bring Pa? And look at Judy—like a little beggar kid! Am I supposed to tell my friends she's my sister, he's my father? Crying out loud!"

He had led her toward the back of the store, and Pa had followed. Vincent, frozen to the spot, suddenly looked at her father. She saw baggy pants, cigarette ash on his tie and jacket, an embarrassed-looking, short man sidling after his wife.

Nate's whisper had burned in her chest like a pain. She was conscious of her dress, clean but old, shapeless as all the dresses Ma made for her, caught to her hard stomach by a dime-store belt. She was wearing the long, black, ribbed stockings which never stayed up. Her hair was shaggy.

From a far distance, she had heard Nate's impatient voice: "There's nothing in the back—just telephones and tables. Come on, you'll have some coffee."

"Where's Shirley?" Pa had asked.

"She stepped out." Nate had come to Vincent then, but she did not look up from the floor. "How about some candy, kid?"

She had shaken her head, and Nate had said with a laugh, "Come on, I'll cook you a hot dog."

But she had just shaken her head for no. Ma and Pa were drinking coffee out of glasses because Nate's stores were never kosher, but it was okay to drink out of glass if you were in a not-kosher place and you were Jewish. He brought a carton of cigarettes to the table for Pa, and some chocolate bars and gum for Ma. Then they had gone home.

Shortly after that, Nate had closed the store. And Shirley had run away with Johnnie. Night after night, Ma crying and Pa hollering: "It wasn't enough, my son a gambler. He always ran with gentiles, but did he have to give his own sister to one?"

And then Nate had disappeared, to New York, and Vincent was glad, glad! She hated him. He had disappeared, and she had begged until Ma had shortened the pants he had left behind. Then she had created the gang—she the leader, she the tough *kuter* with no need or wish for a brother!

In the kitchen now, her mother said, "You wrote that there are no Black Ones in the street yet? All right, now send him love from everyone in the whole family. And write: 'When are you coming for a little visit? Fish, cutlets, pancakes—I'll make you anything you want.'"

"Okay, Ma," Vincent said, quickly scribbling the end of the letter.

146

"And you'll sign: 'Your loving mother, Sonia Vincent.' Now I'll phone Shirley, you'll read her his letter."

When Vincent finally escaped to the porch, Dr. Palay's car was in front of the Golden house. She sat on the top step. As usual, during these regular Wednesday visits, her prayer said itself over and over for Jules, until the man with the black bag left.

## 2

The doctor had gone. Mrs. Golden and Heidi were watching Jules with pure delight as he walked slowly from room to room in fresh pajamas and a bathrobe, the scarcely worn bedroom slippers on his shuffling feet. Becky followed him everywhere.

"God," Mrs. Golden said softly, "to see him on his feet! I better go hang out my clothes. I can't move, I'm so happy."

"Hey, Juley," Heidi shouted joyously, "want your crutches?"

"Sure," he shouted back from the bathroom, "the gold-plated ones."

He flushed the toilet several times, laughing. "Plumbing is a beautiful end of the rainbow, boys and girls!"

"Juley," his mother said, "don't forget you can't do too much, the doctor said. Your bed is all made, clean, when you get tired. You hear?"

"No, I'm deaf," he said as he began walking again, savoring each slow step. He was shaved, his hair brushed back with water.

"Ma," Heidi said, giggling, "did you see how red Dr. Palay got when you kissed his hand?"

"It won't hurt him. All right, the picnic's over—I want you to go to Gold's. Get three ryes, yesterday's, and one fresh white bread for Jules. As soon as I get his clothes on the line I'm going to the butcher. Then vegetables and grape juice."

"Ma," Heidi said, "let's buy one fresh for us, too? To celebrate Juley getting up?"

"We'll celebrate with yesterday's. I'll put it in the oven for five minutes and you'll think it's today's."

"Aw, come on, Ma."

"Take the money and go," Mrs. Golden said calmly. "We're lucky to even get rye bread in this neighborhood. Rosen's and

Mentor's have already moved to the Heights. God knows I never liked Gold's bread but at least it's Jewish."

"I'm ashamed to always ask for yesterday's," Heidi said sullenly.

Her mother gave her a disgusted look. "I'll go to Gold's. You take Papa's shoes to Rinaldi. Heels—not rubber. And I put out Alex's good shoes. It'll be school soon. Tell Rinaldi to put soles and rubber heels, and maybe he can shine them up a little."

"Heidi," Jules called, "help me move to the porch."

Mrs. Golden ran to the basement to haul up her laundry for hanging. On the porch, Jules settled himself on the swing, and Heidi covered him with a light blanket, pushed close the table, crowded with books and pencils, his box of paper tissues, the red notebook.

His nose sniffed the air, his head turned from side to side as he wriggled comfortably against the three pillows. "God, it smells real out here," he said. "Heat, sweat, sun. And the *spunyitze* or Mrs. Rinaldi cooking tomatoes and olive oil. I missed it!"

Heidi grinned to hide her sudden desire to cry at seeing him out here at last.

"How about going to the library?" he said. "Tell Miss Woodburn that last batch she gave you was perfect. Six or seven along that line."

"Okay. She thinks you're brilliant. You know that? She told me."

Jules smiled. "Ha ha," he said, but his face was soft with contentment as he stared at the sky, toward the Gully.

"God," he said in an excited half whisper, and Heidi went quickly into the house to blow her nose.

"Ma," she called out to the yard, "I'm going."

"How is he?"

"Like a kid—he's so happy."

"Me, too! I'll meet you by Braun's—I'll get meat last."

When Vincent came back from mailing the letter to Nate, she was stunned to see Jules on his swing. Becky was sitting on the top step, and Mrs. Golden was leaving, carrying a shopping bag, a big smile on her face as she stepped briskly along the sidewalk.

For a second Vincent could only stare. It was exactly as if her prayers, all summer, had been answered. Maybe everything else would turn out right, too. Then Jules waved at her, and she sped across the street.

"Hi, changeling," Jules cried as she ran up the steps, past Becky.

148

"Jules, you're on the porch!" She wanted to kiss him, to shriek words of happiness to go with the look on his face, but she hopped up on the railing instead, balanced there with a grin on her face.

"Yep. Pretty good for a dying man, huh? You should've seen me learning how to walk again. Stumble bum! Walk, rest, walk, flop!"

"What did the doctor say?"

"I'm a good boy. I'm getting better." The water on Jules' hair had dried, and he pushed at the fallen lock, peering at her. " 'But take it easy, son. Rest, don't get excited.' Who's excited?"

He felt a little hysterical with his choked joy, with all the odors and sensations he had wanted to touch for so long.

"Birds," he said. "Honest to God, a sparrow looks entirely different from inside the house."

Vincent jumped off the railing, turned to look at the birds which could put such a tremble of gladness in his voice.

"I remember when I used to walk in the Gully," Jules said. "There were always birds there. Pigeons, sometimes. Somebody must've been training them—some street near here. They flew like an army. You could hear all those wings beating."

Vincent turned back to him a little dazedly. She wanted with all her heart to tell him about Clara, how Clara and Manny had joined hands, inside of her. That had happened to her in the Gully—yes, it could have been like hearing a thunderous beating of wings!

"Where's Heidi?" she stammered.

"The store, the library," he said jauntily. "Today they could both go—leave Becky and Jules alone." He looked at his sister, who was finishing a piece of bread, and said gently, "Vincent, pull down her skirt, will you?"

She ran to follow his order, glad to be able to let some of her excitement dribble out in movement. She looked into the street, hot with sun, and took a big gulp of the air Jules seemed to be eagerly touching with his restless hands. A dozen houses away, on the opposite sidewalk, a Negro woman was walking slowly, stopping to look at windows, at the address numbers of houses.

"You know," Jules said, behind her, "I used to go for walks in the Gully a lot. Slow—not too far. Becky'd come with me. Sometimes we went at night. And I'd feel the air full of kids. And lovers meeting in the dark, or people just standing and sending dreams up, like—like

149

kites. Just *feel* all that—couldn't see a thing except the stars."

Vincent came back to him, leaned against the railing, and watched his excitement. There was a triumph about him, a quivering of his entire person, from inside out, that awed her. It was like seeing the word "happiness" explained by eyes, by the jolting pulse in a throat, by the beautiful way in which a whole body seemed to open itself to everything in the street.

"I'd send up a kite myself," Jules said. "Always the same one. I'd stand there and dream about being able to run up and down those puny Gully slopes. My Rocky Mountains—to climb like a man. My moon. To touch when I got to the top of the mountain, my beloved at my side."

Vincent swallowed. "That's just like your poems," she said.

His eyes were soft with affection. "Poems? Outbursts, retchings. Let's be honest, changeling. They aren't really poems."

"Yes, they are!"

He smiled. Then his eyes focused on something behind her, changed so completely that she whirled to see what it was. He was staring at the Zigman house. The Negro woman she had noticed a while back was on Dave's porch, ringing the bell.

"What a color, in sunlight," Jules muttered. "I'd forgotten. It's different when you see it from inside the house."

In silence, he and Vincent watched as no one came to the Zigman door, as the woman left the porch and crossed the street· to the Valenti house, pushed at the bell there.

Is she Clara's mother? Her aunt? Vincent thought absently, and glanced at Jules. There was a peculiar, ugly glitter in his eyes as he stared at the Negro woman, one porch over.

She rang the bell again, and the *spunyitze* came striding out of her yard. "Hey, no room, no room!" she shouted, and watched until the woman left her porch and got to the sidewalk. Then she went to her front flower bed and began to weed.

Vincent's heart began to beat very fast, for as the woman walked toward the Golden house Jules threw back his blanket and swung his long legs down. His feet hit the floor and he stood up so quickly that he swayed.

"Jules!" Vincent whispered.

150

He grinned at her, a terrible lit expression, and smoothed his robe, jauntily retied the belt so tightly that she could see his slight hips and meager waist.

"You just watch," he said, and his laugh frightened her, too. "Watch the world come to us, changeling."

He went to the steps, leaned against the pillar and waited for the woman to turn up the narrow walk leading to the porch. "Jules," Vincent said, "what're you doing?"

He did not even look at her. The woman stopped at the bottom step, and Jules smiled. "Good afternoon," he said.

"How do," she said cautiously, and Vincent saw her eyes jump to Becky, to the sign tacked on the porch pillar against which Jules leaned.

"I'm looking for rooms," she said. "Is it your upstairs?"

"It is," Jules said, like a grand announcement, and Vincent saw how hungrily his eyes were taking in the neat clothes, the hat, and the gloves carried with the purse.

The woman just stood there quietly, looking up at him until he said in a jerky voice, "Well, come on. I'll show you the downstairs. It's exactly like the upstairs. I can't take you up, you see. Come on!"

Eagerness gushed into the woman's face. She stumbled quickly up the porch steps. "I sure would like to see the rooms, Mister," she said breathlessly. "I can't tell you. Honest!"

Jules opened the screen door. "Come right in," he said. Becky followed them in, and the screen door slammed. Vincent, still frozen against the railing, watched as the three appeared near the windows inside.

The woman looked all around the living room, her hands clasped to her breast over her purse and gloves. Becky gaped at her, and Jules watched the woman with an intensity that stiffened his long body. The ugly glitter of his smile, the excitement which seemed to pulsate from him, made Vincent shiver. She knew he was doing a bad thing.

For the first time in her life, she resented Jules. She had the dreadful feeling that he was making fun of Clara this way, by watching how this woman's heart came into her eyes as she looked at wallpaper and high ceiling and the shining floor where the rug ended.

She could not bear to go on watching, but she could not look away from the trio. Jules led the way slowly into the dining room. Becky pattered after them, touching the woman's sleeve, her purse, staring up into her face.

As the three walked into the kitchen, then out of sight, Vincent kept herself from crying. It felt so strange to be questioning her brother-teacher-friend, and yet it seemed to go right along with all the other questioning which had run like lightning through her since Friday. Jules, too, had become one of the newly seen people in her life, with their right-and-wrong suddenly sticking out like bones.

The heat of the street poured up on the porch. Her face felt wet with perspiration as she shivered. She had to think of the Grandmother as she questioned Jules this way; and of her father and Manny. Then it was Clara, standing in her mind like a fierce replica of herself. Was that Clara's mother in there, near Jules' ugly smile?

She stumbled toward the steps, with some vague idea of escaping, running away from what Jules was doing. Then, to her horror, she saw Mrs. Golden and Heidi walking from the corner, each carrying a bulky shopping bag. They were almost at the Valenti house, and Vincent lunged to the screen door.

"Jules, Jules," she called desperately. Mrs. Golden and Heidi had stopped to watch the *spunyitze* at her weeding.

"A beautiful garden. Beautiful," Mrs. Golden sang out.

"How's-a boy?"

"Better, thank God," Mrs. Golden said.

The *spunyitze* had straightened; Vincent saw the three faces smiling, nodding in the sunlight, and she called, almost in tears: "Jules—cheese it, the cops!" It was the old gang signal for approaching danger, and Jules knew what it meant, but he did not hear her or would not listen.

She rushed to the window to stare in. He was leading the woman and Becky toward the front door. Calmly, he stopped to open the closet door, pointed inside.

"Jules, cheese it, cheese it!" Vincent whispered, but he would not look at her.

When she turned, the two women were walking, coming closer with each step, and Vincent backed away from the window, grabbed up a book and pretended to look into it. She could hear Jules' voice: "Yes, this is the guest closet. Exactly the same as upstairs."

152

Helplessly, Vincent looked up as Mrs. Golden and Heidi came climbing with their heavy bags. She saw their happy smiles, their faces red and perspired from the heat, the sweat marks on their cotton dresses.

"Hello, Judy," Mrs. Golden said gaily. "Where's the well man? He went running in the Gully?"

As Vincent tried to think of something to say, Jules opened the screen door and the woman came out, Becky's hand in hers.

Mrs. Golden seemed transfixed, only her stunned eyes moving. Then Heidi screamed, "My God!" and ripped Becky's hand from the woman's, pulled her sister toward the railing.

Mrs. Golden said in a peculiar, muffled voice, "What is this, in my house?"

Jules looked straight at her and said in a very quiet voice, "Ma, this lady needs rooms. I showed her through our house to give her an idea of the upstairs layout."

Mrs. Golden's eyes looked glazed with shock; and the woman said, "Your son was real nice. Those rooms are exactly what I want. I'd like to put a deposit—"

Heidi broke in, shouted to Jules, "You dirty, double-crossing snot!"

Suddenly anger poured over Mrs. Golden's face like a dark-red stream of color. "Take Becky in!" she said to Heidi.

As soon as the screen door slammed after the two, she went to the pillar and tore off the sign. Vincent saw a look of exhaustion come into the Negro woman's eyes.

Mrs. Golden, her voice heaving, said to her, "You'll please go from here. This boy is crazy. He's my son but I'll tell you—he's crazy, and we have to watch him every minute. He belongs in the institution. He's not responsible for one word he says."

Jules tottered toward Vincent, leaned against the railing, his face a dirty gray.

"I'll pay anything you say," the woman said softly.

"The upstairs is rented—since yesterday! I forgot to take off the sign, and a crazy boy— Please, you'll go from here this minute."

The woman left. When Vincent looked at Jules, she saw the glitter and elation gone. His gray face, his blinking eyes, turned slowly toward his mother.

153

For a moment they stared at each other, then Mrs. Golden said in an agonized voice, "We? We'll be the first to let them in?"

"That woman has five children," Jules said in a low, squeaky voice. "They live in two rooms. Where should she live?"

"Let her live in the Gully! You think I lied to her? No! You *are* crazy! Becky has more sense than you."

"God," Jules said, "I hate this street."

He went into the house, weaving, and Mrs. Golden glared at Vincent without seeing her, her breast heaving violently. Suddenly she ripped the sign in half and threw the pieces with all her strength, then she rushed into the house.

Vincent ran home, all the way in, shutting the door to her bedroom and dropping on her bed. The woman's face was all mixed up with Clara's, that film of hopeless exhaustion in her eyes coming down over the entire bedroom as Vincent stared up at the ceiling through her tears.

In the Golden house, Jules stood near his bed, looking at his mother. Heidi, wordless with shock, carried the market bags into the kitchen, mechanically unpacked library books, bread, meat, and piled everything on the table. She thrust a piece of bread into Becky's hand. In the other room, mother and son watched each other in a silence that made Heidi's skin prickle.

Finally Mrs. Golden cried, "You'll force me to rent to them—you? After my years of sweating for a sick boy? For Becky?"

"What color is dying?" he said, taunting her. "What color is Becky's poor head inside?"

"Shut up! Why did you take a *Schwartze* in my house?"

"To spoil it," he said, and laughed raucously, spots of red soaring into his face. "I sat her down on chairs—now they're dirty, spoiled. I told her to use the toilet. Now I dare you to sit on it! Becky took her by the hand. Now cut off Becky's hand!"

As she looked at him, her face distorted, Alex ran into the kitchen. His usual shout came with the crash of the screen door: "Eats, eats! Gimme some eats!"

"Now you listen to me, Mister," Mrs. Golden said to Jules in a voice so breathlessly savage that Alex stopped, tightened all through him. "To me you're a baby. Compared to me you're a nothing. In life, in worry, in work. In heartbreak! A nothing, you hear me?"

As Becky's mimicking bellow came: "Ma, Ma, gimme eat!" Alex

said to Heidi, "Hey, what's the matter? Doc said he was better, he could go on the porch. When I left, everything was sugar."

"Sure, he's better," Heidi said. "We left him on the porch and went to the corner. We get back, and he's showing a *Schwartze* our rooms."

"Jesus!"

"He was going to rent out the upstairs to her. We came home and he had her right in our house."

"Wow!" Alex went up on his toes a few times with excitement. He listened as the shouting voices in the living room buffeted each other. When Jules was this way, he was nowhere near dying. To take a colored gal right in the house—how in the hell could you be real sick and do that?

"Ma, Ma, gimme eat!" Becky howled.

Alex grabbed a knife and cut two thick slices off a loaf of bread on the table, one for Becky, one for him. Heidi was staring at her mother and brother, raking each other with daggerlike voices.

"Queen of the street," Jules said caustically. "Landlord of America. With one of my stinking poems I can buy your piece of Ohio."

"You? A sick, spoiled boy with a sewer for a mouth. A genius. Well, let me tell you something. A genius is dumb, dumb! What does he know about day-to-day things? A piece of bread? A mother's heart?"

"Crap!"

"Sure, crap. That's exactly what a neighborhood turns into when they get in. Just go and walk for a minute where they live now. Your skin gets goosebumps. Your heart goes like a hammer. Dirt, saloons. People pushed together like dogs."

"Who pushed them, queen of America?"

"The houses not painted," she went on with furious despair. "In your heart you see the houses falling to pieces. Garbage."

"Who left the garbage for them? God damn it, who dumps all that garbage on them?"

"Talk sense, crazy genius! You won't make garbage from my house. That I sweat to pay for. That I sweat to keep clean and nice. My house. Leave it alone."

"A prison!" he screamed, his fists waving weakly in the air.

In the doorway, Alex saw his brother start to shake all over, and

155

the bread he was chewing turned dry and sour as he tensed to the old feeling of death rushing toward him from Jules' face and body. It was back; he wanted to cover his eyes, so that he would not have to love Jules and run from the icy fear of his death.

"Your house is a prison," Jules went on screaming. "Your heart is a prison. And I'm in it. Choking! Let me out. Let me breathe."

Alex backed away so that he would not have to see his brother's grimacing face. He threw his bread on the table, leaned, unable to move farther.

In the living room, Mrs. Golden grabbed Jules' shoulders. "Why are they so important to you?" she cried. "Why do they make a prison out of me for my own boy? Just tell me! *Schwartze*—why?"

"I don't know," he said, a kind of terror splitting his voice. "You've got to open up your heart. I have to breathe, that's all I know."

"Ma!" Heidi cried in a low, frightened voice.

Mrs. Golden shuddered, her hands dropping from the bony shoulders. "I'm afraid of them," she said. "What do you want from me? I'm afraid of a black face."

"My mother," Jules said. "She's afraid of a black face. What am I going to do, for God's sake?"

"Ma!" Heidi cried warningly.

"Do me something," her mother said pleadingly to Jules. "I'm afraid of them, that's all."

"Do *me* something! I'm afraid to die!" Jules shouted, but his words sounded choked, as if they were beating up through wet, lumpy blobs.

Suddenly Heidi ran toward them, and Mrs. Golden cried, "Juley, no! You're better. Don't—the doctor said you're better."

Alex rushed to the back door and tried to gulp air. He pounded his arm with a fist, as if he could break things to bits, all the lousy things converging on him: Jules dying, the niggers coming at you all the time, and Jules hollering those crazy things, letting them in the house finally. Right in this house!

His mother's entreaties beat in the air, against his back. Later she would sit in the dark kitchen, crying with no noise. And Jules would be a white face with closed eyes floating in the room as you passed. And you would hear the big coin dropping in the *pushke*, Ma muttering to herself as she pushed it into the slot, and he would be punching inside until he could not stand it, until he had to grab somebody and let the noise come out of him.

Alex left, easing the screen door shut before he ran into the backyard and scrambled over the fence into the Rinaldi yard. Then he was across that yard, too, climbing the taller fence Ross and the *spunyitze* had built. He dropped lightly into the tomato patch, crawled the rest of the way to the house so that no one could see him from a window. Then he whistled, the signal that Santina could always hear, no matter where she was in the house.

Come on! he prayed. Come on out here. Touch me, grab me, I can't stand it!

# Chapter ten

That evening, well after dark, Heidi Golden went for a walk in the Gully. She was intensely disturbed about Jules. Was he going crazy, finally, because of being sick so long? She could not forget that moment on the porch, when a black woman had come so suddenly out of their house. And the quarrel; Jules and her mother had never before, in all their shouting, loving fights, been like that with each other. Everything had been different and terrible, their faces, their hating voices lashing out, the queerly baffled things Jules had screamed out.

As Heidi walked slowly under the low stars, her eyes adjusting to the open stretch of darkness, she grieved about Jules. She could not forget how he had lain in bed after her mother had wiped his face and given him his drops and how, suddenly, in a kid's voice, he had cried out: "Ma, I don't want to die! Ma, please!"

He had never talked that way before. He had mentioned death, yes, but proudly or scornfully, using it as a whip, a poem. This time he had meant it. This time, the word "die" was as ominous and real and black as that woman he had led through the house.

Remembering the woman standing so near him, Heidi shivered. And she thought, as she wandered deeper into the Gully, how bitterly she wanted to love somebody, to be safe and married, to be together with a man who wanted her. Chip, she thought yearningly, love me. Come to me before it's too late. Look at Jules!

She came to a turning, then into the cleared, level niche where the kids had their clubhouse. She stopped for a moment to look up at the sky, to let the velvety heat of the night touch her face and neck. Often, on walks in the past, she had seen the bonfires the kids had built here, had paused to listen to them arguing, their faces excited in the light of the burning wood they were poking.

Tonight the place was deserted, but as she turned to retrace her steps she heard whispers. Then a muffled, moaning cry jammed with passion drifted toward her. As she peered across the dark stretch, a woman's whispering voice uttered words she could not make out except for the tones of pleasure, like a breathless pulsing in the air. It was a woman's open, sensuous joy coming out of the clubhouse, and the sound made Heidi's skin tingle, drew her on tiptoe toward the shack.

The door was open. As she came closer, the whispers turned into the sounds of thrashing bodies and a shrill, stifled laughter so meaningful that Heidi's face burned with excitement.

"Oh, Blacky baby," the woman whispered, "you sure do it to me!"

Heidi recognized Santina Valenti's voice. As she strained to hear the man's voice, her body felt flooded with a gush of heat, as if she had been touched by grabbing, ardent hands.

Santina's voluptuous whispering went on and on. "You handsome, big black thing. Oh, my strong, black baby face. Harder, Blacky. Love you, Blacky, love you!"

That open pleasure, the bodies moving in there with such vivid sound that Heidi could fairly see them in her mind, the puffing out of a man's voice, not in words but in guttural sounds like groans, drew her senses like a magnet. For an aching, wonderful second, she was in the little hot house, on the floor, passion pouring down on her until she felt an intolerably exquisite pain spiraling up into her stomach, a heat that rammed up hard and coiled; hands on her breasts, on her neck, a fierceness mounting in her, rising, tightening.

Santina screamed in an ecstatic, clotted whisper, "Oh, you black man, oh, you sweet black sweety man, Blacky honey!"

Then actual words hit Heidi, as if she had just managed to isolate them from the thick, sensual mist swirling about the voice. She

158

backed away, horror cutting through her excitement. When she got to the turning, far enough away from the clubhouse not to have to tiptoe, she ran, in a panic.

She came into her house the back way. The kitchen was empty as she stared wildly about, her breath catching in her throat. The radio was on, low music; in the dark living room, Jules lay motionless in his bed. Heidi tried to get her bearings: Papa's on the porch, asleep. Alex in the street. Ma's giving Becky a bath. Jules is just sleeping. Just sleeping—not dead.

Then, crawling into all the open windows from the hot street, the *spunyitze's* voice called: "Sahn-tina! Sahn-tina!"

Heidi began to shiver all over again. This is what she's been hollering her name for, she thought. All summer, every night—hollering into the Gully, where that girl's laying and laughing. . . .

She ran to the open door of the bathroom. Her mother sat on the rim of the tub, leaning, scrubbing Becky's square-looking body, the woman's breasts, the puffy arms.

"Ma!" Heidi whispered.

Mrs. Golden looked up, her hand freezing on the soapy washcloth. "What happened?" she said with alarm.

Heidi burst into tears.

"Juley!" her mother cried, jumping up. "What happened with Juley?"

"No, no," Heidi said, trying to stop crying. "Ma, I just saw something terrible. In the Gully. Santina Valenti and—and—Ma, she was laying with a *Schwartze!* They—Ma, they were doing the whole works!"

"My God."

"Right in the kids' club. Ma, I almost died!"

"I expected anything, but not that. Sh! Not too loud. If Juley hears such a thing—"

Mrs. Golden stared numbly at Becky, splashing water with both hands. Then, her voice shaking with disgust, she said, "With a *Schwartze*. Thank God she's not a Jewish girl, that's all!"

Heidi's weeping was almost under control. "Ma, what're we going to do?" she said.

"I don't know. I have to think! My God, in our street."

The washcloth she held dripped soapy water on the floor. "Not

159

one word to Juley—he's sick enough." Then, abruptly, Mrs. Golden whispered, "Here, finish up Becky. I'm going to wake up Papa."

She pressed the cloth into Heidi's hand and left, drying her hands on her apron. Mechanically, Heidi scrubbed her sister. She dried her, dressed her in the clean nightgown and cotton robe her mother had laid out on the stool. She led her into the kitchen, sat her down with a chunk of bread in her hand. Then she went back and cleaned up the bathroom.

When she stole past Jules' bed and got out to the porch, she saw her father sitting on the swing, rubbing his hands together in a helpless way. She felt embarrassed suddenly, muttered, "Where's Ma?"

"She went to the neighbors," he said, his voice shaken. Then he got up, saying under his breath, "God!"

"Where you going, Papa?" Heidi said.

"I'll do a little work. I have a coat— Becky will keep me company, I'll sew a little."

He went into the house, closing the screen door without a sound. Heidi stood at the porch railing, staring out into the street. Her breasts felt hard and achey, and there was a burning sensation of emptiness in her stomach. As she pressed her hands against the hurt within her, she heard the fast, noisy night games under the lampposts, and people sprinkling their lawns. There was talk on the  porches, the droning voices and occasional laughter of every night.

It seemed impossible to her that everything could sound the same in the world. She stared across the street at the Levine house, her head bursting with the memory of Santina's urging, joyous words— and that man, the sounds he had made—was that what. . . .

She saw Chip and Moe come down from their porch, stand talking. As Moe lit a cigarette and set out for the corner, Heidi suddenly left her porch and ran across the street.

"Hello, Chip," she said, her voice too fast and shrill. "See my mother anywhere?"

"She went up to my house," he said. "In one hell of a hurry. Hollered for the Vincents to come up. Jules sick again?"

"He was, yeah," she said, trying to talk naturally. In the light from the nearest lamppost, Chip looked tall and muscular in his slacks and sport shirt. She had difficulty not touching him.

"So what's new?" he said, looking toward the corner.

160

"Nothing! It's so hot, that's all. And I— Well, you fighting again this week?" she said, trying desperately to sound gay.

"Yeah," Chip said. "Some bum—nothing to write home about."

He wondered how he was going to get rid of Heidi before Ruth came home from the pawnshop. He had looked forward all day to the moment when she would come into the lamppost light, all beautiful and dark; and if her old man had stopped off at *shul* they could stand and talk for a few minutes before he walked her home.

"Well," he said, "I'm on my way to the corner, and—"

"Hey, Chip," Heidi cried, "I better tell you what happened. That's why my mother's up in your house. It's terrible!"

"Yeah? What is?"

"I was walking in the Gully. You know the kids' club? Well, I was right outside it, and I was cooler already and I was just going to go home, and—my God!"

As he stared at her, she stepped closer to him and whispered, "Santina Valenti was in there with a *Schwartze*. Right on the floor of the club."

Chip whistled. "Oh, baby! How about that guy they got her engaged to? Wait'll Ross finds out. Between him and the *spunyitze*, they'll bust her in half, and—"

Suddenly it hit him, and he stopped. The grin left his face. When he swallowed, his throat hurt. "A *Schwartze*? Jesus, is that what you said?"

Heidi nodded, and he grabbed her arm. "You were right there, huh? What he look like?"

"Gee, I don't know! It was all dark, Chip. I didn't want to get too close anyhow. What if he'd seen me? He would've got right up and killed me, I'll bet."

"Jesus," he muttered, his fingers tight on her arm.

As she pressed closer to him, her entire body shivering, he became aware of her intense excitement and of the pounding burn all over his own body, the tingling in his fingers as they pressed her arm.

"Isn't it awful?" Heidi whispered. "How could any girl do that with them? Gee, Chip, I almost died."

"Her brother'll kill her," he said, and he could not stop pressing her arm or keep himself from staring into her eyes, which were suddenly as intent and coarse as an open question.

161

Boy, he thought as his insides lunged, she's hotter'n a forty-five.

"Want to go for a walk or something?" Heidi mumbled.

His face felt wet and clammy. "Where at?" he said slowly. "The Gully?"

"Sure, if you want," she said, her voice barely audible.

She was so close that he felt her breasts, heavy and solid, as they stared into each other's eyes. Her quick, warm breath fanned his mouth; he could taste her ardor.

Suddenly a feeling of nausea sucked at him. His hand dropped from Heidi's arm as he was swept by a yearning to be near Ruth; just standing with her, or walking slowly in a cool, dark night somewhere.

"Wow!" he said, quickly faking a groan, and pressed at his stomach.

"What's the matter?" Heidi cried, and above them one of the kitchen windows opened and her mother shouted: "Mr. Zigman! Mr. Zigman, come over a minute if your wife isn't too sick. It's important. Right away."

"All day long—this lousy bellyache," Chip said, doubling over. "I drank Seltzer till it came out of my ears."

"How about calling Dr. Palay?" Heidi said alarmed.

"Uh-uh! Before you turn around, I'll be in the hospital," Chip said, pretending to writhe. "Jesus, what'll I do?"

"Why don't you go and lay down?" Heidi said. "Maybe it'll go away. Go on, Chip. Then—well, you can come down later if it goes away, huh? I—I'll be on my porch. Okay?"

"Yeah," he said. "I better do something. Hurts like hell. I'll see you, Heidi."

"I'll see you," she said plaintively, and watched him walk slowly into his yard before she turned and crossed the street.

In the yard, Chip could hear the excited voices floating down from his open kitchen windows. He walked up and down in the darkness. He thought of Heidi for one more second, nervously amused at himself. It was the first time in his life he had turned down the chance at a free piece of skirt.

He tried to contemplate quietly the news she had brought, but he felt only a renewed yearning. Ruthie, love me, he thought. Look

162

what can happen—anything!—while we waste time fighting each other.

Santina and a colored guy; again he tried to visualize the fact, the scene, but the only part of it he could feel was the way it was all tied to Ruth and him, as if some mysterious force in life had blown up near them, and he had to grab her and run, save her, be with her.

He heard the women out front now, on his porch, their shrill, tense gabble reaching into the yard. Boy, the street was already stinking. In an hour or two, every punk was going to have something to dream about tonight! And Heidi, waiting on her porch; how in the hell was he going to get out of here?

Suddenly the back door slammed, and Vincent ran past him. He watched her get to the fence, way back, clamber over it like the *kuter* she was. Grinning wryly, he followed her, climbed the fence, and dropped into a yard in the next street. When he ran out to the sidewalk, Vincent had disappeared. He set out rapidly for Woodlawn. He had to get to Ruth before she came home, before the smell of the street hit her. He had to tell it to her himself, soft, holding her arm, tell it to her right, or. . . .

Or what? he asked himself earnestly as he began to run. There were no words for his feeling. All he knew for sure was that he had to tell her before she got it from the street, or from her old man.

He was on Woodlawn now, slowing down to a fast walk, crossing the lighted avenue to take a short cut down a side street toward the pawnshop. The entire summer seething with nervous talk, which had focused that night in Heidi's blurted announcement, was like electricity in him. He was charged with a peculiar strength and tenderness, as if the mysterious Negro figure stalking the mind of the street so long had turned familiar enough to see, to know as intimately as he knew his own desires.

And it was like knowing for sure tonight that Ruth needed him. He would walk into the pawnshop even though her father was there, still leary of the guy, still aware of the way the bastard looked down on him like garbage. He would go in, all right. He knew his strength tonight, the way he knew and sourly acknowledged the desire in people that made them as familiar as his own face—Santina, the guy she had gone with to the Gully, Heidi.

As he came closer to the pawnshop, Chip saw Dave Zigman staring into the big window. He walked up behind him out of the semidarkness of Central Avenue, looked in at the cheap bracelets and rings the kid was studying. The good stuff had been taken inside, he noticed automatically, and that meant the store was about to close for the night.

"Hey," he said, smacking Dave on the back, "thinking of buying the *kuter* a ring?"

Dave turned fast, his fists up, his face distorted in the light streaming from the window. Chip saw his eyes trying to focus out of a queerly glazed look, and said, "What's the matter, champ?"

"Nothing!" Dave said. "Just looking. I—I took a walk."

"Hear about Santina?"

Dave nodded, and Chip whistled softly. "Je–sus. Trouble, huh?"

"Yeah!"

The kid looked broken up. Chip said quietly, "Why don't you go home? Take the *kuter* to a movie or something?"

Dave's face twisted. "They came in my mother's room," he said, almost stammering. "My old man brings them right in, to her bed. And they tell her about Santina. I—I took a walk. It's like— What the hell are you supposed to do now!"

Abruptly he darted away, ran off into the darkness of the nearest side street. Chip looked after him, oddly touched, and remembered Vincent's wild plunge past him toward the fence. Kids and sex, he thought; what the hell *are* they supposed to do?

He turned back to the store. Then, quickly, he walked in, slamming the screen door briskly as he spotted the two. Mr. Miller was at the safe in the office, Ruth behind the counter as she cleared stuff for the closing.

"Evening," Chip said carelessly, waiting for the man to turn on the ice. He felt shaky as a kid as the bearded face swam up in the grilled window at the back. Funny how he had always been afraid of him, the beard, the stern and wrathful eyes—Moses, or God, huh? How would it be to have a father like that, instead of one like his?

He slouched to the counter, leaned on it. "Just passing," he said into the silence, into Ruth's amazed eyes. "Thought I'd walk you home."

Ruth saw how tight his face was, suddenly thought with a

164

frightened excitement: I never thought he'd have the nerve. Dad's here!

"Oh, I have to help close up," she said breathlessly.

"I'll wait for you," Chip said.

Unaccountably, her father said, "Go, go. I'll put up the gates myself. I have to stop at *shul*, anyway. There's a meeting."

Ruth went back to wash her hands, then took off her smock. Her father closed the safe, twirled the knobs, went to the cash register before she could see his face. She felt choked with nervousness, and yet the excitement of knowing that Chip had walked in tonight, knowing her father was here, was stronger than her fright.

"Dad," she said, "isn't there something you want me—"

"Go home," he said sullenly. "I don't need you."

She flushed as she picked up her book and purse. "Good night," she mumbled, but he did not answer.

Chip slouched ahead of her, held the door. They were no sooner out on the street, walking fast toward one of the short cuts to Woodlawn, when Ruth cried, "Why did you come to the store? You knew he was there."

"Hell with him," Chip said. "Let him get used to me."

"You know he never will," she said, trying to sound scornful, but Chip took her arm in such an odd, gentle way that she was more confused than ever.

For a while they walked without talking in the dark, hot side street. When they could see the first bright lights of Woodlawn, Chip said, "Listen, Ruth. Something happened in the Gully tonight. The Goldens are spreading it all over. Heidi saw it, and the whole street's yacking by now."

She stopped, to look at him. The air seemed too quick and full with her, as if it moved with her alarmed breath, and he said hoarsely as he held her arm, "I wanted to tell you. Before you got hit over the head with it, coming home."

"Chip, what happened?" she cried. "Oh, I knew! When you actually came to the store—Dad right there."

"I wanted you to be with me when you heard," he said. "Not with him."

"Him? You mean Dad? Chip, what is it?"

"Listen," he said, very gently, "Santina Valenti and a colored guy.

165

The works. Heidi was walking in the Gully, and she saw them in the kids' clubhouse."

"My God!"

He felt the shivering start in her, and she swayed, seemed to stumble toward him, dropping her book and purse. He caught her, half held her against him.

"Ruthie. Ruthie, it's all right," he called to her as she gasped.

She did not hear him. For some reason, her father's enraged voice was bellowing in her head: "Whore! Where have you been? My daughter—you will not whore around the city this way. Are you listening to me?"

At the few dates she had made, those few times she had gone to evening parties while at school, coming back to the house by ten o'clock at the latest: she saw his ugly, livid expression now as he got up out of the big chair and came toward her. Why, why had he always called her that awful word? Whore, whore!—but in Yiddish, from the heart, from the ugly gut: *kurveh, kurveh!*

She struggled against his hands on her. First they would clutch her arms, her shoulders, and shake her as that word was slapped against her. Then the embrace, then the tears, the lamenting: "I just want you to be a good girl. Nothing must happen to you. Nothing must happen to my daughter."

Then his kiss, his tear-wet beard pressing against her face, the kiss full on the mouth; Ruth struggled to get away from the clinging hands, the heavy body.

"Ruthie. Ruthie, listen to me. It's all right!" It was not Dad's voice, at all.

Her eyes opened as she struggled; she looked up into Chip's pleading eyes. What did I ever do? she wanted to ask him. What does he want of me?

"All right, Ruthie," Chip said.

As she became conscious of his strength, of how tenderly he was holding her, she pushed at his chest uneasily, murmured, "It's so hot. That was ridiculous of me. I'm fine now. Thank you."

He held her arm until she was steady on her feet. Then he picked up her purse and the book, offered them to her.

"Okay?" he said softly.

She felt intensely, strangely close to him. "I'm fine," she said curtly.

166

Again they walked in silence. This time he did not hold her, but she could still feel his gentle touch, and she thought confusedly that there was a part of Chip she had never known existed.

When they turned into their street, she said faintly, "With—a colored man. That little girl."

"Yeah," Chip said. "Only she's not a little girl, I guess."

As they came closer to the second-last lamppost and their part of the street, they saw clusters of people, heard the hard beat of voices. In the group surrounding Mrs. Golden, Chip saw his mother. She had shoes over her bare feet, the laces dragging, and still wore her suppertime apron. Her face looked exhilarated, her eyes keen and businesslike.

He shrugged, then was astounded to feel Ruth's hand clasp his with a nervous eagerness as they passed the first cluster of people.

They were almost at her house when she murmured, "Poor kid."

"Who?" he asked.

"Santina," she said, her voice tired.

# Chapter eleven

The next afternoon, as Vincent sat on her bed with her treasure box, she tried to shut out the voice babbling into the telephone. Mrs. Levine was speaking to her sister, and the Yiddish had been pouring for almost half an hour through Vincent's closed bedroom door.

"All right, she's not Jewish," Mrs. Levine said for the third time. "But on our own street! I have a daughter, too. I tell you, when Moe heard! Thank God he didn't have a gun in his hand. He would have gone right out and shot the first Black One he saw."

Again Vincent tried touching the things she had taken out of her box and laid out on the bed: the lucky stones, the snapshots of Manny, of Shirley and Johnnie at the park, of Shirley holding Manny in front of Johnnie's birthday cake with all the candles lit. The medal still lay in the box. She tried not to look at it.

"The whole street is crazy," Mrs. Levine said. "That such a thing could happen so close to the High Holy Days. We all thought of it last night—all of us mentioned it. Such horror, such sin—and it's almost the Day of Atonement. It's enough to frighten the strongest heart, Sarah."

Dishes clattered in the kitchen, and Vincent thought of her mother's pinched, frightened face. She wondered if Jules had written a poem about Santina yet. She wondered what he had said when the terrible, dirty words had roared in from the street.

"All right, I'll see you tonight," Mrs. Levine said. "You'll be at the meeting? Thank God it's Thursday and we are going to the lodge. It will be good to get away, to play cards for a few hours—I'm so nervous. All right, good-by. Regards to the children."

The telephone slammed, and Mrs. Levine walked into the kitchen. "Let's go early tonight, Sonia," she said. "Moe will walk us to the corner and wait until we are on the bus. My brother-in-law will drive us home. Sarah just promised me. You don't have to be afraid."

"Oh, it will be wonderful to be on the Heights tonight," Vincent heard her mother say. "Fresh air. You can feel the coolness right on the bus. Halfway up Center Hill, it hits you. I can hardly wait."

"My husband was sick all night with his stomach," Mrs. Levine said. "He could hardly drag himself to work. What is going to happen now?"

"I don't know!"

"Did you see *her* yet today?"

"No."

"They must have locked her up. You know how Italians are about their sisters. I wonder who told them? Oh, they know it! One look at that brother's face. I can see in their yard from my porch, you know—he did not go to the market today at all. He's standing in the yard, with the Big Skirt. Near her tomatoes. Their faces are like thunder, so black. They did not come out to the front all day—I kept looking. Well, I would die of shame, too, if it were my girl. Do you think he beat her?"

Had the man been Clara's uncle, one of her cousins? Vincent wondered desperately. Dave ought to tear down the clubhouse, break it to pieces. What if Clara was there, watching? She goes there a lot—hides behind the club. Watching, laughing?

"Well, I'll start supper," Mrs. Levine said, in the kitchen. "Did you say something to Judy yet about staying out of the Gully?"

"Not yet."

168

"I'm reminding you, Sonia. Even in Nate's old trousers, a man would know her for the girl she is!"

The back door slammed. "God!" Vincent heard her mother whisper, and then her hurried steps to the telephone. It was her fourth call to Shirley that day.

Quickly, Vincent put everything back into her treasure box. She would leave now, while her mother was too busy to turn on her with some of that crap Mrs. Levine was throwing around like garbage.

"Yes, yes, I told Judy," she heard her mother say. "She'll come—you know how she likes to baby-sit for you. I'll remind her before I leave for my meeting. Do you think I should go tonight? To be afraid to go out after dark in your own street—"

Vincent put the box away in its hiding place and tiptoed out of the house the back way, then ran across the street. But the minute she knocked on the screen door and walked into the Golden kitchen, she knew she would get no reassurance from Jules today. He was in one of his dramatic, gesturing, shrewish moods as he lay back against his three pillows.

"Welcome," he called. "Welcome to the house of God, where the world is being deloused of all sin."

In the dining room, Mrs. Golden was on her knees, washing the ornately carved legs of the table. She glanced up at Vincent, her eyes angry and hurt.

"Go to the king," she said. "He needs another pair of ears for his philosophy. Mine, he burned out."

"Look at her," Jules said. "You know she's going to see the mayor? 'Mr. Mayor, I have come to discuss the rape of an innocent, young girl by a *Schwartze*. All right, she's not so innocent—but a *Schwartze*! In our white, beautiful street. In our magnificent, white Gully. Mr. Mayor, I demand. . . .'"

"Shut up," his mother said. "Don't think we won't make a petition. They'll have to fill up the whole Gully now. It's time. For years they promised us. Now they have to. We'll get a lawyer."

"The mayor's waiting for you. Don't forget to take Heidi—she can give him all the wonderful details."

Jules smiled cynically, the glasses too big and heavy for his bony face. As she walked toward his bed, Vincent saw the jumping pulse. It identified the world for her, and she thought pleadingly: Jules, be

169

different from the street. Say a poem or something—real quiet. Don't be like you were yesterday with that colored woman!

"Listen to him," Mrs. Golden said. "It's not enough the street is dirty now, he has to talk dirty in our own house."

Vincent sat down on the chair next to the windows and looked at the red notebook.

"Well," Jules said ironically, "I suppose your mother is crying too? Tearing her hair, scrubbing the house for *Yom Kippur*, praying to God to forgive us for letting this happen in our street?"

"Who isn't crying?" Mrs. Golden answered him as she wiped. "One girl lost the war for us!"

"What girl, your daughter?" Jules said, his voice so cruel that Vincent bit her lip. "That Peeping Tom. What she needs is a good roll in the hay herself, so she doesn't have to gossip about—"

"I said shut up! Thank God she's in the basement. Busy, so she doesn't have to be insulted every second by her own brother. And I don't want you to say such things in front of Alex, either. That's all!"

"That's all!" he mimicked. "Sure, but look what you and Heidi started in the street. You were afraid to tell me first. Afraid I'd holler some sense into your daughter before she could tell what she dreamed."

"It should only be a dream," Mrs. Golden said. "God shouldn't punish us for letting this happen. For losing our whole war in one night."

Jules gestured at Vincent. "Listen to her. A girl got romantic on a hot night and went to bed with a guy—and all of a sudden the street lost a major battle. All of a sudden, this means that every house will go to the *Schwartze*."

"You'll see," his mother said as she moved the bucket of water and began on the legs of the buffet.

"I suppose it'll all happen on the Day of Atonement," Jules said, smiling. "Bang!—every empty will be filled with black faces, the *shul* will float away, and East 120th will be finished. All because Santina got hot pants—or Heidi had a dream that she did."

Vincent saw him very clearly at that moment, sensing him as strongly as she had the day before, when he had led the colored woman into his house. Each mention of Santina excited him. He was enjoying himself, and each time he lashed out at his mother he enjoyed himself more. And she thought, with desperation: This is the

170

lousy part of a person. This is when Jules stinks as bad as some of the people in his poems.

Mrs. Golden shook a puckered, red fist at her son. "You think the *shul* will stay in dirt and sin like this? I don't want to hear one more word about Santina! Let me clean in peace for the holidays."

She attacked another leg of the massive piece of furniture, and Jules said jeeringly, "Where'll you go on the holidays? Santina gave away the *shul* last night, didn't she?"

Mrs. Golden leaned on the bucket. "Ask him what he wants from me," she said. "Why do I have to say it's good for a white girl to go to the Gully with a *Schwartze*?"

"Ask me," Jules said tauntingly; and Vincent thought: What if I told him about Clara? If I showed him the medal? Would he be the wonderful Jules, instead of this one?

Mrs. Golden's face looked slashed with streaks of red. "I'm trying to clean, and he throws a knife. It's going to be *Yom Kippur*; I want to clean my house, that's all! At least my house should be clean for the New Year even if the street is dirty with shame and sin. So close to *Yom Kippur!*"

The secret thoughts went right on inside Vincent: What's Santina and that guy got to do with a Jewish holiday? They're all nuts—my mother and Mrs. Levine, too. And look at Jules! Even Jules.

"From top to bottom, my house will be clean. Let the Gully be dirt. And the street. We will be ready for the Day of Atonement."

"For what will you atone, Ma?" Jules said, beginning to sound annoyed. "What will you say to God on the big day?"

His mother stood up, rubbed her sore knees. "None of your business what I'll say to Him."

"Crap," Jules said. And to Vincent, he added with mounting irritation, "A gal goes to bed with a guy and Ma's temple is destroyed."

Vincent suddenly wanted to run away from him, from the cruel look in his eyes.

"When I think that *Schwartze* will sit in our *shul* some day," Mrs. Golden said.

"Some God you have if you think they can grab Him that easily."

Vincent jumped up and walked toward the front door. Yesterday and today—Jules was a stranger. She could scarcely remember the words of her changeling poem.

171

"Wait a minute," Jules said. "Where you going?"

She could not bear to look back at him. "Got to go to the store," she mumbled, and ran.

## 2

Early that evening, after her mother had taken her bath, Vincent came into the bathroom with the kitchen shears to cut her toenails and the thickened thumbnail on her right hand, which her mother was never able to trim by herself. The room smelled steamy and of the perfume her mother always used for ladies'-auxiliary nights.

"When are you going to Shirley's?" Her mother winced as Vincent snipped carefully at the hard, distorted toenails. "She wants to leave early, as soon as Manny is ready for the night."

"Soon." Vincent was on her knees, her mother sitting on the rim of the tub. She had done the thumbnail first, very slowly because her mother was always afraid of being hurt. Now she held each callused foot hard because it jumped so at the touch of the shears.

"Wait until we go. Moe is going to walk with us to the bus."

"Ma, I'm not afraid to walk to Shirley's," Vincent burst out.

"Sh! I don't want Pa to know where you are going. He's upset enough as it is."

"He's on the porch, he can't hear," Vincent said defiantly.

Her mother hesitated, suddenly said, "I don't want you to go to the Gully any more."

"Why?" Vincent said, looking directly up into her eyes.

She saw her mother blush. "It's not safe for girls," she said, almost stammering.

"Why?" Vincent repeated, like a dare. In the old cotton bathrobe, her mother's body looked puffy with fat, sagging, her arthritic legs held stiffly in front of her.

After a moment, her mother said helplessly, "Go see if you can find my good leather belt."

She looked so old and scared that Vincent wanted to punch out at the whole street as she jumped up and ran to the closet. She brought back the belt, helped her mother tighten the strings on her good corset, which was still stiff because she saved it to wear only on special occasions.

Then, still in a turmoil, she went out on the porch, glanced at her

172

father's gloomy face as he sat on the swing, reading the paper. She hated everybody in the street tonight, every scared and dirty-mouthed adult on her horizon.

In the beginning dusk, a few Negroes were walking, looking for empties. Leaning against the porch pillar, Vincent watched the people of the street watching the Negroes in an entirely different way tonight. Over their lawn sprinkling, over their gossiping, the street people looked a little crouched, too intent on each step that passed them, each step up to a porch, to a doorbell.

In one night we lost our war, she thought as she remembered Mrs. Golden's hurt, angry eyes.

Suddenly, as she looked toward the corner, she was startled to see a familiar figure coming toward the house.

"Pa," she said, "the Grandmother is coming."

"What!" he said, jumping up. "On a Thursday? Go tell your mother. Put on water for tea."

When Vincent came back to the porch, the Grandmother was just sitting down in her favorite chair, pulled out near the steps, so that the street could see her and she the street.

"Mother," she heard her father say, "is something wrong? You come on a Thursday?"

"Is there a law against it?" The old woman's cold eyes met Vincent's, and she held up her face. As Vincent kissed the lined cheek, the Grandmother grasped her arm tightly and held her, studied her closely. The shaking, spotted hand was so strong that Vincent stared at it in amazement.

"Do they still call you the black alley cat?" the Grandmother said, and Vincent flushed with a confused dislike as she looked into the stern eyes.

"It is a nickname for a child," her father said, his voice flustered. "She no longer climbs roofs."

"An alley cat knows how to protect itself." The Grandmother released Vincent's arm, gave her a little push. "And that is good in these times."

Vincent went back to the pillar, stared into the street. As her face cooled, she felt the fierce, guilty dislike prickling over her like goosebumps.

"You heard what happened last night?" her father said unhappily,

173

and she hated it that he acted like a kid with the old woman, a kid who was scared to talk. Scared to see Manny, she thought harshly.

"It is all over Woodlawn," the Grandmother said in her sure, disgusted voice. "Perfect talk for the coming High Holy Days, I must say. One does not have to wait for the Day of Atonement to start fasting."

There they go again, Vincent thought resentfully. What in hell does Santina and a guy have to do with a Jewish holiday?

Without being aware of what was happening, she noticed vaguely that people had straightened up and were looking at the Grandmother. There was a lighter, faster note to people's voices, laughter where there had been none before she had come. Across the street, Mr. and Mrs. Golden came out on their porch and stood looking. Next door, Mrs. Zigman came out on her porch and said, with a little bowing motion: "Good evening, Mrs. Vincent!" Then she went to sit on her swing, where she could watch the chair and the solid figure in it.

When her mother came out with two glasses of steaming tea, Vincent saw the Grandmother examine her with a kind of disinterested scorn—the thin hair so awkwardly curled for the evening, the stiffly corseted body in the good dress, the silk stockings, and the white, high-heeled shoes.

Taking the tea, she said dryly, "I see the women are still gambling in the name of Palestine."

"It is our regular meeting," her daughter-in-law murmured. "How nice to see you twice in one week, Mother. I'm so glad I was still here when you came."

And look how she makes Ma act, Vincent thought. I don't like her!

"What do you hear from Nate?" the Grandmother asked as she pursed her lips for the first sip of her tea, and Vincent slipped off the porch, ran into the yard to climb the fence and escape that way.

Sure, I'm still the *schwartze kuter*, she thought defiantly, as if speaking to the old woman. And I'll show Manny all the tricks. He'll be the smartest *kuter* you ever saw! So what'll you do about that?

When she got to the apartment, Shirley and Johnnie were downstairs with Manny. There were a few people standing around languidly on the sidewalk, but Shirley and Johnnie looked fresh and young, not hot at all.

"Hi, kiddo," Johnnie said, his smile wiping out the Grandmother's cold, wrinkled face. He had been leaning over the buggy, making fun

174

faces at Manny, who liked to grab at his big ears and nose. He was wearing slacks and a sport shirt, not his uniform.

"Honey," Shirley said to Vincent, "it's so hot upstairs I thought you'd take a nice walk with Manny for a while. We'll be home in a couple of hours. The key's under the hall rug and there's cake and stuff; help yourself."

Johnnie slipped a big coin into her blouse pocket. "Have some ice cream on me," he said.

"How's Ma?" Shirley said as she took her husband's arm. Not one word about Santina and the Gully; Vincent was so grateful that she wanted to jump and hop.

"Okay," she said, and did not mention the Grandmother.

She watched Shirley and Johnnie walk away toward Woodlawn, slow and close to each other. She loved to see them together, the way they liked being close to each other.

When they had disappeared into the darkness, she leaned over the buggy until her face was only an inch away from the baby. Nobody was watching them, or too near, but she whispered it anyway: "Hey, Manny. Hey, your name is Manny and I—love—you."

He grabbed at her nose and she let him, grinning at his excitement and bouncing joy. She burrowed her head into him until he chortled, then she gave him quick, pecking kisses on the cheeks and nose and chin.

"Okay," she said finally, in a brisk voice, "let's go. Next year we'll run, huh? All over the Gully. We'll climb fences, jump off—one, two, three, boom! Me and you, huh?"

She started off toward Woodlawn, running a moment and then lurching the buggy in the sudden stop-and-go pattern of the game she and Manny played so often on walks. She loved the way he chuckled, then laughed out loud as if with his whole little heart, at certain steps of their game.

Just before they got to the corner Vincent turned the buggy around with a swoop and started back down the dark street. Behind her, someone called, "Hi, changeling!"

It was Clara, stepping eagerly from the bright lights of Woodlawn into the dimness of East 110th.

"Hi," Vincent said breathlessly, and glanced around to see if anybody she knew was watching.

Santina! she thought wildly. Santina and Clara's—uncle, her

cousin? Who was that big black guy with Santina last night? And Clara watching?

"How's the *schwartze kuter?*" Clara said, with her funny accent. She had a sparkling, wicked grin on her face, and Vincent had to laugh.

"Boy, your Jewish smells," she said. "What're you doing here?"

"Waiting," Clara said. "In case you came to your sister's. I was here last night, too—just in case."

Vincent felt a gush of relief. "Last night? You didn't—you weren't over in the Gully then?"

"No. Not since Tuesday. You know, when we talked." Clara added casually, "Figured I'd have a better chance of seeing you here. On your sister's street. Ever going back there, to the club?"

"Sure—when I feel like it. Some day," Vincent said, staring at her.

It was their first meeting away from the darkness and secrecy of the Gully, and Clara looked both unreal and familiar. She was in pants, and her swagger and proud stance seemed the same, but her skin looked more black than brown in this light.

Uneasily, pretending to be casual about it, Vincent stepped back, dragging the buggy, so that Clara and she would be farther from the lights of the avenue.

"You remembered where my sister lives, huh?" she said, still moving back slowly.

"Sure. You said you go there a lot, so I thought I'd hang around. In case you came."

Clara moved, too, stopped when Vincent finally paused in a safe, dark stretch between the avenue and the first lamppost. "I got hell last night from my father," she said, laughing. "Hung around here until almost ten o'clock."

"Well, I came tonight," Vincent said, her voice rough with shyness.

"Yeah!" Clara motioned to the buggy. "Whose baby?"

"My sister's. His name's Manny."

Clara leaned, peered under the shallow top. "Boy, what a cutey baby. Hi, Manny. How you doing?"

With one of his chortles, Manny reached up both hands. Clara laughed. "You want my nose? Go on, take it. It's all yours."

Vincent waited, with a kind of dread, for Clara to reach in and touch Manny. But she just leaned, with her hands clasped behind her. She just looked, just laughed, just let Manny do whatever he wanted to do with her nose and ears and hair.

"Ouch," Clara said calmly. "You're a big, strong boy, huh? Where'd you get those muscles—from the *schwartze kuter?*"

She peered around at Vincent, that devilish, sparkling smile in her eyes, and Vincent laughed. "He hardly ever cries," she said.

"Yeah, you can tell he's a laughy kind of baby," Clara said. "I like him."

"He likes you, too," Vincent said, as Manny grabbed up again.

"Yeah," Clara admitted in that calm way.

Vincent watched Manny touch her face, exactly the way he touched hers, and Johnnie's. And suddenly, her stomach turning over and over, she thought of Pa and the Grandmother on the porch at home. They did not want their faces touched by this fat little hand. They did not want to lean and say the name, "Manny," into this round face with a button of a nose stuck comically into it. They never said his name to each other, even!

"You know what?" she blurted. "Manny's father isn't Jewish, like me and my sister. Manny O'Brien—that's his name."

She wanted to say, He's a Catholic, like you! She waited for Clara's words of amazement, disgust, scorn. The girl had straightened, was looking at her, as if waiting for anything else Vincent wanted to tell her.

"Yeah?" Clara said casually. "What does that make Manny—half-and-half?"

"I guess," Vincent muttered.

Again Clara leaned to the buggy. "Hi, little half-and-half," she said, and her chuckle bumped into the baby's rising chuckle. "Hi, little half-pint."

Warmth rushed through Vincent. Suddenly she said, "Go on, pick him up. Want to?"

"Yeah. Should I?"

"Sure! He likes it when people pick him up. Go ahead."

She watched approvingly Clara's way of supporting Manny's back and head as she swung him up, then the affectionate way in which she helped him nestle into one arm as the baby studied the new face so close.

"Hey, little half-and-half," Clara said, "you weigh a ton."

Manny laughed at her, or at the comic, tender tone of her voice. He grabbed at her neck, and his hand fisted around the cord, and Clara said with a wonderful jeer—as to a grown-up friend: "Oh no you don't! You can't have my medal, Manny."

Vincent watched her disengage the tight clasp, look at the little fist she had straightened out, and laugh.

"Boy, look at those dimples," Clara said, and kissed Manny's hand.

Vincent felt a peculiar, soaring elation. The medal made her remember the one Clara had taken off and given her for protection—and here was Manny grabbing at it. She liked seeing his face so close to Clara's grin after that impulsive kiss.

Clara and she looked at each other, over Manny's head. They laughed at the loving, amused baby, and Clara said, "He sure is a sweetie."

Then, with reluctance, she said, "I better scram home. See, I was out so late last night. If I do it again, he'll give me hell in a wheelbarrow."

Carefully, she tucked Manny back into the buggy. "Good-by, half-and-half," she said, and then eagerly, "See you, Vincent? In the Gully, or here, huh?"

"See you," Vincent said. She had forgotten all about Santina. As Clara ran off toward Woodlawn, she cried, "So long."

"So long!" Clara waved, then turned the corner.

But as she whirled with a smile back to the buggy, Vincent thought of her father and the Grandmother again, of their faces if they could have seen Clara holding Manny. A bleakness careened through her happy excitement as she looked down at Manny, his bouncing motions.

"Hey, you ought to be falling asleep," she said. "Stop acting like it's morning. Your daddy's going to give you hell in a wheelbarrow, too."

Looking at him, her bleakness deepened. She thought with a kind of despair: Pa, won't you ever know Manny? Won't he *like* you? Sure, the way I don't like the Grandmother! When he thinks about you—oh, Pa, don't you want him to like you?

She stood there, her hands tight on the handle of the buggy. The street seemed very dark, and she wanted to cry with this confused,

178

anguished feeling she could not understand. It was all mixed up with Clara and Pa, with the medal, the kiss, and with Johnnie—the way she had seen him kiss that dimpled hand so often; and God damn it, why did her father always act like a scared little kid when the Grandmother came to visit?

Why, why? she repeated savagely. Why is Shirley as if dead? Why is it like Manny never was even born? Pa, if you kissed his hand just once! Like Johnnie does. Like Clara did. Pa, if he ever touched your face once!

Suddenly, her jaw aching with clench, Vincent turned the buggy around toward Woodlawn and started walking fast. In the hot night, she felt an icy cold shivering all through her. It was like a sleepwalking, fast, so fast that she seemed to move with a dream speed; almost at once, she was inside East 120th.

Pushing the buggy toward her house, past heat-soggy voices and laughter, the hissing of water from hoses, she found herself saying over and over, out loud in a mutter, her magic words: "Dear Lord, kind Lord, gracious Lord, I pray Thou wilt look on all I love tenderly tonight. Weed their hearts of weariness, scatter every care, down a wake of angel wings winnowing the air. And with all the needy, oh, divide, I pray, this vast treasure of content that was mine today. Amen."

She was at her house, still saying her prayer, not pausing for an instant but turning fast into the narrow walk which led to the porch steps. Amen, amen, amen, her head thundered in time to her steps; the yellow light from the lamppost cut across the porch and, as the buggy came to a stop against the bottom step, she saw the shadowy bulk of the Grandmother still in her chair, the blotch of deeper darkness made by her father on the swing.

Vincent was aware of their murmurous Yiddish, but the words made no impact on her. It was like being numbed by that intense drive which had grabbed her in Shirley's street and forced her to bring Manny here. She heard the beggary in her father's voice, a particularly disturbed timbre to the little-boy quality. She felt, like a clammy sweat, her own fear of facing the old woman.

"But Mother, why, why?" she heard him say. "Don't do it. Your children are all here. You are not a young woman. I beg you again. So far—a whole world away from us."

Vincent took Manny out of his buggy. Now the lamppost threw

179

its diffused light across the blinking eyes, the round, perspired face of the little outcast she had brought here. At the swooping motion upward into her arms, Manny smiled.

She heard the Grandmother say in a slow, somber voice, "Yes, a whole world away. But I have never felt at home here. Where I belong, I will go. Why should I die among strangers, enemies?"

Vincent climbed up the porch steps, walked past the Grandmother, straight to her father. The yellow light showed her his suddenly staring eyes, and she said roughly, "Pa, I brought him."

"Whose baby is this?" he said sharply.

Behind Vincent, a chair scraped and the Grandmother said in a bewildered mutter, "What is this little black alley cat doing now?"

Vincent thrust Manny into her father's arms, waited until she felt the awkward tightening of his grasp on the baby before she straightened up. Her father peered down into Manny's face, and then one of the dimpled hands grabbed upward at the nose, so near. The familiar chuckle of delight, now so sleepy, struck through the silence of the porch.

At that sound, her father said hoarsely, "Why do you put a baby in my lap? Whose is it? Judy, whose baby is this?"

Her legs trembling, Vincent said loudly in Yiddish, "Here is your grandson."

"Mendel?" he cried.

In the drifting, faint light, Vincent saw his suddenly tighter grasp on the baby. He leaned, stared into the upturned face. There was a wild longing in his eyes, a fearful yearning. She felt rather than saw or understood his quick, almost merging emotions.

Her heart beat very hard as she heard him murmur entreatingly, in a choked voice, "Little father. Tiny little father."

Never had she heard such tenderness from him. Not knowing what to do with her bursting, screaming feelings, she turned away. The Grandmother was sitting there in her chair, eyes closed, her face sagging. As Vincent stared at this strange face, her father's broken, joyous murmur came again: "Mendel, little father."

And the Grandmother, eyes still closed, whispered with an intense grief, "Abe, are you insane?"

Never had Vincent heard anything in that voice but queenly dignity, disdain, sternness. This tone of exhausted sorrow stunned her.

180

Her father's entreating whisper beat at her back: "Mother! Mother, look at him!"

The Grandmother made a slow, rocking movement in her chair. Again her grieving whisper came: "My son, are you insane?"

As Vincent stood between her father and the Grandmother, battered by their conflict, she sensed the long moment between generations, the hurt of it, the way it could go on, endlessly, like a clock stopped by a senseless, groping hand. And she was ripped with the feeling not only of her father pulling, still trying to pull away from his mother, but of Nate pulling away from Pa, and of Shirley struggling, and of herself fighting to pull away from Pa's talk about Johnnie, from his stern *shul* God, and from the way he could agree to fires and never mention Manny's living name.

It was she herself standing in this enormous moment between generations as she sensed how her father was struggling to stand by himself, to end his own long moment. When she turned back to him, her throat ached with a pity she understood as little as any of the other emotions clawing at her.

He was standing, still staring into that little face of gladness turned up to his. Vincent saw her father's wet eyes. She saw for the first time, and still without the words to interpret it, a man's hunger of spirit. The tears gushed into her own eyes, and she wanted to touch him.

Suddenly he groaned and pushed Manny into her arms, ran into the house. The screen door slashed noise across the thick heat of the night, and still the Grandmother sat like a statue with closed eyes. She looked dead.

Vincent rushed past her, down the steps. She put the sleepy baby into his buggy and started out quickly for the corner.

Her face was wet, but she did not know for whom she was crying: her father, who had wanted Manny and yet pushed him away, or for the Grandmother with her strange and pitiful grief, or for Manny—still the outcast child.

# Chapter twelve

The next morning, at a little past seven-thirty, Mrs. Golden came running from the bakery. As she pounded into the kitchen with her shopping bag, her eyes shone with happiness.

"Juley! Heidi!" she cried in her hoarse, vital voice as she began emptying her bag onto the table. "What do you think? The old Mrs. Vincent is going to Palestine. She will die in the Homeland. Isn't it heart-warming?"

She was speaking Yiddish, her heart's language, as she did so often in moments of real happiness or grief. As Heidi came to help with the food, Mrs. Golden paused to wipe her perspired face.

"Alex and Becky are still sleeping?" she said, opening the bag of rolls.

"Yeah," Heidi said. "And Papa went. When's she going, Ma? How do you know?"

"I met Mrs. Levine at the bakery. Mrs. Vincent told her. It is all over the neighborhood—in every store, Lizzie told it. To every neighbor in our street. You can see the beautiful news in every face you pass."

From his bed, Jules called, "What's so beautiful?"

Mrs. Golden's laugh was a little hysterical with joy. "What would a boy know about Palestine—home? Wait, I'll butter you a fresh roll, you'll eat. Heidi, take in his cocoa."

She was moving with a fast, elated step despite the heat, putting away butter, eggs, grape juice, bread. Heidi, back from serving Jules, sat down at the table and bit into a roll. Her eyes widened as she heard the low song on her mother's lips.

"Aren't you going to eat something, Ma?" she said.

"My heart is full. Milk and honey!" Mrs. Golden cried. "When she came into the street last night, I felt better. A tribal chief, sitting there. Even if she came to judge us—it was new strength just to see her sitting among us. She was already a weapon in our hands. She lifted our hearts—the whole street. And now!"

"Listen to her," Jules called with amusement. "I inherited my poetic gifts."

"Everywhere I went," his mother said. "On every face I saw it:

She is going to Palestine, to live and die in the Homeland! Even the gentiles—there is happiness even on their faces. Even they know this is a triumph over the Black Ones."

"What?" Jules said, suddenly alert.

"It is the talk of the entire neighborhood." Her dramatic Yiddish rolled through the house. "An old woman has the strength, the courage, to go to her true home. It is a sign that our street will be victorious. That we will keep our homes. In peace."

"My God, you're crazy," Jules called, starting on his breakfast with new vigor. His mother's philosophy, the street's thinking, as she voiced it, fascinated him.

"Hah, what would a child know?" she called back, and laughed with such a rich sound that Heidi felt good just listening to it.

Mrs. Golden poured herself coffee, tore a roll apart and buttered half of it. "There is a new strength in the street. Now we can fight. An old Jew has the strength to go home? All right, we will have the strength to keep our homes! How often does this happen? Wait till Papa hears. It is like new blood into the heart."

"Hey, listen," Jules said, "what in hell has the old lady's rushing off to Palestine got to do with us?"

"You'll see! Even the gentiles—they feel, they know. It gives them strength, too." Mrs. Golden was too excited to eat. "I'll buy another for-rent sign, put it back. It has to be now, it has to be."

Jules laughed, half in anger. "I suppose the *spunyitze* stopped you and congratulated you? Gave you the gentile reaction?"

His mother's eyes glistened. "You think not? I passed, and she was working in her garden. She says to me, 'Hey, Missus, that old lady goes on the boat, huh? To the Jew land? Nice, nice! No more trouble, huh?' You see, it is magic—such news. It goes into every heart."

"Did you see Santina?" Heidi asked.

"Who has to think of Santina today! Next to this wonderful news, the Santina garbage becomes nothing. This takes away the dirt. Don't think the Big Skirt does not realize that. If you saw her eyes—happy. She knows this is a good sign."

"Crap," Jules said. "Vincent's grandmother's been here forty years —more. What's the sudden rush to leave her own country?"

"How would *you* know about Palestine?" Mrs. Golden said calmly. "It is the top of life, the pinnacle. The greatest triumph for a Jew.

183

Think of it! One Jew can go home, and my heart is young and strong again. Overnight, I am a woman with hope again. One Jew can go?—then anything is possible."

"Honest to God," Jules said helplessly, "I think you're nuts."

She was listening not to him but to some inner voice of great happiness. "I'm going to telephone Papa at the shop. He has to know right away. Heidi, wake up Alex and Becky. On such a day nobody should be sleeping!"

## 2

At ten-thirty that morning, Vincent went down to the basement with her mother to help her get the Grandmother's things ready to ship to Palestine. She was taking all her possessions with her.

As they walked down the steps into the dark, cool cave of the basement, her mother said solemnly in Yiddish, "It is an honor that she is going to Palestine. An honor for the entire family."

Vincent was silent. She was still raw with memories of the scene on the porch. If the Grandmother was going away, forever, why hadn't she at least touched Manny last night? Why hadn't she permitted Pa to go on holding him?

"She is a rich woman," her mother said, halfway across the basement by now. "She owns down pillows and feather beds, the best of linens, bolts of goods left over from the days when she was a business woman. Why, the remnants alone—velvet and wool—are worth plenty. I wonder if she will sell her things in Palestine. They say American goods are worth a fortune there—and a smart woman she always was!"

Thinking of the Grandmother's deathly face the night before, Vincent followed her mother past the cold, gray bulges of the two furnaces to the storage lockers. An enormous old trunk stood near the doors, its curved top dusty.

"Boy, she's got a big trunk here," she said.

"That's my trunk," her mother said, opening one of the lockers and pulling on the tiny light inside. "I brought it from Europe when I came with Pa. God, where do I begin in here? I'd forgotten how much she stored with me when she sold her house and rented a room."

Vincent peered into the locker room, saw boxes and crates stacked high. "Wow," she said, "is this all hers?"

184

Her mother sounded bitter. "This is a spit in the ocean! She has just as much stored in the basement of each of her children. And do you think she gave even one pillow to a son? One remnant for a dress for a grandchild? Not she! Pa is sleeping on a pillow like wood while the whole city's basements are full of her pure-down bedding!"

Vincent stole a glance at her. She wanted to tell her mother what had happened on the front porch last night. Would she be glad? Or would she start crying and moaning?

She wanted to tell her about Pa's eyes when he looked into Manny's face, but she said, "Well, what should I do, Ma?"

"You start with the trunk and I'll get together these things. Take out all the remnants, and you'll find fur and some whole bolts of goods, if I remember right. Make a pile. Spread out paper first."

She disappeared into the locker, and Vincent swung open the heavy, curved top. From the crammed trunk came the choking smell of mothballs, and she coughed as she went to the stacks of unsold newspapers Mrs. Levine saved to sell to neighborhood stores.

"Such beautiful linens," her mother muttered from the locker as Vincent spread paper. "You know, she took a trip to Palestine once. Years ago, when conditions there were very bad. Everybody warned her not to go but she went—she always does what she wants to. She stayed a year, and she was sick and weak when she came back. But they say conditions are fine now, especially if you bring American goods and money."

Wiping her hands on her pants, Vincent lifted out neatly folded remnants and several bolts of heavy material; then she found pieces of soft, lustrous fur tucked into corners of the trunk and she shook out fragments of mothballs before adding the pieces to the pile she was building on the floor.

Under the separator, she found a pillow. Then she came upon a pile of photographs, a large prayer shawl with some of the fringe gone, and a set of worn-looking phylacteries like the ones her father sometimes wore in the morning when he said prayers. There was a big, ragged-looking book near the bottom of the trunk, and when Vincent opened it she saw that the first page was partly filled with names, many in different handwritings, the inked words spidery and foreign.

The photographs were oval-shaped, pasted on thick cardboard. One was of an old white-bearded man, standing very straight in a long black coat and a round black hat, with one gnarled hand resting on a table next to him. Another was of a laughing young man in old-fashioned clothes. Then she recognized her father in a photograph, his face eager above a hard collar, his hair slicked back. He looked like Nate.

"Hey, Ma," Vincent called, "here's a picture of Pa."

Her mother came out of the locker, bent toward the trunk and shuffled the photographs. "Oh, I have not looked in here for so long," she said softly. "Here is my father. Rest in peace."

She held up the photograph of the good-looking, smiling young man. "My beloved brother Hymie," she murmured.

Vincent handed her the ragged book, open at the page of names. "What's this, Ma?"

"My father's Bible. His father gave it to him when he was thirteen. And he gave it to Pa and me when we went to America. See?" And she pointed to the list of names. "Pa's name and mine—we are the last. My father wrote them in when I was married. Below the other sisters, the brothers, all their children."

Vincent's heart began to beat heavily. Why were Ma and Pa the last? There was plenty of room left on that page! Where was Nate's name? Shirley's, hers? And—no, Manny, not you, not you!

Her mother was peering with sad affection at the spidery list. "My whole family is here," she said with a sigh. "When you were born your name was put in the Bible; when you were married, your husband's name—then your children. My sisters, my brothers—their children. All, all murdered by Hitler."

With difficulty, Vincent said, "How come Nate's name isn't there? Or—or Shirley and me?"

Her mother shrugged. "In America the habits are different, I guess. Pa never did it. He never wrote in the names of his children."

She handed the Bible back and took up the photograph of her father. The book felt solid in Vincent's hands, the binding soft as velvet. She loved it, suddenly, the idea of it, the feeling of many hands worn into the shabbiness. Her skin prickled at the thought that she was touching generations, the beginnings of her family. She seemed to feel names through the closed book.

Her mother was nodding and smiling as she looked at her father's photograph. "He ran a flour mill. People came from miles around to

186

have him grind flour for them. They ate and drank in our house—my mother was a wonderful housekeeper. There was so much singing, evenings. My father liked to sing. The people who came for the grinding—sometimes they stayed overnight. What singing and laughter."

She looked now at the photograph of her brother, and such a look of youthful happiness came into her eyes, changing the very shape of her face, that Vincent watched her with fascination.

Finally she said, "Ma, your brother is real good-looking."

"Nate is a lot like Hymie. Look how handsome. Nate is just like him, inside—exactly. So jolly. Such a one for dancing, for loving life. Oh, how I adored my youngest brother. Just like all the other girls in town. He was such fun to be with. Nate is his image in the soul and heart!"

How bright her eyes looked. How gay and young the tilt of her head, as if she were back in the dancing years with her adored brother, Vincent thought.

Her mother giggled, like a girl. "That restless, wild Hymie. Always looking beyond the skies for excitement. And he found it, too! Exactly like our Nate. Do you know what he was doing just before I left Russia to come to America?"

Her bright eyes danced with a devil-may-care expression that reminded Vincent of Shirley.

"He was twenty-two years old, but already a businessman. Oh, when my father found out what his business was! He would not talk to his own son. Hymie had to sneak home when he wanted to give presents to his own mother and sisters with the money he was making. My father had forbidden him to come."

Again that gay, young giggle came. "Hymie was operating a house of bad women. Can you imagine?"

Vincent grinned. That uncle of hers seemed very real, here in the basement—that laughing, handsome uncle whose memory had turned her mother into a girl again.

"I'll bet the Grandmother didn't like him," she said.

"Hah! How she talked—even on the boat, after we were on our way to America. That *her* son had married the sister of that Hymie!"

She sighed, reluctantly put the photographs down. "I had better get busy," she said. "Once the Grandmother decides something, it has to be done at once."

Back in the locker, her mutter drifted out: "Palestine. It is an honor, an honor."

But in a moment she was humming under her breath as she scurried about, as if she were still back in her singing, dancing girlhood. Vincent opened the Bible again, tried to make out the names tying her down the years to a family, to religion and birth and marriage. What would her name look like at the bottom of this list? And Shirley's?

Hey, little half-and-half! It was Clara's amused, casual voice in her head. Yeah, but could a half-and-half's name ever be in a Jewish Bible?

She wanted to run with that open book to Jules, and cry: "Look at my family—in a Bible!"

And she wanted to run in to that young-girl, happy mother she had seen for a few moments and tell her about last night—how she had brought Manny to his grandfather. Names, names, Ma! Look how you can hold names in your hands. Ma, Manny has a name. I made Pa say it last night!

As she stood there, bursting with all these words, the back screen door slammed and Dave's voice announced the delivery of the Sabbath chickens: "Zigman's!"

He clattered up the steps to Mrs. Levine's kitchen. Vincent put the Bible back into the trunk, pretending that she had not heard him. Mrs. Levine's voice floated down: "Dave, tell your mother I need a fat chicken every week—not only for Passover or *Yom Kippur*. She knows how much fat I use in my cooking. I'm a good customer—I have been taking from her since I live on Woodlawn."

"Okay," Dave's poker voice replied.

"Tell her to take off for my chicken when Moe brings her the papers. I have a lot this week—more than enough to pay for my chicken."

"Okay," Dave said again, and began the clatter downward.

"Judy," her mother called from the locker, "go up and pay for my chicken. Put it right in the icebox before it spoils in this heat. Look in the cereal set for money."

Vincent went upstairs. Without a word, she passed Dave in the hall and opened the door. In the kitchen, she went to the canister on the shelf, marked "Sugar," where her mother kept things like pins, receipted bills, rubber bands, and special money for bills.

"How much?" she said stiffly.

Dave had followed her in. "Three forty-seven."

Without looking at him, Vincent put four dollar bills on the table and carried the package to the refrigerator. She moved slowly, giving Dave a chance to make change and leave.

She heard the clink of coins as he put them on the table but no footsteps. When she turned, Dave was looking at her with a grin, his hands in his pockets, his blond head way up.

"Well," she said, mocking his way of saying it, "why don't you cop a sneak?"

"Hear about Santina?" he said, still grinning. "I knew those hot pants would come sliding down some day, and—"

The sudden twisting of her face stopped him instantly. His own face turned gray as their eyes met, horrified.

"How the hell do I know anything?" he stammered. "This God damn street! There's going to be a big, fat explosion one of these days, Vincent. Everybody! It—it feels like we're all just waiting to explode."

She stared at Dave's strangely broken expression. That was the way it felt to her sometimes, but since when did a tough guy like Dave feel that way?

He grabbed at the edge of the table. "Jesus, Vincent, why'd it have to be our club?"

"That's what I thought!" she cried.

Again their eyes met in that look of horror, and Dave wanted to beg her: Take back the gang. Let everything be the way it used to. You and me—the strongest, the best.

"My mother's sick," he told her.

"Gee, bad?"

"I don't know!" he said, and the old frantic bellow started up in his head: She'll die, she'll die—I got to get the bracelet right away.

"Hey listen, Dave," Vincent said, "maybe it's not too bad. My mother gets these headaches sometimes. Nervous—you know."

"Yeah," he muttered. "It's funny, that's all. She's so weak since —well, she tries to kid me."

His eyes were raw with fear. "See, she passed out last Saturday. Right in the store. Then she gets up and walks home. Laughing! But she's been funny ever since. Weak or something. I—I feel like picking her up and carrying her half the time. She's sick—I know it!"

Vincent saw a lost, sad kid, as if Dave's old face had been a mask and it was off now. And suddenly she could hardly remember that tough, narrow-eyed face: some long-ago Halloween mask, as far away as the Gully fires and the gang raids on stores.

"Don't worry, Dave," she said. "Maybe your mother's just real tired."

He looked at her with pleading eagerness. "Yeah, maybe she's just tired. She's always working. In the store, then when she gets home. She'll rest up today, huh? It's Friday—she goes home early on Fridays."

"Sure. Your father'll drive her home and—"

"That dirty sonofabitch," Dave broke in. "Wait'll I get my driver's license some day."

Vincent swallowed. The mask was back, only it seemed different; hatred, a bleak and despairing hatred. What if she talked about Manny and her father to him? How she had met Clara last night?

She tried to change the subject: "Hey, Dave, you all ready for school Monday?"

"I guess so." He added slowly, "Summer sure went fast."

"Yeah."

"It was a funny summer, all right," he muttered. "Next summer —it sure won't be the same."

Her heart sank at his tone. It was true; nothing would be the same.

Outside, a horn sounded, and a satisfied smile came to Dave's face. "Ha ha. My old man's blowing a gasket—we got plenty of orders to deliver."

He turned to go, hesitated. "Hey, Vincent, how come your grandmother's going to Palestine? For good, that way?"

"I don't know," she said.

"The way my mother told me," he said, puzzled, "it sounded like she was going up to heaven or something. With a million bucks in her hands."

The truck horn blasted into the open windows, but Dave went on in that puzzled way: "Sometimes I think they're all nuts."

"Me too," Vincent agreed.

Again the horn sounded. "Bastard," Dave said. "I better cop a sneak. I don't give a damn if he squawks at me, see, but she's sick. I want it quiet in the house."

"You better go," she said.

"Yeah." The blond head came up, and he said quickly, "Going to be at the club tonight?"

It was Friday, the gang's regular meeting night. Last Friday. . . .

"No," Vincent said, her face hot.

"Me either. I'm going to stick around with my mother."

There was a sudden tight silence. Then Dave said in a very low voice, "See you?"

"See you," Vincent said after a minute, giving him the forgiveness he was begging of her.

He ran out, whistling as he took the hall steps in one leap, and she felt a strange softness all through her. She liked this Dave, without his mask. Today he reminded her of the poem Jules had written for her.

Hey, she thought with wonder, is Dave a changeling, too?

## 3

Early that evening, as Vincent sat on her bed with her treasure box, she heard her mother say, "Abe, I'm going next door. Mrs. Zigman is sick."

"What, Fanny Zigman?" her father said with surprise. "She's always worked like a man. What's the matter?"

"Nobody knows. One of those mysterious illnesses—she gets weaker and weaker." Her mother's voice lowered. "They're talking about cancer."

"Who's talking?" her father said with irritation. "Mrs. Levine? As soon as anybody gets sick, one would think she has a patent on the word and gets a dollar each time she says it."

"Well, I'll go see if I can help out."

Vincent put the medal back into her box, on top of the snapshots. She had been thinking with longing of taking the Bible out of the trunk, putting it in the drawer up here, next to her box. But how could you snitch a Bible? It sounded like a sin or something, even if nobody ever used it and it just lay there in the basement.

Her box put away, she snapped off her bedroom light and tiptoed into the hallway. Without making a sound, she stood in the dark hall and eagerly studied her father as he sat at the kitchen table, leaning over his library book.

At the supper table, he had talked only of the Grandmother's departure. She would leave by train Sunday night, and in New York his brother Morris would meet her. It was Morris who would put her on the boat—none of her other children could afford to go to New York for the actual moment of leave-taking. But at least, he had said gloomily, she would see the face of one of her sons in her last sight of America.

Vincent had waited tensely for him to mention Manny. Not one word! It had been her first glimpse of him since the porch episode the night before; he had been in bed when she had come home from Shirley's, and this morning he had gone off to work before she had awakened.

She had felt his eyes on her several times while she was eating, and she knew he was remembering how that laughing, little boy had felt in his arms. Not one word! Instead, he had talked about how he would miss his mother, how far the trip, how holy, how people had stopped him all the way from the corner to tell him how happy they were to hear about his mother's journey to the Homeland.

Vincent stared out into the bright kitchen. When she had taken the fish and soup over to Shirley's that afternoon and played with Manny, she had not been able to shake off the picture of him in her father's arms on the shadowy porch. The broken yearning in the man's voice had echoed in her head. She had not told Shirley, but it seemed to her that she loved her sister even more because of last night's emptiness. And Manny—she loved him twice as fiercely today.

Her father laughed at something he had been reading. The sound of enjoyment made a little pool of softness in Vincent's chest, drew her out into the kitchen.

She walked past him warily, landed at the stove, and studied his back for a minute. Then she said, "Pa, want some tea?"

He blinked up at her in a startled way. "Yes, I'll take a glass of tea," he said.

Her hands fumbling with eagerness, Vincent put on the teakettle, got a glass and saucer ready, the bowl of lump sugar. Waiting for the water to boil, she watched him while he read his book. She felt breathless with her big wish.

"What are you reading, Pa?" she mumbled.

192

When he looked up, she searched his eyes for Manny's name, for a left-over fragment of last night's love and yearning.

"It's a book by Sholem Aleichem," he said. "A wonderful writer. He takes you right back to the old days. Every line is a memory."

He turned back to the book, and she thought hungrily: And after we talk about Manny, about last night, maybe we can talk about our family Bible. Those names. And the missing names, too!

The kettle was boiling. Vincent poured his glass of tea, took it to the table. An exquisite shyness made her heart beat too fast as he pushed the book aside and took a lump of sugar, broke it expertly. It seemed to her that the whole kitchen clamored with Manny's name, still unspoken between them.

Her father sipped his tea. The shyness began banging hard in her side, like a big booming heart, as she went on groping awkwardly to touch him.

"Everybody's talking about the holidays coming," she said. "The whole street, Pa. You know, how it's going to be *Yom Kippur* soon, and—and everything."

Take Manny, she thought with excitement. Take Manny to *shul!* And then we'll all be here that night to eat, after you and Ma fast all day. The whole family, huh? Maybe Nate'll come. And—and Manny and Shirley and Johnnie!

Her father nodded, and she studied his eyes eagerly. She could see Manny's name there!

"The holiest day of the year," he said darkly. "To fast, to atone. Of course the street is talking about it."

And, waiting for the word about Manny, Vincent remembered how he and Ma came home that evening after sundown, and how they sat down at the table to break their fast. Soup, and then Ma would look around, as if for missing people. She would sigh, and say, "I'm not even hungry. One would think I ate all day."

Her father stirred his tea. Then, instead of talking about Manny, he said in that gloomy voice, "This will be the first time in my life that the Grandmother and I are not fasting together."

A violent anger flared in Vincent's head. I don't care about the Grandmother! she thought. Why are you talking about her instead of Manny? It's Manny's name in your eyes. What are you lying for?

193

She ran out of the house. There was a bitter, empty feeling in her as she stood on the sidewalk. What was the use of having a father? A brother? That bastard!—no wonder Pa'd never written his name in the Bible! Why didn't Nate come back here and stick up for Manny?

Mr. Miller's Sabbath chanting and singing came through the open windows of the house next door. A screen door slammed across the street. From the Valenti porch came the *spunyitze's* angry voice: "Sahn-tina! Sahn-tina!"

Vincent sauntered across the street to Jules, as she had so often on a wave of longing and hatred for her brother, or on a helpless surge of contempt for her father. As she crossed slowly, she looked in the direction of the Gully. The regular meeting would be going on, the plans for tomorrow's raid, the door of the club open so they could see the last of the glow in the fireplace outside.

Sure, and Santina doing it in there, she thought in tune with the *spunyitze's* calls. Well, good-by, gang!

Mr. and Mrs. Golden were on the front porch. She heard the creak of the swing, their low voices in the hot night as she walked into their yard. Through the mesh of the back screen door, she saw Becky on the floor, cutting up newspapers, and Heidi at the kitchen table, looking at pamphlets.

"Hi," Vincent said. "Jules around?"

"Sh, he's sleeping," Heidi said, very low. "He had an attack today."

Vincent came in, leaned against the table, cluttered with the booklets in all sizes and colors, each with the word "Florida" printed across it.

"He's been kind of sick," Heidi whispered, "ever since Santina did you-know-what."

Vincent whispered, too. "What did the doctor say?"

"He started to talk about the hospital again. But Juley doesn't want to go! My mother—you should've seen her face when Dr. Palay said that about the hospital."

With a throb of fear, Vincent stared at the queer shapes Becky was cutting. Jules in a hospital? What would the street feel like, without him in it?

She moved on tiptoe to the doorway, peering across the dark dining room to see the bed. His lamp was on, but his eyes were closed,

194

his head back on the pillows. She saw his glasses on the table, on top of the red notebook.

One of Becky's abrupt bellows started up: "Ma, Ma, gimme eat!"

"Sh, sh," Heidi whispered. "Here's some bread."

She had the big loaf of bread on the table in a second, started cutting, but Jules was awake. He licked his lips as his head came up, and reached for a tissue. "Give that poor thing something to eat," he said.

"I did," Heidi cried, and Mrs. Golden's voice came in at the open windows: "Darling, Judy Vincent came to visit you. Did you see her yet?"

"Vincent?" Jules said eagerly.

Heidi pushed past Vincent, said coaxingly, "How about some cocoa?"

"Go stuff your own face," he said with sudden good nature. "Go fly a kite to sunny Florida. Vincent? Come on in."

Heidi went back to her pamphlets, a smile on her face. Mrs. Golden came in from the porch, her eyes shining with relief, and her husband came quickly after her as she said, "Ah hah, you're hollering? You feel better! Judy, congratulations about your grandmother. Isn't it wonderful? She'll be there for *Yom Kippur*."

"Congratulations, congratulations," Mr. Golden said in his fussy way, and went out to the kitchen.

"Juley, a little grape juice?" Mrs. Golden said, leaning to push back his hair, and to plump out the pillows.

"Champagne or nothing," Jules said airily.

In the kitchen, Mr. Golden said, "You're still sitting here with your Florida? Look how a woman eighty years old can go across the world to Palestine. But a young girl sits and waits for the world to come in her kitchen! Why don't you go somewhere? A party—a club meeting?"

His wife strode toward the kitchen, said in a soothing voice, "Come, we'll go to the show. Juley feels better, he's got company. Herman, it'll be good for you to sit in the show. Heidi, go put on a good dress while Papa changes his shirt. Juley? Juley, we'll leave Becky with you?"

"Certainly. She's happy here—she doesn't have to run away."

His face seemed all bone and beaked nose tonight, the unshaved

195

fuzz dark in little feathery blotches on his cheeks and chin. He peered like a half-blind old man as he listened with a smile to the bustling activity. Vincent could see the little deep scar his glasses had made on the bridge of his nose, the red marks at his temples.

Mrs. Golden strewed fresh newspapers near Becky, in the kitchen. "Herman," she called, "you got change in your pocket? For candy? Heidi likes to eat in the show."

"So do you," Heidi said, laughing.

"It's true," Mrs. Golden said. "Good-by, Juley. If the bell rings, don't pay attention. I locked the screen."

"Have a good time," Jules called affectionately. He groped for his glasses as the back door slammed, put them on and looked at Vincent.

"Let's see you," he said. "I didn't want to look at the world today, so I took off my specs." His eyes were quizzical as he said, "Forgive me for yesterday? I was a stinker, wasn't I?"

"You sure smelled," Vincent said, thrilled with the closeness he made between them. "I could've cracked you one."

"So," he said with a grin, "congratulations on your grandmother's holy trip."

"What the hell for?" she said.

He shrugged. "Don't ask me. But will you just look how excited everybody is? My dumb, sweet mother—paradise has opened for the whole street."

"Not the kids," she said quickly. "I was talking to Dave. He thinks they're all nuts."

"So do I," Jules said. "Religion, my God."

"Yeah," Vincent said, frowning. "How come it's so important to die in Palestine?"

"Home. People want to get home—die in peace." An odd kind of smile trembled around his mouth. "How would you know? You're not ready to die."

"Neither are you," she said hotly.

"No." With an effort, he said, "Take a look at Becky, will you? See if she's okay."

Vincent ran to the kitchen doorway. Becky was still happy with her scissors and paper. "She's okay," she told Jules when she got back.

"Sit on the bed," he said. "All ready for school Monday?"

"I'm going to look over my supplies tomorrow," she said. "You know, pencils and notebooks and stuff."

His mouth pursed with disgust. "My religious mother! First she makes a big speech about Palestine, then she talks about how school's going to be crowded with *Schwartze* this fall. Poor little Alex'll have to sit in the same room with them—imagine!"

Vincent wished she could see Clara right now. What if she walked in this room, and they would all three start talking about things? The way just she and Jules did sometimes? Things: the Grandmother going to Palestine, Manny, that wonderful book of names in the basement trunk. Would Jules read her poem to Clara? If she were to tell him how Clara kissed Manny's hand last night? Hi, little half-and-half! Hi, half-pint!

Jules was sucking one of the orange halves from the plate on his table, watching her with interest. "You look like you just swallowed a rainbow," he said.

As he put back the orange and wiped his hands on a tissue, the doorbell rang.

"Forget it," he said in a low voice. "Nothing to do about it."

They did not talk until they heard the footsteps down the porch steps. "Nuts!" Jules muttered.

"Hey, listen, Jules," Vincent burst out. "You don't know it, but I got this new friend—she's colored. We got together in the Gully, see? I was there all alone this one night and she just came over and —well, we started to talk. Nobody was around. Nobody knows. She—her name's Clara Jackson."

"Colored?" His face flushed with excitement as he stared at her. "You mean you got yourself a *Schwartze* friend?"

"Yeah!"

"Changelings!" he cried with a wondering happiness. "See, they'll do it. Over hell and high water."

"Hey, you know what? She *is* like a changeling," Vincent said. "Honest, Jules. When we got to talking—well, she was just like me, kind of! I mean, the way her mother and father act to her, and— I even told her about you. Our poem. We were like—hey, isn't it funny? We were like pals."

"My God," he cried, "that's wonderful! Vincent, you did it. The hell with this street—you did it!"

His tired, sick face seemed to shine. His eyes were as bright as if he had just taken a spoonful of some magic medicine. "I can't get over it," he said incredulously. "It's wonderful, impossible."

Then, her heart sinking, Vincent saw the snoop in Jules take over. "Clara, huh? That her name?"

She nodded, watched the gloating curiosity swallow the happiness in his eyes.

"Say," he said, lowering his voice as if they had a nearby audience, "what's a *Schwartze* girl like, anyway?"

"Like me!" she said.

"No, no," he said, still probing. "I mean, what does she look like, close up? Does she talk different? You know—Southern? How'd she act when you first talked?"

"Hell," Vincent said resentfully, "you make it sound like she's— you said they're just like us! Not different. But now you're acting like she's all different. What's the big idea?"

Jules was silent. He was looking down at his hands. Vincent did not know what to say as she saw the color drain out of his face. The anger puffed out of her; she struggled with her old, stifled feeling that Jules was trapped by sickness, able to run only with his red notebook. She wanted to tell him about the book so suddenly in her own life, the names written in it and the names never written.

"Hey, listen," she said stumblingly, "something happened last night. I was taking care of Manny. Shirley and—well, Shirley had to go away, and I go over there and take care of the baby when she goes. So I was wheeling him in his buggy and I bumped into Clara, see? We talked. I told her to pick up Manny, and they laughed and had a good time together. Real good! She knows how to hold a baby right and everything. Well, then she had to go home. We were on Shirley's street, right near the corner, see? Clara waved good-by and she went home. Her father gets sore if she's out late a lot. And I was standing there. With Manny in his buggy."

Jules was looking at her, his eyes startled at her breathless lunge of words.

"Jules!" she said. "All of a sudden I pushed the buggy over to our street. Fast—real fast. I got to the porch. My father was up there, and my grandmother was still there. I grabbed Manny and went up there and— Well, I just put Manny on my father's lap."

198

"Oh, Vincent," he said tremulously.

She had never talked much about her nephew, but he knew a great deal of her impassioned, painful feelings. Looking at this kid's face, the blurted story written in her eyes and in the tight shape of her jaw, he felt stunned with happiness. He tried to remember the first clumsy, sullen words she had ever said to him, the possible steps over the years which might have helped her grope blindly toward the incident she had just described.

"Your grandmother was there, too?" he said, his voice choked.

"Boy, was I scared," she said.

It seemed to him that he could sense her shadow in the street—as heretofore he had sensed one of his poems there—an inch-by-inch lengthening and darkening and strengthening, until that shadow touched the walls of every house, tapped at doors and windows like an insistent wind full of questions and accusations.

His eyes were moist with gratitude as he sat up straight and shouted out his excitement: "Vincent, it's proof! A changeling can change the world, huh? There's hope, Vincent. Thanks, thanks! Look what you did last night—you and your little *Schwartze* friend."

He stretched, as if reaching sharply for something, his raw-looking wrists high above his stupefied grin. He did not ask her what had happened on her front porch after Manny had reached his grandfather's arms. He just looked happy, his eyes wet and shining, his gestures electrified.

"Hey, you crazy?" she said elatedly.

"I feel wonderful," he cried. "Thanks! I'm drunk; you poured a big glass of wine into me. Changeling, you made your father look. You made him open his guts. As for the old lady on her way to Palestine! Both of them, huh? You made them see the shape of your soul, changeling! They'll know you in the dark after this!"

He sounded hysterical. Vincent felt a little frightened, but his reaction was proof that she had not done a bad thing last night. She was breathlessly glad she had told her secret.

"Go get some grape juice," he said. "We'll have a party. Becky, too!"

Vincent tore off to the kitchen, got his bottle of grape juice out of the icebox, three glasses. "Come on, Becky," she said. "Eats."

Jules poured the juice, put a glass into Vincent's hand, one into

199

Becky's. "A toast!" he said, laughing, and clinked his glass against his sister's, then against Vincent's. "I propose a toast. Here's to the changelings. May they change the whole world!"

The bell rang. They could see the man standing on the porch. Jules nodded at Vincent. "It's all right," he said. "Some day, changeling. Some day."

## Chapter thirteen

Herb drove up to the pawnshop well after ten-thirty, when Ruth had given him up for the day. Her heart sank when she saw him come in. A full week had passed since last Saturday's violent words; he had not even telephoned her.

"Hi, honey," he said casually. "Sorry I'm too late to carry in the gates. Everything else done?"

"Want to open the safe?" she called from the office. "I had two customers right off the bat. Don't forget the gun. How's Alice?"

"Fine," he said. "Mom okay?"

"As usual. She sent along a drumstick for you—in case."

"Good," Herb said. He was leaning now, twirling the knob on the safe, and he said very quietly, "Did Ben open today?"

"No," Ruth said, and quickly carried a tray of jewelry to the front windows, began to set the pieces out in a decorative display.

It was cheap, gaudy jewelry, what Herb called "*Schwartze* bait," their father's way of attracting Negro customers. Once they were inside the store, he sold them the jewelry at give-away prices but often managed to dispose of the expensive, unretrieved items like radios and luggage which crammed the store.

Herb swung open the doors of the safe, took out the heavy books for Ruth, and placed the gun within easy reach. Then he came to the front and pushed out a wardrobe trunk, brought in his invention and set it up in the tool section, a few feet away from the window where Ruth was working.

"What's new, honey?" he asked as he took off his jacket, rolled up his sleeves, and loosened his tie.

200

"Well, the street's still up in arms about Santina. Mom said she told you all about it when you phoned."

"Yeah," Herb said. "I suppose Dad's disturbed?"

"Terribly," Ruth murmured, and a shiver went through her at the thought of that girl lying near a big, dark body.

"Such a moral man. He always did get a bit rabid about sexual items."

Ruth's scalp tingled. As she set out the last piece of jewelry, she said faintly, "Well, good heavens, do you think it's right?"

When she turned, Herb was studying her. "It's none of my business," he said, "if a gal decides to go to bed with somebody in the Gully. It's none of Dad's business."

Ruth tried to laugh. "Anyway, there's been an antidote in the street. Old Mrs. Vincent is going off to Palestine, for good."

"Ah. And Dad's green with jealousy."

"Of course he envies her," Ruth admitted. "The whole street does, Mom says. But Dad's thrilled that someone can go. He talks about it a lot, and—well, it seems to have depressed him," she finished lamely.

"He's jealous," Herb said with disgust. "Why do they insist on making specials of Jews? Homeland—that word makes me sick! So do Dad's letters to the President, to Congress. A big man—he has his fingers in international politics! 'My dear Mr. President: We, the Jews of America, ask for your help in getting the Homeland back for the Jews of the world.' And the way he's always showing off those careful, polite answers—that say nothing. Dad's medals!"

"Oh, Herb," Ruth cried, "please don't start on Dad again. What do you want of him?"

His intent eyes looked sad. "Ruthie, Ruthie, you're a confused girl. My baby sister—I forget age! You're a woman. Ask Chip, he'll tell you."

"That roughneck," she said, but she had to think of the new, gentle Chip she had seen Wednesday night.

"I like him," Herb said. "He's got stuff. Stack him up against Dad—then pick your America." Wryly, he added, "Stack Chip up against me."

"I will not!"

"Afraid to?"

She felt close to tears, said indignantly, "You don't really want me to marry a—well, practically an illiterate, do you? A man who hustles newspapers? He's a—a peasant!"

"A Jew, a peasant?" he said with gentle sarcasm.

"There isn't a Jewish thing about him. Believe me, Herb, I know what a Jew should be."

His eyebrows shot up. "The cultured, intellectual man—with a soul? Music, books, a little *gelt*, maybe on the poetic side in bed?"

Ruth flushed. "At least aware of—of beautiful things."

Herb said nothing for an instant. Then, very softly, he told her, "You know, honey, our simple brother tried to tell me once what he means when he says 'the Jewishness' of a person. It all boiled down to the fact that Jewishness in a man means that he's good, decent, compassionate. Little, simple Ben—he said that."

"And yet he can't take care of his own family! Ilona cries, and he goes right on closing the store on Saturday."

"Ruthie," Herb said, his eyes somber, "what is all this crap about people having to be Jews? With their own God, their own Homeland —to live and die in? What the hell are you doing to yourself?"

"First Dad, now me," she said miserably. "What do you want of me?"

"God damn it, I want you to get some happiness out of life! Don't be afraid to live it. I remember when we came to America. You were such an eager little beaver. Not even eight—a skinny little thing with the sun for a face. What happened to us? Mom, Ben, me—I can still remember how happy we were on that boat, coming over. Singing. Looking forward to Dad's meeting us. A new country, a new life."

Ruth walked to the counter and began blindly to dust.

"Does Dad still call you *kurveh* when you come back from a date?" Herb asked, his voice flat.

"No," she said, not turning. The sickening, frightening thing of Santina in the Gully leaped at her, and she remembered her father's reaction to the news, his fury, his words like a sermon of vengeance.

Then Herb was at the counter, one of his hands lifting her chin.

"I'm sorry, honey," he said. "I don't know why the hell I started to go back almost eighteen years. These days, I—why am I thinking about the way we sang on that boat? Maybe—well, I went over and saw Alice this morning. Brought her a little something. And you

202

know?—all of a sudden she reminded me of you, the year we came from Europe."

Ruth patted his arm, managed a laugh. "But Alice isn't a greenhorn, like I was. She doesn't have to go to the store every day after school."

"Thank God. Yeah, he made a pawnbroker out of you right off the bat, all right."

"No parties, no football games," she said, her laugh suddenly wistful. "Isn't it funny what a kid will yearn after? With me, it was the football games I had to miss by rushing to the store right after the last bell. I was madly jealous of one particular girl at school. The cheerleader. She could go to every single game of the season."

"Ruthie, Ruthie," Herb said tenderly.

"Poor little greenie—me. Imagine leading cheers with that accent it took me so long to shake!"

"Was that the year you wanted to study music?" he said.

"No, music came the next year. I had a new dream every year, I guess." She frowned. "I can still remember the way Dad laughed at the very idea. Well! Even today—when I dust the violins here, I get the strangest feeling sometimes."

"Violins? College?" Herb said harshly. "God, when that man lost his temper."

Ruth's eyes closed. Unthinkingly, she burst out, "Herb, why *did* he scream *kurveh* at me whenever he got into a rage? It used to kill me. For years—I was fourteen, fifteen, and he—he kept calling me that."

"A filthy mind, that's all." Her eyes flew open at the phlegmy sound of his voice, and she saw his scar darker, the puckered edges very sharp. "Come to America and learn new ways. A new vocabulary, O holy man!"

She felt the sudden, alarmed battering of her heart again. For weeks now, she and Herb had come closer and closer to something dreadful about their father. She could not bear the inevitable way every sentence, of late, seemed to twist away from Herb and catapult toward a chasm of some kind. It was as if he could not help himself and something dragged him into these bitter denunciations, toward that frightening brink.

"Those rages," he muttered. "I think the man was crazy for a

203

while. Guilt, filth—something. His actions toward Mom. Toward all of us."

Ruth broke in quickly, with a shrill gaiety. "Well, he's stopped all that. I grew up, became an expert pawnbroker. He admires my business ability."

And, as if to help her, a woman entered the store, carrying a bundle wrapped in newspaper. Herb sauntered to the portable phonograph and began to look over records as the customer came to the counter and threw down her package.

Her hands shaking, Ruth unwrapped the bundle and said mechanically, "Good morning," thinking of the years when all of them had walked in wide circles about the quaking ground of hints and half-shouted secrets. She would not think of it—whatever it was, happening in Herb's mind after all those years! His violence, coming on top of the ugliness of the Santina affair, was more than she could take.

"Well, well?" the customer demanded as Ruth examined the fur jacket.

"How much do you want?"

"What'll you give?" the woman asked.

"Sell or pawn?" They were the stereotyped questions and answers Ruth had lived with for so long that they seemed part of the dust and odors of the store.

"Pawn. I'm broke now but by Monday I'll have plenty."

"Three dollars," Ruth said.

"Hey, that jacket cost me sixty bucks," the woman yelled.

"Three is all it's worth to me," Ruth said. "It's stained under the arms, a seam is burst, and the fur is badly rubbed down here."

"Make it six, will you? I need the dough."

"Give her four," Herb said in Yiddish, his voice barely audible.

"Four do you any good?" Ruth said crisply. "That's top price."

"Okay," the woman said, hating her.

But hatred, whining, threats, all were part of the dusty years, too, and Ruth walked back to the grilled window, began to fill out the police forms and the store receipts.

"Like it cleaned?" she asked.

"Hell, no. I got my own gyp joint for that." The woman signed with a flourish, counted the money carefully, and left.

Ruth hung the jacket, then washed her hands. When she came

204

out of the office she saw Herb's face pale and stern as it hung over the records.

"Should we have a concert, Herb?" she said, still trying to sound casual.

He turned, holding one of the records. "Why are we afraid to talk, Ruthie? Have you forgotten the years we were always together? Always jabbering to each other?"

As she looked at him, half afraid, Herb said softly, "We were talking about Chip. Versus Dad or me. But I was really talking about a person's insides. You know, honey, Chip reminds me of—me. Strong, young. Sure, a peasant. Wasn't I a peasant in Hungary? Gypsy songs, working the ground when I could get an inch of it, the fastest *czardas* dancer for miles around. A guy with an eye for the girls. Life felt good to me then, even though it was tough to eat."

He put the record on the turntable of the phonograph, stared down at it for a second. "So in America I got stuck in a pawnshop. I married a phony. A very cultured girl. Chopin on the piano after supper—excuse me, dinner! I was on my way to being a well-to-do, intellectual phony myself."

When he turned around, his expression was so undisguised that she swallowed.

"But Ruthie," he said, "the warnings were there, even though I didn't know how to see them. At my store I was never happy unless there was a lull—no customers—and I could putter around with those big-dream inventions of mine. At home? I always wanted to sleep. Brahms, people dropping in for musicals, literary discussions, white napkins and candles at the table. And I'd fall asleep—in a chair, right after dinner, while Flo was putting Alice to bed. In the middle of a sentence from Flo, in the middle of the Chopin waltz, in the middle of a hot discussion by her friends on Eliot. People are sick— for years—and they don't know it. Until something punches out at them."

Ruth crouched over the counter, afraid a customer would walk in and end this intimate talk she had so longed to hear from Herb. She was afraid to say anything, even to make a sound of agreement or pity.

"This whole *Schwartze* deal, for example," he went on musingly. "I don't know—lately, that's been really punching at me. A thing like

*Schwartze* coming into a neighborhood—you know, it can smack you like a psychiatrist's talk–medicine. It has an effect on stuff that's been there all along—hidden. All that poison starts bouncing up to the surface."

"You mean," Ruth said, unable to keep from saying it, "a thing like Santina?"

Herb gave her an odd smile. "I mean you and me, Dad. I mean all the kids in that street—Alice's age, a little older. Chip, and don't think I'm skipping Ben and Mom. To all of us the *Schwartze* came. Who are they? What are they?"

He shrugged. "It doesn't matter. What matters is, they came, and all of a sudden we can see who we are, what we are."

"Herbie, what kind of crazy talk is this?"

"Is it so crazy?" he said very quietly. "They say in a war certain soldiers break down because they've been ready to break down anyway. The guns and bombs just start the ball rolling. Well, I'll tell you. Right now, I'd like to go out and say thanks to the first colored guy I see in the street."

"Why?" she said breathlessly.

"For busting through like a bomb to my rotten little hiding place. Am I going to break down—like one of those soldiers? No, Ruthie. For the first time, I know it. The answer is no. Like the *Schwartze* put a big searchlight on me—I can finally see Herb Miller's insides. Is he a punk, a failure, a guy who married blind and even became a father, without giving his kid a thought? Is that really me?"

"No!"

"That's right—no," he said. "I just thought it was. That's a strong searchlight I'm talking about. What's Dad look like in that light? And you—are you going to keep your back turned while it burns down on you?"

He was like the Herb she remembered so often, so longingly; like the oldest, the beloved brother who had led her by the hand, talking to her when she was frightened, singing with her when she was lonesome, bringing her a tidbit he had sneaked somewhere or a rough toy he had made. A thrilling sense of closeness went through her at this talk he was offering her again, after all the years of silence.

"Oh, Herb darling," she said, "don't let me! I mean, don't let me turn my back—on anything. You never let me go, in Europe. Some-

206

times I feel like that little girl. As if I stopped, right then—or maybe on the boat coming over. Herb, I do feel like that sometimes!"

"Yeah, I know," he said. "Sometimes I see you like that, too. Little and scared—with a big hand on you. Stopping you, pushing you into the store, a dark hole. You're like my kid—inside of me. Alice and you. I want you both to have something out of life. It's got to be, honey!"

She listened eagerly as he said, "I've been telling Alice about Europe. That village of ours. Remember the bands of wandering gypsies, Ruthie? The wonderful, gay thieves?"

She nodded, smiling.

"Alice and I are becoming good friends. On Sundays. We drive to a park, to the country. We roast hot dogs over a fire. Sometimes we go to see Mom. Mostly, we talk." Then, without a pause, he added quietly, "Last Sunday I told her what made me leave the store. And her mother."

"Herb!" Ruth cried.

"She's old enough," he said. "Are you?" He smiled at her expression. "Let me tell you, too. It was a small thing, Ruthie. Wouldn't even make sense to most people. Even if I told them how it punched into me. Like the *Schwartze* have started punching lately. But you know what? My gal understood me last Sunday. I made sense to her."

His eyes were wet, but he was still smiling. "I took a big chance, telling her, huh? But she understood. My own kid."

He leaned to start the phonograph, saying, "I'm glad I found this record here. I want Alice to hear it. She doesn't know much about Hungarian music—only what I've whistled to her. In the park, in the car."

The record started, tuned low. It was one of those sentimental, half-mourning Hungarian love songs which, at a halfway point, go into the faster and faster music of the dance known as the *czardas*. The haunting, familiar tune, Herb's sudden brotherliness again after his long silence, made a dreamy happiness in Ruth.

"And so I told Alice," Herb said in a musing way, the love song a plaintive background to his voice, "that one day I was walking on East 9th Street, to the bank. It was a little past noon. I had locked the store for an hour—figured I'd get the bank over with, grab a sandwich, then rush back to business. Well, I had to park my car

207

way down because of traffic, and walk past the ratty part of down-town. Near Hamilton, you know?"

She nodded.

"I passed a store—there are a lot for rent down there. And inside that store—gypsies, Ruthie. They'd rented it for the week, I guess. They were living there, telling fortunes—and probably going out every night to steal the town blind, like our Hungarian gypsies used to do. There were a lot of them in that store. I could see the costumes, a pack of beautiful, dirty kids on the floor, playing. And there was a lot of singing going on. Some kind of instrument—the music came out at me as I started to pass. I had to stop. Ruthie, such a feeling of homesickness!"

Herb smiled. "Homesick for the me I used to be. Young, laughing, clean, like boys are. Full of boldness—for girls, for dreams and life. I never got to the bank that day. Or opened the store that afternoon."

The traditional *czardas* began, like a gay pulsation around them.

"I went back to my car, Ruthie. Drove way out to the country. Walked, smelled things, stood at the edge of fields and just looked. At suppertime, when I came home, I knew I had to get out of the store, out of my marriage. That I was a dead man in both places. My daughter? I didn't even know her—she didn't know me."

Suddenly Herb lifted the needle, set it back to the start of the dance part of the record and tuned the music blasting-high. With a smile, he held out his hands. Ruth came out from behind the counter and walked into his arms, and they began to dance a *czardas* in the narrow floor space left over from the clutter of the store.

Herb guided her skillfully; they danced faster and faster to the insistent demands of the quickening music. It was wonderful to take the perfect steps with Herb, as if they had danced together only yesterday. It was wonderful to be laughing, whirling with his hands on her waist to lead her in the most detailed intricacies of the dance.

At the height of the whirling, Chip walked in with his bag of fruit. He stopped to stare, to listen to this unfamiliar, hilarious laughter. The passion, the warmth and joy he had suspected in Ruth all along were now openly displayed. For a few seconds, he filled his hungry senses with her sparkling grace and the wonderful sound of her pleasure.

Then he whistled the long, piercing wolf-call sound of the street, called, "Hey, gypsy queen, meet me in the Gully?"

Herb grinned. The dance went on another moment until the record ended, then Herb said pantingly, "Wow! To think I used to do this all evening when I was young."

He staggered to cut off the phonograph. Ruth, her face glowing, walked back of the counter and sank down on the stool, leaned her elbows on the glass, and tried to catch her breath.

"Grandpa," Chip said admiringly, "I could use that legwork in the ring. Any time you say."

"It couldn't happen twice in a row," Herb said, still panting. "Toss me an apple, I'm going back to a sitting job."

Chip threw him an apple, and Herb went to the tool section and sat down heavily, laughing to himself as he bit into the fruit.

Pushing the bag toward Ruth, Chip said in a low voice, "You look like you're on fire, gypsy. I never thought you'd let this part of you loose."

She tried to frown but she felt too good. "Don't embarrass me in front of Herb," she said. "Aren't you early today?"

"Yeah—God must've come out of *shul* and told me to get here, huh? Hey, why can't you be this way all the time?"

The screen door slammed, and Herb said, "Well, well. Don't tell me we're still in business? I'll get him, Ruthie."

He walked toward the man, who asked to see some work pants. "This way, sir," Herb said, and led him around the tool section to the front wall where Mr. Miller kept a supply of cheap, new work clothes.

"Have some fruit," Chip said. "Listen, gypsy, I got a new come-on. Marry me and I'll take you to Palestine for our honeymoon. Like Old Lady Vincent."

Ruth looked into the bag. "Bananas again? . . . Why waste your money?"

He tasted the delight of her rare smile, leaned closer to her across the counter, and said, "Diamonds. They cost like diamonds, like stars—so they're for you, from me."

"My, where'd you learn the poetry?" she said lightly, and reached into his bag for a banana.

Chip laughed. "I forgot to tell you! I snitched one of those fancy books you're always reading. Been keeping it in my *torba*, studying it on the job. Think it'll do a low punk like me any good?"

"Aren't you funny," she said absently, staring at the banana in her hand.

She felt the old repugnance, but for some reason she found herself thinking of old Mrs. Vincent, of her journey to Palestine. That old woman an immigrant again—or maybe the word was "still." Did a Jew have to be an immigrant all his life, looking for home?

"Hey," Chip said softly, "what's so terrific about that banana? The way you're looking at it, huh?"

She glanced up at him. Her body felt strangely alive from the dance. And her mind, her heart, felt that same freshness and elated youth, as if Herb's intense talk had replenished them.

"Bananas. They always make me think of this country," she said. "America. What America meant to me when I came here from Europe. A scared kid, a little greenhorn—big eyes, big imagination. When we got off the boat, my aunt put a banana in my hand. She came with my father to meet us. 'Here, eat a piece of fruit,' she said, and embraced me. Then my father grabbed me and—and kissed me. So hard. I was still holding that banana. I'd never seen one before. I—well, you know, I'd never seen my father before. He'd come to America before the rest of us. I was almost eight before I even saw him."

Uneasily, Chip became aware of the quickening of Ruth's voice out of the brooding with which she had begun to talk.

"America," she said. "It's odd what you keep remembering, after so many years. In the taxi, on the way to my aunt's house, I still had the banana. I was scared—in that fast car, I guess, and all the strange sights. Confused, I guess. Anyway, I began to eat the banana—skin and all. How my father laughed! Then he showed me how to peel it, explained that one ate the hidden part—not the skin that hid the fruit."

Her laugh sounded hurt to Chip, in some peculiar way that made him wince.

"I took a bite—it was delicious. And as I ate, I made myself an exciting little picture. This is how America must be, I thought. You peel a strange, thick skin from the new country, and inside you find the sweet fruit: education, friends, love. How wonderful! All you have to do is study and work hard—and you'll find out how to peel off that skin. That armor hiding the beauty, the—the heart of everything this country stands for! And I ate the whole banana, very slowly. How sweet it was. Delicious!"

"But you don't like bananas," Chip said, trying to figure out why she was so upset.

"I hate them. They always make me think of what I could have been. How far I could have gone in this country."

Ruth looked around the store, her eyes almost bewildered, so that Chip felt again that uneasiness for her.

"Well, well," he said carefully, "I never knew you were born in Europe."

Ruth flushed. She was astounded that she had told him. It had always seemed an inadequacy to her, something to be ashamed of, and yet she had just confessed this flaw to a man who loved her.

She tossed the banana back into the bag and said, "Well, now you know. So?"

"So nothing. Am I supposed to give a damn where you were born?"

"Don't you?" she said in a low voice.

"Listen, baby," he said, "all I ever wanted was for you to be born, see? For you and me to get together."

The customer left, and Herb called as he went back to the workbench, "Honestly! Not even a pair of two-dollar pants, and on a Saturday. If this goes on, the Millers are through."

"I'm crying for you," Chip said, but his eyes were eager on Ruth's new tenderness of expression, the beautiful twist of her lips in some kind of wistfulness.

"Damn me, anyway," Herb said suddenly, and put on his jacket. "I'm missing a piece. I was going to go downtown right after seeing Alice, pick it up, but she talked a blue streak this morning. Got me thinking of everything but."

They looked at him so absently that he grinned. "Well, so long, kids," he said gently. "I'll bring back some lunch. Chip, it's early—you'll eat with us."

They watched until he roared off in the car. "I love Herb," Ruth said.

"Yeah, I know," Chip said.

She played with the bag of fruit. "In Europe," she said, "it was Herb who—you see, he was always there. My father had gone to America. I was born after he'd gone. He was going to send for us in a year, but—well, no money, I guess."

"So he strung it out, huh?" Chip said.

"He was getting the store started," she said quickly. "His first store—every dollar must have gone into it. Time, hard work. When we came here, Herb was eighteen. Imagine! Ben was thirteen, and Mom—oh, she was so pretty! So strong, always laughing—with Herb."

She stopped abruptly at her memory of her mother so soon after their arrival. She tried not to think of that tearful face and the accusing eyes, as the confused outcries about Dad came babbling all those times. Poor Mom, who had gone a little crazy in the America where her husband was so respected and. . . .

"Of course," she plunged ahead, "I knew all about my father, even though I had never seen him. Mom and Herb would tell me stories about him. Every night. What he looked like, how brilliant he was, what a scholar. Like fairy tales! You know, I dreamed about him a lot. I was such an imaginative child. Not even eight when I got here. I—he seemed like a king, a handsome prince, in all the stories."

"He send any dough to your mother?" Chip blurted.

"I don't know," she said, after her instant of surprise. "After all, he was saving money to send for us. And he had to get the store started, didn't he? We didn't starve! Mom worked in one of the big houses—cooking and cleaning. Herbie would bring food home, too. From somewhere. He was wonderful. I'd sit in his lap and eat, and Ben would sit on the floor, with his mouth stuffed, and Herbie would tell us another story about Dad."

"So you finally came here and saw your old man for yourself," Chip said thoughtfully. "Must've been some minute for little Ruthie when the king walked up to her and gave her a big smile."

"He was crying," she said, her voice jerky. "My aunt gave me the banana, and then all of a sudden this sobbing man grabbed me. So suddenly—just picked me up and kissed me. So hard I—I couldn't breathe. I couldn't get away. The hard touch—his suit, or something, and the smell—I mean, I was jammed against him so hard! I can still remember the feel of his beard—it was wet with his tears. And he kept kissing me, and—and crying."

212

Chip saw the shiver go through her. "Hey," he said gently.

Ruth looked at him, her eyes dazed, and Chip said, "Let's get back to 1945, okay? How about if we talk about you and me now? Just us?"

The screen door banged, and Ruth slipped off the stool quickly and went toward the customer. He was a middle-aged Negro in work clothes, and he asked to see a second-hand alarm clock.

Chip ate an apple as he watched her dealing with the man. The black skin of the customer made him think of Santina and the guy in the Gully. Was that the first time, or had Heidi just happened on them after a whole summer's worth?

And then he thought, in that idle way, that Ruth had not mentioned Santina today. The woman of ice, huh? Maybe he had dreamed Wednesday night, when he had told her about Santina and she had clung to him, so scared and shaky. Pure ice—he had never even had the nerve to kiss her. But Jesus, when she had been dancing with Herb!

But when he tried to remember the vivid, laughing girl in the gypsy dance, her full mouth and sparkling eyes, the tall body twisting in the sensuous rhythms of the dance, he could think only of the little girl off the boat Ruth had described so excitedly. He could see that kid clutching the banana as she was swept up into the hard embrace of the stranger, bearded and sobbing old Moses himself—God damn him!—who had scared the guts out of her.

He stared angrily into the bag of fruit at the bananas, and the door slammed for another customer. Another colored guy, Chip noticed automatically, as he took a pear out of the bag.

It was impossible to shake off the haunting little girl who had stepped off the boat looking for the king, her father. And he thought of his little brother Louis, who was going out again tonight to hustle papers—even though Moe didn't want him to—because Chip had promised to keep an eye on his toilet habits.

God damn it, Chip thought as he bit violently into the pear, kids got a right to live, too! Pishers or not. They want to grow up, be like everybody else. They got big dreams—education, dough, be somebody. Then help 'em, for Christ sake!

For a second, he had Louis and the little immigrant Ruth mixed. He wanted to pick up the yearning composite figure and carry it, love it, give it a big bag of toys and laughter, promises.

"Yes, sir," Ruth said easily to the later customer, "these are genuine, gold-filled good-luck charms. From Harlem. Only seventy-five cents, never been worn by anybody. Better than horseshoes for luck."

Chip watched her wait on both guys, quick and glib, the friendly little business woman. She sold the clock, she sold the charm, she filled out the forms, and rang up the money like an efficient, smart Miller.

When the customers left, she straightened a pair of crutches somebody had pawned a long time ago, and went to wash her hands. Then she came back to Chip, so brisk and poised in her smock that he might have dreamed the Ruth who had talked so intimately a short while before.

"Hi, gypsy," he said, and put the core of his pear into an ashtray. "Want to get married?"

"I'm an old maid," she said casually. "Hadn't you heard? I'm twenty-five, sir."

"Me, too," he said. "Before you turn around, it'll be too late to have kids. And I really want kids with you, baby."

She stiffened, but he went on, his eyes suddenly somber: "Before you turn around, I'm going to be on the floor, kissing your feet. Shoes and stockings off. All those damn clothes off, and just you there, all twenty-five years of you. Right next to me, with my clothes—"

"Don't be so crude!" she cried. "You talk like a—well, certainly like no decent Jewish man would!"

He laughed. "I'm one of those dirty, low Hebes. I can hardly talk English."

"Oh, stop that!"

"You're living right in the middle of a lot of us low types," he said tauntingly. "We're not so bad. We've all got stomachs and a big sex urge. Just like fancy Jews."

As she stared angrily, he reached across the counter and grasped her arm. "How about a kiss?" he said, grinning. "Did you ever kiss a low-type Jew, baby?"

He felt her cringe. She cried, with such panic that his heart dropped: "Don't! Don't grab me!"

When he released her arm, she said shrilly, "We're not in the Gully! I'm not—that girl!"

Chip looked at her intently. She was shivering, and a feeling of pity and tenderness rushed through him.

"So when I touch you," he said a little thickly, "you think of Santina and her *Schwartze?*"

"Just don't grab," she said faintly. "I can't stand that."

"What the hell have I got to do with a *Schwartze?*" he said. "Or you with Santina? I'll bet *she* doesn't kid herself. I'll bet when she wants a lay she goes out and gets it."

"Chip, no. Don't."

"So it was with a *Schwartze,*" he went on deliberately. "So what? She wanted a guy—she got one. Some gals don't need a fancy reason out of a *shul.*"

"Would it hurt you to step into temple once in a while?" she said frantically.

"What for? I don't even understand any of that stuff they throw at you in *shul.* I'm low-class, all I know is English. And a little dirty Yiddish—the kind my folks talk."

"Chip, I'm not joking!"

"Me, neither," he said, his voice very quiet suddenly. "Listen, Ruth, stop trying to mix me up. I'm just a guy who wants to marry you and go to bed with you. Make you a living, have kids with you. I'm so nuts about you that I want us to be married before I have you. I mean, you aren't just a piece of skirt, see? So what's it got to do with this Jew business? This is just us. Me and you."

Looking at his square, set face, she had the confused feeling that she could love this quiet, almost ominously sure man. She walked away from him, toward the front of the store, pretended to rearrange a display of rifles. When the door opened she moved instantly toward the customer, smile and words all ready, as if she were the old Ruth instead of this woman shaken by too many new thoughts. The customer wanted to redeem his radio, and she went to the office with his receipt. Chip was staring at the bag of fruit as she passed him.

Why on earth did I tell him about the boat? she asked herself as she found the radio and processed it for release.

She had not remembered the scene in years: her first glimpse of that bearded, corpulent stranger who was crying—the grabbing embrace, being pressed against that big, harsh body—the kisses pouring onto her mouth until she could hardly breathe for fright. . . .

The customer left, and she went to wash her hands. When she came back to the counter, Chip smiled at her. "Hi," he said.

Ruth saw that he was peeling a banana. He threw the skin into the bag, broke the fruit into two pieces.

"Let's get this banana deal over with, okay?" he said casually, and gave her one of the pieces.

He bit into his half. After a second, she took a bite of her portion. Chip watched her, smiling as he ate all of his.

Then he said, "Not bad, huh? A piece of fruit. Right?"

## Chapter fourteen

At noon that same day Vincent had taken all her school materials into the living room, and was sorting the things she would need for Monday. The long, narrow table near the porch windows held notebooks and pencils, the clean three-ring paper she had bought that morning, clips, and several erasers.

She filled her pen, then clipped it carefully to the inside of her blouse pocket for safekeeping until she could get the neat stack of supplies back to her bedroom. Shirley had given her the pen on her last birthday. She used it only for school, and it still shone like new.

As she leaned over her notebooks, she smelled the chicken and soup warming, heard snatches of the up-and-down talk between her mother and Mrs. Levine, shouting from their kitchens into the back hall as they prepared the Sabbath meal for the men who would soon be coming from *shul*. They were talking about cleaning the basement and the attic for the coming Jewish holidays.

A movement outside caught Vincent's eyes. A colored woman had stopped in front of the Zigman house. The woman looked up at the sign, then turned into the little walk leading to the porch.

Dave answered the bell. He shook his head, and the woman left. He just stood there, behind the mesh of the screen door, looking out, and Vincent could see in his lost eyes how sick his mother was today.

When his face disappeared, Vincent turned to see where the colored woman had gone (Clara's mother, her aunt?). She was walking toward the Gully, studying each house she passed.

216

Suddenly Vincent was thrilled to see Jules come out on the Golden porch, a slow figure in pajamas and bathrobe, followed by Heidi carrying pillows and blankets. She watched him lie down on the swing, and saw Heidi tuck the blanket around him; no matter how hot it was, Jules needed a blanket.

Some of the men were coming from temple. Vincent saw her father and Mr. Levine, Mr. Miller. The colored woman was on the sidewalk in front of the Golden house, her eyes searching out the telltale, curtainless windows despite the absence of a sign on the porch pillar. But as she started to turn in, Heidi ran toward the steps.

Vincent heard her voice, clear across the street: "No rooms here. We rented them out yesterday."

She could not see Jules' face. Heidi stood there, hands on her hips, until the woman (Clara's mother, her cousin?) started to move toward the corner. Vincent saw her father turn to stare at her as she went up on the Valenti porch and rang the bell. Nothing happened. Nobody came to the door, or even out into the yard to see who it was, and Vincent felt a throb of anger.

God damn it, she thought, come out and tell her no! You know she's there, answer the God damn bell and say something!

After a while the woman (Clara's mother?) went away. Mr. Levine and her father turned into the yard, in their dark suits and hats, each carrying a newspaper-wrapped package of prayer shawl and book. The colored woman was two or three houses up toward the corner when Santina came out on her porch and began shaking out rugs.

Vincent watched her for a minute, but there was nothing different about Santina. She looked exactly the same, as if Wednesday night had never happened.

In the kitchen, her father and mother were sitting down to eat. "And Judy?" he asked heavily.

"She had a late breakfast," her mother said. "What's the matter, something happened at temple?"

The colored woman had walked out of sight, and Vincent wondered what Clara was doing today. As she began to stack the pile for school, she wondered what Clara's church (Manny's, too!) looked like inside. Did the men sit downstairs, the women upstairs, like in *shul?*

"Today my mother sat in our temple for the last time," her father said. "Tomorrow she leaves. All day—I can't believe it!"

"Abe," her mother said quickly, "can you stop the ocean? The sun? All her life she did exactly what she wanted to."

"All her life."

Vincent heard her father's voice turn into the plaintive, weak one she hated so: "And her children followed. Wherever she went, whatever she did. She led us to America. Then here, from New York. Who will lead us now?"

"Abe, at least she will die in Palestine. Can't you think of that? My father and mother—may they rest in peace—it was their dream all their lives to go there, to die at home. I remember when I was still a girl how they talked of only that. How many people can make such a dream come true? Only your mother! How did my family die—when a Hitler came into existence? Not in the Homeland, believe me!"

"Yes," her father said, his voice choked, "she was always able to get what she wanted. A strong woman. The strongest person I have ever known."

Strong, Vincent thought with scorn. Sure, so strong that she can keep Manny from being born? People from saying his name? Right here, in our own house—nobody can say his name?

She stared out the window at Jules' long, skinny body on the swing. She wanted to talk to him, ask him. . . . Well, what if Manny ever wanted to go to this Homeland everybody got so excited about? They wouldn't even let him in, would they? The way they wouldn't let him into *shul*.

God damn it! she thought, if Manny came up on our porch and rang the bell Pa wouldn't let him in. Or even answer the bell! Like that *Schwartze* on Valenti's porch.

She listened with a sneer as her father said, "The whole family will take her to the train tomorrow."

Yeah? she thought. Not Shirley or Manny. Or even Nate. Not me!

She slipped out of the house, closing the door soundlessly. Then she jumped effortlessly over the short porch railing, landed on the driveway, and ran in her tennis shoes toward the side door. In a second, she was inside the hall and on her way down the stairs.

In the always dusky, cool basement, she ran across the floor to the

218

trunk and opened it, holding her breath against the strong odor of mothballs. She groped past the pictures and prayer shawl until she found the big, ragged book. When she had it out, and open on the edge of the trunk, she struck a match.

The list of names shimmered in the light, and the book looked very solid and thick. The blank part of the page swam up at her as she thought of the Grandmother's departure tomorrow—never to be back. A strong woman.

The match burned out, and Vincent carried the open Bible over to the washtubs, where some light came down through the high, cobweb-covered windows. Again she stared at the names.

Suddenly she took the pen from her blouse pocket. Very carefully, in her best school writing, she wrote under the last spidery name on the page: "Emmanuel O'Brien."

An excitement, like a shock of delight, came into her as she saw his name there, part of the list. Gee, Shirley's pen writes nice! she thought.

Then, in that painstaking way, she wrote: "Shirley V. O'Brien (Manny's mother)."

Then, without pausing, she wrote the next name: "Judith Vincent."

She blew on the ink to dry it. The new names, inked in so darkly on the page, made her heart beat very fast. They looked so permanent. Hers, too; her name looked—nice.

For a second she thought of Nate, instantly said to herself: No, let that bastard take care of himself. He went away, didn't he? From all of us.

Then she had to think of Johnnie. A troubled frown came to her face as she studied the entire list of names. How could she put him in? Manny was half Jewish. (Hi, little half-and-half!) But Johnnie? (Oh, God, that our Shirley could marry a goy! A Jewish girl—she is as if dead now!)

Better not, Vincent thought as every memory of her father and the Grandmother loomed like a threat. It's a Jewish book.

She capped her pen, clipped it back into her pocket. She took another gloating look at the three new names, staring longest at Manny's, then she carried the Bible back to the trunk.

In a few minutes she was upstairs, out on the driveway. Taking a deep, exultant gulp of the heat and the glaring sunlight, she ran across the street to Jules, making the porch in two jumps—the *kuter*, the strong one!—and rushed toward his grin.

"Hey, you're on the porch again," she cried, and perched on the railing near him, balanced herself skillfully.

"Sure, I grew the right heart in the night," he said. "You did it yesterday, you know that? Did you ever think you'd be medicine for a guy?"

She laughed. She had never felt so strong and sure, not even when the gang had jumped to her slightest order. Teetering on the railing, she looked at his red notebook on the table, surrounded by books and pencils, the bottles of medicine, the halves of an orange. The red notebook; well, she had a book of her own now, too! Would she ever tell him about the names in her Bible?

"Hey, changeling," Jules said, "what are you looking so happy about?"

Because I wrote in his name, she wanted to shout. And Shirley's, too—mine. So let the Grandmother go to her old Homeland! Who gives a damn?

"Because you're better, I guess," she said.

"God, it's wonderful to be out in the world again," Jules said, his head back on the pillows, his eyes closed. "Even the heat feels different."

Mrs. Golden came out on the porch, stood for a moment with her hands on her hips and surveyed the street.

"How do you like that?" she said placidly. "Not one *Schwartze*. They're resting up for the parade—tomorrow's Sunday!"

She looked fondly at Jules. "Papa and Becky both fell asleep after eating. You should see them, Juley—side by side on the bed. You want some grape juice, darling?"

"Later, Ma," he said, his eyes still closed. "It feels good just to be here. Not even move."

Mrs. Golden turned triumphant eyes on Vincent. "How do you like him today?" she said. "Look how he's better, even in this hot weather. On the porch. Like anybody. It's for the New Year—a sign."

"Sure," Jules muttered with a smile. "And God looked down on East 120th. And God said: 'For the coming High Holy Days, Jules

Golden will walk the earth like any man.' Come on, Ma, I'll walk you to *shul*."

She laughed. "Listen to him. I always know when he feels better. He hollers, he talks like a *goy*, he makes my life miserable."

Jules' eyes popped open. His mother and he grinned at each other.

"Well, Judy, you'll see," she said smugly. "Soon he'll be all better and we'll go to Florida. Heidi's in the kitchen, reading a new bunch of books the mailman brought today. We're all ready. Today I can look at him and feel how we're all ready. It's a New Year's present!"

Vincent smiled calmly. She knew better; Jules would never, never go away from the street, or from her.

Mrs. Golden came to the swing, straightened Jules' blanket. There was deep contentment in her face as she swept the street with slow, sure glances.

"*Nu*, Judy," she said, "your mother is all ready for *Rosh Hashonah?* The house is clean enough for the biggest Jewish holidays of the whole year?"

Vincent saw the sudden slyness in her eyes, a veiled amusement that made her think of the cruel thing in Jules' eyes sometimes. The word "Jewish" had been stressed in such a way that she was immediately on guard.

"Sure, I guess so," she said.

"Your whole family is going to *shul?*" Mrs. Golden asked with a broad smile.

Vincent's heart plunged: was she actually talking about Shirley and Johnnie? What if she made a crack about Manny?

"Well, well," Jules said with relish, "listen to the religious woman. She goes to *shul* once a year, on *Yom Kippur*, so this makes her an expert."

"Shut up," his mother said calmly. "The worst Jews in the world go on that day, so I shouldn't go? Gangsters, gamblers, even Al Zigman. Even Ziggy, when he wasn't in jail. Maybe he goes even in jail. They got rabbis there—I read it in the paper."

Vincent had a flashing picture of Dave's sad eyes, unmasked, and wondered for the first time if his brother Ziggy hurt in his heart when people made cracks, like Shirley and Manny hurt in hers. Her hand slipped into her blouse pocket, and secretly she touched her shining pen.

Then Mrs. Golden was attacking her again with a sly, probing question. "Judy, your brother is coming from New York for *Yom Kippur?*"

"Well, I don't know," Vincent muttered, and got down from the railing. She dreaded further questions. Don't let her, she thought frantically. Don't let her say it, dear Lord, kind Lord, gracious Lord!

But the questions came, with cruel, hidden laughter in the voice: "Your sister and her family—they'll be by you for the holidays? To eat with your father and mother after the fast? The baby? The—uh— Shirley's husband?"

Vincent stared at her, hung on hard in her mind to the names in her Bible, the new names she had written in her best handwriting.

"Ma, you sound like the rabbi's wife," Jules said, his voice as cruel as hers had been. "Are you clean? Have you washed out the sin of Santina from your street for the New Year, O Sister Golden?"

His mother's face darkened. "Don't think we forgot that, my little wise man! Nobody talks about her, but it's in every heart like a rusty nail. Parents don't forget such a thing."

"Cheer up, parent," he said. "The New Year will fix everything, if you pray. Heidi will find a doctor for a husband. Alex will turn into a smart, good boy. Becky will never cry again. And I—I will climb mountains and write books and bring you home six beautiful grand-children—"

He stopped as she winced. A split second later, she laughed tremulously. "Listen to him! Every word is golden. This is a sick boy? Never! Not while he calls his own mother names."

She leaned to smooth his hair. "I'll go in. You're warm enough?"

"God keeps me roasting, Sister Golden," he said.

With another uneasy laugh, she went into the house. As the door crashed, Jules said, "Listen, Vincent! She doesn't mean it, you know. She just likes to hear herself talk."

It was not Mrs. Golden's face that hung in Vincent's senses, but a mysterious face of shame, dark and fleshy, the eyes narrowed with laughter. And she thought despairingly of the Bible, of the names she had added to all those others. Her feeling of joy, of strength and sureness, had gone like a puff of wind as soon as the woman had started to insult Shirley and Manny.

"Why do they hate everybody who isn't Jewish?" she stammered. "She—damn it, *your* mother!"

"Come on, don't be that way," Jules said urgently. "She didn't mean anything. She—well, it's the parents against the kids. Old-fashioned notions against—just think about changelings."

"Crap!" she said savagely.

"No kidding, Vincent. I mean, look how your grandmother goes to Palestine and to my mother it's like God handed her a present. And then—well, look at my brother. What's 'Jew' to him? Nothing. But Alex would kill five *Schwartzes* in a row before he'd let them move upstairs. It's her fears in his blood. Her—her tears."

He tried to smile. "See? I made you a poem."

Her hands clenched tighter. "This whole New Year's stuff! Yeah —your mother, too. What's she so excited about? Clean the house, clean the street! My grandmother'll be in Palestine for the Day of Atonement. So what? She wouldn't even *look* at Manny when I brought him up on the porch."

"Sure," Jules said doggedly, "but you got yourself a new friend out of the whole mess. A *Schwartze*—and the hell with parents and your grandmother, and their stupid reasoning. You won, didn't you?"

She looked at him with such desperation that a sick, depressed feeling spurted through him. He wondered bitterly how this kid had managed to give him all that hope yesterday, that elated feeling that she had touched hands with a black girl and—presto!—the world was changing.

"What the hell was your mother laughing at?" Vincent demanded.

Jules looked at her coldly. His heart was wallowing in self-pity by now as he remembered the false strength and laughter of yesterday. Damn it, she had come to him and shown him what he wanted of his own mother, his own self! Why was she taking it all away from him today?

"Go ask her," he said sullenly. "Go in there and tell her you're going to change the world, she should stop laughing."

Vincent held herself from running away. She could not bear the helpless way in which she permitted people to laugh at a little boy. She could not bear to think that it had not done Manny or Shirley any good to join their names to the family list in a holy book.

223

"What's that, a joke?" she said, sneering to hide her feelings.

"Sure," he said. "Everything's a joke—I just forgot about yesterday. Was that a joke, too? That you thumbed your nose at the street and made friends with a *Schwartze* girl?"

She stared at the clamorous pulse of anger in his throat, at the blinking eyes that suddenly were just like his mother's—prying, sarcastic, cruelly amused.

"Sure, that was a joke," she said. "You want it to be a joke?"

"God damn it!" he shouted. "What's the matter with you? You got a friend—stick up for her! Talk the same two days in a row."

They glared at each other. "So how is your *Schwartze* girl friend?" he said cuttingly.

"Go ask her!" The thought of Clara was just another burden, like Manny and Shirley.

"Some changeling. Thought you were pals with this girl. What were you doing yesterday, just trying to impress me? Bet you made up the whole pretty story."

"Hey, you calling me a liar?" Vincent stammered.

"Well, you certainly talked different yesterday! What did you do—get cold feet about that girl? What do you think you're doing to me?"

To Vincent's horror, her eyes filled with tears. She lunged away from Jules, not hearing his suddenly entreating cry: "Vincent, wait a minute! Where you going?"

She rushed down the porch steps, stumbling as she fought to keep her crying inside. Suddenly she found herself over the lip of the Gully; she had run there blindly. She slowed down and wiped her eyes, glanced about to see if anybody was there to watch her cry.

The Gully looked empty. She found herself headed for the clubhouse, thinking with a sharp yearning of the old days when she had been the acknowledged leader in a fast, clear-cut world. She began to walk fast as she remembered those simple days of fun and excitement, the time before questions had begun to rip her to pieces.

Vincent was running now, her eyes wet again. She was peering for the first sight of the clubhouse, the fireplace, the happy free time. Around the last bend, into the familiar cleared space; and there—as if Jules' angry, distrustful outburst had dragged her here—was Clara. She stopped abruptly, for a second not believing the girl was real.

224

Clara had built a little fire in the fireplace, was standing over it and poking at the wood with one of the gang firesticks. At the sound of footsteps, she looked up quickly, instantly on guard. Then a shy grin came as she saw who it was.

"Hi, *schwartze kuter*," she called in her comical Yiddish. "I sure was wishing you'd get here. Today—I knew you would today! I brought some potatoes—they're almost done."

It isn't even dark, Vincent thought. How'd she have the nerve to come here in the light?

"How's little half-and-half?" Clara said. "Boy, what a sugar."

The question brought another gush of tears to Vincent's eyes. Clara was walking toward her, smiling eagerly. "Hope you're hungry," she said. "I got eight big fat potatoes in there."

Vincent walked past her quickly, wiped at her eyes with the back of her hand. Then Clara was back at the fire, looking into her face.

"Hey, what's the matter?" she said. "Why are you crying?"

Her concern infuriated Vincent. "Crying? You're nuts."

As the startled eyes studied her, Vincent said roughly, "What the hell do you think you're doing here?"

Clara's face turned expressionless. "I told you," she said slowly. "I brought some potatoes."

"Yeah? You been in the clubhouse! Whose firestick you using?" Vincent grabbed the stick out of Clara's hand. For a second she stared down at the V carved in the stick. The fury—half the same confusing grief and anger which had shoved her from Jules' porch—erupted in her again.

"You've got your dirty nerve," she said.

"Yeah?" Clara said in the slow, guarded way.

"Lay off my stick!" The senseless anger made a roaring in Vincent's ears. "Nobody uses *my* stick! You saw my initial—it's mine. What do you think you're doing, snitching my stuff?"

"What the hell's eating on you?" Clara said.

"Lay off me! Lay off!" Vincent shouted, and kicked wildly at the fire until the potatoes flew out.

"Hey, save your shoes, white folks!" Clara shouted back. "I don't want nothing of yours, hear me?"

Vincent stopped. The hatred in Clara's voice had come through the roaring anger like a jab. Her head ached suddenly. When she stumbled around, Clara was standing like an enemy, a little crouched, her hands in fists.

Her face looked distorted with the same hatred that had been in her voice, but Vincent saw the hurt in her eyes and she stammered, "Hey, listen."

She wanted to tell Clara what a crazy thing had happened: she had hollered and cursed her because of Jules. No, because of the Grandmother and Manny! Because people laughed at babies and beloved sisters. Because—look!—because she had written in the names and nothing was different. Nothing!

"Listen, yourself," Clara said. "You take your clubhouse and stick it! You take your fireplace and stick it, girl! Because I don't want it. I don't want nothing of yours, hear?"

At the heart of that brown face, it's jaw clenched with disdain, was the hurt. Vincent could almost touch it in Clara's eyes, its open rawness.

"I'm going, all right," Clara said. "Don't worry, white folks, I won't bother you in school, either. If I see you coming, I'll go the other way. Where it smells better!"

She jumped over the smoldering fire. Then, her body scornful in every line, she sauntered across the cleared space. She took her time and she did not look back once, though Vincent begged her with all her heart.

Clara disappeared into the turning, and Vincent thought numbly: school? Sure, they would be going to the same school. Monday, the day after tomorrow.

She glanced at the clubhouse. It looked abandoned, like some little toy house she had never seen before. Once she had planned to bring Manny here, let him sit in the club, some day teach him the running, jumping, tackling, punching skills of the gang. The *kuter* and the kitten. Hi, *schwartze kuter*, how's little half-and-half?

Vincent's head ached intensely as she remembered Clara and Manny together that night. The world was swollen with secret reasons for cursing, for slamming doors in people's faces. That night on the porch, the Grandmother sitting like a dead person while Pa and Manny. . . .

All of a sudden she had the stunned feeling that she understood the old woman. That night, the Grandmother must have wanted to put her arms around Manny and hated him and loved him and wanted to cry—all at the same time.

Like me just now with Clara, she thought incredulously. Why did I do it? Why did the Grandmother do it with Manny?

She walked slowly toward the stick she had thrown away. She picked it up, rubbed her finger over the V. Clara had chosen this stick to use, out of the whole bunch in the clubhouse. She had brought eight potatoes. Nobody could eat eight big fat potatoes by herself, so she had brought enough for Vincent, too—like a party. With nerve enough to come while it was still light, to act as if it was okay, like it was a party. . . .

A party? And suddenly Vincent remembered that today was Clara's birthday. I didn't even say anything, she thought heartbrokenly. Happy birthday or anything. She thinks I forgot.

# Chapter fifteen

Three weeks later, the heat was still pressing down on the street. On this Sunday afternoon every porch was full, most of the lawns were being sprinkled or languidly weeded. The walkers had no need to come up and ring a bell; the shake of a head, the "No rooms here!" came to them as they paused on the sidewalk in front of a house.

The empties were well guarded. Mr. Zigman sat on his porch swing, and Dave and Chip were boxing on the lawn. At the Golden house, where Jules lay on the swing, Mr. Golden sprinkled and Becky dipped her hands into the flow from the hose, or tried to catch the gushing water. At the Valenti house, as Santina hung over the railing and watched the boxers across the street, the old woman in black weeded her lawn with a short, stubby tool.

Vincent sat on the top step of her porch and watched Dave punch so hard that his jaw quivered. His face was furious and sweaty in the bright sunshine as he created fast, dancing steps, but at each violent movement of his arms she could hear him crying inside: "Ma, Ma, don't die!"

The usual audience had assembled on the Zigman sidewalk, but it was too hot for wisecracks. Even Moe Levine had very little to say. The boxers themselves danced in silence, except for the padded smack of a glove hitting and the heavy breathing puffing out of them. Every once in a while one of Dave's blows landed, and then Chip grunted: "Nice going, champ."

Swings creaked in the heavy, still air. Vincent heard her mother say, "But what does Dr. Palay say?"

"She will not have him," Mr. Zigman said. "I think she has given up. She lies there."

Their gloomy Yiddish was part of Dave's furious dance, too, and Vincent wished all three would beat it and leave him alone; but her father said, "When a woman like that stays in bed. . . . Who ever saw her even sit down, until late at night?"

"It is the heat," her mother said with a sigh.

"I can't remember such weather," Mr. Zigman said. "Here it is, after the holidays. At home, it is almost past the harvest by now."

"Will you ever forget the Day of Atonement?" her father said. "The temple was like a sweatbox. I was glad my mother was not here."

Then he added casually, "Zigman, here comes another Black One."

A woman had halted near the little crowd watching the boxers. Without getting up from the swing, Mr. Zigman called: "Hey, no rooms here, lady."

She moved on, toward the Gully, and Vincent watched her brown face go past—expressionless, like Clara's had been when she had grabbed the firestick from her on her birthday.

Funny! Vincent thought. It was just as if Clara had disappeared out of the world that day in the Gully. She had watched for the disdainful brown face at school, she had looked for her every time she had gone to Shirley's apartment, had taken a careless walk into the Gully evening after evening. But there was no Clara anywhere. Sometimes she felt as if she had dreamed the few meetings, the briefly flaring friendship and closeness—except that there was the medal in her treasure box. And there was the name, "half-and-half," to whisper to Manny when she was alone with him, and the question gushing up in her: "Clara's mother, her father, her aunt?" each time a Negro walked in the street, looking for empties.

Members of the gang lounged in the crowd on the Zigman side-

228

walk, and she could have dreamed their faces, too, all the days of adventure, the candlelit evenings of planning raids on stores. Leo, Angelo, Joey, Dan, Alex; there they stood, watching their new leader punch.

On his porch, Jules lay back against his hill of pillows, the library book closed on a finger to mark his page. He watched Vincent, the figure in white blouse and pants and tennis shoes, hunched on a porch. She looked withdrawn from the entire street, as lonely as he felt for her.

In the three weeks since their quarrel she had come to see him a few times, but she had seemed very different. He had read her a new poem, had had only silence from her where always, in the past, a new poem had ripped words from her. She had said nothing about her nephew, her friend Clara, not one word of the inside girl behind the little, freckled poker face.

His mother came out on the porch, stared up and down the street with her owner's eye. "Ah hah," she said, "the parade has started. God, if only people worked on Sundays, too."

"Do you have to say the same thing every Sunday?" Jules said, but he was too dispirited to carry it further.

"Herman," Mrs. Golden said to her husband, "a lot of *Schwartzes?*"

"Enough," he said, and suddenly played the hose over Becky's wrists, smiling at her delighted laugh.

"Look at the *spunyitze*," Mrs. Golden said. "She doesn't even give them a chance to open their mouths and ask her. Becky isn't too wet?"

"In this heat, can you get too wet?" her husband said. "Should she take off her shoes?"

"No. She'll step on a nail or glass." Leaning over the railing, Mrs. Golden called toward the boxing tableau: "Alex, don't you want eat?"

"Later," he yelled back.

"Herman," Mrs. Golden said, "did Herb Miller come with his little girl? While I was inside?"

"Don't you see Sam Miller is on the porch? Herb wouldn't come."

She looked toward the corner wistfully. "I miss the old Mrs. Vincent this time on Sundays. The way she would sit—a queen, a mother to all of us—on that porch."

"Me, too. It felt good just to look across the street."

"So was Al Zigman here yet?"

"Not yet. She's still so sick that he would come every day?"

"Terrible," she said. "That I should live to see Fanny Zigman lay down and wait to die. She never sat in her life."

Mr. Golden frowned, played the hose over Becky's hands. "Maybe," he said uneasily, "she rented out her upstairs and now she's afraid?"

"Rented to *them?* Herman, are you crazy? The woman has cancer —everybody is saying it. All right, to us the *Schwartzes* are a cancer, but don't take a joke too far."

Jules' eyes closed. He felt exhausted with the steady, day-after-day sameness of the words which came so mechanically from his parents. The Negroes walking in the street, from empty to empty, exhausted him today, too. Sometimes he felt trampled all over his body by those stubborn steps approaching so eagerly, departing so reluctantly.

The screen door slammed, and Heidi came out with a glass of grape juice. Her mother felt the glass, nodded. "Juley, it's cold enough," she said.

"Thanks, just put it down," he muttered.

Heidi put the glass on his table and went to the railing to watch Chip. She loved to see him box, even with a kid. He was so lithe and graceful, a dancer and yet a powerful and muscular man at the same time. Jules, watching her flushed face, felt a bleak pity.

A movement on the Miller porch, across the street, flicked at his eyes. Yes, it was Ruth. She had come out on her porch, beautifully dressed in cool white, her head bare so that he could study her smooth, black, coiled hair, so that he could again visualize the entire head on its lovely column of throat as a living picture out of the Old Testament.

She lingered to talk to her mother and father, sitting on the swing. She looked up the street, her gaze staying for a minute on the boxers, then she walked down the steps and looked up to the porch above, where Ilona Miller stood near the closed railing and held one of her children.

Ruth waved, and the little boy laughed and waved back. They called back and forth to each other, and Ilona pretended to throw him to his aunt, who stood with outstretched arms to catch him. Jules saw

Ruth's smile, heard the child's laughter, and warmth trickled through his bleakness.

As Ruth waved for the last time to her nephew and moved off slowly toward the sidewalk, a middle-aged Negro man in neat Sunday clothes stopped in front of the Valenti house and read the sign on the porch pillar. He took off his hat as he turned eagerly toward the old woman kneeling on her lawn, but before he could shape the words of inquiry she shook her head and said loudly: "Hey, we got no."

He blinked at her accented voice, then he noticed Santina leaning over the railing. He smiled, stepped into the little walk leading to the porch and said, "How do, Miss. I see you got a sign out for rooms to rent."

Mrs. Valenti pushed herself up, in such an alarmed flurry that her long black skirt was tangled and held by her shoes. Santina shook her head at the man, but he came on toward the porch, holding his hat, still smiling.

"Could I see those rooms upstairs, Miss?" he said, and started up the porch steps. "My family sure can use some nice big rooms."

A flood of Italian clanged in the air, so frightened and shrill that everybody in the street turned instantly to see what was happening. The boxing stopped. Ruth stopped, a few feet from the crowd on the Zigman sidewalk. On every porch, men and women leaned over railings to stare.

"My God," Mrs. Golden cried, "what's with the *spunyitze?*"

The woman was running, her weeder clutched like a weapon, and the man was all the way up on the porch. "Ross! Ross!" she screamed.

As the street watched, Ross Valenti rushed out the front way and immediately got between the man and Santina, pushed his sister back so hard that she almost fell.

"What do you want?" he shouted.

At that wild movement of protection, at his question like an accusation, the street had an instantaneous picture of Santina and a black man lying in the Gully.

Another rush of Italian came from Mrs. Valenti, who stood near the bottom step now. The Negro looked at her with puzzled eyes, looked back at Ross, and pointed to the sign.

"That lady don't understand English, I guess," he said patiently,

231

smiling again. "You got a sign out for rooms. I'm looking for rooms for my family. Could I see your upstairs, Mister?"

"Get out of here!" Ross shouted in a choked voice.

"It's empty, ain't it?" The man sounded surprised. "You got a sign out says it's empty."

"You getting off my porch?" Ross demanded savagely. "No colored here! Get out!"

"Why don't you take down that sign?" the man cried. "You got no business putting it up if you're going to—"

Ross pushed at him, so violently that the man fell against the narrow railing near the steps, and his hat dropped from his hand and rolled down the steps.

"Hey, what's the matter with you?" he said to Ross as he rubbed his bruised back. "You better cut that out, Mister."

Ross punched his face. Suddenly blood gleamed in the sunlight, trickling from the man's nose. A second later, the two were fighting, grappling, their grunts and curses audible on every porch and lawn.

A dreamlike, thrilling moment came to many of the watchers as they saw the battle they had been fighting so long in secret, now abruptly in the open. The air throbbed as if their own hidden emotions had burst out and shattered in the hot sunshine. After the months of inner violence, it was like enormous, soaring relief to see actual bodies struggling, to hear the curses and outcries they had stifled so long.

Ross was giving the Negro a lot of punishment, but the shorter, older man fought back doggedly. Though the blows sent him reeling down two or three steps several times, he panted back to the porch, clutching and wrestling until he was up there solidly enough to trade punches again. The afternoon sunlight showed the street his curled-tight black hair, a sweating brown face with blood very red on his lips and chin.

Only a few minutes had gone by. Vincent, nailed to the top step, could not look away from Clara's father-brother-uncle being beaten to a bleeding pulp. Dave, standing in a trance on his lawn, felt his stomach rocking with the nausea of panic. The explosion—here it comes! he thought. Run, where's Ma, run! His arms felt numb, the boxing gloves hung like big weights at his side.

Only a few minutes. . . . Alex Golden stared at that porch. He

232

could see Santina's eyes as she crouched near the punching and the bleeding and the hard, tight excitement. Their eyes said it for both of them. He knew how her whole body felt, right now—just like his —right now, as if they were touching, right across the punching and the blood and the *spunyitze* screaming her head off.

Only a few minutes: Jules cried out as the fighting began: "No! No, don't do it!" He was half off the swing, his eyes back on Ruth's face from the bloody, brown one a porch over. He saw Ruth stop, her face so frightened it looked like a different woman's. He struggled to run, to help her, to help the man. He was staggering toward the steps when his mother seized his shoulders, supporting his weaving body with hers.

"Juley, no," she cried. "You'll kill yourself. God, look how white he is! Come, lay down."

He stared into her face, still trying desperately to run as she held him. "Ma, go help that poor man! Show some decency. Go help him."

"What?" Mrs. Golden said fearfully. "We can't mix in. Lay down, Juley. God, look how he's sweating!"

"Help him!" Jules bellowed. "Don't be dogs. Pa! Heidi! Alex! Go help him, for God's sake!"

The whole street heard him. Nailed to her step, Vincent heard him, and the fast, imploring words began spurting through her head: Dear Lord, kind Lord, gracious Lord, I pray Thou wilt look on all I love. . . .

Ruth heard Jules. A dizziness broke over her like a wave of that past which was always nipping at her mind. The thick books in English, the word "culture," the smug and snobbish language she had learned for social evenings, all were submerged by the compulsive wave. She was the little, frantic immigrant again, the child caught between fairy tales and hunger of body and heart, and yet she was the woman of the present moment, too, so that child and woman made the dialogue of pain within her as she stared across the street.

No! This, *this* is America. Chip, I was wrong! The banana—the sweet, hidden fruit— Dad! Dad, stop them! Herbie, help me, make them stop! Chip, I lied to you! Here is the truth—the other America. Oh, you knew! Your eyes knew when I talked of home—the place every drifter in the world wants to call home. With tears and fists, his own heart's desire. Well, here are the fists! My God, look how Amer-

233

ica crumbles, while the drifters themselves watch! Where is home now? Dad, Herb! Stop them! Chip, you stop them!

Ruth whirled, to run back to the safety of her house. Searching for the familiar family faces on the two porches, she saw her father's at once, excited and gloating; then her mother's, the petulant, fretful expression changed into one of wrath, of queer satisfaction. She stopped, looked up. Ben's face was pale, thoughtfully quiet, as if it hung like a rabbi's over a foreordained act of God; Ilona's was frightened but fascinated.

Her mind clogged with her dizzying confusion. Dad, she thought, you look like a *goy!* Dad, please, they're beating Herbie! Why are you happy?

As she stared, horrified, the faces of her family seemed like the village faces out of her childhood, the faces of the gentiles, called the *goyim* by the village Jews. She searched for Herb's face among the gloating, excited, vengeful expressions of her family. Where was Herbie! She turned back, looking for him on the Valenti porch. Was it Herbie being beaten up there? Herbie, again? With his own father, his mother and brother, fantastically changed into the *goyim* who used to catch Jews and beat them when they wandered into the wrong streets?

One of Ross's blows landed directly on the man's face, sent him backwards off the porch. He tottered onto the first step down, then fell past the others, a choked scream of panic torn from him as he groped for something to hang onto, something to break his fall. The scream cut off as he struck the cement walk and lay still.

The blood on his face glistened very brightly in the sunlight. On the porch, Santina's head went down on the railing, her face hidden in her arms. Ross, panting hard, stood at the edge of the steps and looked blankly down at the man. Mrs. Valenti was voiceless at last as she clutched her weeder, and in the street there was an instant of thick, sucked-in silence.

In that instant Ruth was back inside the day Herb had been attacked by a group of the village peasants. There had been rocks and heavy chunks of wood in their hands that hot, sunny afternoon. Herb's face had been boyish and smiling one second, gushing blood a second later. "Ruthie, run!" he had shouted, without turning to look at her.

She had been four years old, and she and Herb had gone on a

234

berry-hunting trip to the outskirts of town, where the fields stretched like a green, rippling dreamland before a little girl. That morning, their mother had gone off to work at the big house, looking like a pretty, young gypsy in her full, gay skirt, with a strip of the same material binding her hair. She had taken Ben along, as she sometimes did, to help her in the kitchen.

Herb's tense, watchful face was stained with the berries they had eaten earlier. His hands, up in fists, were stained, too. "Little sister, run home!" he had cried again, and a great plank of wood had come down against his cheek, opening it as if someone had sliced his face with a knife. Blood fountained out of Herb's face as he screamed; there was just red in the sunlight, instead of his laughing eyes, instead of his hair and nose and chin. He fell dead. All the laughing *goyim* sauntered away, and the little girl screamed, "Father, Father!"—calling to the fairy-tale figure of strength and nobility she had never seen except in the beautiful stories told her so often.

The wise, strong, loving father had not come. The little girl had crept closer to the dead brother who had been her laughter and singing in life, her finder of tidbits and giver of toys. She had thrown herself on him, hiding and holding, until he had stirred and sat up groggily, somehow alive again.

In that one instant in the American street, the pretentious mannerisms and the empty values Ruth had made for herself were wrenched from her as if that tiny, frightened girl had clutched them away. And it was like starting all over again, stepping from the boat in a shabby, foreign dress, looking for the fabulous land Herb had told of in the fairy tales, waiting for the first sight of the fabulous father. Except that she was the grown woman, too, and now the face of a gloating *goy* was her father's face, and the grown Ruth struggled with the little Ruth to find Herb's face in that bloody, brown one on the sidewalk.

Herbie! Herbie! In her mind, she was screaming his name.

Then somebody was supporting her, holding her with strong arms so that she would not fall. It was Chip, not Herbie. It was Chip, saying softly, "All right, I'm here. Stop it—stop calling my name that way. I'm here, I've got you—it's okay now."

For Vincent, who had heard Clara's father-brother-uncle call out in fear as he plunged backward to the sidewalk, that instant went on

235

forever as she sat staring at the motionless-like-dead body. Then, terribly, it was like seeing her father lying there, the short stocky body, the middle-aged face with lines of worry in the forehead even now, even dead in the sunlight. Only her father's face was brown, like Clara's. If I'm late he'll give me hell in a wheelbarrow . . . hi, little half-and-half; hi, changeling; hi, *schwartze kuter*; hi, little half-and-half; hi. . . .

Vincent took the porch steps in one leap, was running toward the sidewalk.

"Judy!" her mother screamed.

A choked, startled call came from her father, and on the upstairs porch Mrs. Levine cried piercingly: "That girl, my God, where is she going?" but Vincent kept running, past Ruth and Chip, seeing the big, padded gloves incongruous against the delicate white dress as he held Ruth in his arms.

She was cutting across the street toward that flung body on the Valenti walk, running as fast as she could; and Jules, on his porch, felt her all through him like a shock of life—that taut, freckled face, the dark hair tousled over intent eyes, that clenched body and hands and jaw.

His eyes closed. Oh God, he thought, thanks, thanks!

Then, suddenly, Dave was running across the street after Vincent, trying to unknot his boxing gloves with his teeth. He was on solid ground again; that first glimpse of Vincent running—the familiar figure in pants, the fast, daring leader of all the fighting and snitching years—was like knowing, for the first time since the break-up of the gang, where he belonged.

When he got to Vincent she was kneeling beside the man, digging for her handkerchief, saying: "Hey, come on, get up. Come on, Mister, I'll help you get up."

"Vincent!" Dave said, kneeling by her.

They looked into each other's eyes intently, sharing a togetherness again that held all the old freedom and gladness of companionship, all the fiercely shared danger.

"Help me get these damn gloves off," Dave said.

She fumbled the strings loose, and he flung off the gloves so violently that they flew onto the lawn, falling near Mrs. Valenti, who had backed away from the fallen man.

Vincent was wiping the man's face with her handkerchief. Dave shook his shoulder gently. "Should I get water?" he said.

"Stick around," she answered. "They wouldn't give us any water."

Dave saw the man's hat, scooped it up, and began fanning air across his face; and Vincent said, "Yeah, that's good."

Carefully, she wiped each streak of blood on the brown face. "He's starting to move. Give him some more air, Dave."

The man's eyes opened. He blinked up at the two kneeling figures. "That a boy," Dave muttered, and Vincent said, "If we pick up his head a little, huh?"

They raised the man slowly to a sitting position. Dave fanned him again, and Vincent said, "Don't worry, Mister, we'll help you get up."

She dabbed at a bloody spot she had missed on his chin, and the man winced and smiled at the same time as he attempted to push himself up from the walk. Immediately, Vincent and Dave jumped up, leaned, and pulled gently at his arms.

He was standing uncertainly, and Vincent saw that he did not look like her father at all. She brushed some leaves from his jacket, and the man peered at her.

"Thank you, child," he said.

Dave handed him his hat, and the man said, "Thank you, boy."

They watched him walk slowly down the narrow walk, turn into the sidewalk, and go off toward the corner. Then they both became aware of the eyes of the street on them.

"Oh, boy," Dave said under his breath. "We better cop a sneak."

"Hell with them," she muttered back. "Get your gloves, huh? Before the *spunyitze* grabs 'em. Remember how she used to keep our baseball when she got it first?"

Dave swooped down on his boxing gloves. Out of the corner of his eye he saw Ross still standing on the porch, and Santina crying, and the *spunyitze* staring at him two inches away.

"Let's scram home," Vincent said. She was on the sidewalk, the bloody handkerchief balled in one hand, the other hand in her pocket. She had her poker face on, the face he remembered so well from past moments of danger when they were ready to leave a store, their pockets jammed with loot.

"Okay," he said, making it careless.

He joined her, the gloves swinging from one hand. Together, they swaggered across the street. Mr. Zigman was on the lawn, eyes narrowed; his was the first greeting from their world.

"Go in the house," he shouted to his son. "You got a sick mother! You want to kill her?" Then he spat on the lawn. "Pheh!"

"See you," Dave said to Vincent, as if his father was not there.

"See you," she said, and he sauntered past his father, toward his porch.

Vincent walked toward her house. Ruth Miller and Chip had disappeared. She passed Leo and Anna and Louis, standing in a huddled group on the grass strip, their eyes big and scared, as if she had turned into a peculiar stranger. The urine smell wafted out at her as she turned into her yard, but even that did not make anything more real.

Her mother and father, standing on the porch, had shocked, staring faces. Moe Levine was up there, too, leaning on the pillar nearest the steps. He looked at her as if she smelled; from the porch upstairs, his mother muttered: "The black alley cat plays with the Black Ones these days?"

Vincent kept walking in that devil-may-care way toward her side door. She was in the house, up the back steps and into the kitchen. But when she got to the sink she felt funny, as if she were falling. She hung on to the drainboard, discovered the bloody handkerchief in her hand. She stumbled into the bathroom and washed it, hung it on a towel rack to dry, took a drink of water.

The screen door slammed. Vincent heard Moe's whistle, the kind he made sometimes as through clenched teeth, as he rushed to the telephone and dialed a number. He cursed and slammed down the phone, ran out with big, pounding strides, the door slamming. In a dazed way, Vincent wandered into the living room and looked out of a window. Her porch was empty. People stood on the sidewalks in tight clusters. The Valenti porch was empty. Across the street, Mr. Golden stood on his porch and stared toward the corner.

Suddenly Dr. Palay's old black car came careening down the street and jerked to a stop, and Mr. Golden shouted, "Sophie, he's here!"

As the doctor walked rapidly toward the porch, his bag swinging, Vincent saw Moe leave one of the clusters of people and sprint in her direction. She ran back into her bedroom, afraid that he was coming after her with that threatening face. But as she pressed her body against her closed door, she heard him dialing again, heard his tight-
238

jawed whistle as he waited, then: "Let me talk to Al Zigman. Tell him Moe Levine—it's important!"

Vincent sucked air into her lungs, stopped guarding her door. She wandered around numbly for a minute, then she ran to her drawer and pulled out her treasure box. She groped for Manny's picture. As she studied it desperately, she tried to remember the sound of his laugh, the way his strong legs kicked against her when she held him. But all she could think of was Clara, the look of her face in the Gully, on her birthday, her eyes all hurt and hate. "Don't worry, white folks, I won't bother you in school!"

She tried to remember Clara leaning over Manny, saying, "Hi, little half-and-half," but she could not remember that other voice with its eagerness and friendship. She picked up the medal, felt its cool actuality, but it brought only the grief-hate of Clara's eyes, not a memory of the shy grin which had accompanied the gift.

"Al?" Moe said at the telephone. "Moe. Well, it finally happened! A *Schwartze* got beat up here. . . . Ross Valenti. He got sick of the whole thing. This guy came right up on his porch while the *spunyitze* was trying to stop him, and—well, Jesus, after what they did to his sister! And she was right up there on the porch when this guy walked up. What the hell do you expect Ross to do, shake hands?"

Vincent remembered the man's uncertain smile, his soft voice. He had said, "Thank you, child."

Moe's excited voice rolled into her bedroom: "And your kid brother goes over and helps the guy get up! Him and the *kuter*. Can you beat it? How do I know?—maybe this guy gets together a gang and they come back. Beat up on the whole street. Ross knocked the crap out of him, see? So they come back after dark, maybe, and get us, huh?"

Vincent began to shiver.

"Maybe you'd better line up some guys, just in case, huh? I told you—your kid brother and the *schwartze kuter!* Ran over and picked him up like he was a pal or something. Sure."

All of a sudden Vincent was able to remember Clara's other face —the smiling one with which she had said, "Hi, *schwartze kuter.*" And she could remember Clara's other voice, the low intimate one of a friend, saying, "See, I never knew no white kid."

"No," Moe was saying; "just your old man. Your mother never

even came out. Yeah, your brother went right in the house, after."

Vincent hid away her treasure box and stole out of her room, into the kitchen. On tiptoe, as Moe's voice beat in back of her, she left the house by the back door. She had to find Clara; she knew that, now. She had to tell her something—she didn't know what, exactly—about their last meeting in the Gully.

From the driveway, she could see the groups of people in the splashes of late sunlight and shadows now in the street. She could hear the throbbing of the voices as she ran into her back yard and climbed over the fence, dropped into the yard behind hers. In a minute, she was out on East 121st and running toward the corner.

## Chapter sixteen

Now Vincent was in a *Schwartze* street.

Trying to saunter, she put on a rigid poker face as she looked about her. There were mostly colored people either on the porches or sprinkling the lawns; but every once in a while she would see white faces on a porch—no kids, just grownups. She wondered about that for a second until she noticed that everybody seemed to be staring at her. She began to walk faster, her poker face shivering like a loose mask.

There were a lot of colored kids, some of them playing baseball in the middle of the street, others playing kick-the-stick at the curb. Still others were just standing around near the lampposts, dressed in good clothes. She was conscious of all their eyes as she walked along looking for Clara, and kept waiting for a barked-out, cursing challenge, or the sudden rushing attack of one of the groups.

Within her head, a square lit with harsh sunlight held the motionless, bloody man who had been stretched out on the Valenti walk only a short while ago. It was as if a photograph in color had been pasted in her head, and she had to keep looking at it. She wondered if the man lived on this street. Maybe everybody knew about it! And maybe everybody watching her knew she lived on East 120th, where it had happened to the man!

240

She was about halfway down the street when she thought humbly, as her heart rammed thunderous blows into her chest: This the way Clara felt when she came to our Gully? But she never looked scared. . . .

Instead of turning and running back toward the corner, Vincent stopped in front of a cluster of boys and said gruffly, "I'm looking for Clara Jackson. You tell me where she lives?"

They looked her up and down. Then one of them said, "That's that tomboy girl, Chuck's cousin, ain't it?"

"Sure," one of the others said. "She's right down the street. About —let's see—yeah, seven houses. You cross the street, they're in the back. Ain't no bell—go on in the yard, last doorway in."

"Thanks," she said, pretending nonchalance, and crossed the street. Her legs were shaking as she started to count the houses—but nobody had punched out, or ganged up on her, or asked if she lived on East 120th.

Then, like a rush of air into her body, she saw Clara sitting on the bottom step of a front porch, playing chubbies by herself with the knife she had loaned Vincent, that first time in the Gully. Vincent stopped to stare. Clara was wearing a soft, blue dress, white shoes, stockings. She looked different, much older. Vincent looked quickly at the porch behind her to see if there were grownup *Schwartzes* up there, but there was no one.

The sight of the familiar game steadied her. For a while she stood on the sidewalk and watched Clara throwing the knife dexterously into the air and directing it in a perfect plunge downward, so that it hurtled into the grassy earth at her feet and stood quivering, blade half buried. Clara flipped the knife from her thumb, from her shoulder, then—all the ritual steps of the same game they played on East 120th—from her head; and each time the knife made its perfect arch. She was as intent on her movements as if she were in a closed room.

"Hey, Clara," Vincent called finally, in a low voice.

Clara's head jerked up. She looked astounded, pleased. But a second later her eyes went on guard. She did not say one word as Vincent turned into the short walk and came slowly toward her. It was hard to keep moving toward those wary, suspicious eyes. Their last meeting in the Gully, the past weeks of looking for Clara and never finding her except in her head or in her treasure box, made it harder step by step.

There was a clicking noise as Clara shut both blades of her knife.

241

She was standing now, putting the knife in her pocket. She looked taller, very graceful in that dress. In daylight, there was a reddish color in her skin.

"What the hell you think you're doing here?" she demanded.

Vincent stopped. "I'm looking for you," she said, her throat so dry that her voice sounded different.

"Yeah? What for? Why don't you get the hell back where you belong?"

Vincent tried to think what to say. Clara studied her flushed, perspired face. After an instant, she said roughly, "What's the matter? Somebody chase you or something?"

Vincent shook her head.

"The gang beat up on you again? That blond guy who thinks he's so good?" Clara said sullenly.

"No, nothing happened to me." Then words burst from her: "Listen, you got to excuse me! That lousy stuff I pulled on you in the Gully—last time—you know. I didn't mean it. Honest to God! I'm sorry! I been thinking about it every day, and—listen, excuse me, will you?"

She saw bewilderment seeping into Clara's face and she stumbled on: "I went back to the Gully—every day. As soon as it got dark. To see if you'd be there and—and I could tell you."

In a very still voice, Clara said, "I couldn't go back there. Hell, would you?"

Vincent shook her head, said miserably, "After you went away that day, all of a sudden I remembered it was your birthday! I felt twice as bad. Real bad—honest. I didn't even tell you 'Happy Birthday' or anything."

As Clara stared at her, she said, "You believe me?"

"I guess," Clara muttered.

"You believe me when I say excuse me for that time in the Gully?" Vincent said, starting to shiver all over again with the effort to get the yearning out of her. "It means a lot to me if you'd believe me."

Clara took a few hesitant steps toward her. "Yeah?" she said.

"Yeah." Vincent took her own few blind steps toward the girl. Suddenly she cried, "Listen, don't hate me!"

"I don't!" Clara said. Then she thought about it, a puzzled frown

242

coming to her face as she said slowly, "But I did. All of you—the whole damn Gully, your whole street."

"Don't hate me any more," Vincent begged.

Clara thought about it. Then, surprised, she said, "I don't."

They walked toward each other slowly, meeting on the narrow walk. "How's that little half-and-half?" Clara said.

"Fine. He's swell!"

"How's your sick friend?" Clara said, making the second sign that they were friends again.

"He's okay," Vincent said, with a soaring gladness.

"I think about that a lot," Clara said. "You know—that changeling stuff."

"You do?" Vincent said eagerly. "Hey, you want to go up on your porch? Talk or something?"

"Well, it's not mine," Clara said. "My aunt hasn't got a porch. See, we're in the back. They cut up the whole house, kind of. We're way in the back."

"Oh," Vincent said, not understanding.

Carelessly, Clara said, "They don't like it when somebody from the back comes on their stinking old porch. They pay more rent, see? On account of having a porch and a front door. So I figure they can stick their porch. I don't even want to go on it when they're not home."

"Well, you want to take a walk or something?" Vincent said.

"Sure."

They turned into the sidewalk, went off together toward Woodlawn. After they had walked for a few minutes, Clara said, "How do you like my dress? Bet you hardly even recognized me, huh?"

"You look pretty," Vincent said.

"Me?" Clara guffawed with embarrassment. "Well, the hell with it. See, my father likes me to wear it all day Sunday. Sure is a long day! What can you do in a dress?"

"You play a good game of chubbies in a dress," Vincent said, laughing.

Clara gave her a pleased look. "You were watching me, huh?"

"Boy, you'd beat anybody on my street."

They walked in silence for a while. They passed the staring clumps

243

of kids, porch after porch where people sat and watched them. The third time Vincent's eyes swung back from watchers, Clara said with a wicked chuckle, "Feel funny about being on my street?"

"Kind of," Vincent admitted.

"Don't worry," Clara said, swaggering. "I didn't get too palsy with anybody around here—not yet—but nobody'll bother you when I'm around."

"Who in the hell's worried!"

A delighted grin came to the girl's face. "I always was—in your Gully."

They both laughed. Vincent felt wonderful all of a sudden, full of a million things to talk about. "Hey, have you got a lot of homework so far?" she said.

Clara groaned. "That's the toughest school I've ever been at. How about you?"

"Plenty. Takes me until I go to bed, some nights. Especially math. I hate it."

"Me, too. Do you like history?"

"Yeah, a whole lot."

"Me, too," Clara said. "And English—when we read out loud. Those plays. That's when I really like it. That guy Shakespeare."

But she sighed. "I didn't have a chance to do my homework yet. Boy, I hate Sundays. No work—everybody's home. It's so crowded in there. No place to do homework. Yackety-yack, all day, all over the joint."

They turned into Woodlawn, walked toward Shirley's street. "Well, what'll you do?" Vincent asked. "If I couldn't do my homework I'd be plenty worried."

"Oh, I'll do it," Clara said. "Later. The kids go to bed, and everybody gets all through cooking and eating and running back and forth to the bathroom. Then I get the kitchen to myself. Sometimes, if I'm lucky on Sunday, they go somewhere. Dancing or something. It's pretty quiet then."

Vincent thought about that as they walked. She tried to visualize a house so crowded that there was no place to do homework. She tried fitting Clara and her books into her own bedroom, or at the table near the windows in the living room, but she could not visualize that, either.

244

Across the avenue, St. Joseph's loomed, huge and stone, stretching almost a block behind its stone wall, rising in turrets and towers into the air.

"Hey, there's my church," Clara said. "Come on, let's cross, huh?"

And Manny's church, Vincent thought as they cut across between cars. She followed Clara to the open part of the wall, through which the broad steps and the heavy, wooden doors could be seen.

"Pretty, huh?" Clara said proudly. She looked up, until her eyes came to the enormous cross at the very top.

"Yeah," Vincent murmured.

"I think it's the prettiest church in the whole city," Clara said. "It's real old. My father says it's one of the first churches ever built in this city. I just love it. Walking in there—boy!"

Vincent stared at the steps, tried to imagine Manny climbing them some day. "Are there a lot of colored people who're Catholic?" she said absently.

"I don't know," Clara said. "I guess. Why?"

Vincent flushed as she became aware of Clara's intent, cold eyes. "Hey, don't be sore," she said miserably. "I was just wondering. What makes some people be Catholic. I mean—well, how come you are?"

Oddly enough, Clara began to laugh. "That's real easy! My great-grandfather was. See, he was a slave but he was crazy about his master. His master was a Catholic so my great-grandfather decided he'd be one, too."

"A slave?" Vincent said, amazed. The exciting thing happened to her of having history books turn alive.

"Sure," Clara said. "Then after he was freed, he decided to stay Catholic. He came up North and raised his family. It's my father's side. You should hear the stories he can tell about all that stuff. Before he was born, even. After they got up here, they helped a lot of other slaves run away. See, not every master freed his slaves. This guy who owned my great-grandfather, he was a wonderful man. A real Catholic, my father says. He freed all his slaves. Even gave them money and helped them come up North. My grandfather was named after him."

The pages of history books turned fast in Vincent's mind. Clara had just stepped right out of one. So had Manny's religion—one half of it! And she thought of the book that held the other half of Manny.

245

She wanted to show it to Clara, take it out of its hiding place in the basement and open the shabby cover, show her the list of names.

"One thing about our family," Clara said thoughtfully. "My father told me that right away. Said I didn't have to be Catholic if I didn't want to. He said I could choose, just the way my great-grandfather picked what he wanted to be. See, my grandfather decided all for himself, too. And so'd my father. He told me if a slave could pick, so could we."

She nodded as her eyes went back to the church. "I picked it. Then, after a while, I picked going to regular school, too. I wanted to transfer out of parochial, and my father said that was okay—if that's what I decided."

Slaves! Vincent thought. When I show her that Bible some day, she can see all those pictures, too. Does she know how a lot of guys in Russia ran away from the army there, and came here? That's like slaves!

She thought of one of Ma's stories that she could tell Clara some day. The family had picked America to go to. On the boat it was Passover, and all the Jews had made a Seder supper, a great big one, and then the very next day they saw the Statue of Liberty. All the Jews began to sing that important Jewish song, "Hatikvah"—all except Ma. She was so overcome by the Seder on the ocean, and then by the sudden beauty of the Statue of Liberty, that she began to cry. And then the Grandmother came over to her and hollered: "Is this a time for tears? Sing, you stupid girl—we have escaped from starvation and tyranny, passed over into a golden land. Sing!"

But, remembering that story and the way her mother had smiled at her young, sentimental self as she had told it, Vincent now thought quietly: So how come the Grandmother went to Palestine? If she called this a golden land, and called Ma dumb for crying when she saw it for the first time?

She stared at the church, Manny's church. Would he choose it, too, some day, when he was big enough to pick a God and prayers? Would he cry because the other door was slammed in his face? Would he want the solemn *shul* chant that he was not permitted to hear? Then she would show him the Bible! She would point to his name, among all the others!

246

"What's the matter?" Clara said. "You look like you're going to cry or something."

"Who, me?" Vincent said dazedly.

"Yeah. What's the matter?"

"Nothing." Then Vincent said abruptly, "Do you know what all the prayers are in your church?"

"What?" Clara said, puzzled.

"I mean—well, do you understand all those Catholic things they say in there?"

"The prayers? You mean, do I understand about Jesus?"

"Yeah, maybe that's what I mean." With wonder, Vincent saw the affection and tenderness in Clara's eyes, as if she were speaking of a person, somebody she was crazy about.

"Sure I do. I know all about my Lord."

Clara's words tipped off others in her mind: Dear Lord, kind Lord, gracious Lord. Yeah, and if Manny wanted to pick her prayer some day—when he was choosing God and prayers?

"Is your church pretty inside, too?" she said.

"Boy, is it?" Clara said. "Want to go in and see?"

"Me? I don't know! I—well, is that okay?"

"Sure," Clara said. "There won't be too many people this time of day. But I'll tell you what—we'll just kind of look in. We haven't got hats on, and—well, you're wearing pants. Know what I mean?"

"Oh, sure," Vincent muttered uneasily.

"Come on." Clara led the way toward the stone steps.

It was a journey into the secret heart of Manny-land. Vincent climbed the steps slowly. Inside the heavy doors was a kind of narrow, long hallway. She saw stone statues, little fat candles burning. From the corner of her eye, she caught tag-ends of movements from Clara: fingers dipped into—what, water? Clara's hand made a quick gesture in front of her as she seemed to bob up and down. When Vincent looked away from these half-seen mysteries, she became aware of the dark, glowing wood of walls, heavy stone insets. It was so quiet, so—solid.

"Come on," Clara said. "Let's look in, huh?"

She held open one of the double inner doors, and Vincent peered into a huge, shadowy place. There was a high, high ceiling, there were long windows of colored glass that made the late sunshine quiet as it came through. There were life-size statues that made her think of the trip to the Art Museum her class had taken. Down at the front there was the gleam of velvet, of golden objects. Amazed, she recognized vases of flowers down there. She saw three women kneeling, their backs motionless as the statues. There was the shine of a cross, glittering even in the shadowy light. Her eyes flicked back and forth: seats, aisles, stone pillars soaring up toward that high ceiling, little curtained alcoves at that wall, the muted gleam of metal at this one.

It was so completely different from the stark inside of the *shul* that she blinked. Here again were the books coming alive, all the pictures she had studied of great, tapestried castle rooms with life-size statues and the gleam of old, old precious jewels, rare metals, and cloth.

"Isn't it pretty?" Clara whispered behind her.

Vincent nodded as she looked into that place of splendid possessions. Suddenly a breathless fact hit her: this was Manny's, too. This rich stillness and beauty belonged to the little boy, as well as to Clara and her great-grandfather and to all the people who came here for their kind of dear-Lord-kind-Lord-gracious-Lord. Then how could Manny be a shameful little outcast?

Hell! she thought jubilantly, they *can't* say he was never born! Look what he's got!

A choked sound of delight escaped her lips, and Clara whispered, "Sh. What did you say?"

"Do the men and women all sit together?" Vincent whispered back, trying to get a picture of Manny's church when it was full of people.

"Sure. Did you see enough?"

"Yeah." Vincent followed her, and they stood outside the heavy doors, on the top stone step.

"Isn't it pretty?" Clara said.

"Sure is," Vincent said, taking one last look over her shoulder at the Manny-land she had finally seen.

Dusk had begun to blue the air while they were inside, and the thicker light of the coming night hovered close. As they lingered another moment, Vincent blinked hard; Dave was walking past the opening in the stone wall. Had he seen her, up here with Clara?

248

"Hey," Clara said as he disappeared, "there's that bastard who told them to take off your clothes."

"So what?" Vincent said, shrugging, but there was a sinking sensation in her stomach. Was Dave spying on her? She could hear in her head: Hey, cop a sneak, *Schwartzel*

But remember today? she thought almost at once. Dave and me, together on a job, pals again.

"Does he go to our school, too?" Clara said.

"No, he's almost fifteen," Vincent said. Then, abruptly, she blurted, "How about meeting me in the main hall tomorrow? Near the water fountain. Right after the last bell, huh?"

Clara did not answer, and Vincent thought of a hundred white faces in the main hall, all turning, all staring at her as she met Clara, all watching as she pushed the button that squirted the water while Clara leaned to drink. She felt a little scared.

"Will you?" she said.

"What for?" Clara's voice was wary. "I'll meet you in the Gully if you want. Right after dark."

"No!" Vincent said harshly. She could not fashion the words for her feeling that she wanted to come out of the dark, secret corner of the Gully with Clara.

"I saw you a couple of times," Clara said, feeling her own way. "In the hall, between periods. I went the other way."

"I never saw you," Vincent said.

"Did you ever look?" Clara said eagerly.

"I look for you all the time. See, we could go somewhere. The library, or get some ice cream cones and take a walk."

Clara played with the knife in her pocket. She frowned. Then she said, very carelessly, "You really want to?"

"Yeah."

"Tomorrow?"

"Right after school, okay? Near the fountain, first floor."

Suddenly Clara grinned. "Okay, *schwartze kuter!*"

Vincent laughed. "Boy, your Jewish sure smells," she said.

"Yeah," Clara agreed. "Well, listen, I better scram. It's getting good and dark, and I'll sure get hell in a wheelbarrow if I'm not home."

They walked down the stone steps, stood for a moment longer in the deepening dusk. Then Clara said, "Tomorrow, huh?"

"Right after the last bell."

"So long."

"So long," Vincent said, and watched Clara dart across the street, shrewdly gauging the traffic, then disappear.

She looked back at St. Joseph's, remembering the opulent stillness and beauty inside and the way Clara had tied this church to history and to generations of people picking and choosing, how she had said her love out loud, as if her God were a friendly person. And it all belonged to an abandoned, nameless baby, too.

Funny! Vincent took a deep breath. Somehow, her journey into Manny-land, her sudden discovery there of the riches the little boy possessed, had given her back something: the powerful, happy belief she had felt so briefly when she had written the new names in the big book in the basement.

Somehow, Clara's story about her great-grandfather, the slave, had brought a vivid life to Ma's stories about her grandfather and his Bible, her father and the flour mill, her gay brother and his house of bad women. Clara's great-grandfather, his free journey North—some day she would tell Manny how people had picked and chosen the church he belonged to, but she could tell him at the same time how Ma had cried and the other Jews had sung on the boat, and how sometimes when you sat in *shul* and listened to the chant of the prayers it was like a sad, thrilling feeling of goosebumps—as if you recognized the sound even though you did not understand the words, or the meaning of a prayer that made Pa strike his chest slowly with his fist as he stood there swaying, wrapped in the long, tasseled prayer shawl.

But there was another important thing to tell Manny some day, Vincent thought as the fact hit her. Clara, who loved "my Lord" and understood all the prayers in there, who possessed all the riches of this church, felt just as much like a changeling as she did. Clara's mother and father, with all these possessions they had picked and chosen, were just as afraid of white people as Ma and Pa were of *Schwartze*.

Yeah, but don't ask me why, little half-and-half, she thought wryly as she started off for home.

At the end of the church property, Dave suddenly stepped out of the dark shadows of the stone wall.

"Hey, Vincent, I was waiting for you," he said hesitantly.

She tensed, waited for snarling words: What the hell were you doing with a *Schwartze?* In a church! I saw you coming out of there!

"Want to walk or something?" Dave said.

His eyes looked queerly glazed in the dusky light, his pallor hitting through even in the shadowy place where they stood. Had his father or Al beat him up for what he had done this afternoon?

"Okay." She still felt that fierce, intense togetherness between them, as if they were still kneeling near the man. The feeling stayed with her as they crossed Woodlawn and turned east toward their street.

"I couldn't stay in the house," Dave said. "Just thinking. My head feels—like it's smoking inside. I walked around. See, I saw you cop a sneak over the fence. And I—took a walk."

His voice sounded so lost and dazed that Vincent wished she could tell him of her new, wonderful knowledge about Manny. Let the Grandmother go to her Homeland! Let Pa never, never say Manny's name out loud! He was okay, anyway.

"How's your mother?" she said as they walked past the Sunday-dark store windows.

"She's just laying there," he said in the same spiritless voice. "My father rushed in and told her about me and you picking up that bloody guy. Sick as she is, that bastard yelled right in the bedroom."

They turned down East 119th, mechanically avoiding their own street. As in the old days, when all roads led to the clubhouse, they headed for the Gully and the little house.

"What did your mother say?" Vincent asked.

There was a little life in Dave's voice. "She said it's good to help people when they're sick. In trouble. And—and she said, 'I always liked Judy.'"

"Thanks," Vincent muttered.

When they came to the mouth of the Gully, they stopped and looked into the massed blackness which had always seemed luminous because of the reaches of sky overhead.

"Want to see the club?" Dave asked in a low voice.

"Yeah."

They stepped over the sidewalk, turned on the incline toward their own part of the hill. In a few moments they were in the familiar

251

cleared space, standing at the fireplace. The little clubhouse made a darker blotch nearby, and Vincent thought, with almost no sensation, of Santina and that guy inside. Would Dave make a crack?

"Boy, the fun we used to have," Dave said in a twisted voice.

"Yeah."

There was a rustling, crackling series of noises near the shack. They stared across the dark area, but the sounds had gone almost at once.

"Cats, maybe," Dave said. "Remember that big one that used to come all the way across the Gully, every time he'd see our fire?"

"He liked potatoes," Vincent said. "If you blew on a piece first."

"He must've died. Maybe somebody poisoned him." Dave kicked at the charred pieces in the fireplace. Suddenly he said, in a mumble of pain, "Vincent, I'm sorry as hell about that day we did it to you! Honest, Vincent! You believe me?"

And Clara had walked up to her, right here. Would they ever have known each other if it hadn't been for that day? Would she ever have gone to a *Schwartze* street, into a church? Would she ever have discovered that Manny was not really an outcast but could stand as big in the world as any. . . .

"Vincent, you believe me?" Dave begged.

"Yeah, it's okay. Forget about that day."

"I can't!"

"Everything's different now," she said awkwardly. "Like—well, from that day on—like it started right here, and— Dave, it's okay, honest."

"All right," he muttered. Then, in a little while, he said, "Want to go in the club for a second?"

"Yeah." When she turned to follow him across the familiar stretch, she felt a queer, sweet gush of homesickness.

The door was half open, and Dave said, "Who the hell's been using our club, you think? Kids, huh? I ought to come around and make 'em cop a sneak."

But his voice had no heart in it, no real flare of anger or proprietorship. He struck a match and lit the stub of candle set in the bottle. Without a word, they sat on the orange crates, and Vincent picked up the old cigarette box.

"Remember those long butts?" Dave said. "Only a couple of drags on 'em?"

She nodded as she put the box down. The little tongue of light made the same old shadows in the room, and she remembered not Santina and a man in here, not her terrible farewell to the gang, but a thousand candlelit nights of free and easy dreaming, timeless; no calendar, no clock.

Dave took up the box and opened it. "I should've bought a pack," he mused. "Newman's was still open when I went past."

She noticed the shakiness of his hands on the box, and took her first good look at him, saw how pale and twitching his face was, his lower lip bitten-looking.

"Quiet, huh?" he said, and there was such a lost look in his eyes that she wanted to blow out the candle as he went on in an aimless way: "I forgot how quiet it used to be in here. When the gang wasn't around."

"Hey, Dave," she said softly, "isn't your mother better? Any?"

His eyes jerked up at her from the box. "I don't know! She gets out of bed and cooks, gets back in and just lays there. It—she keeps looking at the ceiling. I mean, her eyes open—she ain't sleeping! She —she called me Meyer yesterday. See, that's Ziggy's real name. I walked in her bedroom, and she was looking at the ceiling, and she said, 'Meyer, you're hungry?' Jesus Christ, Vincent!"

His anguish glared in the candlelight. "I wish I had a sister. Somebody to—with soft hands. Mine are—I keep thinking my hands must scratch her face!"

Suddenly his fist was pounding on the crate. "My God," he cried, "I can't stand it when I think what she went through. Sometimes I don't think about it for a day, maybe two days. But then it's in my head again. Like a knife! And today—after we picked up that bloody guy. I went in the house and took a look at her laying there, and— It was the worst yet. I mean, in my head—a big knife. And all day to-day—I'm going nuts, just thinking about all that crap she went through for him. For that rotten bastard!"

"Who?" Vincent said, breathless with his naked grief.

"My old man. And he's a crook on top of everything else. He's just a low, dirty crook."

Again he pounded on the crate, his white face gleaming in the uneven light, his blond, rough hair gleaming.

"Ever since I heard it. Jesus Christ, it's about a year, almost! I heard my aunts and uncles telling the whole God damn thing—nobody knew I was in the kitchen, listening. That day—it was kind of a family party and I promised my mother I'd go. See, my old man was out by his Polacks so I told her okay, I'd go. So I hung around the kitchen, just eating, see, and they must've figured I was out in the yard or something. I heard them talking: 'Fanny, you remember this? Fanny, you remember that?' I heard every stinking word! Vincent! You just don't know!"

"What?" she said.

"And—and now! I look at her and I want to cry. Lay down and—and kiss her feet. I want to give her everything in the whole world. Tell her! But I can't talk to her. I want to ask her. I want to say to her, do I *have* to be like Ziggy? Like Al—and *him*? Sometimes I feel like my father's pushing me—the whole street, the whole world—they're all shoving me, making me be like Ziggy. Do I have to be?"

"No, you don't have to be," Vincent cried. "What's the matter with you, Dave?"

"You don't know! I've got to make it up to her. Vincent, what should I do? I'm going nuts. He took away that bracelet, and—Jesus, Vincent, if you'd heard what they said that day. I mean, my aunts and uncles. I didn't know what to do. I sneaked out of that house. Then when I got home there was all the *Schwartze* trouble starting for my mother. And then the Rosens moved and we had an empty upstairs, and I kept thinking every day about what she'd gone through already, and here was more trouble for her—the *Schwartze*, and how they'd move in and she—she'd cry. I didn't want her to cry any more! God damn it, she had enough!"

And suddenly, sitting there and staring into Vincent's eyes, Dave was blurting out the story he had been carrying around inside of him for almost a year.

His mother! Fanny Zigman; the year she came to America with her husband and two kids, they had their picture taken in a studio in Brooklyn, a couple of blocks from where they lived. She was beautiful! Kind of thin, her long brown hair up real nice with two of those colored combs. Her eyes straight into yours when you looked at the

254

picture—so soft, so friendly. The two kids, Al and Meyer, six and four, hair combed with water, short-pants suits, round fat faces, and her husband Morris sitting there in the picture, too. Good-looking guy, all right, blond hair and mustache, big smile: he was doing all right, see? That was the year he'd brought his wife and two sons from Poland, and he had a job, and he was in America, and look me over! Ain't I the nuts?

But she—she was beautiful. All soft and brown and young, with a hand touching each kid in the picture, and her eyes looking straight out at you and liking you, asking you to like her.

Well, for a couple of years everything was swell, see? Morris worked in a slaughterhouse—he'd go into New York every day to the job. They had nice furniture, and the kids were clean and healthy, and Fanny took care of the third-floor apartment and cooked a lot and baked a lot—stuff Morris liked to eat. He brought her home pieces of jewelry from New York once in a while—he was a sport, a big shot, see? Once he brought her a bracelet with a real diamond in it. Boy, did those dimples of hers go in and out, in and out, with the way she laughed!

She was crazy about that bracelet—she couldn't believe it was really hers. She wore it only for Jewish holidays or special parties. She was so happy sometimes she didn't know what to do—so she put on the bracelet and sang to the kids, danced around the kitchen until they laughed and clapped their hands to see her. I mean, when your husband buys you a diamond bracelet—Jesus Christ! She even forgot how lonesome she was, sometimes, for her mother and father and sisters. She'd left them all in Poland when she came to America with her husband, see? Well, all his brothers and sisters and his mother were in Brooklyn, and they liked her, and he loved her, so what the hell? When she got too lonesome for her own family she used to take her beautiful, wonderful bracelet out of the drawer and put it on. She'd sit there and look at it, or she'd walk over to where the boys were having a nap, and stand there looking at them and then at the bracelet and back at them until she felt better and didn't want to cry any more.

Well, one Saturday night Morris didn't come home from work. Fanny wasn't too worried because he had a lot of pals in New York, guys he'd run around with in Poland, and sometimes he'd play cards with them and just sleep at their house, see? So she ate some supper and put the kids to sleep. After a while, she went to sleep, too.

Sunday came, but no Morris. Sunday afternoon, then suppertime. There wasn't any phone, so she got the kids dressed nice and took them over to her mother-in-law. "Where's Morris?" she said to the old lady. "Was he here today?"

No. Well, they got a little nervous and the old lady puts on her coat and all four of them start traveling around Brooklyn, from one brother to another, from one sister's house to another: "Is Morris here? Have you heard from him, about him?"

No! Nobody had seen Morris since Friday. Well, by that time Fanny was crying and fainting, and the little boys were screaming their heads off, and the old lady was moaning and praying. Everybody figured he'd been in an accident, he was in some hospital, or dead or something.

Well, Monday night after work, one of his brothers went all the way in to New York to see Morris's pals. Yeah, he got the right story! That sonofabitching Morris, that big-shot lover boy—he'd just packed up and gone back to Poland. Went to all his pals, said good-by like a good friend, then got on the boat and copped a sneak—back to Poland.

Little by little, Fanny Zigman got the whole stinking story. Stuff she never even knew about even when she was in Poland, married to Morris. See, he'd been in love with a babe there. Not Jewish, so they couldn't get married—some gal who whored around for dough. Hell, that's where he'd met her, in a whorehouse. She was a hundred-per-cent *kurveh*, for Christ sake! Morris would see her two, three times a week—in the whorehouse—even after he was married! Even after he had kids! But Fanny never knew. Fanny'd never seen a *kurveh* in her life, let alone figure a dirty deal like that one!

So when Morris's mother and his brothers and sisters and their families decided to come to America, and he had to come too because his father was dead and his mother always ran the whole family, and she was paying their way across anyway, Morris told this *kurveh* he'd come back to her. In fact, he swore to her he would. This pal of his in Brooklyn finally told Fanny the whole story: how he swore he'd come back as soon as he had enough dough.

He did, too! Three years after he hit America, Morris Zigman got

256

on a boat and went back to his *kurveh*. Not one word to his wife and kids, not one word to his mother, even. Just copped a sneak, see?

About a week later, Fanny kind of snapped out of it and looked around her home. She was so scared and tired and lonesome that she didn't know what to do. So she went to her drawer for her jewelry. She was just going to sit at the kitchen table and look at it, remember the happy days when he used to bring home presents for her.

But Morris had taken all her jewelry with him! Even her wonderful, beautiful bracelet—he'd grabbed that, too. And he knew how she felt about that bracelet! He knew she loved it with a special, way-down-deep-inside feeling. He knew it! But that big shot from America was going to arrive in class, see? With presents for his *kurveh*—real fancy American presents, see? A sport, a lover-boy with class!

So, hell began for Fanny Zigman—like that missing bracelet had really smacked the truth at her. Maybe she didn't really believe it would go on. That he'd come back. Maybe! She waited. She sold the furniture one piece at a time. She took charity from his mother, from his brothers—stuff to eat, the rent. She started getting letters from her family in Poland: all about Morris, how he was driving a taxi again like he did before he went to America, how he was drinking like a *goy*, living openly with his *kurveh*, having one hell of a good time—the talk of every Jew in town and the hell with it. Fanny's dimples just disappeared—like she never had any. No more laughing. There wasn't any left in the whole world.

But she still waited. Maybe she figured she was having a bad dream. If she stayed real quiet, in a little corner, it would end, and everything would be the same as before. Maybe! Because she still loved this dirty sonofabitch, see? She'd go to visit his family, his mother. And the old lady would read her another letter she'd just written to Morris and was going to send that day: "My son, come back. You are a wicked man but if you come right away we will forgive you and take you back. Come, your wife and sons are waiting for you."

But he didn't even answer those letters. And stuff finally caught up with Fanny. Because how long can you go on waiting, and how long can you go on taking charity from people? Yeah, how long do people go on giving it—even to two little boys—without griping?

Fanny sold the last piece of furniture and bought Al and Meyer

257

new suits, then she took them to an orphan asylum. She got herself a furnished room, and another piece of her heart broke off, and she buried it in the same hole as the piece that died when she went to look for her bracelet and found out he'd taken it to another woman. Fanny went to work, cleaning and cooking for people, getting tired enough so's she wouldn't have to think about the kids. That was the year her hair turned gray.

Well, time passed, life pushed everybody around a little bit. Morris's mother died; one brother moved to Ohio, and things were so good there—jobs for painters and carpenters—that the rest of the brothers and sisters moved there, too. Fanny Zigman went along. What else could she do? She didn't have anybody else for a family, and she hated New York like poison by that time, anyway.

The day before she left New York, she took a big basket of candy and cake and toys to Al and Meyer in the orphan asylum. She spent the whole day with them, told them exactly where she was going and then swore to them that she would work like a horse until they could come to her, to a new house, with new furniture, new clothes, and plenty always to eat. She swore it to them by God.

They'd stopped asking where their Pa was, by that time. They looked at her when she explained all these things and they started to cry, but she quickly took them into her arms and made them laugh. She stuffed candy into their mouths and told them funny little stories and got them to eating and giggling and having fun. She cried later, after she got back to her room.

So Fanny Zigman got to a new city in America. It was a different kind of city—cleaner, lots of trees and grass; and she kept thinking of her boys playing on this grass, climbing one of these big trees. She kept thinking of Morris, too, how in Poland they used to walk under the trees while he was courting her, how they would look up into the tall, leafy trees and find the stars caught at the top in the thick branches.

She was working—like a horse, all right! Scrubbing, cooking, cleaning toilets, but thinking about the trees. She was saving every dime, never spending for face powder, a holiday dress, cake, even chewing gum. She didn't send the kids much, just on Jewish holidays. She'd think of them, all three of them, going to a park and sitting on

258

all that grass, and that was like sending them presents, see; that was like buying herself new shoes.

One day she took her savings out of the bank and opened up a poultry store with Morris's brother Joe. Maybe she wanted a business for her kids. Maybe she wanted it for Morris—still waiting for him in her heart, where the picture of grass and trees was, her and Morris and the kids in a park, see?

They opened the store, and Fanny Zigman really worked. She'd get up at four in the morning and go down to the market with Joe, work like a man to haul the crates of chickens and ducks, the cases of eggs. Then she'd open the store, work there all day—selling, *flicking*, making good customers out of everybody with her peppy talk and laughing. Late at night she'd fall on her face—even a horse gets tired!

But it worked, see? One day she had enough money to send for Al and Meyer. She had the rented downstairs of a house with a yard full of grass ready for them, nice second-hand furniture, their own bedroom, a kitchen full of stuff to eat, two used bikes, even. She had been up most of the night, baking honey cake and sponge cake and bread—the braided Sabbath loaves of white bread she used to bake when she had a family and a home. When she met her sons in the bus station, saw their faces turn up to hers, a strange, wild feeling ran through her blood and lifted her heart like a big country wind. It was happiness, the first she had felt in so long that she couldn't recognize it. All of a sudden there were deep, flashing dimples in her cheeks. She felt them, as if Meyer had stuck his little hard fingers in each cheek, the way he used to when he was a tiny, kissing boy.

Well, Fanny's kids were home, with plenty to eat, and grass to play on. And time passed, and yet it didn't, see? Because she was still waiting. She was still in love with her husband, for Christ sake! One day Joe got on the war path again to his brother. Letters, letters: "Come home, Morris. You've got a business. Your boys are big. Your wife is a regular business woman, but first of all she is a wife. She says it, herself. So come."

And the bastard came. Six years had gone by, a long time and yet a minute. Who knows why he came? Maybe his *kurveh* had given him the pitch, or maybe he felt like he was getting old, or maybe he wanted to see his wife, his sons. Maybe! He never told why; he just came. He didn't have a dime. Fanny sent him the money to come. And when he got here he was sick, and his hair and mustache were white, and somebody had given him a bum leg for a present. Maybe his *kurveh*—who knows?—he never said, and Fanny never asked.

She just took him back. She gave him his kids and her half of the business and a clean, nice house. The day he got back, there was fresh-baked bread and a holiday meal, as if it was *Rosh Hashonah* in that house, the first day of a New Year. She called a doctor and he got better, except he still had the bum leg for a souvenir and always would. They worked hard, together for a change, and one day they bought out Joe, and the business was all theirs. One day they had another kid, name of Dave. And they lived happily ever after— like all the stories in books end!—with Meyer named Ziggy by the street, and Ziggy ending up in jail, and Al turning into the best card dealer in town and never quite making jail. And Dave? Yeah, what about Dave? He wants to know! He wants to ask his mother—Fanny, with the sad eyes fixed blankly on the ceiling of her bedroom. He. . . . Yeah, he wants to ask her what. . . .

In the candlelit clubhouse, Dave was crying harshly, his face twisted with hurt.

"Why'd he have to take that bracelet away from her?" he said, his voice choked with sobs. "I have to snitch one for her. I have to! What if she dies before I get her another bracelet? Make it up to her?"

"She's not going to die," Vincent whispered. Her chest ached with the way he had told his mother's story.

"What if she does? I'll kill him! I've got to go and snitch that bracelet, that's all. Downtown somewhere? Or Miller's pawnshop? They got bracelets in the window. My God, Vincent, what should I do?"

The hard sobs began to pull at him again, and he put his head down on his arms, sprawling across the crate as he cried. Vincent moved the candle; it was too near his hair. She sat very still, waiting for his convulsive crying to stop.

She knew what he had to do. She could not tell him about Clara or Manny, but she knew exactly what he would have to do. No matter how terrible the enemy street was, he would have to walk into it.

His crying was lower, tired. Vincent put out her hand awkwardly, and patted his head a few times. "Hey, Dave," she said, "she'll get better. You'll see. She's just got to."

"Yeah!" he muttered against his arm.

She thought of his mother's dimples, in the story he had told with such furious grief and pity, and she thought of how long it had been since she had seen Dave's dimples, that big grin with which he had welcomed the highest roof to climb.

"Dave," she said, "you've got to talk to her."

His head jerked up. "What about? Jesus Christ, you mean about *him*, and that stinking dame of his? The bracelet?"

"No," Vincent said, groping for the right words. "No, not the bracelet. About you. How you feel—way inside."

His eyes looked red in the candlelight. "I can't! I don't know how to show her that— Jesus, I love her so much it—it cuts me."

"Tell her," Vincent said. "Can't you?"

"I don't know! It's so God damn funny. I mean, the way everybody expects you to be exactly like your brothers. Maybe she does, too! Maybe she thinks I'll turn out to be like that dirty crook who copped a sneak on her—stole her bracelet and gave it to a—a *kurveh!*"

"Listen, Dave," Vincent said, "I just know you've got to talk to her. About your brothers and—well, how you know for sure you're not going to be like that."

"She never talks about Ziggy," he burst out. "She can't stand to— I know it. She's crying inside. It's my old man who does all the talking, and—and she just looks. Crying inside, I know it. Boy, I hate him! After I found out, I—I was going to kill him. Steal her the prettiest bracelet in town, walk in there, and put it on her. Make him look, and—and kill him."

"Yeah," Vincent said doggedly, "but try and talk to her, huh? And you know what, Dave? Maybe she wants to talk to you, too. About inside stuff. How you feel way inside, and maybe how she feels, too."

"Think so?" he said, a little breathless with the idea.

She nodded, thinking of her father and herself in a room, only their eyes talking about Manny; the glitter and flash in a room of all the words unsaid—like a bracelet.

"Some day," she said, knowing it for the first time, "I'm going to talk to my father. About inside stuff."

They watched the candle for a while. Dave blew his nose, wiped slowly at his face. Shadows, long and short, flickered across the walls and the ceiling, and Vincent's eyes followed them for a while as she thought of the real Dave—the entire mask off now, not one piece of it left to hide the boy who was so torn with love.

With quiet excitement, she suddenly contemplated another new fact: others must be like this, acting one way with people but being an entirely different way inside of them, under the mask. Her brother, maybe. Had somebody (like Dave's father) made Nate put on a mask and show its cynical, sneering face to the whole world—even to a sister who had worshiped him?

"Vincent," Dave said, "you think they can *make* you be what you don't want to be?"

"No," she said fiercely—to him, to Manny, to Shirley, and to herself.

"You sure?" he said. "How do you know?"

"I just know! You believe me?"

He stared back at her. "Yeah," he said, taking a deep breath. "That guy Ross knocked out today—when I saw you running to him. Jesus, you don't know how it felt, inside of me! I started to think about my mother and was she going to die. And the bracelet. And what the gang did to you. Me—what I did to you! And how we never used to be afraid of anybody! Nothing in the whole damn world!"

Vincent nodded. "You know that red notebook Jules writes in all the time?" she said abruptly.

"Yeah?"

"He's got one certain poem in there. It's—maybe you can come with me sometimes and he'll read it to you, too. It's about how people have to be not afraid. Free—in the world. Strong, and it's okay to love a lot of other people even if your own family is—well, all different than you are inside."

"Jules, huh?" he said. "He's a pretty smart guy."

"Yeah! And that red notebook—well, wait'll you hear that poem. He'll read it to you, too, some day, Dave—you'll see."

Dave looked at the candle for a while. Then he said in the unmasked, gentle voice, "Want to take him some ice cream? I've got some dough."

262

"That'd be swell," Vincent said. "Sometimes he can't eat his supper. When he feels real lousy. Ice cream is cool."

They were silent for a while. Then Vincent said, "Going to talk to her?"

"Yeah. Tomorrow—after school. My old man won't be there." Dave played with the candle, said in a low voice, "I'll get her that bracelet some day."

"Yeah, I know," Vincent said.

Again she followed the uneven shadows with her eyes. There were planks loose in the wall opposite her, and a hole in the roof.

"The club's kind of falling to pieces," she said.

"Want me to fix it up?" he said.

"What for?"

Their eyes met, and then Dave nodded. "But it was swell, huh?" he said somberly.

"Yeah," she said, and they got up to go.

She blew out the candle. He closed the door carefully, and they started out of the Gully.

## 2

Later that evening, when they walked across the street from the Golden house, Dave said, "Your house is dark—even the kitchen."

"They're probably upstairs," she said.

"Talking about *Schwartzes*," he said. "You going to get hell?"

"Yeah," she said absently, still thinking of Jules. "So what?"

They lingered in front of her house, seeing each other in the yellow light coming from the lamppost. "Well," he said, his voice gruff with shyness, "I'm going in and see my mother."

"Okay," Vincent said. "Maybe she's better."

"Yeah!" He leaped away, ran into his yard, and Vincent went up on her porch and sat on the swing.

The street noises seemed to make a faraway, almost gentle accompaniment to her thoughts: a screen door slamming somewhere, and men and women talking on porches, the game of kick-the-stick at the Gully lamppost. She was thinking of Jules in his bed, the pulse banging and speeding, identifying the world of his room for her again.

She had come to him alone from the kitchen, leaving Dave there with Mrs. Golden and Heidi. Through the windows near his bed, she

263

could see his father and Becky on the swing. His father's arm was about Becky, who was lying against him, and the swing creaked slow and regular as one of those lullabies Shirley sang so often to Manny.

"Hello, changeling," Jules had said to her. Their eyes—in their eyes they had been close again, as if their strange quarrel had never happened.

Now as she sat on her porch, Vincent saw Anna dash out of the yard with the empty pitcher, heard her shout toward the Gully game as she headed for the corner: "Lou, Lou! Ma says she wants you in the house."

How beautiful and strange Jules' eyes had seemed, Vincent thought. All restlessness was gone, the wild push and pull of inner feelings. She had never seen his eyes so quiet; they looked just as quiet as she had felt after finding Clara that afternoon.

Jules had patted his bed and she had sat near him in the light falling from the lamp on his table, so close to the bottles of medicine and heaped books and the red notebook that she felt at the very core of his life.

"When you went to that man today and helped him," Jules had said to her. "You know what you did? You pulled me up, too—over the mountains. I was climbing, Vincent."

And she had cried out to him in a whisper, so that they would not hear in the kitchen: "Jules, you know what I did—after? I went to find my friend Clara. In her street. I found her, too!"

He had smiled in a dreamy way. "Your friend. And you talked—"

And I found out how much Manny's really got, she had thought excitedly. And Dave's going to talk to his mother. And tomorrow, right after school, Clara's meeting me. . . .

But she had become all choked with the million things she had to tell Jules some day, had looked away from his tender eyes. The red notebook was right in front of her on the table. She had touched it, for the first time feeling the knubbly grain she had looked at so long.

Jules' eyes had closed. He had said softly, "I'll read you poems—lots of new ones, all for you. Later—tomorrow."

Then Dave had come in, and behind him Mrs. Golden saying softly, "Juley, Dave Zigman brought you ice cream."

Jules' eyes had opened. Suddenly his old, glinting grin was there.

264

"Another changeling yanks at the world!" Catching Vincent's eye, he had winked and then said, "Dave, you understand Yiddish?"

"A little bit," Dave had said, startled.

That grin had deepened and Jules had proclaimed, as if reading a poem: "*Erscht schwartz is weiss und weiss is schwartz. A gantze welt tantzed und freyd sach!*"

His mother had just looked at him. Glancing at Dave's perplexed eyes, Jules had said, "Vincent, tell him. Only it sounds better in Yiddish!"

" 'Now black is white and white is black,' " Vincent had translated for Dave. " 'A whole world dances and—' What does '*freyd sach*' mean again, Jules?"

"It's got joy in it," Jules had said. " 'A whole world dances and is full of joy.' "

As Vincent sat now, remembering how he had said "joy," Anna came back with the pitcher of Seltzer. Shortly afterward, she rushed out of the yard again and ran toward the loud game at the Gully lamppost. Then the screen door slammed on the porch over Vincent's head, and she heard Mr. Levine say, "Sit down, Abe. Let the women talk in the kitchen."

One of the rolling belches came, and Mr. Levine said, "Ah! Seltzer is a boon to mankind's stomach."

"Here it is, fall, yet the evenings are still warm enough to enjoy the porch."

Vincent heard the nervous tension in her father's voice, but she did not feel like sneering tonight. Did her father wear one mask for Mr. Levine, another for the Grandmother, and still another for Nate and Shirley and her?

"But it will be cold soon," Mr. Levine said. "My coal was delivered Friday."

"Yes, mine, too."

"Only half a ton," Mr. Levine said. "To start."

"Yes. Half a ton."

Listening to her father's depressed tones, Vincent's heart began to beat too fast. But they always order five tons a piece, to start, she thought. More later, if it's a long winter. No, no! Pa's just scared— he's kidding that bastard. So there won't be a lot of hollering. Pa hates all that hollering.

"You know, Abe," Mr. Levine said thoughtfully. "Today, when the Italian beat the Black One, I was thinking of Hitler. It makes a man shiver. It makes a man realize that time is going fast, fast—and nothing stands still."

"Nothing. Things get either better or worse."

"Worse, worse!" Mr. Levine said impatiently. "Hitler was not enough for us? Look—in our own street. And Abe! If the Black Ones get angry enough over what happened here today to one of theirs? If they get together—five hundred, a thousand—and march in here? Remember what happened in Poland, in Vienna, in Berlin!"

Crap, Vincent thought, anger flaring in her. If Pa ever talked to Clara he'd know it's crap.

"I was talking to Sam Miller today," Mr. Levine said. "Did you ever know him to be nervous? Before today? A leader, a man who built our temple!"

"I was talking to Morris Zigman," her father said. "He told me that the board has called a meeting for next Sunday morning—to vote on selling the temple building. Do you think it is possible?"

"Certainly! Today was like the first bomb. Next is the crematorium. Well, I am not going to wait until they come and push me and mine into doom, that's all. Today, when that Black One started the trouble, I made up my mind. I am warning you."

"You—you're warning me?"

"I made up my mind! If nothing happens, I move. That's all!"

"You would do that to my family? To Jewish neighbors?"

Instead of answering, Mr. Levine drank his Seltzer noisily.

Pa, Pa, Vincent thought, close to tears at the man's threatening bluster, don't let that bastard scare you!

Mr. Levine's voice began its inexorable pushing again: "We don't have to talk about it. Let us discuss, rather, how to save money. Afterward—you understand me, Abe?—afterward, I could repair much of the house myself. Pick the cheapest materials. You could do the painting—maybe with one other union man. There are plenty of cheap leads on the market—we don't need Dutch Boy. We spend just enough to make the house look good, then sell. What do the Black Ones care, as long as the surface glitters? They ruin a house—everybody knows that. They never paint, make repairs. All they want to do
266

is fill up a house with five, six families. Do they care if a house is solid, a joy to its carpenter, its painter?"

Joy. The whole world dances and is full of joy. The words beat through Vincent's head, and she thought grimly: Okay, dirty old Mr. Levine! Burn it up, sell it! Clara can move in and you can go to hell. She can do her homework and everything. Just leave my father alone!

Then, with a kind of panicky sorrow, she heard her father say hesitantly: "And you're sure banks lend money to the Black Ones?"

"Abe, even they are working these days. There is no depression. A bank will do business with anybody who has money."

"And—and Moe really knows what to do?" her father asked, his voice so tremulous that Vincent winced with shame for him.

As Mr. Levine chuckled meaningfully, she jumped up and grabbed the porch railing, shook the heavy wood. Over the weeks, the overheard talk of a fire had sharpened and mounted in her senses. From a low, ominous drumbeat, it had come closer and louder, ever more clear; now, suddenly, it was gunfire all through her.

No, Pa won't do it! she thought. She knew with a dreadful certainty how wrong the fire was, even in his thoughts. It was as wrong as the beating of the man that afternoon. It was completely wrong, as wrong as he had been about Shirley and Johnnie, about Manny.

As if Jules had just written it out for her in a poem, she knew how wrong Pa and the Grandmother had been, the two of them entwined into one figure of wrath—ordering her to feel ashamed and frightened, never to say beloved names in their presence.

Then, as if the poem suddenly lit up with its real meaning in the glare from that planned fire, she shivered. That entwined figure had only a single voice, the Grandmother's. It had only her sternness, her overbearing, sure way of ordering life and the world and God. Where was her father in the figure which spoke for them both?

"I wonder," Mr. Levine said thoughtfully, "how a Jew would feel in permanent safety. In the Homeland, finally."

"Is such a feeling possible?"

"You know, Abe, I thought of your mother today. While the Italian was beating the Black One."

"I, too."

Her father's voice was so low that Vincent had difficulty hearing

267

it. What came down to her powerfully was the unhappiness, the lost-ness, in his voice: "I thought of how she fasted in Palestine this year. I here, she across the world. Apart for the first time in my life on that holy day. I thought of how I prayed for our sins to be forgiven—and, across the world, she was praying, too. Our sins—this afternoon, when I saw that man falling, bleeding, I had to think of a word—sins."

"Hah! You know what I was thinking when he fell? If a Jew gets *almost* to Palestine and they keep him out at the last minute—by beating him—does that make other Jews stop trying to get in? That's what I was thinking."

"What do you mean?"

"Isn't this street like a Palestine to the Black Ones?" Mr. Levine demanded fiercely. "Do you think that because one was kept out to-day, beaten and pushed away from a golden place, the other Black Ones will stop trying to get in? Oh, no! Every man has his dream of a Homeland. You know that!"

"My mother—I will never see her again. That one thing I know."

Vincent heard the loneliness in her father's voice, the mourning and yearning, and suddenly she ran from the porch, raced toward the side door.

On her way down to the basement, headlong into the blackness and sudden coolness, she groped in her pocket for matches. At the open coal lockers, she struck a match, looked into the Levine locker. Then she thrust the lit match into the other locker.

It was true! There was a small hill of coal in each locker, instead of the usual mountain of craggy lumps. She went upstairs very slowly. The door to the kitchen was open, and light blazed out into the back hall. When she stepped into the room, she saw her father at the stove, lighting a fire under the teakettle.

His eyes looked frantic, and she strode past him scornfully, went back to the porch. The shouts of kids and the sound of laughter and voices, the noises of full summer, came at her from the street as if there never would be a time for furnaces. Across the street the lamp in Jules' window was lit, and that proved it! It was summer! In cold weather, Jules' bed was always moved back to his own bedroom from the living room. It was summer, and there would never be a furnace lit, never!

268

Vincent's stomach lurched as she glared into a screened window, across the dark living and dining rooms. In the bright kitchen, her father was pacing and muttering while he waited for the water to boil.

Now her mother came in through that open back door. Vincent could hear her cautious voice: "Why did you rush down that way? Without one word? Lizzie thought you went crazy. What's the matter?"

"Sonia, telephone Shirley," he said in a strident, shaky voice. "Tell her to bring Mendel here. I want to see Mendel."

"What did you say?"

Vincent saw her mother's shocked expression, and a queer mixture of elation and fear tore through her.

"But not *him!*" her father cried. "I want only Shirley and Mendel to come here. . . . Well, why are you standing?"

Her mother rushed into the dining room, flicked the light switch. In a daze, Vincent saw her fumbling at the dial. She saw her father scowling as he poured his tea, and she thought incredulously: It's like he walked into that church with me today! Took a good look around, saw that Manny isn't a poor little punk who was never even born!

He had said Manny's name. Right out loud—right in their kitchen. Vincent sat on the swing, and her eyes were wet.

Her father carried out his glass of tea, sat in the rocker, and sipped. She heard the crunch as he bit into a lump of sugar. Then her mother came out, closing the screen door soundlessly, as if somebody were lying sick.

"She's coming with the baby?" her father said, his voice gritty.

"Right away. She'll pick him up and dress him, and come right away."

Her mother sat down in the other chair. Vincent saw her clasped hands, her set face as she stared at the street. In the faint lamppost light, she saw her father purse his lips to drink, his eyes, too, straining toward the corner, for the first glimpse of Shirley's car.

Vincent blinked as the tears kept coming to her eyes. Everything seemed tied together, all at once: the beating of the man that afternoon; the talk of fire; the departure of the Grandmother; Dave's

269

unmasking; the search for Clara today which had led Vincent into Manny's church; the solemn meaning of the Day of Atonement for her father—that made him think of his mother gone forever, after seeing a bleeding face on the sidewalk. They were all tied together so closely that her father had *had* to say Manny's name out loud!

She visualized the baby on her father's lap soon, the sound of laughter on the porch, the way those little fat hands would reach up to the man's face. Manny won't let Pa do it! she thought. He'll kiss Manny and hold him, and he'll never, never again even think about a fire.

As the three sat in silence, waiting for Shirley and Manny, the *spunyitze* began calling from her porch, "Sahn-tina! Sahn-tina!"

A little, quick song started up in Vincent's head and chased itself around and around in Jules' gayest voice: Now black is white and white is black. A whole world dances and is full of joy!

"Sahn-tina! Sahn-tina!"


# Chapter seventeen


On Tuesday morning the beautiful, exciting adventure of the world ended for Santina. She walked a few steps behind the Sister. In the long, dusky corridor stood the mysterious-looking Christs, tall as men, the stone eyes glinting secrets she could not understand.

For comfort, as she walked behind the stiff–robed figure, Santina remembered Woodlawn on a summer night. The show, its high sign in the air seeming to steam with hundreds of electric light bulbs. The guys in front of it, in front of the big colored posters about the next attraction; dark guys and blond guys, dressed up for night, hair slicked back with smelly stuff; the way guys laughed when you passed —one of the wonderful shiver-sounds of the world in summer.

She remembered the long, exciting stares of guys as you passed the poolroom and gym, next to the show. The laughter of the avenue, the fast and slow walk of people on both sides— And you could look into store windows: Rinaldi's, the drugstore, Newman's with its salamis hanging and its garlic and sweet-chocolate-soda smells com-

270

ing right out at you, and the Café so dark on the outside but the nickel music coming and singing and dancing as you passed.

"This is the geography and history classroom," the Sister said. "Use plenty of soap, child."

Then Santina was alone with the pail of water in the middle of the big, tiled floor. Only the paintings of the saints were there, hung in their smiting colors upon all the walls.

"When the bell rings," she whispered to the saints with a grin, just for the hell of it, "come on down and scrub the floor for me, huh?" But then, at the instant pang of fear, she crossed herself.

Everything was done by the bell. The girls awoke to the gong–gong–gong. They said morning prayers, kneeling at the narrow beds. Sister led the prayers, her robe mysterious as the early morning in the big room, her robe black as the night out of which Santina had fought awake.

They put on the gray, striped uniforms. They washed themselves, made the beds, swept rooms. Gong! Prunes and cereal, cocoa, dishes to wash and dry. Gong! Chapel, drone of voices. Reading, history, daily chores, gong-gong! Laundry, spelling, afternoon exercise, but most of all because they offend Thee, Who art, gong!

And Santina remembered the Gully, far and velvet-black from her own house as another world. You are standing close to Blacky. You don't have to see him—you can smell him, hair and damp hot body. His hand has you. It is summer. It is nighttime, dance time, bright wonderful summertime of your life, and his hand—then the other hand! Touching like a cool wind, a laugh, a tickle, a bruise you want.

In the clubhouse, you are lying next to Blacky. It is like a dance. His hand touches to some exquisite place and back, back and back in a curved, rocketing plunge through dark velvet.

After the shouting Sunday night, after the furious words and the slap of hands against her face and head, there had been silence in the house. Grandma had sent her to bed, and Ross had locked the bedroom door; she could hear them in the basement room, their voices like a beating and vibrating in the furnace registers. From her bed, Santina had watched the stars outside her window, how they made a green-white, blue-white dance in the sky. Then she had drifted, like the stars dancing, into sleep.

In the morning, at the table in the basement room, Grandma had shouted, "Well, was it this same Jew neighbor boy last time? When they all said it was a black man you were with? Maria, Maria, the shame!"

Her eyes were red from crying—Grandma, who never cried. After breakfast, she had done the dishes and Ross had locked her up in her room again. It was like jail, but she just kept remembering Blacky and Sunday night, and all day she laughed and danced on tiptoe, just remembering.

Then it was Tuesday. After breakfast, Grandma said, "Come." And all three of them had walked. Down Woodlawn, far, past St. Joseph's and down a side street. They came to a big building inside a high fence, fire escapes all over it, all the windows barred, and above the door, in a square like a picture frame, stood a little tiny Christ dressed like a shepherd, holding a little tiny lamb.

"Come," Grandma said, and pulled her inside.

"Sit down!" Ross said.

He and Grandma went to a desk, talked to the Sister there. Then they came back to the bench, pulled her up. They were embracing her, Ross too. Funny to feel your own brother's arms around you—hard, like a guy's.

"Santa, Santa," Grandma said, crying again, "be good! Here you will be pure and good. We will pray for you every day. Be pure in your heart."

"Good-by," Ross said in English. To her astonishment, she saw tears in his eyes. "Don't be a bad girl. Be good. Like my little sister! Then you'll come home and get married, huh? Good-by, kid."

They went away. Santina and the Christ and the saints were alone, all together. Then Sister came to get her, and they walked. All the statues they passed had sad faces. All the girls they passed wore the same gray uniform. Santina could see the bars across the windows, and she thought quietly: Blacky'll get me out of here.

They walked, but in her head Santina walked back into the beauty of night time. She remembered the sound of cats Sunday night—hot, the heat still pouring like a dark, pervasive scent, even though it was fall.

Blacky and you in the club (Vincent and Dave had finally gone, and Blacky had tiptoed back to where you were hiding and said,

272

"Okay, they scrammed."), lying close-close. "Listen to those damn cats," he had muttered. "They give me the wim-wams." You had giggled, blown in his ear. "They give *me* goosebumps!"

"Boy," Blacky had whispered, "when your brother beat up that guy today! All I wanted to do was grab you and run. Then my brother gets so sick, after. When I looked at him I thought he was going to— And my mother sitting there and crying—boy, I wanted to bust up everything in the world. Took a year to get dark, before I could whistle for you, babe. A year—boy, put your hand on me, gorgeous! Come on!"

"Blacky. Me, too, Blacky!"

You murmured his name. Down through the Gully, from every house in the world, your murmur was told again, repeated in every woman's throat, deep, laughing, a name like dancing.

No more loneliness now, close to him. And no more fear. You were safe with Blacky, in a world like dancing, the hours dancing past both of you and never changing. Only you changed, from kiss to kiss becoming a more beautiful dancer, whirling from finger to finger of his hands, like a butterfly dancer, ever-deepening colors, ever slower flutter of wings—and from far away, in that other world, Grandma was calling your name from up there, far away.

Then Ross came, somehow. Right to the Gully, right into the club, into your own secret dancing world. He grabbed Blacky, hollering and swearing. He tried to beat the hell out of Blacky, but couldn't hold on to him. Blacky ran, and Ross grabbed you and slapped you so hard that the stars came down to dance in your head. After Ross had pulled you through the street, still full of people in bunches talking about the bleeding, brown face, Grandma had slapped you and slapped you, screaming: "Maria, help this girl!" And you could still hear the cats, as if you were still with Blacky.

Now, in the room with the barred windows that Blacky would break through tomorrow, or the next day, soon, Santina sat and hummed a song you could dance to. It was rest-prayer period. She looked at the saints on the wall, and they were all looking back at her.

No more Blacky, the saints told her. Never again.

In her heart she would not believe them, even though they were saints. She crossed herself, just in case, but she went on not be-

273

lieving them. Sitting there, she remembered the last time Blacky had taken her to the show.

He had bought her some candy from the machine in the lobby. The picture was called "All the World's in Love," and she and Blacky had sat inside, hands touching every once in a while on the box of candy.

Soon, watching the screen, she had felt the dancing begin in her heart, then all over her body. The people in front of her and behind her had gone away, and then even Blacky had gone away. Then she had gone—into the big screen she had gone, and there she was, dancing better than anyone in the picture. The dancers swirled, in red and orange and rainbow costumes. She was the leader, the best. She was a bird, a flower swaying, opening, lifting to the sky.

Santina, Santina! a thousand little silver voices called. And there was no today, no barred windows, no Grandma or Ross or even Blacky. There was nothing but beautiful movement and delicate laughter in a great open place of summer night.

Santina, Santina! a thousand little golden voices called. And she was floating in the never-ending, soft hours of a summer night.

### 2

The next afternoon, after waiting since Sunday night for Jules to come back from the far land of his spirit, Mrs. Golden decided on action.

She had watched him with deepening fear. It seemed to her that he had embraced a strange peace (she could not call it, even to herself, Death, the dread figure so often disguised as a beautiful woman offering love, or as a tranquil old man holding out stillness).

Directly after lunch, she sent Heidi and Becky to visit Uncle Nathan. Alex had been there since early Monday morning, when his father had grimly escorted him all the way into the house on the Heights before he took the bus to his job.

When they had gone, Mrs. Golden washed her face and combed her hair. She felt like an old soldier at the moment of his most important battle. Every weapon she had ever mastered, every trick of war, must be used to rescue Jules.

She could see him from the kitchen, propped against his pillows, the pencil in his hand and the red notebook open. God, why was he so quiet? He had not talked much since Sunday night, or even listened to radio music. He had not read a single book—he who could devour one in a day.

Smiling, she went to him, stood on her old battleground at the foot of his bed.

"Listen, Juley," she said, "I just had a good idea. I'll rent out our upstairs to my cousin Sam. You don't like rooms to be empty. Wasted—you said so yourself. See, I know what to do!"

Jules smiled at the flagrant bribe. "Don't be silly, Ma."

"Silly? He'll do it if I tell him. He's a poor man—he never found out how to make money in America. They always lived in terrible rooms. It'll make you happy to have people upstairs?"

"I'm happy right now," he said.

"You think he won't move here?" Mrs. Golden dragged out humor, mimicry, the crafty weapons with which she had amused him so often. " 'It's my house,' I'll tell him. 'You think I would let anybody, just anybody, live in my house? Oh, no!' So maybe he'll want to know why he should move in this neighborhood. 'Sam,' I'll tell him, 'is it all colored? Should I count the Jews who're still here? I would have to have twenty hands, at least, with plenty of fingers. Don't be a fool, Sam! Look at the rooms in my upstairs. And did your wife—since all the years you live in America—ever have a modern sink? With Chicago faucets? A front porch like mine? She can sit like a queen and look out on the whole world.' "

She spoke to her cousin, as if she had pulled him into the room. Her hands on her hips, eyes spitting, she said: " 'So what if there is a couple *Schwartze* around—ten, fifteen streets away? Can they bite you? Hah! Do you think for one minute that Sophie Golden would live in a neighborhood that's no good for her children?' "

She turned in triumph back to Jules. "Sold! I'll go to Sam right after supper and tell him my upstairs is waiting."

"Ma," Jules said, "you hate your cousin Sam. He's stingy and cheap. His wife keeps a dirty house. Remember?"

Mrs. Golden winced. "So I'll give them lessons!"

"Come on, Ma," he coaxed gently. "We don't have to kid ourselves any more."

"Who's kidding?" she said, staring down at his thin face with that terrible quiet in it, down to the bone.

"Listen!" she said with a fresh spurt of eagerness. "I'll go call your little *kuter*. As soon as she's home from school. You'll talk, you'll argue. All right? A party—cake and grape juice. I'll serve pretty, the way you like it—white napkins, real—not paper."

He shook his head lovingly. Quickly, with a pitiful cunning that made him swallow, she said, "I'll invite the whole street later—after they come from work. Ruth Miller—you'll see, she'll come! All the young people, the house'll be full of talk, big discussions—exactly how you like."

"Oh, Ma," he said, his voice choked, "I'm all right. Don't you see? I'm happy."

"No! You can't fool me! I know when you feel good. Juley, listen." Her hands gripped the foot of his bed, and she began to sweat as she offered him the enormous bribe: "Should I rent to *Schwartze*? I'll do it—honest to God. One word from you. I mean it, Juley!"

He knew she meant it, and he said very softly, "Ma, I'm not going to tell you what to do. I don't have to worry any more."

"Why?" she cried, terrified. "What happened? What was so terrible Sunday that you—just tell me, what happened?"

"Nothing. It's just that I feel all quiet, not worried any more. Let me feel like that. Quiet, not afraid. Let me."

She came around the bed, studying his face frantically. "I—I'll let you. All right, sure, I'll let you."

But suddenly she cried, "Juley, fight with me! Call me names, holler. Please! Don't lay there like—like—"

She sank to her knees at his bed, sobbing. Jules smoothed her hair, calling tenderly to her, "Ma, please. Come on, Ma. Get up. It's all right to feel this way. All peaceful like this."

She peered up at him. "No! It's not all right. Not for you—you're a person who talks and hollers when you're all right."

Jules wiped her wet face with a tissue out of his box. "Ma, get up, please," he said. "Sit here, on my bed."

She pushed herself up, sat near him. "Ma," he said lovingly.

Red splotches appeared on her face, and she cursed. "It was Alex! He, he made you sick this way! I won't leave him in the house. You'll hold the clock—you'll say when it's time for him to come home again. A month, a year—you'll say when. All right?"

276

It was the biggest sacrifice she could offer. Jules grabbed her shoulders and shook her. "Ma, stop that," he begged. "It was not Alex! You've got to believe me. I told you that Sunday, damn it!"

There was real anger and disgust in her as she said, "That Gully. It made garbage out of children. When I think that it was Alex that first time, too. God!"

"Ma, don't do this to yourself," Jules cried.

"God, to do such a thing. That same night! While you were still so sick from that fight by Valenti. While the street was still waiting for a whole army of *Schwartze* to come back with guns. That—that dog went to lay with Santina. Alex—my son! All right, I hit him plenty when I found out, didn't I? And Papa hit him—with the strap. He couldn't move when we got through with him."

"Stop punishing yourself," Jules said. "It's enough."

"Enough?" Her teeth gritted for a second. "Sure, the whole street knows. When Ross came on my porch Sunday night and hollered for the whole world to hear—all right, the whole street knows that it was never a *Schwartze* in the Gully with her—it was *my* son all the time! It's enough? Alex—me—it's enough suffering? Then they should leave you alone now!"

"Ma, you listen to me. Please! Alex'll be all right, but you've got to help him. Not this way. Ma, it's not the end of his world—help him know that, will you?"

"He made you sick," she cried, as if her reiteration made it a fact. "What he did with that girl. It made you sick like this. You never liked dirt, garbage. All right, I won't let him in the house. You won't have to look at him. Just get better."

Suddenly Jules put a hand at each side of her face, framing it, turning it so that she had to look at him.

"Listen, Ma," he said gravely. "Alex is a good kid. He made a couple of mistakes—you going to break him to pieces for it? No—I'm telling you that. He's not a man, he just tried to act like one. So you're going to give him the electric chair?"

"Juley!" Her voice was trembling.

"Explain to him, Ma," he went on in that earnest way. "Help him get ready to be a good man."

"Juley, he's my baby! My son!"

"I know, Ma. He'll be all right—give him a chance. He's a good kid, under all that crap he throws around. I know him, inside. So do you."

She nodded, the tears trickling down her face. Jules released her head and handed her some tissues. "Wipe, Mrs. Golden," he said gently.

After a while, he said, "Ma."

When she looked up, he said, "I feel real peaceful. Happy. You always wanted me to be happy."

She stared at him, her eyes pitiful with her attempt to understand, and he said, "Ma, I don't want you to be afraid. Please."

"I'll try," she said. "Honest, I'll try."

"I love you," he told her. "All in my heart."

"My heart is in you!" After that choked outburst, she got up blindly and said, "I'll go and start supper."

Jules lay back against his pillows. He listened to his mother walking softly about the kitchen, then the plunk of a coin falling into the *pushke*. And he thought tenderly of how she had tried to bribe him with Ruth—as if she could offer him love along with a party full of white napkins and cake and discussions and Vincent.

He listened to the sounds of a knife on the sink, a pot lid clashing, the rush of water. Through the open windows the street sounds came to him. He was still not quite accustomed to the utter quiet inside of him. He had been tired and in pain for a long time. The terror had become confused in him, yet all the while it had held the seeds of the real fear which had kept him from resting.

Even today, as he tried to get used to the peace, he was still deciphering the last fragments of that wild fear he had fought so long. His family had frightened him. His street, the only world he knew, had frightened him. It had become more and more intolerable to contemplate the cheap, rotten values, the barren spirit, of this world —headed always by his family. They were his beloveds, and he was frightened for them, for the empty and meaningless shadows they would cast.

He lay there resting, the red notebook open under his hands, and thought of the way people could change. He had seen it, finally.

"Ma," he called.

She appeared in the kitchen doorway; he saw her deep-lined forehead, her tired face.

"Come and talk, Ma, huh?" he said.

"All right. I'll make a little fire."

When she came to him, he said, "Sit on the bed."

He saw her eyes turn wary as she sat down, knew she was groping again among her weapons. He shook his head, said, "Ma, I want you to know for sure. I'm not afraid any more."

"Afraid?" she said, attempting a jaunty laugh. "You? I heard better jokes from Becky!"

He looked at her steadily. "You know what I mean, Ma," he said.

He's not holding his sickness over me like a club any more, Mrs. Golden thought. He's not begging me with crazy eyes: Pity me, save me! Look how quiet he is. Like a religious man. Oh, God, he has taken Death into his arms like a sweetheart. God, save him!

"Juley," she said fiercely, "I got plenty to do—"

"Ma," he broke in, "help me tell you. I've got to tell you the way I feel. It's real important. It's hard to find the right words, so help me, Ma. Don't fight me."

She winced. "Juley! All right, I'm going to help you. You know I always tried my best for you."

"I know it. Now listen, Ma, let me get it out in words. I've got to know that you understand."

Jules pushed himself up straighter. He felt excited, on the verge of some deeply penetrating moment he had never thought possible.

"Ma, you always asked me why the *Schwartze* were so important to me. We hollered, we argued, but I didn't ever know. Not really. Not until Sunday. Ma, when Ross began to beat up that man! When my heart flew out of me for a minute—so scared—like all the hope was flying out of me! Ma, then I started to know. When Vincent ran to help that man, so fast, like her heart was flying, too. But not like mine—not scared—oh, no! When I said thanks to God, then I started to know why the *Schwartze* were in me like that. Eating out my guts."

Mrs. Golden listened intently to his stumbling voice, her hands absently pushing through her hair, so that it looked tumbled and youthful above her bewildered eyes.

"Ma, this whole *Schwartze* business. I knew, finally. It's only a match—to start the real fire in people. Their real fight with themselves in life. Ma, the big fire that makes you sweat, and change—for better or worse. Either you burn up or you come through—pure, good. Ma, I want you good. My whole family—good people."

"Juley," she muttered, "what is it? I can't understand you. It's like you're talking a different language to me."

"I'll teach you this language," he said glowingly. "It's beautiful—when you know the words. You're never afraid again! Let me tell you."

"Tell me, tell me. I'm listening to you."

"That a girl! All right, Ma, look. The *Schwartze*—what are they? Just a name you gave to a lot of stuff you're afraid of. You gave it a name and then you were able to curse it. Hate it. All right! Here's another way to look at it. The *Schwartze*—they're a wall that you made yourself. You made it, and it—well, it stands between you and—and the right kind of world. Do you understand?"

She shook her head, and he patted her arm. "A wall, Ma—higher than any kind there is. Higher than the no-money wall, the sickness wall. Like you made it yourself, brick by brick. A mistake! People make mistakes. But now you've got to climb over it, Ma. You first, then the whole family—after you show them how. You're the smartest, the strongest—you'll show them how! Even Alex. Even Becky. You'll say to them, 'Climb, climb! Watch me, don't give up!' You understand, Ma?"

Yes, she felt that she was beginning to understand him, though it was more a sensing of the powerful emotion he was holding out to her than any actual realization. She leaned toward him, as if she could breathe in his wonderful certainty.

"Ma," he said, "you know what's outside that wall? Flowers, the sun. The whole beautiful world. And Ma, your heart is just as beautiful—only you put a wall around it. You made yourself afraid, and you made me afraid. With the *Schwartze*."

His quiet eyes looked magnified behind the glasses, and his joy and love seemed magnified. "You made me so afraid that I thought—my God, Ma, I was afraid you couldn't ever change. My whole family—they'd stay ugly and—and weak. I couldn't stand that. I felt how all of you were pulling at me, your hands—so scared of life. I had to go on trying to help you. Change you, so you could stand up by yourself

280

—all of you, my family. But especially you, Ma. With your beautiful heart. I had to holler and fight, and I was so afraid all the time. I couldn't lay back and rest. Not while you were afraid."

Mrs. Golden took one of his hands. Their eyes clung over the intense feeling of closeness, over the understanding she was beginning to touch.

"I'm nuts about my family," he said. "I love every one of you. Every time I said I hated you, I loved you more. You know that."

She nodded, and he said, "I want my family to be tops. Over any wall! I want you to be people the world is proud of. Not only me—the world, Ma. The world has to be proud that you climbed over the wall and came down—to be a part of it. Not scared to live in the world, to work in it. Not scared to change, if you have to. Not scared to show you got just as beautiful a heart as anybody alive. Ma, you getting any of this language?"

"I think so," she said tremulously. "I'm trying, so I think I'll know, Juley."

"And Sunday," he burst out. "You know what I mean about Sunday?"

"How the *kuter* went to him? And Dave, too? And—and you thanked God?"

"Yes, Ma! A kid from this street—two kids. They ran to help that man. That *Schwartze*—that curse and hate and wall. Oh, Ma, then I knew it was all right. People could change. They could climb over the highest wall—like those kids did. You, Ma—and you'll pull the family with you."

He took a deep breath into him. "And Ma, it was so wonderful. All of a sudden I could lay back and rest."

Mrs. Golden pushed him gently against the pillows. "So rest," she said. "Show me."

They smiled at each other. "Ma," he said, his eyes shining in the pale face, "you do know what I was talking about!"

"Maybe," she said very quietly. "When you were talking, I remembered something. You know, when I was a girl in Russia, I climbed the highest walls in our village. You know what was on the other side? Fruit, nuts—such trees! I was never afraid of the watchman, the dogs. I climbed like—like your little friend, the *kuter*. Who could stop me? Who could catch me? Nobody."

She shrugged. "When I was little, I always knew what was behind those walls. Is that why a girl was not afraid? She knew what was there?"

He looked at her with delighted wonder. "Mrs. Golden," he said, "you're terrific."

"Thanks for the compliment," she said wryly. "Maybe I can bring you some grape juice, Mr. Golden? Before I start to climb again? And maybe break my neck?"

He laughed. "Later."

"All right," she said, watching him open his notebook, the new softness on his ravaged face as he glanced at a page.

He looked up at her. "Want to hear a poem?" he said.

"Didn't I always want to?"

"I wrote it yesterday," he said, and looked at her searchingly. "I didn't think I'd ever read it to you, Ma."

"You changed your mind?" she asked, her voice steady.

In answer, he began to read:

"I will no longer be afraid to die
When I know I can live in my mother's heart,
Be there, for always, in my brother's heart
The way I dreamed I'd be.
The way a man is born to be:
A love, a song to hum, a good fine memory.
I will no longer be afraid of death
When life has opened for all to see
My mother's heart—the beautiful flower,
The song, the dream that never dies."

It was the first time he had ever mentioned death in this way. In the past, he had thrown the word at her in bitterness or in panic. Hearing it this way, with such a meaning of opening doors, Mrs. Golden felt no fear. She felt, instead, the strength he had found for himself, and she thought: Some day I'll understand the whole thing, the whole quiet boy.

Jules touched her cheek. "Like it, Ma?" he asked.

"Beautiful. I want Papa to hear it. Some day, huh?"

"Okay. You know? It feels good to read my poems to you. I mean, like now. It's like talking real near." He turned back a page, then a few more. "Want to hear another one, Ma?"

She smiled at the living poetry of her boy, which she was at last beginning to understand.

"Read, read," she said. "It feels good to me, too."

# Chapter eighteen

It turned cold early the following Sunday morning. Snow whirled through the air for an hour or two, but melted as it hit the ground. On his way home from the board meeting, Sam Miller shivered, his bearded chin burrowing down into his coat for warmth.

He felt dazed with mortification as he strode toward his house. The street looked deserted and dirty, the lawns cluttered with wet leaves and bits of newspaper; it was like an illustration for the cynical things which had been flung at him in the temple. Dr. Palay's car, in front of the Golden house, completed the picture.

A dying street, he thought. A dying neighborhood.

As he came into the kitchen of his house, he bellowed toward the upstairs: "Ben! Ilona! I'm here from the meeting."

His wife came running from the bedroom wing. Her anxious, blurred-looking eyes fastened on his, and he said heavily, "Riva, they did it to me."

"They are selling? Impossible!" she cried. "You told them you forbid it?"

He made one of his dramatic gestures. "I? Who am I these days?"

"God! It's because of the Valentis and the Black One. I knew something awful would happen."

Slowly, with a sigh, he removed his coat. His wife took it at once and shook the wet drops from it. Smoothing his hat, she scurried to the closet.

Ben came down the back stairs, and his father's head jerked up. "They are selling," he said.

"I heard you tell Mother," Ben said quietly, speaking Yiddish, too.

"Where is Ilona?"

"Simon is not well," Ben said. "She is with him."

His father glared. "At a time like this, a man wants his whole family with him!"

Mrs. Miller had come back into the kitchen. She, too, knew he was referring to Herb, and she said quickly, "Ruth will be home from the store soon. We'll sit and talk."

"Talk about what?" Again a heavy, dramatic gesture came. "They humiliated me. They made me small—even after I reminded them that it was my money that started the temple. I asked them not to sell. I told them I had to stay in this neighborhood—I had no choice. Surely I, as *the* founder—I said—surely I have a certain influence? Do you know what they told me?"

He looked at his son, at his wife. "They told me—in so many words! —that my five thousand dollars is an old story. Others have put in more money by now. They have more to say than Sam Miller! It is the wish of the majority to move to a better neighborhood. To a Jewish neighborhood, they said!"

"And we?" Mrs. Miller cried. "Are we to be abandoned?"

He paid no attention to her. He went on with his angry monologue: "They made me a nothing. I, the founder of this very temple. The owner of three stores—at whose home the visiting cantors, the rabbis, used to stay. They disregarded me. They have decided—they will run before the hurricane of the Black Ones."

"I wonder why," Ben said softly, as if to himself. "We are people. Our need is here, right here."

"No philosophy, please!" his father said. "These are hard-headed men. Money, prestige—God, those words! When a man no longer possesses them he is a nothing in the eyes of his community."

Ben felt stunned. It seemed to him that he was seeing his father's soul for the first time, empty, overly proud, seething with envy. He had always been awed by this man, full of admiration and respect. Now an unfamiliar sensation of pity crept into him.

"Sam," Mrs. Miller said timidly, "there was talk of merging with another congregation, joining it on the Heights. Did anyone bring that up?"

"Stupid!" Mr. Miller shouted. "And I said as much when Izzie Diamond stood up with the idea. A lot he cares! He has no store in

284

this neighborhood, he was not a founder. Why should we be swallowed up?—this is what I asked the board. Made a nothing by some other congregation? It would be their name, their building. And we of the Woodlawn Jewish Center? It would be as if we had never existed."

"Maybe they would take our name for the merged congregation," his wife said eagerly. "Elect you chairman of the board."

He gave her a look of scornful fury. "Am I the rich man I was? The owner of three successful business establishments? They would never take our name. Already it smells of a slums. My temple and I— both are condemned by the Jewish community. We have lost our reputation, here among the Italians and the Black Ones, so they take even our God away!"

"No one can take God away," Ben said very quickly, his face pale.

His father sneered. "Not even the rich Jews on the Heights? They are the new kings now."

Mrs. Miller began to cry. "How dare they?" she wailed. "It was you who brought the first rabbi here. Fed him, gave him a bed, pocket money even—until they could afford to pay him."

Her husband nodded. "Go tell it to the board. Remind them."

"Father," Ben said suddenly, "let us start a new congregation here. There will be enough Jews."

Mrs. Miller stopped crying, her eyes astonished and hopeful, but her husband said, "Hah! They are moving faster every day. And when the Center is sold, this will become a black slums overnight."

"Some Jews will stay," Ben said eagerly. "Others will move here— if we have a temple. We can even start in a little store. Save money, build a new Center some day—a beautiful new temple."

Mr. Miller stared at him, breathing heavily. "In a little store? Like the Black Ones and their store churches? I? I should go and pray in— in a store?"

Then the shocked expression in his son's eyes struck him. With a great effort, he said, "I am too old to start over."

"I am young," Ben said instantly. "I will help you. God will help us both. Is it so impossible?"

His son's gravely flashing eyes, his pallor and look of asceticism— as if he were a fanatic young student of the Talmud instead of a busi- nessman—made Mr. Miller uncomfortable.

"Why should we start over in a dying neighborhood?" he said,

285

trying to shrug. "It will soon belong completely to the others. Let us face the situation: any Jew will run from here as soon as he has the money. An entirely different world of people is swallowing this area."

"But Father," Ben said, so earnestly that he was stammering, "why can't we keep Jewishness here? There are many people left, to live here. Their children. Why can't we keep our neighborhood decent, dignified? A place where we can meet together quietly. Work together, talk of—of good deeds. God does not move out with a temple building. There can be Jewishness here."

His son made Sam Miller taut with nervousness. The boy had been strange and different, and the man was even stranger. What kind of holy reasoning was he trying to put into words? He was in America, not in a school for scholars of mystic, higher-than-man thinking! What was this interpretation of Jewishness that would salvage a neighborhood plunging toward decay?

"Listen, Ben," he said uneasily, "I feel better. You don't have to worry about me. What will be, will be. When the time comes we will move to the Heights, too. I am not dead yet. I made money once in America—I'll make it again. They will listen to me again in the temple."

His wife was nodding eagerly. Ben said nothing, his eyes downcast, like an abashed boy, and Mr. Miller began to feel more like himself.

A vindicative, satisfied thought came to him, and he said it to them: "And what will happen on the Heights, some day? In fifteen, twenty years—watch! This same Heights where the Jews are crowding so excitedly, mortgaging their lives for a fancy house? The same thing! A few Black Ones will manage to sneak in, and again the panic will start. Mark my word! Again the Jews will start running—to still another neighborhood. This is America for you, eh? And when I think how we ran here from Europe—God! For this?"

"After all," Ben said, his voice husky with feeling, "the whole world is a constant migration. A man makes a home for his family and tries to keep it a good home. He tries to keep his small place in the world decent. Is it different in Europe, anywhere?"

"Yes," Mr. Miller said, slapping his hands together. "In Europe there are not any more new places where Jews can run. They can go only to Israel—if they are lucky. And in America? The new places are running out here, too. Only Israel is left when our own temple abandons us."

"I am sorry you feel abandoned," Ben said in a low voice.

"Oh, I am not dead yet! They will listen to me again, don't worry!"

The feeling of pity struck deeper in Ben, and he wondered how he could have once been frightened of his father. He saw the aging face and paunchy body, the gleam of gray in the reddish-brown beard. He saw the empty soul, and he thought: Does it take the imminence of another world of people to make a man see his father? Is this why these other people came, asking to enter our world?

And he went on with his simple, earnest reasoning: They will enter our world. For is it ours, after all? For is this not my father, after all, this man I have just seen? Yes, it is the real, inner world that I must accept. The real world, the real father—

His father said suddenly, "I am going to the store for a while."

"But you haven't eaten yet," his wife cried. "It's after twelve. I have your dinner ready."

"I'm not hungry," Mr. Miller said. "Where is my coat?"

As his wife ran to the closet, he thought almost with yearning of how it would be at the store. Maybe many customers would come, two and three at a time, as they used to on Sundays. And Ruth would be there; he wanted to be with Ruth, suddenly. He had told her that he would not be in at all today, because of the board meeting, but the restlessness in him was like a homesickness.

In a few moments he was back in the street, taking deep gulps of the cold air. The doctor's car was still in front of the Golden house but he turned his eyes away, refusing to think of death of any kind. Passing the Zigman house, he saw Dave and Chip boxing on the lawn. They wore heavy sweat shirts, and their faces were red and youthful.

Sam Miller glared at Chip as he passed. The powerful, hard body made his eyes narrow, but he thought scornfully: That scum? Sure, they can be married in Ben's new temple—in a store! But first I'll have to be dead, Ruth, so don't worry, he won't pull you under.

Near the corner, he passed a Negro couple peering at windows as they walked slowly. He cursed them, thinking: Maybe it *is* time to

287

move. I'll buy a car, Ruth will drive me to the store. I can afford to live! Why am I saving my little money, she should marry that peddler of papers? Ruth and I—all right, a new house, a new temple, we'll drive to business every day.

But on Woodlawn, walking fast with the excitement of these new plans, Sam Miller came to his temple. A bleakness swept through him as he stopped to look at the familiar little building. He had created it. Could life actually do such things to a man? Take away his—heart, and for no reason that made sense?

He walked on, before he could weep. But then a gnawing emotion drove him toward Herb's former store. In the old days there had been a meaningful path of life for him each morning; he had stopped at Ben's store briefly, then at Herb's for a nice visit, then he had gone on to his own store, which Ruth had already opened.

Herb's place was now a bar. He looked with bitterness at the size of the store, the two large display windows, the corner location: all the shining advantages which had made him pick it for Herb. He had chosen the best, stocked it with the finest things from his own store. And now it was a saloon!

His excited feeling that he would soon start all over again toward success left him as he moved away from Herb's store. How was it possible? he brooded. Why had he lost so much—his son, his wealth and reputation, and now the temple itself?

When he came within sight of his store, he saw Herb's car at the curb. It infuriated him: small, old and shabby—as the man's whole life had become. He almost ran the rest of the way.

The screen door had been removed for the coming winter. The big electric heater was on, and a blast of warm air hit him as he banged the door shut. Ruth was sitting behind the grilled window in the office, making entries in the books. In a moment, Herb's face came into view as he got up from the bench in the tool section.

As his eyes met his son's, Sam Miller felt the painful mixture of love and yearning and blind anger. "What are you doing?" he shouted. "Still playing with your toys? While my whole life falls to pieces around me!"

"Dad, I was afraid," Ruth said very quickly. "I phoned Herb and asked him to come and stay with me. Told him I'd be alone, and—"

"Stop lying, Ruthie," Herb said. "It was a good chance for me to
288

work with the store tools, Dad. She phoned that she was going to be alone."

"But I *was* afraid," Ruth said tremulously as she came toward the front of the store. "You warned me—to have the gun handy. Since last Sunday—"

"So you can still protect women?" Mr. Miller interrupted with a sneer. "That much of a Jew is still in you?"

Herb watched him for a minute. He saw how tense Ruth was, standing behind the man, her hands clenched on the counter, and felt his stomach lurching with the old, helpless despair. He turned to wrap his belongings, so that he could leave as quickly as possible.

"Talk!" his father said. "They stole your glib tongue in the gentile world? Talk—it's time!"

"The gentile world?" Herb said, still stubbornly speaking English. "Where should I live—in Palestine?"

"They wouldn't spit on men like you in Israel. They haven't the time, or the space to waste. And please!—how many times do I have to tell you? Call it Israel! That will be our name when we are recognized by the world."

"We?" Herb muttered. "Include me out."

"You're not a Jew?"

His package wrapped and tied, Herb straightened. "I live in this country," he said, not looking at his father. "I'm going, Ruthie."

"All right," Ruth said breathlessly. "Thanks for the help."

But Mr. Miller went right on, in a bitter, strident voice: "You'll know, some day. When the gentiles remind you—with clubs, with fire, and with guns—that a Jew has only one home. Look in the mirror at your own face, if you want a reminder! Then look at the neighborhood, where once a beautiful temple was created. Yes, let the Black Ones remind you that only in Israel—"

"Shut up!" Herb shouted.

"Herbie," Ruth cried, "for God's sake!"

Herb's scar looked like a welt in his pale face. "Let's cut the propaganda. Please!"

He picked up his package and rushed toward the door.

"So you'll walk out on me, too?" Mr. Miller called after him, his voice frantic. "You don't care what happens to your father? You don't care if they take my temple away?"

"Oh, Dad," Ruth said, "they're not selling?"

"Oh, yes! They voted, they made a whole democratic process of it! Sam Miller lost."

Herb had stopped. He turned and stared at the dramatic, posturing man.

"Dad, it's impossible," Ruth said. "What happened?"

"They gave me a slap with every word. They told me I'm a nothing these days, a nothing. The whole board of trustees—" The words seemed to choke him. He took off his hat, threw it on the counter, and wiped his face.

"So they have decided to sell the building," Herb said, his voice harsh with excitement. "The congregation is going to move out on you. Well, well!"

Mr. Miller sensed a queer elation in his son, another mystery in this man whom he had never been able to draw close, and he said with real despair: "The end of my life—and where were you, to hold me up? An oldest son. A man's support in his old age. Who will I look to—Ben, with his mad ideas? I need my son! Where have you ever been when I needed you?"

Herb's chest pinched with hurt. He fumbled his package down on the floor, thinking: Need, for God's sake! Even now, I could bawl like a kid. Even now I want him, I need him.

Ruth ran around the counter, touched her father's arm. "Dad, please," she begged. "You're just upsetting yourself. Come on, take off your coat and lie down in the back. You'll just make yourself sick."

Mr. Miller pushed away her hand. "He has made me sick. Sick and old! Nothing is left to me now—just a wilderness of Black Ones. He—my own son."

With that wondering grief, Herb said, "So I'm responsible for the *Schwartze*, too? I'm the one who brought them, who surrounded your *shul* with them—until it fell?"

"I say you are responsible for all my misfortunes," his father cried. "They began the day you left your store."

"The day of wrath," Her said, and suddenly he felt full of words, of burning and flashing thoughts, at the electric end of all the years in which he had walked away from his father in helpless silence.

"I suppose," he said caustically, "it's my fault, too, that you and

290

your street said it was a colored guy in the Gully with Santina. When all the time it was one of us. And a boy, at that."

"A mistake!"

"I'll say. So did you go and apologize to the first *Schwartze* you saw? Sex—grabbing the wrong woman—that's some crime! Did you tell that *Schwartze* you accused the wrong man?"

"You can still laugh?" his father said ominously, and Herb realized that he was smiling. He saw the shocked surprise in Ruth's eyes.

"You walked away from a business, from a marriage." The familiar rage had grabbed his father's voice, and it was shaking. "From your own religion. You lost everything—the store, even your child! And from that day, bad luck followed us. My store, Ben's. We stopped making money. The holdups began all about us. The Black Ones came."

A customer was at the door. Herb waved him away, called, "Closed, closed."

His eyes were glittering when he turned back to his father. "Blame it all on me, go ahead. Even the way they calmly took your *shul* away."

"Don't talk of the temple!"

"Don't talk about my child," Herb said grimly.

"Oh, Herb," Ruth said, horrified. "Please go home!"

"You stay out of this," her father shouted at her. Then he said, "What are you saying? That I'm not good enough to talk about my grandchild?"

"That can't be news to you," Herb said, his jaw aching with the tightness of his smile. "Ruthie, *you'd* better go home. There's a hell of a lot might be said here. Go on, beat it."

"She'll stay right here," Mr. Miller said. He searched Herb's face, his heart pounding so that he felt breathless and ill.

A man stopped in front of one of the windows. Herb locked the door and pulled down the shade.

Mr. Miller stared, demanded, "What are you doing? There's a customer—let him in."

"Later you'll let him in," Herb said. "You'll have your store all to yourself. You can make a *shul* out of it."

"Ruth," Mr. Miller said hoarsely, "you hear how he is talking to me? A Jew should have no respect for his father?"

"Good Lord," Herb said, "can't you stop that? Even now? A Jew!

Stop pointing it at me like—like a gun! The big deal, the big threat. God damn it, you could've made religion clean, a—a refuge where a man could go sometimes for quiet."

"Listen to him! Thank God I have one child left to respect me."

"But she can't get your *shul* back for you, huh? Even Ben can't. Go on, write to Congress. To the President."

"Why are you laughing at me?" Mr. Miller shouted.

"I'm not. I just wonder what you'll do now. With nothing left but the store. Will they welcome you in Israel when you've flunked out in an unimportant place like America?"

"Don't talk to me! You're no son of mine."

"I suppose not," Herb said pleasantly.

Ruth had been watching the two in complete helplessness. It was all so unreal: the way it had exploded out of the sale of the *shul*—out of the *Schwartze*, really—exploded right into the secret war Herb and her father had been fighting so long. Only it was in the open now, being uttered out loud in angry, bitter words that were appalling between a father and a son.

And the two seemed so different. Herb was no longer the silent man who had walked away abruptly when Dad had said one accusing word. Her father—he had no dignity left, somehow. His coat looked too tight for the big, bulky body as he gesticulated so dramatically. His face was red and perspired, and the beard looked suddenly awry.

"Stupid!" he began to shout again. "It's not enough that you spoiled everything you touched? Ruined your own daughter's life?"

Ruth saw Herb's face turn a pasty white, the scar throbbing dark red and livid. When she looked back at her father, the ugly memory slashed through her of his expression last Sunday when the Negro was being beaten in the street. Oh, Chip! she called in her head. Please, please, Chip!

"You are stupid. A weak, stupid fool. Yes, you are a replica of your mother! She was never more than a peasant. Superstitious, ignorant—like that whole village. I shouldn't have left you there with her. Look what she made out of an oldest son who—"

Ruth cringed as Herb lost control and broke in on their father with hatred: "No, you shouldn't have left me with that poor little peasant girl! While you slept with sophisticated city women in America. That's right! It was a mistake to leave me!"

292

With a gasp, Ruth ran away from them. But when she got back of
the counter she did not know where to go or what to do. Here it was
at last. The secret, the nightmare she had tried to squeeze out of the
tiniest dark place of her mind; but it had stayed, like a germ hidden
in her over the years, to spring out at once to Herb's call.

Sam Miller was staring at his son with a sick fascination. Herb's
eyes loathed him. He seemed to see, for the first time, a big young
man, strong, with a shining and direct glance—an oldest son.

His voice thin, he managed to say, "You're talking to your father."

"Don't call my mother names, you," Herb said, his hands gripping
the edge of the counter. "Just don't do it."

"Didn't I have enough today?" his father said uncertainly. "They
broke me to pieces. What do you want of me?"

"Leave my mother alone. That's all I want."

Both men had forgotten Ruth. "You took a pretty, happy girl,"
Herb said. "Free, barefoot, like a little dancing gypsy. You broke *her*
to pieces, inside of her. You broke her good, where it counts."

"I! What are you talking about?"

"What! My God, you slept around, like—you chased women
until you made her crazy. You made me crazy! And all the while
you hollered Palestine up and down the streets."

"No! What are you saying?"

"Yes, yes. Before we got here from Europe. For years—ah, the
secret life of Sam Miller! And after we came, even after Mom got
here, you went right on sleeping around. You dirty, low— Even after
we came."

"Liar!" Mr. Miller cried, and slapped Herb's face.

Ruth screamed, and the men looked at her. She saw her father's
eyes, stunned with shame and fear, and covered her face with her
hands.

Herb's voice came after a while, too quiet, as if the slap had
knocked everything out of him but exhaustion.

"Dad," he said, "I followed you for a while. I had to, finally. A
man has to see if his mother is crazy, or— A man has to listen, finally,
when his own mother keeps crying. Dad, I saw you. That redheaded
woman. And the one with a kid."

Ruth waited for denial, knew it could never come; never, even after
all the years she had denied it in the darkest, smallest place left in her.

293

"Honey," Herb said.

She looked up, saw with surprise that there were tears in his eyes. "Get your stuff," he said in that tired voice. "I'll take you home."

"Ruth!" her father cried hoarsely. His face was twisted, and he was crying.

"Yes, Dad?" she said mechanically.

But he did not answer. He was watching Herb unlocking the door, bending for his package. Suddenly Ruth ran back to the office and gathered together her things. Chip, please! she said to herself, but she did not know what she was asking of Chip.

Through the grilled window, she saw her father still staring at Herb, who stood at the door, looking out into the street. She remembered her brother's gypsies. She remembered the tall, gentle, laughing boy who had told her the golden fairy tales. She remembered how the father she had dreamed about so often had always had her brother's face, his eyes and voice.

Herb turned and looked for her, and then she was able to move. She ran toward him, past the showcase stretching the length of the store with its hundreds of dusty, pawned objects, past her father. Herb opened the door, and in an instant she was out in the cold air.

Then she was in the car, and they were riding up Central Avenue; the long, rolling shivers were still in her body, and Herb, driving slowly, lit a cigarette and passed it to her. She smoked it, staring dazedly out the window at the people walking all bundled up against the cold.

"Want to know something, honey?" Herb said, a breathless curt quiet in his voice. "I'm glad the *Schwartze* came shoving. Would I ever have opened my mouth today, otherwise?"

She could not answer; the feeling of sick fear was still in her. But Herb seemed really to be talking to himself.

"For a year—more—that's all we heard. *Schwartze, Schwartze,* they're coming, they're here. So exactly what happened? Did they rob, murder? Only in our heads. What finally happened? A half-ass thing like Ross getting nervous enough to punch one of them."

He pulled the wheel jerkily, and they were in one of the side streets leading toward Woodlawn. The curtness in Herb's voice, quiet as it was, held excitement.

"The houses are still there," he said. "Some empty, some full. The street's in exactly the same condition. Only we're different! Only we did something—inside. God, it's funny!"

Still she could say nothing, and Herb seemed to become aware of her daze for the first time. He was silent, driving faster.

When it was time to turn into East 120th, he said, "It'll be all right. I'll sit with Mom—eat with her, she likes that. You lie down for a while, honey. You'll feel better."

The curtness was gone from his voice, only the quiet there like a hush. When he pulled into the driveway, to turn around, Ruth looked next door for Chip but saw only Judy Vincent. She was sitting on the top step of her porch, huddled in a sweater, staring intently at the Golden house. The tragic tenseness of the girl's face struck through to Ruth, and she seemed to stir inside and to start feeling real. She followed the child's frozen glance, saw Dr. Palay's car.

"Oh, Herb," she murmured, "poor Jules must be very sick. The doctor's back. He was there when I left this morning."

Herb put a big, gentle hand on her arm and shook her. "You okay now?" he asked.

Ruth looked at him, saw him as real as the girl's watch over that house of sickness. His battered face looked different, since the shouting and the violence at the store. His eyes were deeply quiet.

She nodded and opened the car door. They went into the house, Ruth directly to her bedroom and Herb to the kitchen, where his mother looked up from her game of solitaire at the table and cried, "Herb, have you heard they're selling the temple? Your father—oh, Herb, what will he do?"

Ruth lay down on her bed. The shades were drawn, and the room was blessedly dusky. She heard the low mutter of Herb's voice, then her mother's—first a moaning, then an accusing, scolding shrillness. She remembered her father's weeping face, and a terrible pity surged through her.

Herb came into the room and sat down on the bed. "Thought I'd take Mom for a ride," he said. "She's pretty upset. We'll pick up Alice."

Ruth took his hand. He pressed hers hard. Suddenly, from the kitchen, their mother cried, "Herb, I'm not going with you. I'm going to the store. He needs me there. I'll sit with him."

"Wait, I'll drive you," Herb said, getting up.

295

"No! I don't want him to see you drive me. He had enough!"

The back door slammed. Ruth sat up, said, "I—do you think I should go, too?"

"No, honey," Herb said in a low voice. "God, did you hear her? She still loves him."

After a moment, he came to her and kissed her cheek. "I'm going to Alice," he said. "We'll be together—talk. It's my Sunday to have her."

He left. Ruth became aware of the silence all over the house. Ben must have taken the family out, she thought, and got up, went to the bathroom mechanically and washed her face.

She was sitting in the living room, staring down blindly at an open book, when Chip appeared. He did not knock, simply came in by the back door and walked to her chair, stood there until she looked up.

It was the first time he had been in her house, but it was the room that looked strange, not he. His boxer-dancer body was taut and graceful and alive against the background of drab drapes and heavy furniture.

"Ruth," he mumbled, pain wrenching at him as he saw her eyes. "Ruth, I'm sorry. Herb just told me. I mean, your father and him— he told me."

Her eyes went back to the book, away from the golden young apparition of him in that gloomy room.

"Ruth, I'm sorry for you! He was—your rabbi, your everything. I know it! I'm sorry it killed you like this."

She started to cry and to try to explain at the same time. "No, not me," she gasped out. "I just feel so sorry for him. I—I never pitied him before. Oh, Chip! Chip, that poor old man."

He went down on his knees before her, took the book and tossed it behind him. "Don't cry," he said. "My Ruth, don't cry like that. Here, cry on me."

She leaned into his arms and buried her face against him, and he rocked her. Oh, God, he thought, this why a guy looks at a star all his life? To pick it up when it falls?

"Ruth," he whispered against her hair. "My Ruth."

When she sat up, he wiped her face with his handkerchief. She looked at him, so close, and it was like being able to see underneath

296

so very much that she felt breathless. She saw his dreamer eyes; the dream was love, togetherness, two people together.

She saw his whole dreamer self, and she called his name.

# Chapter nineteen

After school on Tuesday, Vincent met Clara at the water fountain and they walked home. They both wore jackets over their middies and skirts; the morning snow had turned into blustering dampness.

They walked in silence, then Clara said softly, "You still feel lousy, don't you?"

"Yeah," Vincent said, the lump back in her throat.

"Was it today?"

Vincent nodded. Again they walked silently, slowly, until they came to East 112th.

"See you tomorrow," Clara said, and she patted Vincent's arm.

"Okay."

They stood looking at each other on the windy corner. Then, with great delicacy, Clara said, "Want me to pray?"

Vincent thought about it for a minute, then she said, "Yeah."

"Okay," Clara said. "So long."

"So long."

Clara turned into her street, and Vincent went on toward hers. When she got home she heard her mother upstairs talking to Mrs. Levine. She changed into pants and a blouse, moving numbly. It was the emptiness that was so frightening. Big chunks of space; even thinking of Manny did no good.

"Judy, you're here?" Her mother had come downstairs. "There's a letter from Nate."

Vincent wandered into the kitchen. Her mother was fixing her bread and butter, turned to say gently, "Come, you'll eat something. You want to read the letter? If not, I'll wait."

"I'll read it, Ma," Vincent said. "Only I'm not hungry now."

She took out the letter and a ten-dollar bill, began to read very fast: " 'Dear Ma, here's ten bucks for after the holidays. How about a new hat or something fancy? Even if it is after New Year's. Get it for Christmas and pretend you are a *goy* like your son.' "

"Now isn't he terrible?" her mother cried, her eyes shining.

" 'Sorry I got the holidays screwed up,' " Vincent went on. " 'I suppose I wouldn't even remember now except that I bumped into Uncle Morris the other day. In this Jewish restaurant I go to when I get a yen for a piece of fish or a plate of your potato pancakes. But they're not as good as yours.' "

A pleased laugh came from the listening woman. "He's lonesome!"

" 'Uncle Morris bawled the hell out of me for not coming to his house over the holidays. He said even the lowest Jew goes to *shul* on *Yom Kippur*. So I told him I was in Chicago, on business. So then he's all smiles and wants to know if I'm making money. I told him sure, and picked up his check. I guess that proved it to him.' "

Vincent paused while her mother giggled. Then she went on: " 'How's Shirl and the kid? He must be quite the boy. Sure would be good to see him, bring him a few presents from Uncle Nate, in person. Does he dance on your lap, the way Judy used to when she was little? How is Judy? I passed a school the other day, with a million kids playing ball in the yard, and I got to thinking about Judy's high marks and how she'll be in high school soon. I'll bet she goes to college. I sure am proud of that kid. Think about her a lot.' "

"See?" her mother said happily. "He's homesick. He'll be here soon, for a visit. Read, Judy."

" 'Well, Ma, that's it for today. How's Pa? Take care of yourself and the whole family. Wait till you see the collection of silver I got for you already. You'll love it. Regards, from your loving son, Nate.' "

"A boy," her mother cried. "It's like he's here, talking."

Vincent pushed the letter across the table, and her mother said very gently, "You feel like answering? If not, I'll wait for Shirley."

"Okay," Vincent muttered, "let Shirl answer him."

The lump was back in her throat as she left quickly. But when she got to her room and closed the door she could not cry, after all. She opened her books, spread her notebook, and began her homework.

Suddenly, like a piercing ache, she wanted to see Nate. His letter had sounded lonely—for the whole family, for her. There had been an empty hole in it; she had touched it, in the midst of her own gaping emptiness.

298

She tried to remember his face, his exact expression. She thought of Dave, for some reason, of the face-mask he showed the world and the different face she had seen underneath. Did Nate wear a mask, too?

He had never talked the same language as their father and mother, even though he had been able to reach Ma always, her hidden laughter. Maybe he loved Manny, too—the way she did! Hollering his name out in his head every day, like shaking a fist at everybody.

Then another faltering thought occurred to her: Would Pa be different if Nate lived here and they were pals? Real pals—the way a father and a son were in books? Look how Pa and Manny got together. And maybe Nate'll come home, too, some day?

The gush of yearning broke through her feeling of emptiness like a name called over and over. She grabbed her pen and some of her notebook paper, went quickly out to the kitchen.

"Ma," she said, "I feel like answering Nate's letter."

When they were sitting at the table, she said in a shaky voice, "I'm going to write him about Pa and Manny."

## 2

When Vincent finished her homework that evening, she put on her sweater and went out on the front porch. The darkness held a wet, chilly smell, and she shivered as she sat on the swing and looked across the street. Jules' room was bright. The ceiling light was on, and she thought: He hates that light, he likes just the lamp on.

The street looked gloomy. No kids played under the lampposts, no fast games were being called out. As she looked in the direction of the Gully, she saw a Negro man rounding the dead end of the street, walking into the lamppost light that was like yellow mist tonight. He looked huddled, as if it were a colder night than it was, as he walked and peered for empties.

Her mother and Mrs. Levine came out of the yard, talking in low voices, and crossed the street. They went into the Golden yard, and the Negro man watched them from the sidewalk, then walked up on the porch and rang the bell. The lights from the windows lit him up, a short slim man in a coat and hat. Then the front door opened a crack and he took off his hat, but in a moment the door closed.

He left the porch. On the sidewalk, he stood looking up at the dark, second-floor windows for a little while, then he resumed his walk toward the corner and became a slow shadow in the darkness. Maybe Clara was praying right this minute, Vincent thought.

Upstairs, the door opened, and Mr. Levine said, "I told you, Abe. It's getting too cold. When it's too cold for Seltzer on the porch, the summer is over."

"Let's sit for a little while, anyway."

"Believe me, I hate the thought of locking myself into the house for the long winter! All right, let's sit for a few minutes."

Their Yiddish drifted down to Vincent, made a familiar warmth in the lonely night. She hugged the sound to her.

"Quiet," her father said. "There is a sadness in the street."

Mr. Levine said, almost as softly, "A death stays for a few days. It hangs in the air, like a soul reluctant to leave."

Vincent looked up wonderingly. Was that really Mr. Levine talking? But in a moment she heard his usual coarse, gloomy tones: "Well, now they will sell and go to Florida. She'll put the daughter in the institution, and they'll go."

"Is it so easy, just because of a death?"

"Now it's easy! I know Sophie Golden. Now that the joy of her life is gone, what does she care about black, white, neighbors?"

"I'm not so sure," her father said gently. "When a mother has buried a son from a certain house—I don't know."

"My wife says he was buried in the new cemetery, on the West Side. A world doesn't live forever, eh? Only a year ago, my wife's brother was buried in the old cemetery. Now all that ground is taken."

"She will have a long way to go when she visits the grave."

Jules, Jules! Vincent called into the emptiness. It was like being lost in it. Everything was swallowed by that emptiness, and even a prayer disappeared in the swirling, thick fog of it.

"Ah, why shouldn't she sell?" Mr. Levine said drearily. "How much heartbreak should people have to bear? Sell—regardless—for the best price! Go to a warm land, live a little."

Vincent heard her father sigh. "But could she go away from a houseful of memories? In each room a memory, and a son in the grave? Yes—good-by, good luck, may you become millionaires, may you stand under the canopy at your daughter's wedding! But is life really that clear-cut?"

300

"Sometimes it takes a dead hand to push the dream out of a house."

"But it can never again be the whole dream. I wonder—is it possible to forget part of a dream, take what's left? When you have dreamed for years about walking into a golden land with a son. Hand in hand. Then the son disappears—all of a sudden the shining star has gone out, like a candle. How will it be in the promised land without him?"

Vincent had the feeling that her father was talking about Nate and himself. It was an uncanny sensation, as if she had seen into his heart. It scared her.

"In a street like this, a dream?" Mr. Levine said, his voice oddly wistful. "Maybe when the children are young. When you comb a little girl's hair. When one of the boys runs in from the game outside and calls for a big sandwich in that happy voice—then maybe you have a dream. For an hour! How long does it take a man to throw away half his dream, Abe?"

"What is the difference? As long as he doesn't throw away the whole thing. Florida, New York, Palestine—even the name of the place does not matter, as long as you know it means hope, a tomorrow."

Vincent remembered last night. Shirley and Manny had come, and Pa had stayed home from his lodge meeting. All evening, Manny had been in his lap. In the living room, Pa had danced Manny up and down, and Shirley had served the tea and cut up Ma's cake, had watched Pa and Manny with a smile. But the smile still had Johnnie's name in it. And Ma had said, "Abe, I'll hold the baby while you drink your tea." And Pa had said, "Since when do I need two hands for a glass of tea?" And Manny had laughed and bounced. But though Vincent had tried desperately to swim up through the swirling mists of her emptiness, they had swallowed up even the wonderful baby chuckle.

Mr. Levine sighed. Then her father sighed. Their old, scratchy voices drifted down like mourning lullabies.

"Well, the boy is dead," Mr. Levine said. "The whole dream of a mother and father—gone out of a street. The rest will go, too—you'll see. Smiles, tears—gone. A family—gone."

"No," her father said. "Something has to stay in a street where a family used to live. A radio playing—the window open, a song comes out. All right, the years pass and the street changes—but still the songs come out. You'll hear them when you walk."

It was a lullaby, a lament, and Vincent tried to put Jules' name to its soft music.

"Yes, a street changes but the same sky is over you. This time of year, the same leaves blow over the sidewalk when you push a baby in the buggy. And when you walk, when you think about people, you hear the same songs. The baby laughs—maybe he hears the songs you are remembering? Maybe, for him, the whole dream is just starting?"

After a while, Mr. Levine said in a bleak voice, "Songs? Not for old men, Abe. It is too cold to sit here and remember things. Come in, we'll have a glass of tea. Summer is over—we might as well admit it. Tomorrow I am going to light my furnace."

Their footsteps boomed over Vincent's head, then the door up there slammed. Mr. Miller came walking from the corner, passed very slowly, and turned into his yard. A dog barked somewhere.

Jules, Jules? Vincent called into the emptiness. But he was all mixed up, in her father's gentle old voice, with Nate, with Manny laughing in a buggy. No matter who lamented, she could not cry.

The funeral had been at two that afternoon. At school, by the big round clock in her English class, she had closed her eyes at two o'clock and tried to say her prayer. The words had made no sense. When she had opened her eyes again, the emptiness had not gone at all.

She stared at his house, at his windows bright with too much light, and she could not understand how that quick, leaping pulse could possibly be quiet. She tried to think of Clara praying to help her out, like a real friend. She tried to think of Dave, mask gone, another friend; of Manny on her father's lap, his name spoken out loud in the house. Nothing touched through the loneliness.

As Vincent watched the Golden house, Heidi came out of the yard and started across the street. Huddled in her coat, she looked for a moment like another of the continual, slowly walking searchers for empties, on her way to investigate the dark, upstairs windows of Dave's house. Then she turned into the walk leading to Vincent's porch.

"Judy?" she called in her hoarse voice, so like Jules' and her mother's.

Vincent met her at the top of the steps, then did not know what to say. In the bunched shadows at that side of the porch, Heidi thrust something toward her. Vincent's heart began a violent thudding as she touched the red notebook.

"Juley said I should give it to you," Heidi told her. "It's for you, he said. I couldn't come before. Alex was carrying on so bad, ever since— I had to take care of him. He finally fell asleep. So I brought it to you."

"Thanks. A lot," Vincent stammered, holding on hard to the red notebook. Heidi's-Jules' voice: she remembered her father saying, ". . . the street changes—but still the songs come out."

"You going to go now?" she blurted. "Away from our street?"

"What?"

"To Florida?"

In the shadows, Vincent saw Heidi's hands picking absently at her coat as she stared across at her house.

"Florida?" she said, as if she could not understand.

"Yeah," Vincent said, her throat starting to ache.

"I don't know! My mother—" Heidi began to cry softly. "I got to get back. I—I'll tell her you got his poems now. Like he wanted."

She went away, back into her yard like one of the huddled searchers. The street was the same, but the notebook pushed against Vincent's hands like a sudden touch in the emptiness. She rushed into the house, to the first lamp.

In the light, the red of Jules' notebook glowed richly. She saw the worn places on the knubbly binding, where he had opened and shut the book so many times—in the night, during the day when he wrote in it, when he grabbed at it to read aloud.

The words he had written on the first page came surging into her loneliness like the sound of his voice:

"Dedicated to Judith Vincent,
My Beloved Changeling"

She stared at the page, which gave her the poems as actually as if Jules were sitting up in bed and holding them out to her. She could see the speeding pulse, his hand brushing back his hair, and she began quickly to turn the pages.

Then she found her poem, gulped the words.

"Come, Changeling, let us look into our hearts for identity!
Let us know how they put us into the barred baby cribs, deep inside
the walled homes of these strangers who call themselves our
mothers, our fathers.
Let us know that we speak a different language of dreams, of thoughts,
of love—we children who are never their children in the heart.
Yes, though they feed us with bread made of their fears and ignorance,
we cannot grow into their dark images: we are changelings in
our hearts, we must be free.

In our hearts, in our hopes, World is our mother, and Life our father!
In our hearts we are free, as these strange parents can never be.
In our hearts we embrace the whole World, our mother,
We look into every face of Life—they are all those of our loving
father.

Come, Changeling, be a son of World, a daughter of Life!
All doors are open, Changeling-my-brother, Changeling-my-sister.
All doors are open to us, for we are young and strong and full of hope.
We will take the big footsteps of faith, leave behind the narrow corner
of our stranger parents, our frightened elders.
We will journey to our own street—to the free and sunny room of
our dream.
The clean room: doors open, windows open on the singing laughter
outside.
Oh, beautiful World, our mother.
Oh, beautiful Life, our father."

There were tears in Vincent's eyes. She leafed through the note-book, remembering how he had said, "I'll read you poems—lots of new ones, all for you. Later—tomorrow."

She found a new one among many he had read her, another piece of the changeling poem, as if he had thought of this one afterward and written it down for her.

"But a street marches upon the rest of the world.
The rope knotted by shivering people chains all of us, enmeshes our
minds.

And who will untie the knots of rope?
The Changeling!—coming upon her parents' wailing wall, hearing the
    chant of all her grandfathers and their fathers in her parents'
    lamenting prayer.

And who will pause to sing at that wall?
The Changeling!—meeting all the world there, taking her place, lifting
    her voice, so that the prayer will be anyone's now—love with-
    out fear—music so strong as to soar over the wall."

Crying hard, Vincent found the last poem in the notebook: "I
will no longer be afraid to die . . ."

She cried for a long time, the emptiness filling and filling with
the poems until they sang all over the house and the street for her.
She heard them roar past the opening at the corner—out, like a powerful rush of sound, into the world he had described.

Dear Lord, kind Lord, gracious Lord; and the meaning was there
again, as if Jules had given her back her prayer along with the elation
and certainty of the poems he had sent her tonight.

After a while, she carried the red notebook to her room and put
it with her treasure box. I'll show the poems to Manny some day, she
thought. And to Clara. She'll know what Jules means.

As she went to wash her face, she thought of the girl bending over
the little boy in his buggy. Hi, little half-and-half! She could make a
picture, if she wanted to, of Clara and Manny some day walking together into that beautiful church of theirs.

She could make another picture, which included herself. They
would sit in a room, the three of them, and she would read the poems
aloud, the way Jules had to her. And on that day she would have the
Bible in the room, too. Names, Manny—see all these names, and
yours, too? This family book, Clara—remember when you told me
about your family down South, the slaves? Well, here's mine—from
Russia. Mine and Manny's. And here we are! The way we met in the
Gully once, and—and were friends! And here's the red notebook.
Come, Changeling, let us look into our hearts for identity!

Vincent changed into a clean blouse, then put on her sweater again.
She was going across the street to visit Mrs. Golden; she had been
afraid to, before. The doorbell rang as she was smoothing down the
collar of her blouse.

She ran toward the front door. It was Dave. Through the window, she could see him shadowboxing with hard, excited motions as he waited for her.

When she opened the door, he cried, "Vincent, my mother's better!"

"Hey, that's swell," she said, coming out on the porch.

"She even went over to visit Mrs. Golden," he said. "That's how better she is. Want a cig? I got a whole pack. Nobody's around to see us."

He led the way to the swing. "I'm getting paid at the store now. My mother had a knock-down fight with my old man today. Said he had to pay me or—boy, you should've heard her!—or she wouldn't come and work there herself."

In the light from the lamppost, Dave's dimples flashed deep as he said gloatingly, "My old man looked at her like she was a ghost."

He struck a match for their cigarettes. They sat back, watching the brightly lit windows of the Golden house as they smoked. They could see people walking in Jules' room.

"You know what?" Dave said. "The funniest damn thing happened today. Some guy came in the store for a duck. It was after school—I was loading the truck. So he asks my old man if he knows where there's any rooms for rent. See, he's from out of town—got a job here in some factory and now he wants his wife and kids to come. He's white but not Jewish."

He chuckled. It was a sound of ease, of relaxation, that made Vincent feel good.

"My old man says to him, 'Your wife isn't here? So who's going to cook the duck?' This guy says, 'Me. I'm in a place with kitchen privileges. But I want five rooms, so's she can come and cook the duck next time. You know about rooms?' My old man stands there and scratches his head like a jackass! Can you beat it? He's got *Schwartze* on the bean so much that he doesn't even figure this guy!"

"Your empty, huh?" Vincent said.

"Sure. Our empty is rooms, ain't it? Five rooms? Hell, if my mother'd been in the store she'd have had that guy sewed up so fast he'd have been dizzy. So I hollered in from the truck, 'Hey, Pa, our upstairs is empty.' He looks at me like I'm nuts. Grownups are so damn dumb sometimes! Then he jumps, like I kicked him, and says,
306

'My God, our upstairs!' This guy breaks his neck to give my old man a deposit. Without even looking at the rooms."

"A white guy," Vincent said, and thought dreamily: When Clara moves upstairs of me, Dave's going to like her. We'll sit here and smoke. Maybe we'll read the red notebook, and we'll talk.

"Wonder if he'll cop a sneak when he finds out the *Schwartze* live so near? And how they're trying to get in our street?"

"Maybe he knows," Vincent said.

Dave snickered. "Maybe he doesn't even give a damn. As long as the wife and kids can come and cook him a duck, huh?"

"Sure!" Vincent laughed, too.

"Want another cig?" Dave said. "Don't nurse that butt. I told you —I got a whole pack. And money for more. I'm getting a salary!"

"Okay," Vincent said, and flipped away the end, took a fresh cigarette from the pack he held out so eagerly.

Again they smoked in silence, until Ben Miller walked past the house and into his driveway. Then Dave said, "Wonder how Chip's making out. You know he got himself an inside job at the paper?"

"Yeah?"

"He told me he never would've had the nerve to ask for it if— well, Ruth, you know. Guess they're going to get married or something."

"Yeah," Vincent said softly.

After a while, Dave said, "Wonder how Santina's making out. I went past that place they got her in. I was on the way to the market for eggs, and— You know they got bars on all the windows in that joint?"

"No," she said cautiously, thinking of jails and of Ziggy, how Dave used to swear and punch at any mention of his brother in prison.

But Dave laughed. "They ain't going to keep her in there long! Not Santina. Want to bet she cops a sneak right through those bars?"

"Think so?"

"Hell, yes!" Dave tossed his butt over the railing. "You should've heard my mother today. We were talking—a lot of stuff. You know, about Santina and Alex? How everybody figured he was a *Schwartze* at first? Boy, was that a stinker! Anyway, my mother said Santina ain't going to be in that place long."

"No? How come?" Vincent said.

"Because she's too full of life, and—and ripe for love. My mother said it in Jewish, but I didn't get it, so she starts in teaching me Jewish—we had a lot of fun. Ripe for love—wow! That's Santina, all right."

Vincent grinned. "Your mother—I can just see how she looked when she said that stuff. Dimples, huh?"

"Yeah! Big as nickels." He peered at Vincent; she heard him take a breath, then he said shyly, "You know what? When I got home from the store today—well, we were all alone in the house. We sat in the kitchen and ate. See, she'd baked a couple of breads to take over to Golden's, and she baked some for us, too—even though it ain't Friday. So we had warm bread and butter and tea, and—well, I told her about this guy with the duck, putting a deposit on our empty. She got real happy and excited. And—well, we got to talking."

His voice turned gruff, too fast. "Vincent, all of a sudden I was talking to her. I mean, real stuff! Ziggy and Al—me. Jesus, it was so wonderful. Because then she started to talk, too—both of us jabbering. Because—well, it's so damn funny, Vincent!—she was worried about the same things I was. You know—what I'd be in the future. What Ziggy and Al would do to me—inside of me, kind of, you know? She was so worried that she even quit visiting Ziggy! Can you beat it? She used to go a lot—bring him stuff to eat, spend the whole day there. But she just quit. In case I'd—well, want to go up with her and—hell, I don't know, catch it from him or something! She started to cry when she told me that, and I said, 'Aw, Ma, cut it out. Ziggy ain't got the flu or measles, that I can catch it!' So I made her laugh again."

Vincent remembered a poem Jules used to read aloud:

"There's a fire that burns between mother and son, too bright with
    pain to see one word.
Yet the words are there for the blind to see, all love and gold as
    they burn.
Oh, tell me, please, as the fire burns high:
Mother or son,
Who blinded me?"

Dave and his mother, Vincent thought very quietly. The bracelet and the dimples, and it's okay now. Did changelings ever find their mothers or fathers, get together with them? Maybe they did.

He was laughing, a low sound of wonder. Vincent watched the play of his dimples in the lamppost light as he said, "Hey, you know what? My mother told me she always wanted me to go to college. Can you beat it? Boy, I—well, we just talked our heads off! And we kept on laughing. I mean, even after my old man came home. He must've thought we were nuts."

"So what if he did?" she said.

"So nothing," he said, shrugging airily.

They watched Jules' bright windows for a while. Then Vincent said, "I'm going across to see Mrs. Golden. Want to come?"

"Yeah," Dave said earnestly. "Let me go with you."

They started off the porch, and Vincent felt the poems moving with her into the street, like a singing.

## Chapter twenty

"Judy, I'm ready," her mother called from the bathroom.

Vincent finished adding before she jumped up from the table in the living room, where she was doing her homework.

It was the Saturday night of the big yearly party given by the lodge, and she could hear the Levines running back and forth upstairs as they got ready to go. As she walked into the bathroom, steamy from her mother's bath, Vincent could see her father in the bedroom across the hallway. He was knotting his best tie, frowning at his clean-shaven face in the mirror.

"That thumbnail," her mother said, holding out the kitchen shears. "I almost tore my good stockings. Why does it grow so fast?"

Vincent took her mother's right hand in hers and began to trim the nail she could never cut by herself. She sniffed, thinking with a grin of Nate's letter: "Here's five bucks, Ma, buy some perfume for a good-looking gal."

"You smell good," she said.

"Does my hair look all right?" her mother asked anxiously. "I don't know if Shirley used enough curlers when she gave me the permanent."

"It looks swell." Then, as her mother winced, Vincent said firmly, "Don't jump, Ma, I'm not going to hurt you."

As she snipped off bits of the thickened nail, she felt an unaccustomed tenderness for the woman in her best dress, harshly corseted, the carefully curled hair about her eager face.

"When are you leaving for Shirley's?" her mother said.

"After I finish my homework. She said there's no hurry."

In a whisper, her mother said, "Don't forget the fish and the sponge cake."

"Okay," Vincent said, winking at her; it was their secret from Pa that Johnnie ate most of Ma's little gifts of food.

Smoothing off the last bit of ragged nail, Vincent went back to her homework. She glanced out the window at the Golden house, saw that the lamp had been lit in the living room. Jules had been dead almost two weeks, but in her head he was not gone at all. Like tonight; he would go with her to Shirley's. He would sit there with Clara and Dave and her, listen to their talk.

She leaned over her math problems. At the back of the house, her mother and father talked. Tag-ends of thoughts chased around at the back of her mind, in tune with their voices as she added and subtracted.

The party would be fun for them. It always was, because the men and the ladies' auxiliary joined for this one, and it would be way up on the Heights. A little orchestra would play dance music for the young folks and Jewish music for the mothers and fathers. After the big feed and a lot of wine and beer, all the older people would start the Jewish dances. A huge circle of laughing fathers and mothers and even grandparents suddenly drew itself in the middle of the floor, slow steps and joined hands, a perfect circle in perfect time, then faster and faster, and the singing would break out to the quickening music and the clapping of hands from those who were watching, the rhythmic words cried out at the end of each line of song and dance. Then, later in the evening, there would be solo dances by some of the men: their arms crossed at their chests, they would crouch and leap, their feet flinging out faster and faster to the music in the traditional

Russian dances they had learned in the village where they had been born.

Vincent wondered absently if Clara's parents belonged to a lodge for people who had been born in the South. But her mind jumped from this thought to the evening ahead. She was waiting for the house to empty so that she could get the Bible from the basement and no questions asked—and then it would be time to whistle for Dave, and go meet Clara!

What would Clara say when she heard the changelings poem, word for word? And Dave?—it would be all new to him. What would they say when they saw that long list of names in the Bible? See, here's Manny's name; and maybe Manny would be right on her lap when she said it—or on Clara's lap, or Dave's. Dave had told her he had never held a baby on his lap. What would his face look like—holding Manny?

She started another problem. At the back of the house, her mother said, "They had a telegram upstairs from Chip. He's in New York with Ruth Miller. They're married."

"By a rabbi?" her father asked dryly.

"Ask the mother of the groom!" Then, eagerly, her mother cried, "Oh, I hope he remembers Nate's address. I long for a personal regards."

"Yes, that would be good to hear."

"Lizzie is going to have a good time tonight," her mother said, laughing. "Imagine—the biggest event of the year, and she will be able to announce that her son is married to Sam Miller's daughter!"

"My ears ring, just thinking of how much she will talk tonight."

"Oh, Abe, be glad for her. Did she ever expect him to marry anybody but a gentile? And now—not only a Jewish girl, but Sam Miller's daughter. Let her talk."

"Let her, let her," he said darkly. "But watch how quickly Sam Miller will sell now. Move out of this street."

"You really think so?"

Let him! Vincent thought jubilantly. No talk could bother her this evening. She was happy. Just thinking about friends, she was warm and happy.

There was a knock at the back door, and Moe Levine called, "Hey, okay to go? All I have to do is settle the furnace for the night."

Vincent heard his wolf-whistle, and her mother said in a pleased voice, "It's a new dress, Moe."

"We're ready," her father said flatly. "Save your whistling for the party."

"Where's the *kuter?*" Moe said. "I want to see what she looks like in a fancy dress instead of Nate's pants."

"Stop calling her that," her father said, so furiously that Vincent grinned and remembered Clara's comical accent whenever she called her *schwartze kuter*, her funny little gleamy smile.

"Judy's not going," her mother said. "She never liked parties anyway, and tonight she's—"

Moe broke in, his voice sullen. "I'll call her any nickname I want. How come she's not going? It's a family party, all our kids are going. The whole damn house is going, so how come the *kuter* thinks—"

"I said don't call her that!" her father shouted. "She's not a baby any more. She's going to Shirley tonight, that's what. She's even sleeping there—because Shirley expects to be out too late. Now go tend your furnace and tell your father we're ready."

Moe laughed. "Yes, sir! Hey, how's Shirl's fire chief doing?"

The door slammed, and Vincent heard Moe run down the basement stairs, then the sound of the furnace being shaken.

"Sons," her father said curtly. "Sometimes I wonder if I would not rather look into the face of a Black One, instead of his!"

"I'll remind you, Abe. There are new tenants at Zigman's—white. Don't feel so depressed."

"So are they Jewish? And how long do you think they will stay? After they learn the real situation of the neighborhood?"

"How do we know?" her mother said softly. "And Abe, did you notice? The sign is out at Golden's again."

Her father sighed. "I knew she would not go away to Florida. So do you expect a white family to move in there, too?"

Her mother came into the living room, got their best coats out of the closet. "Judy," she whispered, "don't forget the fish and cake."

"I won't, Ma."

Her father came, to put on his coat. "When are you leaving?" he said.

"Oh, about eight-thirty," Vincent said. "Shirley said they're not in a hurry. See, it's a late dance." And she thought dreamily: Hey,

Shirl, this is my friend, Clara—and you know Dave, huh? Johnnie, hey Johnnie, meet my friends: Clara, and this is Dave.

"Tell Shirley," her father said stiffly, "that I'll come for the baby tomorrow at eleven o'clock, for our walk. Dress him warmly—it's cold in a buggy."

He still flushed when he spoke of Manny. "Okay," Vincent said, and then shyly: "You look swell, Pa. Both of you look swell."

He smiled. "Don't forget to lock the door and leave the key," he said. "We'll put on the hall light before we go."

Turning back to her homework, Vincent remembered how he had gone over to Shirley's last Sunday, to take Manny for a walk. Tomorrow would be the second Sunday. He had not gone upstairs, Shirley had told her. At his ring of the bell, she had brought Manny down to him, and Johnnie had stayed up in the apartment. "But honey, it's okay," Shirley had told her. "They'll bump some day. You'll see. Pa'll come up and have a drink with Johnnie one of these days. You'll see, honey!"

"Come on, come on," Moe suddenly yelled from the back hall. "It'll take us forty-five minutes to get up there. Why the hell people don't ever take a cab!"

"A millionaire," Mr. Levine said with a dry laugh. "Let's see if you can still sit in a bus, like a working man's son."

"So long, Vincent," Leo shouted. "I'll think of you when I'm eating all that fancy stuff. You dope!"

"Who has the tickets?" Mrs. Levine said nervously. "Moe? And you have the telegram from New York in your pocket? Show it to me."

They were gone. The stillness washed snugly around Vincent as she made herself finish one more problem. Then she stacked her homework and snapped off the lamp, carried the pile of books to her bedroom. Whistling, she took the red notebook out of her drawer.

For a few minutes, she leaned over her treasure box, glancing at the snapshot of Manny, the medal; touching them was like tasting the whole, wonderful evening to come. They would look at Manny—he was so sweet when he slept, on his stomach that way and his hands in fists like a little fat prize fighter. If he woke up, they would take him out to the party in the living room.

She carried the notebook out to the kitchen table, then ran out

313

into the back hall and down to the basement for the Bible. She had opened the door leading to the basement and was four steps down before she realized that she had forgotten to snap on the light.

"Nuts," she said, and giggled at her excitement, continued down into the blackness as she dug a packet of matches out of her pants pocket.

At the foot of the steps, Vincent lit a match and got her bearings, started out for the big trunk at the far end of the basement. She passed the furnaces, with their merry little gleams of coal behind the slotted doors, and then the match burned out. Too impatient to light another one, she groped the rest of the way, past the piles of left-over newspapers waiting to be sold by Mrs. Levine, past her father's overalls hanging stiff with paint from the basement clothesline. Then one hand touched the trunk, and she straightened to light a match.

A mysterious, tiny gleam of light caught at her eyes from out of the blackness. It seemed to come from the floor, from somewhere close to the coal lockers. Puzzled, she struck a match and went to investigate.

For a few seconds, what she saw made no sense. There was a peck basket on the floor, and in it sat a stump of burning candle. All around the candle, half filling the basket, were torn papers, slivers of wood, masses of curled shavings such as collected when Mr. Levine planed a two-by-four. It was this shaded candlelight she had seen, standing at the trunk.

Details etched themselves painfully and slowly into her mind: the kindling piled all around the basket, the balled-up newspapers—a nest of paper, ready to ignite at the first touch of the burning basket.

The match burned Vincent's fingers, and she dropped it. Instantly, her hands fumbling, she struck another match. More details appeared, her head aching with them: there was a sort of path made of paper and kindling, leading from the basket to the wooden door of one of the coal lockers. Leaning against the rickety door were thicker pieces of wood, more balled paper.

Pa! she thought dazedly, trying to remember how long it had taken a candle stump to burn down in the bottle, in the clubhouse, on a long summer night.

Suddenly a pungent odor hit her as she stared down at some dark, wet-looking stains on the basket, on crumpled paper. Anna Levine's

314

hair—the same smell—the back hall had reeked of it, remember?—
that time the school nurse had sent her home with a yellow slip
—Anna bawling and her mother hollering as she had washed her hair
with kerosene to get rid of the nits. Why kerosene now? Oh!—sure, it
burns—remember that book about farmers, how they cooked on a
kerosene stove and it lit so quick?

Pa, no! Vincent screamed in her head. No, no, you wouldn't do
it, Pa!

The match went out. She completed the picture in her mind: the
candle burns down until it touches paper, shavings, kerosene-soaked
basket. Poof! The fire starts, runs fast, fast along the path, hits the
leaning wood, ignites the locker door and mounts with a roar into the
walls.

In a sudden panic, as if the house was already burning, Vincent
ran to rescue the Bible. She crashed into things, almost fell, but found
the trunk and flung it open. Blindly, she pushed through soft goods
and pictures and things that clung to her hands, the odor of mothballs
blending horribly with the stench of kerosene in her nostrils. She dug
and tore at everything in her way until she had the big book.

Afraid to look behind her at the candle burning down so steadily,
she banged the trunk lid and began the stumbling flight across the
dark basement. One outstretched hand smacked into the hot-water
tank. Then she tangled with the hanging overalls, cried out in hoarse
fear before the smell of paint identified the enemy. Somehow, she
found the steps and plunged upward, the horror chasing her, and the
kerosene-mothball smell, the candle stump burning hot and steady in
her instead of in its soaked nest.

As she ran, she thought: What if Shirley and Johnnie tell Clara
to get out? When Clara rings the bell and comes up their steps and
I open the door and let her in? "Shirl, here's my friend, Clara. . . ."
What if they insult her, make her feel bad?

Vincent was now in the dimly lit hall. She took the remaining
steps two by two and got to the kitchen doorway. The room was an
abrupt, blinding light after all her groping and fumbling. It was somebody else's kitchen, full of unfamiliar things she had never seen
before.

But then, as her terrified eyes fell on the red notebook lying on
the table, the room seemed to focus. Her father's stained teapot on
the stove, the week's stack of newspapers on top of the refrigerator,

the pieces of her mother's cereal set bright on the cupboard shelf: the kitchen was home again, and she was able to move.

She ran to put the Bible on the table, then tore into her bedroom to rescue her schoolbooks, the pen Shirley had given her, the treasure box. She piled everything on the kitchen table, then tried to breathe, tried to remember what else had to be saved from the fire. Standing there so rigidly, she thought she heard a crackling and snapping, the fire mounting into all the walls.

"Pa!" she screamed.

That stump of candle someone had stolen from out her secret life in her clubhouse and hidden, still burning, in the basement—why, Pa, why? Again panic rose in her, and she grasped the edge of the table, shivering, hanging on so that she would not fall and be burned up by that racing fire. Objects blurred under her glazed stare, colors running into each other—red, brown, the silver-gold shine of her pen, and red-red-red.

Then the red notebook stopped blurring and moving. It was actually there. For a moment longer, the candle burned in Vincent's mind as she put a hand on Jules' notebook, but her heart had begun to quiet down. She could no longer hear the roaring of a fire in her head. Instead, words seemed to come up through her hand, as if a voice within the notebook had said them: Come, Changeling, be a son of World, a daughter of Life.

There was a brackish taste in her mouth, as if she had thrown up, but she went to the switch near the kitchen door and snapped on the basement light.

Dear Lord, kind Lord; the words began in her head, blessedly familiar and steadying: gracious Lord.

In the hall, she began to run. She was shouting as she rushed down the basement steps: "I pray Thou wilt look on all I love tenderly . . . weed their hearts of weariness . . . with all the needy . . . this vast treasure of content that was mine today, amen! Amen!"

She raced past the furnaces. The dingy basement light shone down on the basket, kindling, paper, uneven flicker. No, she had not dreamed it. The candle had not gone out. It would burn forever, and— When a house burned, you moved to a different street—on the Heights —to a different world. The men—the grownups—they'd said that, on the porch. Clara didn't have a porch.

316

Dear Lord, kind Lord, what if Shirley was afraid when she saw Clara at her door? Screamed: "My God, a *Schwartze!*" What if Johnnie cursed Clara, hollered: "Get out of here!"

Vincent stared at the craftily laid materials for a fire. Above her, all the silent rooms waited to be demolished by the hot flames. Her entire evening, so eagerly anticipated, hung above the candle, waiting to be destroyed. Clara, Manny, all the stories she had planned to tell Clara and Dave about Russia, about the boat coming over, about the way the voyagers had sung but her mother had cried—it was all in the fire. And the Bible, the notebook full of poems to be read aloud—the names, the poems—all burning here.

She herself was in this fire, in the evil of it and the question-and-answer of it: leave it, put it out—wrong, right? She was standing in its dreadful glare, an outsider, an enemy of the world. No, no!—oh, beautiful World, our mother. Lit by the roaring flames, she was outlined in some old pattern of ignorance and fear, the shadow of her father falling across her heart as she tried to run. No, no!—oh, beautiful Life, our father.

The Gully, the gang—they were in the fire. The girl she had met in the Gully, the girl who had stood looking at her, fists and flashing eyes and upflung head, as if from out of a mirror. Could you see somebody's heart in a fire? Could you see somebody's dream, exactly like yours?

Suddenly Vincent was crying. She grabbed up the candle and blew it out, threw it violently to the floor. "Damn you, damn you!" she shouted, and jumped on the basket, smashing it. She kicked all along the path of balled paper and soaked wood. Then, leaning against the open locker door, she sobbed helplessly as she looked in at the small pile of coal.

After a long time, she was able to stop crying. She found the basement broom, an old cardboard box, and swept everything up very carefully; found the candle she had thrown and put that into the box, too. Then she carried the box up the steps and outside, to the rubbish barrels near the back fence.

It was snowing. Walking back to the house, she raised her face to the feathers of coolness floating down. She could hear faraway voices in the street, misted by the wet darkness. For an instant, the candle burned down and touched the paper, the shavings in her mind, and the whole basket burst into an explosion of leaping red and gold but she thought steadily: No, Shirl's going to smile when Clara gets there. She's going to say, "Hello, honey. I'm so glad you could come and keep my sister company." And Johnnie'll say, "Don't forget the cake, kids. When Manny wakes up, give him a big piece, too."

When she was back in the kitchen, Vincent turned off the basement light. She went to the table, looked down at the things she had rescued, and suddenly felt a new fear as she visualized facing her father the next day, then Moe and Mr. Levine—and she thought with a shudder of thankfulness that nobody would be able to grab her tonight.

Maybe she would not come home from Shirley's in the morning, but wait until her father came over for Manny. Would he mention the fire? Would he holler, hit her? Maybe they wouldn't even talk about it—only in their eyes, the way they had talked about so many other important things.

She opened the Bible. There were all the family names, the old ones and the ones she had written on the page. She stared down at her own name for a long time.

Suddenly, her mouth dry, she uncapped her pen and wrote: "Nathan Vincent." Then, without pausing, she wrote under her brother's name: "John O'Brien (married to Shirley, father of Manny)."

There! God damn it! she shouted in her head.

She felt very tired as she carried her schoolbooks and treasure box back to her room. Methodically, she took the fish out of the refrigerator and put the dish in a bag with the cake her mother wanted Johnnie to have. She wrapped the Bible and the red notebook in newspaper. She got her jacket, turned off lights, locked the door, put the key in the milk box. It was like doing homework, crossing off one problem after another as she completed it.

Again she was in the yard, her face raised to the delicate touch of snowflakes. She was so exhausted that she stumbled as she walked out to the sidewalk and next door to the Zigman porch. At the steps, she whistled.

Dave was out in a minute. He, too, was bareheaded, his jacket unbuttoned. "Hot dog!" he called as he closed the door. "It's really snowing now!"

318

He took the steps in one leap, said, "Want me to carry some of that stuff?"

She handed him the bag of fish and cake. As they started off toward the corner, Dave laughed and said, "Hey, Vincent, want to hear something? Guess where me and my mother are going tomorrow? Rain or shine, snowing or not. Al's driving us in his Caddy. Guess!"

"Where?" she asked.

"To see Ziggy," he said with elation. "Al's driving us up to the state pen. My first time! My mother hasn't been there in three years, but Al's been a couple of times. Boy, you should see my mother! Cooking, baking—there's stuff all over the kitchen. We're taking chicken and cutlets, cake, pickles, bread—he's nuts about her bread that she bakes. See, we eat with him when we get there. She told me about it. She even takes a tablecloth."

"Boy, that's swell," Vincent said, and she thought of the candle burning down, licking toward the basket of shavings. Dave had been in that fire, too, and his mother's bracelet. But she had not seen, even in that intolerable brightness, this visit to Ziggy in prison.

"How does it feel?" she said quietly. "Going to see your brother?"

"I'm nervous as hell! So's my mother. But Jesus, I'm glad we're going. So's she. See, I never had the nerve before. I mean, to—to see Ziggy. I want to. A lot. It's funny. I used to think about it—you know, going up there with her. And she'd cry—I'd hear her crying. I mean, right in my head! Not there, with Zig—but on the way home, with me."

"Yeah," Vincent said.

"Well, but mostly it was my mother who was afraid. Just like I told you. Boy, we been talking our heads off! Talk, talk—and laugh."

Talk, talk, she thought numbly as the candle burned in her mind. What would she say to her father tomorrow? Pa, I put out the candle before the fire could start. Because—well, cops, jail! They would've arrested you, and—well, so I put it out.

No, that did not sound right in her head. Pa, now you listen! If you ever do that again, I—I'll tell on you! I'll tell the cops. You'd better warn Moe and Mr. Levine. I mean it!

They were almost at the corner, the bright Saturday-night lights of Woodlawn just ahead, when Dave said in a low voice, "Vincent, I

319

want to tell you—well, thanks! When we went to the club that time and talked? What would've happened to me if that Sunday hadn't happened? I mean, if Ross hadn't knocked out that guy and we got together, and—and I told you all that stuff! I would've exploded, I guess. Vincent, thanks!"

"Nuts!" she said intensely, thinking of all the explosions she had talked out with Jules.

"Yeah!" Dave muttered as fervently, grinning as he tossed his head in the thickening snow.

Walking along at his side, Vincent realized now that she had to talk to her father. So many times they had been on the edge of talking, but tomorrow she would step over that edge. She had to tell him how she was in that fire he had helped set. Whatever the words were, she would have to find them before tomorrow. Where were the words? How did you talk to your father—finally?

Her arm squeezed the package tighter, so that she felt the hard outlines of the Bible, the notebook, against her side. Come, Changeling, let us identify ourselves! she remembered out of a page, but she was scared, scared to see her father tomorrow, scared to say the first word that would blast the long, crammed silence between them.

When they turned into Woodlawn, Dave stopped in front of the big, lighted window of Newman's grocery. His hair was powdered with snow, yellow under white, and his eyes were crinkled with amusement.

"You look like a cream puff," he told her.

"Wait'll you see your hair," she said. "Coming?"

But he hesitated. "Hey, what about if I get some ice cream?" he blurted.

There was a shy, strained smile on his face. "Think Clara'd like some ice cream?"

She looked at him, suddenly realized that he was nervous about meeting Clara. "Well, Shirley always has cake and milk when I'm sitting," she said.

"Ice cream would make it a real party, huh? And I'm going to get some cigs, too." He laughed excitedly. "I got paid today. Okay?"

"Okay," she said, and he ran into the store.

Clara's probably scared, too, Vincent thought. About meeting Dave, a strange guy—a white guy. And Shirl, Johnnie—scared they'll maybe say something, insult her. They won't! Clara, honest they won't!

All three of us are scared, she thought. But Clara and Dave are coming tonight, anyway—scared or not. And Dave's got guts enough to go and see his brother tomorrow.

She took a deep breath. I'll just look in his eyes, she thought, and I'll say: "Pa, I put out the fire. I knew it was a bad thing. I don't know—it was wrong, bad. So I put it out, Pa."

When Dave came out, Vincent was standing with her face up to the heavy snowfall, trying to catch flakes on her tongue.

He laughed. "What flavor is it?" he said.

"Strawberry!"

"I got strawberry *and* cherry," he said. "Think Clara'll like that?"

"Yeah," she said, and they began to walk toward Shirley's street.

A wonderful sensation of lightness puffed all through Vincent. Inside of her, she was walking on tiptoe, fast, a free-and-easy soaring step.

"Hey, Dave," she said, making it casual, "I'll walk home with you tonight. Stick around, huh? Shirl said they ought to be home by midnight."

"Thought you were sleeping there," he said.

"I changed my mind. I've got to talk to my father tonight."

"Okay," he said, "I'll wait for you. Hey, look at it snow!"

There was a thick, white fairyland all about them, and suddenly, joyously, Vincent cried: "All doors are open, changeling-my-brother!"

"What?" Dave said. There was snow on his eyelashes as he looked at her, puzzled.

"Tell you later," she said. "I've got lots to tell you, Dave. Later —you and me and Clara. Come on, let's run!"

They began to run, laughing and calling to each other as they plunged through the beautiful, thick whiteness. To Vincent, it was like a dream in snow. She was running swiftly over the gently sloping, known terrain of the dream, no longer an outsider, no longer an enemy of the world beyond her street. There was no one to hate or to fear, no one to weep over, in the dream.

There was somebody running with her, at her side, as fast as she and as graceful, somebody whose face she was not sure she had seen yet; but the laughter was there, the free elated sound of it, and the direction was there—shearing clean through the curtain of snow, as if marked out for her in the dream.

She felt the whole world opening in front of her as she ran. In a moment, she could touch it.

# Afterword

For many decades, the phenomenon of hostile resistance to integrated housing repeated itself in almost all of the major cities across the "liberal" northern section of the United States, the Promised Land to America's dark-skinned children. It did not occur in the South, where black people knew their "place," and where they had no illusions that the descendants of Africans would be able to pursue a way of life other than that defined by open racism and rampant segregation. But in the North, settlers often used extreme means to insure maintenance of exclusive all-white ethnic neighborhoods when it appeared that blacks were interested in moving inside of those boundaries. This behavior on the part of many whites, occurring with painful but predictable regularity, came in the wake of the black migration from South to North, as members of that group sought claims to the same American dream that had brought others of a different color to these shores. The struggle between the races inflicted severe wounds and left ugly, deforming psychic scars on the lives of many, blacks and whites alike.

The significant era of the black migration north began in the early years of this century and continued well beyond its midpoint. The failure of crops, the brutality of the sharecropper system, the unrelenting poverty and ignorance, and the increase of overt racial oppression were some of the reasons that led black people to flee the South in hopes of finding a place where they could be human, and have a chance to improve the conditions of their lives. Their destinations were the industrial centers of the North, mainly large ones like New York and Chicago, but even smaller cities were not immune from experiencing this moving tide. The life that black migrants found in these new places was not easy, and the problems they encountered were unfamiliar and difficult for them to resolve. But outside their old environments, they envisioned greater promise for themselves and an eventual end to the hopelessness and despair they had left behind. It was true that the schools their children attended were segregated and inferior to white schools because of segregated housing patterns; that the places they were forced to live in were substandard, highly overpriced, and already rife with overcrowding and crime; that they were unskilled, considered untrainable, and therefore relegated to the most menial jobs available; that the owners of food and clothing stores provided the worst qualities of those commodities to the black community; and that more subtle forms of racism than they had known or imagined made a searing impact on their collective consciousness. Still, this life held possibilities, the trek north continued, and black people dreamed that one day they and their children would overcome the hardships of their present condition. Significant gains along these lines were slow and painful, and it was not until the civil rights movement of the 1960s and early 1970s began to make an impact on the national life that black people, as a group, were able to begin to measure the distance they had come.

Advocates of open housing, school busing, and the like, have always claimed that the problems of racism in America are largely generated and kept alive by the ignorance and the needless fear that racial groups have of each other. Fear and hatred of the "other" go hand in hand and nurture the cancer that separates Americans from each other. If it is true that "the family that prays together stays together," then proponents of full integration equally maintain that the people who live together, go to school together, and work and play together, soon lose their fear of each other, and are able to commune on a human level. Unfortunately, the road to this solution to the problem has been fraught with many impediments. Not least among them are the deeply embedded roots of racism. From the beginning of their migration to this country, European groups, anxious to hold on to their distinct identities, even as they embraced a new language and new ways of doing things, created self-serving religious, political, and social enclaves that for a time successfully resisted penetration even against each other. But nothing was like the unanimity these groups displayed in their resistance to the presence of black people living in their neighborhoods, or black children attending the schools that they considered their own. The resistance has been at the heart of the American experience for more than a hundred years, confirming the words of W.E.B. DuBois who, in 1903, intoned: "the problem of the twentieth century is the problem of the color-line—the relation of the darker to the lighter races of men in Asia and Africa, in America and the islands of the sea."[1]

Jo Sinclair's (Ruth Seid's) novel, *The Changelings*, first published in 1955, goes to the heart of this problem, exploring the dilemma of the human condition at the intersection of race fear, class consciousness, and ethnic bias, which turns "good" people into racists and bigots. Sinclair is a sophisticated writer who fully understands the complexity of the issues with which she is dealing, and helps her readers to comprehend the intricacies of the motives behind the actions of her characters. This is a novel that does not let anyone off the "hook," but which also does not trivialize or simplify the search for solutions to the problems. Its richly textured layers of consciousness and experiences bring us to a closer awareness of the failures and frailties of human thoughts and deeds, and push us to examine our own interactions with people outside our individual racial, religious, or ethnic heritage.

The novel focuses on a Jewish girl and a black girl who face each other across generations of racial and ethnic differences and hostilities, even as they both stand hesitantly at the line that divides childhood from womanhood. This gives it breadth and scope, and simultaneously, a center in the world of individual experience. This was a crucial work for its time, if for no reason other than that American culture had entered a new age, and technology, mechanization, and urbanization were revolutionary. Old ways were changing rapidly, and the boundaries of space, territory, privacy, and independence were in a process of redefinition for everyone. Racial groups, among others, were no longer able to operate exclusively, as rural and urban patterns of living underwent irrevocable disruption, and for some, violation. The relationship that develops between Judy Vincent and Clara Jackson, the changelings within their families and communities, represents the novelist's vision of the harbinger of possibilities for a new era in American life and culture. Judy Vincent tells Clara Jackson: "I'm the changeling in my house.... I'm not going to run around crying and hating people.... I'm going to be free, so I can go out in the world.... You can't be free if you're scared of everybody."[2] This declaration represents a radical break with her community's ideas.

Sinclair's interweaving of the strands that make up the everyday lives of the working-class, mostly Yiddish-speaking Jewish community, with some Italians, and others indiscriminately called gentiles, gives the novel its rich texture and a realistic background against which to observe the struggles and frustrations of the changelings. These people, like the black people whom they fear, have an ongoing battle to maintain their economic and human dignity. Most of them were born in Europe, and they and their parents fled before the oppression that had plagued Jewish existence there for centuries. They came to America to begin new lives, to search out new opportunities, and with the hope that they would find a safe haven from the persecution and attempts at genocide that perpetually threatened their group. They arrived in America with dreams, and little else. These hardworking people on East 120th Street in a small city in Ohio are much like the people in the nearby black community from whom they are separated only by a partially filled-in gully, which stands "like an ocean" between them. They are still on this street because they had not made it "big" in America and they identify the preservation of their human dignity with preserving and protecting their community from the intrusion of the black outsiders.

The sense of community in the novel is established early through Sinclair's personification of the short, narrow "street," economically defined by its predominant two-family houses. Only a few people occupy one-family dwellings. The street has a life of its own. It watches with a hundred eyes as the Negroes—the black ones—the *Schwartze*, come singly or in couples, in their attempts to rent the three suites left empty that summer just past, after their former tenants moved to the more affluent "Heights." The street watches, waits, and wonders who among the Valentis, Goldens, and Zigmans will weaken first and rent or sell a place to the "invaders," the "enemies." And all the time it hides its fears behind the racist myths of black people's disrespect for property. The street resents and envies the people who have left for the Heights, for those who remain have no resources with which to stay the unwelcome advance. The street is tense, aware that in time there has to be an explosion between itself and those it wants to keep out. In the meantime, the black people, driven by the need for decent housing, come courteously, but "eagerly and stubbornly" to look for rooms, so that their children can have space to do their homework, and their families will have a respite from the overcrowding that drives them to seek those empty rooms. The street is the pulse of the community and represents both its unfulfilled dreams and the remnants of the self-respect of those who cannot leave it. It is the symbol of their failure to achieve a greater share of the American dream, as well as their stronghold to resist the winds of an inevitable change. For these people can take pride in knowing that they built a whole neighborhood, raised their children there, brought in bakeries and butchers, their *shul*, movies houses, doctors, and schools. These institutions give them the right to call the street their own.

But the street is also the place where changeling, street-gang leader Judy Vincent grows up resisting differently from her elders. She rejects the behavior expected of girls (calling herself Vincent rather than Judy is a symbol of this), and the attitudes that her elders have toward the world outside their ethnic boundaries. She understands them as she understands their Yiddish; yet, unable to master the use of that tongue, she achieves only a "stumbling mixture," half in English. In search of yet another language to describe her feelings and the turmoils that beset her thirteen-year-old emotions, in her head and in her heart she lives out, in poetry and music that no one else can hear, the feelings she cannot get put into words. Even after she loses her gang because of fifteen-year-old Dave Zigman's confused emotions, she does not permit anger and bitterness over that event to interfere with her determination to move beyond the confines of the narrow thinking and distorted perceptions of others that characterize the adults on the street. The friendship with her counterpart changeling, also a former gang-leader, Clara, provides the bridge that gives her access to an understanding of those feelings that set her apart from her family and the others.

In Judy, the reader meets a sensitive girl whose world turns upside down during the summer of her thirteenth year. Although outwardly it seems the same, for a long time she is aware that something indefinable, almost imperceptible has changed the nature of her gang. Finally, she traces the sense of her uneasiness to the new and strange behavior of her friend Dave, in whose house there are empty rooms, and who is often the person in his family to turn the black people away. She is unable to explain what has happened to him and to the gang, but her coming to a larger consciousness is born when she realizes that her three worlds—the gang, the street, and her family, which she has so far kept separate—have jumped their boundaries and are intruding on each other. And she knows that Dave's actions, the differences in the gang, and the empty rooms in his house are part of the same whole, and, in an inexplicable way, linked to her worlds. It is a conundrum to her, and no one she knows can enlighten her, not even Jules, who writes poetry to explain the riddles of life. Before, gang meetings had filled Vincent's head with secret music that floated between the fire and each person gathered around it. It was music "like an arch of tenderness over the Gully," where the clubhouse was located, or "a long story chanted with the stars, with the slowly moving clouds and the reddish moon" (p. 4). Now that has changed, and when she loses the gang, it is Clara's protective fierceness and Jules's encouragement and admiration for her to which she turns. They help her to unravel the tangled threads of the interconnectedness between herself, the internal problems of her family and the community, and their hostilities, fears, and anxieties regarding blacks.

Vincent and Clara Jackson face the same world from opposite sides of the racial barrier that separates them but which is not strong enough to divide them from each other. Mirror images of each other, except for the colors of their skins, they are alike in age, size, and dress, in the way they both stand guarding their bodies, and in their pride and arrogance. They also share a similar sense of confusion toward their individual community's attitudes and ideas of others. Their personal interests and sensibilities complement and support their friendship, which is born when Clara offers Vincent her knife, as a gift of protection against male victimization. Their relationship, sensitive and vulnerable to the pressures of their worlds, develops, in spite of those worlds, to offer the hope of reconciliation on which the novel concludes. Sinclair never loses her grasp on realism through the narrative, and The Changelings is no fairy tale. The friendship suffers a crucial setback before it has time to be strong, the move toward renewal is tense and unassured, and at the end of the book the anxiety and uncertainty that Vincent feels as she takes the first step to move Clara out of the "dark" of her life in the gully into the "light" open space of her world reflect the difficulties of standing by the hard choices that count. Nothing but more struggle is promised.

In this book, Vincent's friend Jules Golden usurps the place of the angel in the house. But Jules is no angel. His fragile body, almost at the point of losing the battle with life that he has waged for all his seventeen years, is not able to contain the mighty spirit of his being. Like Vincent, whom he gives the appellation of "changeling," he is searching for a way out of the narrow space that the "street" entombs. The dying Jules is the only person in the community who understands what burns in the inner reaches of his younger friend's heart, and his words and encouragement serve as the guide that enable her to reach out to embrace what she knows is right. Fittingly, Jules is a poet, and his well-worn notebook, holder of all that he has created in thought in his short life, when passed on to Vincent, is more than a collection of adolescent yearnings and frustrations. It is a mandate for her to pursue her dream to the end of the rainbow. The portrait of Jules Golden that Sinclair draws leaves her readers little room to pity the dying boy. Though his life is extremely short, it is well-spent, and regrets would be pointless. Sinclair gives him a keen understanding of his mortality, faced over years of lying in bed unable to participate in the life outside his window. She also gives him insight and vision, which he conveys convincingly to Vincent. His illness too, and his knowledge of the love within his family, give him authority to voice his condemnation of the self-diminishing attitudes the family embraces and is governed by. When he cries out to his mother that he does not want to die, it is not physical death that scares him, but one that is choking life out of the possibilities of a meaningful freedom for them, even more than for himself. "You've got to open up your heart," he tells her, "I have to breathe" (p. 156). But if opening up her heart, even for her dying son, means renting her empty rooms to black people, in the house that she "sweat to pay for," and which she "sweat to keep clean," Mrs. Golden cannot rise to the challenge: "I'm afraid of them," she says, "What do you want from me? I'm afraid of a black face" (p. 156). Keeping the black faces off of 120th Street is "a war," she tells her son, one to save the entire neighborhood—the all-white streets surrounding their own—from falling. Vincent's mother echoes similar sentiments: "I am afraid to look into their eyes," she says. And the girl wonders why the woman would have been afraid to look into Clara's eyes, which she has seen so "proud and fierce with anger at Dave" for his having wronged her as he did. Those eyes have revealed to her that the bond connecting her to Clara is stronger and more reliant than any racial ties.

Dave Zigman and Jules Golden, in all ways unlike each other except in their ethnic background, are Vincent's closest friends until Clara enters her life—the one, on the edge of death, the other, with the prospects of his whole life ahead. They represent the polar extremes of Vincent's world of the street. Among Vincent and the two young men, it is Jules who best understands and also speaks the language of his forebears, and it is Dave who does that worst. Their varying abilities to master Yiddish are a metaphor for their understandings of the world of the street. While Vincent is aware of, and struggles to find rational answers to the confusions that are part of her and her community's thinking, Jules most clearly perceives the nature of the fears that have taken hold of everyone. On the other hand, Dave responds to his inner turmoil regarding those fears with violence against Vincent. Jules's fierce and insulting arguments with his mother, which make it seem as though they despise each other, are ritual concealments of the love the two hold for each other but do not know how else to express. But they understand each other and the meanings of their attitudes toward each other. Mother and son are deeply aware of the bonds of guilt and love that operate between them.

On the contrary, between Dave and his mother there is the silence of hidden secrets, shame, and the inability for expression of human emotion. Dave dearly loves his mother. He wants to protect her and to make it up to her for the years of unhappiness that she has endured because of his father's profligacy and the criminal activities of his two brothers. What is crucial between them is the absence of a mechanism by which he can communicate his feelings to her. His cruelty to Vincent, who has all the qualities of life that he wishes his mother could have, is born out of his frustration at his inability to find a way to let his mother know how much he loves her. For Dave, his mother needs protection from the humiliation that the black presence suggests in the mind of the street and which threatens her in the existence of their empty rooms.

Conversely, Jules loses no opportunity to deride his mother for her lack of humanity in not rising above the racist attitudes of the street and renting her empty rooms to the black people who need them. Philosophically, her relationship with the two young men offers Vincent the choice between following the conventions that govern socially prescribed attitudes toward race and the roles of women, as Dave's behavior indicates through the major part of the novel, or to break with these, as Jules encourages, and embrace a larger world in which what is good and beautiful in each one will be the standard on which her judgments and decisions are made. In search of the good and the beautiful, her acquaintance with Clara makes Vincent aware of the importance of female bonding for women in a world in which men find their identity in dominance over women's lives. She also learns that the "enemy" is not in the color of an individual's skin, but rather in one's outlook on the world beyond the parochial boundaries of one's group. "When you're a changeling," she tells Clara, "you believe in loving a lot of people. Not hate them. You're real strong. You're real free. And—and the whole world is waiting for you to come in. You belong to the whole world" (p. 136).

Within the world of the novel, in spite of Jules's denigration of his mother's attitudes to the black people, Sinclair does not suggest that the Goldens, or their neighbors the Levines, the Vincents, the Zigmans, the Millers, or others are cruel, heartless people. Among other things, they are a group who feel that life has cheated them of the fulfillment of their dreams. In resisting the entrance of blacks into their neighborhood, they are fighting desperately to hold on to an image of American success that they want for themselves, but which has eluded them. Their everyday problems reflect the universal human condition of countless people like themselves: they fear illnesses and poverty, but have the will and strength that keeps them from admitting easy defeat to such adversities; they are anxious over the welfare of their children and desire to give their young ones the best they can afford; and they want stability and continuity in the patterns of life around which they have created their identities. The intrusion of black faces and black bodies into this arena, which is already beset by deep angers, frustrations, and feelings of powerlessness, is the final insult to them, and the one on which they can find collective voice and articulate their outrage against the machinations of a fickle fate. Black people are the scapegoats in the American system, and available targets against which to hurl the deadly arrows of all their pent-up hostilities. Vincent sees the connection between her three worlds clearly after the beating of the black man:

> Everything seemed tied together, all at once: the beating of the
> man that afternoon; the talk of fire; the departure of the Grand-

mother; Dave's unmasking; the search for Clara today which had
led Vincent into Manny's church; the solemn meaning of the Day
of Atonement for her father—that made him think of his mother
gone forever, after seeing a bleeding face on the sidewalk. They
were all tied together so closely that her father *had* to say Manny's
name out loud! (p. 270)

Jules's father, Herman Golden, is a good example of the people who
live on the street. Although only a tailor, he is always neatly dressed,
and he has the manners and speech that exude the qualities of an old-
fashioned schoolteacher. However, his income is never adequate to
meet the needs of his family, and the frustrations of his life are centered in the problems within that family. These strain his tolerance and
his appearance of outward calm. Guiltily, and for the most part
secretly, he longs to find a way to sell his house, even if that means
to the "enemy," to institutionalize his retarded child, and to move the
remainder of his family to someplace far away—to Florida, where the
living would be easier. The coming of the blacks make it possible for
him to put words, however tremulously, to that wish. His desire to escape the blacks is in fact the fantasy of a middle-aged man who feels
his failures, and who, although knowing how futile are the thoughts,
yet wants to believe that he can have another chance at life. The empty
rooms in his house invite both the ultimate affront to his dignity, and
a chance to break away and start again. Nor is his wife Sophie less
complicated in wanting to escape the social pollution she predicts that
black people will bring to the neighborhood if they are allowed to enter. Motivated by intertwining threads of love, guilt, and a sense of
duty, she tends her children faithfully through their various physical
and mental disabilities, and finds release from the anxieties such at-
tendance spawns in the fear she feels for black people because she does
not know them.

Contributing to the sense of failure that pervades the street are the
separations that exist within many families, as the children of these
households reject the rigid standards of the old country. Among the
Goldens, this division, represented by the fights between Jules and his
mother does not destroy the fabric of family unity, largely because it
is acknowledged and accepted with a large degree of tolerance. It does
not interfere with expressions of love between the members of the fa-

mily. The decision not to hide the retarded Becky from public view, either at home or in an institution, is an indication of the family's acceptance of visible internal difference, and their efforts to love in spite of it. As a result, it is not difficult for us as readers to understand why it is possible for Jules and his mother to struggle as they do over their separate views of dealing with the issues surrounding the coming of black people into their neighborhood.

This is not true of many other families, where differences of opinions on internal, familial matters often result in painful physical separations, and even more painful psychological ones. In the Vincent family, for instance, inflexible attitudes toward intergroup marriage banish Shirley and her son Manny. Not only are they denied any contact with Shirley's father and grandmother, they are relegated to the lists of the dead, so that their names cannot be spoken. Vincent's brother Nate, who leaves home largely because his principles of work and friendships are different from those of his parents, is also a symbol of the distance that separates one generation from another.

Among the Zigmans, the separation originates in the past, the shady history of Morris Zigman, and in the illegal actions of two older sons. But while the Vincents, parents and children, present an aggressive resistance to each others' views on deviation from the old ways, with the former standards upheld by an unbending grandmother, the Zigmans are pathetic in their inability to give voice or to act in ways that acknowledge either pain or gladness. The Miller family best dramatizes the force of the generational clash when there are strong wills on opposing sides.

Sam Miller is one of the persons most outraged by the threat that the blacks present to his street. Like many of his neighbors, the internal unity of his family has fallen away, and he attributes the unfulfillment of his personal ambitions to the failure of his children to follow his lead. In his case, the separation between him and them is filled with open recriminations on the parts of all concerned. Miller's dream of establishing a successful chain of pawnshops, operated by himself and his two sons, has dissipated because the sons refuse to take their father's goals as their own. When Herb, the older son, and the one who more directly confronts his father, walks away from his marriage and the store that was set up for him, he deals the old man a blow from which the latter will never recover. When Ben, the younger son, decides that although Saturdays are the best days for business, he will not open on those days until after sundown, the collapse of the father's dream is final. Ironically, only Ruth, his daughter, and as a woman the "lesser" child, is willing to follow in her father's footsteps.

Sam Miller's anger at his sons, one whom he considers willful and vengeful, the other, of inferior mental abilities to himself, is further aggravated by the erosion of his power and prestige in the religious community. An early settler in the neighborhood, he had been influential in helping to shape its nature. A faithfully religious man, he had been among the first to contribute funds toward the construction of the *shul*, and his words had been listened to and heeded in those early days. When the community grows weaker as its more affluent members move to the Heights, Miller finds himself losing the power he imagined had been his. By the time we meet him, he is an angry, embittered man—no longer feared and obeyed by his sons, or influential among the leaders of the *shul*. The final blow to his dignity comes when he loses the fight to prevent the removal of the *shul* from the neighborhood. In her depictions of the confrontations between Sam Miller and his sons, Sinclair exposes the most sensitive aspects of the tensions that exist between generations in an immigrant community. The behavior of their children was a turn of events that those who had come early in the century had not anticipated and were unprepared to deal with without rancor and great disappointment. Old ways of life were disintegrating, and in their place, the new ways threatened the existence of all that they had previously known.

Against this background of a neighborhood undergoing painful internal changes, Judy Vincent and Clara Jackson discover each other and begin the difficult task of trying to understand the meaning of tolerance and friendship within the boundaries of cultural pluralism. That they share the common ground of gender facilitates their meeting when one of them has been victimized because of that gender. Soon they find that in addition to their physical similarities, each of them is struggling to find meaning in her world outside of the limitations that race and gender place on them. It is on this level that the novel assumes its most profound significance.

Although Sinclair does not highlight the black community in her book, she permits her readers glimpses of the factors that lead those people to travel into hostile white territory in search of a decent place to live. The novel is set in the pre-Black Power days of the fiery 1960s, and the home seekers are well mannered and unassuming, anxious not to disrupt, but importunate in their need. Nor are these people the poor and downtrodden of their race. They have jobs and money sufficient to meet the living standards of the community they seek to enter. Clara's father works for the post office, which insures him a permanent, steady income. Her mother is a beautician—no welfare cheaters here. As she listens to Clara's story of the horrors of decrepit, overcrowded housing, Vincent cannot imagine what it would be like if she were deprived of a quiet place in which to do her homework, or private place in which to store the treasures she does not want others to see, or never to have time when she in not hemmed in on all sides by other people. These are basic needs, and Clara and her people are denied them because of their race.

At the intersection of race and gender the two girls, separately and together, explore avenues toward a social reconciliation that will leave them both their full human dignity. For both, the first step is in learning how to be sensitive to, and to respect each other's differences. Understanding and forgiveness have to be important ingredients in their friendship. In addition, Vincent has to come to consciousness of the extent to which racial ethnic intolerance leads to irrational fear and hate. She has to see that her father's and grandmother's denial of Shirley and Manny, cutting them off from family love, is similar to the community's denying an entire group of people the opportunity to have decent housing and the opportunities that all Americans hold dear. She has to see, as Ben and Herb Miller do, that the street's attitudes toward black people is like a mirror held up to itself, and that it reflects their innermost weaknesses, insecurities, and feelings of inhumanity. Vincent has to prevent the fulfillment of her father's and Mr. Levine's plans to burn down their houses and cheat the insurance company at the expense of the blacks, for such action is also intimately connected to her father's inability to speak his daughter's and grandson's names, for no reason other than that Shirley has married a gentile. And finally, she has to see that even though she is a girl, and the world of men constantly tries to deprive women of the power to be autonomous, she has not only to demand her right to be a full human being, but to take the responsibility to show others the blindness of prejudice, unwarranted fear, and hate.

In the building of this friendship, Sinclair gives Clara the role of transcending the damage that racism might well have inflicted on her youthful psyche. Clara becomes the gift-giver to someone she might well have seen only as an enemy. First there is the knife—the gift of protection—although neither girl would have been able to use it successfully had she been called upon to do so. Clara, tougher and more streetwise than Vincent, once second-in-command of an otherwise all-boys gang, had often flaunted it to stay challenges to her authority. "I used to go home after, and throw up," she says. Still, this knife, passed from one to the other, a secret bond between them, symbolizes the psychological repudiation of female powerlessness, and a challenge to male dominance in circumstances where the latter represents the status quo.

The medal of St. Anthony is an even more intimate gift of protection, not loaned to Vincent, but given to her from around the neck of her friend. On this level, it becomes the pledge of friendship and kinship between the Jewish girl, who has to hide it in her treasure box, away from the eyes of the world, and the black Catholic girl, who belongs to the same church as the Jewish girl's nephew. "The medal was the biggest gift she had ever had in her life. Nobody had ever taken a piece of God—right off herself" (p.133), Vincent thinks. Far better than the knife, which addresses outside threats to the self, this gift enables the girls to share important parts of their inner selves with each other, and to learn from each other.

*The Changelings* is a novel that, although centered on a certain period of our national history, is full of themes that continue to be of major importance in contemporary times. Although the civil rights movement, and now the women's movement, have done much to expose and begin to facilitate redress of the problems of race and gender in America, these ills are so firmly rooted in our soil that the struggle to combat them must be ongoing, and the end is not in sight. By focusing on this crucial period in the lives of two young girls who are significantly different, yet very much alike, and forcing them to grapple with the social codes of their communities, Sinclair's novel has timeless value, for the future always belongs to the young. The book reminds us of what it was like for many young people growing up in the 1950s, and of the roles that gangs, single and dual-sexed, played in the lives of young people—useful lessons to be passed on to succeeding generations. Beyond that, it takes a hard look at the forces that motivate our notions of American success, and challenges our moral and ethical standards in pursuit of that goal. When Herb Miller points out to his father that the black people he was so willing to denigrate have been his faithful pawnshop cutomers for decades, or when Vincent writes the names of her nephew and brother-in-law in the family Bible, the novelist has turned the spotlight of searching inquiry, not on a period of time past, but on time present and time to come, by reinforcing the need for constant vigilance against those prejudices that diminish our humanity. Vincent and Clara recognize their sameness to each other, and their differences, not only from one another, but also from those people they are supposed to be like. Girl-changelings both, they are joined in believing that "now black is white and white is black. A whole world dances and is full of joy."

*Nellie McKay*
*University of Wisconsin, Madison*

## Notes

1. W.E.B. DuBois, *The Souls of Black Folk* (New York: The New American Library, 1969), p. 54.
2. Jo Sinclair, *The Changelings*, p. 135. All subsequent references to *The Changelings* are indicated by page numbers in the text.

# On Racism and Ethnocentrism

The story line of Jo Sinclair's novel is straightforward. Two adolescent girls, one Jewish, the other black, are "changelings" in their respective families and societies as they challenge, defy, and conquer the fear and hatred that come to dominate life in a Jewish neighborhood that is "changing" from white to black. *The Changelings* agitates us, moves us, teaches us, and inspires us. As practicing social scientists and teachers, we appreciate the novel especially because it not only exposes differences in the human experience, but also calls forth commonalities in the human condition. The novel is focused both on conflict rooted in social judgments based on race, ethnicity, religion, gender, age, and class; the novel is also focused on the practice, belief, and experience of solidarity in the forms of love, friendship, neighborhood and ethnic pride, and in family attachments. At center, *The Changelings* is about the coexistence among humans of divisiveness and cohesion.

*The Changelings* is about change and the resistance to change, among a variety of people in a single neighborhood, and outside it as well. It is also a story of the changes central to growing up, of an adolescent girl's struggles and dreams. What is required, the novel seems to be asking, for attitudes, bigotries, systems to change—even as neighborhoods do, as people do, if only because they "grow up"?

As social scientists, we propose to look at the novel as a repository of instruction about human behavior and social life, about the nature of society. Sinclair does not lecture to us on these subjects. Rather, she projects us into the midst of a society grappling with the political, economic, and cultural currents that impose themselves on the most intimate of human relationships: "It was all so unreal: the way it had exploded out of the sale of the *shul*–out of the *Schwartze*, really–exploded right into the secret war Herb and her father had been fighting so long."[1] In passages like this one, Sinclair "explodes" and exposes the fragments of racism, family arguments, ethnic identity, and religion in all of their complexities. Never single components, these elements, like the shifting fragments inside a kaleidoscope, form patterns for the reader to disentangle.

As important as the capture of a single moment of time, is Sinclair's effort to project a sense of how change comes about, not from any one source, but from the interaction of many social forces. Change is a process, or group of processes, each deriving some momentum from the changes that have already occurred. And yet, as in the novel, the results can sometimes appear suddenly:

> "Sure," Jules said doggedly, "but you got yourself a new friend out of the whole mess. A *Schwartze*—and the hell with parents and your grandmother, and their stupid reasoning. You won, didn't you?"
>
> She looked at him with such desperation that a sick, depressed feeling spurted through him. He wondered bitterly how this kid had managed to give him all that hope yesterday, that elated feeling that she had touched hands with a black girl and — presto! — the world was changing (p. 223).

But how does change—far more a process than a magical moment—come about? Sinclair often describes it from the perspective of individuals moving and interacting with each other. She conceptualizes transformation in the words of Joey, as he explains to his mother exactly how she can cease to be afraid of "this whole *Schwartze* business":

> "The *Schwartze*—they're a wall that you made yourself. You made it, and it—well, it stands between you and—and the right kind of world. Do you understand?"
>
> She shook her head, and he patted her arm. "A wall, Ma—higher than any kind there is. Higher than the no-money wall, the sickness wall. Like you made it yourself, brick by brick. A mistake! People make mistakes. But now you've got to climb over it, Ma. You first, then the whole family—after you show them how. You're the smartest, the strongest—you'll show them how! Even Alex. Even Becky. You'll say to them, 'Climb, climb! Watch me, don't give up.' You understand Ma?" (p.280)

Jo Sinclair's analysis of society and the process of change is the context for considering the question at the core of her novel: the intersection of racism—particularly as practiced by people who have themselves been victims of a similar form of oppression—and their ethnocentrism. One special contribution of the novel is its meticulous and effective dissection of the cognitive anatomy of racism: Sinclair's purpose, to make palpable the viscera of fear and ignorance. For racism does not rest on knowledge of the despised, the pariah group, the outcasts. On the contrary, it sits on a solid foundation of ignorance and misinformation:

> [Judy Vincent] had never stood as close to a Negro, or talked to one. On lower Woodlawn they were black faces to walk past. In school she had passed them in corridors without looking for the color of eyes or the shape of a face. One or two of them sat in some of her classes, but they had never focused for her outside of vague names (p.24).

Racism involves a complex process of categorizing, sorting, naming, and defining its victims in ways that make it easier to oppress them. African slaves weren't being stolen from their homelands; they were being brought into a New World where Christianity would transform their heathen souls. And even so, said some of the slave masters, black slaves still did not laugh, or feel sad, or love their children, or long for freedom like normal (white) people. "The idea was so horrible that she jumped up and ran. It was too new, too confusing, like looking into the faces of *Schwartzes* for laughter or sadness, instead of for just the color of fear" (p.104).

And since fear is a major ingredient of racism, it is important to understand that those who feel the fear are petrified by it, unable to move to a new perspective, even one that might teach them that there is nothing to fear:

> Mrs. Golden shuddered, her hands dropping from the bony shoulders. "I'm afraid of them," she said. "What do you want from me? I'm afraid of a black face."
> "My mother," Jules said, "She's afraid of a black face. What am I going to do, for God's sake?" (p.156)

Sinclair is relentless in exposing the many sides of racism, including its shameless arrogance:

341

"Mr. Mayor, I have come to discuss the rape of an innocent, young girl by a *Schwartze*. All right, she's not so innocent—but a *Schwartze*! In our white, beautiful street. In our magnificent, white Gully. Mr. Mayor, I demand...." (p.169)

She illustrates how racism is expressed even in humor—using the joke that everyone can surely laugh at—except the central characters who are inevitably the brunt of its commentary: "Then [Judy Vincent] said with rough irony, 'Who's turning your potato? Got yourself a nigger servant all of a sudden?'" (p.8) Sinclair even suggests ways in which the victims of racism become a metaphor for the worst that is imagined in society: "The woman has cancer—everybody is saying it. All right, to us the *Schwartzes* are a cancer." (p.230)

As Sinclair uncovers layers of racism, she also reveals the internal bonds of ethnic solidarity. And then, teaching more by not making all the connections, she leaves the reader to ponder the relationship between the "us" versus "them" upon which racism is built, and the similar dichotomy at the base of racial or ethnic solidarity:

> "I'll tell you," she said, thinking it out slowly. "We feel how we are the owners here. We built up a whole neighborhood. With our sweat, raising our families, worrying. We were the first in the neighborhood with our babies and butchers, our *shul*." (p.115)

The additional intricacies of class bias within ethnic solidarity are also present though the novel, as Jewish characters contrast their condition as working people with that of the "fancy Jews" who have moved out of the changing neighborhood to the Heights. The latter may well continue to sell their labor too, but at a higher price, and less visibly to their former friends. On the other hand, some of the Jews in the changing neighborhood feel superior. Ruth, working in the small pawnshop owned by her father, responds to her brother's defense of a man who sells newspapers: "You don't really want me to marry a—well, practically an illiterate, do you? A man who hustles newspapers? He's a—a peasant!" (p.202) Ruth's cultural attitudes and aspirations separate her from the man who hawks newspapers, and she from him:

> "Don't be so crude!" she cried. "You talk like a—well, certainly like no decent Jewish man would!"

He laughed. "I'm one of those dirty, low Hebes. I can hardly talk English."

"Oh, stop that!"

"You're living right in the middle of a lot of us low types," he said tauntingly. "We're not so bad. We've all got stomachs and a big sex urge. Just like fancy Jews." (p.214)

Gender is also important to the novel, even to its dissection of racism. The novel includes many portraits of women and men both envisioned through the lens that reveals patriarchy. Gender, class, and Jewish identity, for example, are interlaced in a portrait of "a very rich woman—in money and in down pillows and feather beds":

> "They say her sons' basements and attics are overflowing with her possessions, stored for the day when she will give them to her children. After all, until five years ago, she still had that big store. She must have made a fortune, selling remnants to the gentiles. Smart! I should have half her mind. . . .
>
> "It strengthens me to talk about her, to look at her. Religious—she prays like a man in temple." (p.96)

Sinclair later on tells us that this woman even has "a brain like a man's." In contrast to this "extraordinary woman," Sinclair offers another portrait, the female idealized:

> [Dave] wanted a fragrant, young mother with long beautiful hair and white hands, in a cool green dress; somebody like Ruth Miller as she passed on the street, only older, a mother. He wanted someone lovely and happy and full of love, a mother, to hold and worship and kiss right out loud in the house, instead of only in his heart (p.66).

Similarly, Sinclair calls up the social ambivalence of maleness. Herb, constantly trying to sort out his complex relationship with his father, turns to his sister for an answer: "Ruthie! . . . Look at me. Why does that man make me feel like—like a punk? Soft, weak—a nothing!" (p.62) Sinclair is especially sensitive to patriarchy's force when she develops, through the thoughts of Judy Vincent's father, the pain and confusion of a man for whom societal expectations of male and female, mother and son, have been inverted:

343

So he had been a miserable failure. He had gone back with relief to the safe and simple life of working for other men. Why did his mother continue, Sunday after Sunday, to punish him with the memory of how he had disappointed her? Her scorn, her insistent question each week, simply highlighted the way she had been able to walk through America and take from it the success all men sought when they emigrated to a new country (p.101).

There is still another frame for the seemingly chaotic interaction of these disparate elements—gender, ethnicity, race, class—within each individual, family, or in the neighborhood as a whole. Sinclair reminds us of history and historical conditions that give rise to these influential elements and social processes. No social action or individual exists outside of historical antecedents, and no experience or event, whether of an individual or group, erupts full-blown and distinct, disconnected from other experiences and events. In this dialogue between two aging Jewish men, for example, the novelist reminds the reader of the historical context and of what may be constant at the very heart of change:

> "Today, when the Italian beat the Black One, I was thinking of Hitler. It makes a man shiver. It makes a man realize that time is going fast, fast—and nothing stands still."
> "Nothing. Things get either better or worse."
> "Worse, worse!" Mr. Levine said impatiently. "Hitler was not enough for us? Look—in our own street. And Abe! If the Black Ones get angry enough over what happened here today to one of theirs? If they get together—five hundred, a thousand—and march in here? Remember what happened in Poland, in Vienna, in Berlin!" (p.266)

As the novel indicates, the oppression of black people and of Jews has many points of similarity, but also crucial points of difference. The victimization of each group, for example, does not render its members incapable of victimizing others. Judy Vincent sees a resemblance between the bigoted attitudes of her father toward her black friend Clara and those he turns on his own son-in-law and grandchild. In the first instance, his bigotry focuses on Clara's blackness; in the second, on his kinfolk's "non-Jewishness." And Judy Vincent is equally aware of the commonalities between the descendants of slaves and of the victims of tyranny and anti-Semitism in Europe:

> Slaves! Vincent thought. When I show [Clara] that Bible some day, she can see all those pictures, too. Does she know how a lot of guys in Russia ran away from the army there, and came here? That's like slaves! (p.246)

Finally, it is not Judy Vincent, but the sage eighteen-year-old dying Jules who clarifies the differences between the victims of racism and anti-Semitism. He is reading his poem to his mother, *"Die Schwartze"* ("The Black Ones"), which begins:

> The immigrants come to America.
> Freedom, freedom!
> But the years go by—they get fancy ideas.
> Look at them!
> They can't even talk good English,
> They're still greenhorns in their shivering hearts,
> But overnight they're demanding ownership of a street.
> Overnight they dreamed America melted them into a new shape:
> Landlords of a city. (p.32)

Jules's mother interrupts him: "This is a poem?" she interjects, "Go to Public Square for your lectures!" and Jules continues:

> O, fable of democracy!
> Having come, a pilgrim,
> You can now deny a new kind of pilgrim:
> *Die Schwartze!*
> Having stepped foot upon a new shore, like a forefather,
> You can now order off the newest invader,
> The enemy which once you were:
> *Die Schwartze!*
> O, democratic vistas!
> My son's son will have no need to remember
> When his immigrant blood was enemy,
> When his own difference was the flaw
> In the fragrant American night! (p.32)

345

Thirty years after this novel was first published, in the 1980s when again there is heightened tension between certain sectors of Afro-America and of American Jewry, a brief quotation from Barbara Smith's "Between a Rock and a Hard Place" speaks to a similar theme:

> It's true that each of our groups (Black and Jewish) has had a history of politically imposing suffering. These histories are by no means identical, but at times the impact of the oppression has been brutally similar—segregation, ghettoization, physical violence, and death on such a massive scale that it is genocidal. Our experiences of racism and anti-Semitism, suffered at the hands of the white Christian majority, have sometimes made us practical and ideological allies. Yet white Jewish people's racism and Black gentile people's anti-Semitism have just as surely made us view each other as enemies. Another point of divergence is the fact that the majority of Jewish people immigrated to the United States to escape oppression in Europe and found a society by no means free from anti-Semitism, but one where it was possible in most cases to breathe again. For Black people, on the other hand, brought here forcibly as slaves, this country did not provide an escape. Instead it has been the very locus of our oppression. The mere common experience of oppression does not guarantee our being able to get along, especially when the variables of time, place, and circumstances combine with race and class privilege, or lack of them, to make our situations objectively different.[2]

As social scientists, we admire Sinclair's ability to offer to us through Jules's poem and other means a richness that makes palpable the analysis offered directly by Barbara Smith. And yet, we have two criticisms of the novel that raise serious questions for us. First, we would ask why, though many individual characters are presented complexly, all the black characters, including Clara, are not? Why are the black characters, with the possible perfunctory presentation of Clara, almost invisible? And second, why, when most aspects of social life, including the process of change, are presented so completely, is the novel filled with references to the idea that change occurs through an individual's unique action, in isolation from his or her social context?

We can only assume, in answer to our first question, that Sinclair intended the black characters to be invisible as part of her presentation of the psyche of racism. As she demonstrates through the novel, racist perceptions are based on the ignorance of their object. Racist perceptions include, paradoxically, "seeing" black people as invisible.

In response to the second question, we come to the conclusion that Sinclair selects the individual as a focus of change in the society as a whole. She looks at individual social change as a beginning, an entry point into her broader analysis of society.

On the whole, it is not easy to capture the richness of *The Changelings*, or even with the most critical eye, to discern "problems" with the book. Indeed, all of our senses respond to the novel, to its insight and analysis, challenging us to feel and to reflect. It is pure joy to read a book that offers a moving human drama as it educates about society and culture. We have only high praise for *The Changelings* and deep respect for Jo Sinclair.

*Johnnetta B. Cole*
*Hunter College of the City University of New York*

*Elizabeth H. Oakes*
*University of Massachusetts at Boston*

## Notes

1. Jo Sinclair, *The Changelings*, p. 292. All subsequent references to *The Changelings* are indicated by page numbers in the text.
2. Barbara Smith, "Between a Rock and a Hard Place" in *Yours in Struggle*, by Elly Bulkin, Minnie Bruce Pratt, and Barbara Smith (Long Haul Press, 1984), p. 72.

# A Biographical Note

Who is this writer, in her early seventies and still writing—now finishing her seventh novel? Only four have been published: *Wasteland*, 1946; *Sing at My Wake*, 1951; *The Changelings*, 1955; and *Anna Teller*, 1960. Of these, *Wasteland* and *The Changelings* are (like most novels) partly autobiographical. Thus, we know about Jo Sinclair from her fiction as well as from her letters, now available through the archives of Boston University. Jo Sinclair is a second-generation Jew whose parents came from Russia via Argentina; her father was a carpenter and her mother, a seamstress in Russia. She is a Midwesterner at heart: until 1973 she lived in or around Cleveland, and most of her fictional settings are the multi-ethnic streets of a large industrial city in the Midwest. She comes from a working-class background, and she writes about all kinds of poverty. She is a gardener, in a literal and spiritual sense—growing tomatoes is as important to her as weeding minds of prejudice.

Jo Sinclair was born Ruth Seid in Brooklyn on July 1, 1913, the youngest of five children. Her family settled permanently in Cleveland three years after she was born. As with most children, home and school were the most important influences on Jo Sinclair's early life. She felt great kinship with her brother Herman, a press photographer, who was the model for Jake Braunowitz, John Brown, in *Wasteland*. She was always closer still to her sister Fannie, two years older than she, and still living, to whom Sinclair dedicated the unpublished *Approach to the Meaning* (1960-69). Fannie is Sinclair's only living sibling. She helped the young and struggling writer with belief and money. *Sing at My Wake* was dedicated to "my mother and Fannie."

As an adolescent, Ruth Seid led an active life on the street and in school. Like Judy Vincent in *The Changelings*, she led a gang of boys but became single-minded about school and writing after she outgrew the gang. At school she was an honors student; as an athlete, she won many ribbons, particularly in track and field events. She played the lead in a school play and was even a cheerleader until that bored her.[1]

Most important of all, she wrote. She was editor of the school news-paper. She corresponded for years with a high school journalism teacher who had been very supportive of her.

Ruth Seid applied herself very thoroughly to education at John Hay, a commercial high school named after Abraham Lincoln's secre-tary, but she was still a child of the thirties, of the Depression, and she has continued to regret that she was not able to attend a college of her choice. Even though she was valedictorian of her class in 1930, her school could offer her only a scholarship to a teacher's college. And Ruth Seid knew that she wanted to be a writer. So the day after com-mencement she started working in the Higbee Company, a large department store in Cleveland,

> ...where I was to be an apprentice in the adv. dept. Stayed 6 months or so—doing messenger and clerical work, learning how to write ads. Wrote my first adv—about a slip (petticoat)!—saw it in the Cleveland papers. Then quit. Bore, bore![2]

But Ruth Seid never stopped being a student. Through school and the Cleveland Public Library, she had acquired the habit of reading, and she had become a writer. As she recalls in a letter:

> Started writing at 14 or so—poetry. Out of the blue—I didn't "pick" writing; it choose *me*. My kind of screams to the Lord, of course. People scream in different core-ways. *Raison* has to be let out of prison. Mine turned out to be writing, of course. I wrote all through high school: English comp and essays, journalism (the editor kept writing feature stories!) Wrote all through the depres-sion, all through every phase of life. Had to then; have to now.[3]

She wrote furiously after she graduated. The following spring, she went to Brighton Beach in Brooklyn where she lived with an aunt and started writing *The Changelings*, a book originally called *Now Comes the Black*. But she tore this first draft into working pieces around which she built other pieces.[4] Between graduating from high school in 1930 and publishing *The Changelings* in 1955, Ruth Seid rewrote the novel in five major revisions, never losing the focus on race relations.

In the early fall of 1931, Seid temporarily laid *The Changelings* aside and returned to Cleveland and a couple of tedious jobs that saw her through the next five years while trying to get published. For the rest of 1931, she proofread telephone directories and other things for the American Multigraph Company. During the next four years, she worked for a knitting mill, doing a variety of jobs that included typing, bookkeeping, taking cash, and making boxes.

Nineteen thirty-six marked a turning point in Ruth Seid's life. her first published story appeared in *New Masses* one week before she began work for the Works Progress Administration (WPA) on editing and writing projects.[5] She did not get paid for "Noon Lynching," but for the first time "Ruth Seid" appeared in print. She worked for WPA from 1936 to 1940, and her experience with this unique relief program became the single most important source of literary inspiration for her early short stories and sketches. In 1938, *Esquire* published "Children at Play," the first story for which she was paid. This was the first appearance of "Jo Sinclair," the pseudonym she chose because it did not reveal her gender. *Esquire* would accept writing only by men, and it was a magazine that was to accept several of Ruth Seid's early stories.

In an enclosure entitled "Student and Creative Career," accompanying an application for a Guggenheim in 1953 (she had applied in 1942, also without success),[6] Jo Sinclair describes the jobs following her WPA employment:

> The end of WPA came when I got myself a job as a ghost writer to a man who wanted to write a historical novel. Bad idea! Three weeks later, I left. Then I was hired as assistant editor of "National Events," a small trade magazine put out by the National Bindery of Ohio. In addition to helping with layout and ideas, I write poems and articles for the magazine. Money lasted for about six months, then the magazine died & I looked for another job.[7]

Then she spent another half year with the Ohio Adcalendar Company before she started working for the American Red Cross. She worked for the Red Cross from 1942 to 1946, feeling that she was helping in the war effort, and eventually became assistant director of the publicity office. During these years, Jo Sinclair wrote many pieces for *Junior Red Cross Journal* and *Junior Red Cross News*.

In 1946, a peak year of anti-Semitism according to the Gallup poll,[8] Jo Sinclair won the $10,000 Harper Prize for her first novel, *Wasteland*. This unknown Jewish woman had won a competition with seven hundred contestants and had gained national attention by writing a novel about a fragmented and self-loathing Jew who, with the help of his lesbian sister, seeks psychiatric help. Once the war had ended, Sinclair felt she could resign from the Red Cross with a clear conscience. She finished a publicity campaign and then left what was to be her last professional employment, to venture forth as a free-lance writer. She returned to work on *The Changelings*, published less than a decade later.

While *Wasteland* was Jo Sinclair's first published novel and the most feted, *The Changelings* also won acclaim: in 1956 it won the National Certificate of Christians and Jews' Brotherhood Week Certificate of Recognition, the Harry and Ethel Daroff Memorial Award sponsored by the Jewish Book Council of America, and the Ohio Library best fiction award. Her editor at Harper's, Edward C. Aswell, recommended it for a Pulitzer.[9]

*Elisabeth Sandberg*
*University of Massachusetts at Amherst*

Notes

1. Jo Sinclair to Elisabeth Sandberg, November 26, 1983, private collection.
2. Sinclair to Sandberg, June 11, 1984.
3. Sinclair to Sandberg, November 26, 1983.
4. Sinclair to Sandberg, June 11, 1984.
5. Uncatalogued envelope marked "evaluations," found July 19, 1984, at Boston University Special Collections.
6. Ibid.
7. Ibid.
8. Jules Chametzky, "Main Currents in American Jewish Literature from the 1880's to the 1950's (and Beyond)," *Ethnic Groups* 4 (Summer 1982):86.
9. Sinclair to Sandberg, June 11, 1984.

The Feminist Press at The City University of New York offers alternatives in education and in literature. Founded in 1970, this nonprofit, tax-exempt educational and publishing organization works to eliminate sexual stereotypes in books and schools and to provide literature with a broad vision of human potential. The publishing program includes reprints of important works by women, feminist biographies of women, and nonsexist children's books. Curricular materials, bibliographies, directories, and a quarterly journal provide information and support for students and teachers of women's studies. In-service projects help to transform teaching methods and curricula. Through publications and projects, The Feminist Press contributes to the rediscovery of the history of women and the emergence of a more humane society.

For a free catalog, write to The Feminist Press at The City University of New York, 311 East 94 Street, New York, NY 10128. Send individual book orders to The Talman Company, Inc., 150 Fifth Avenue, New York, NY 10011. Please include $1.75 postage and handling for one book, $.75 for each additional.